Praise for *RV There Yet?*

"Diann Hunt is a one of a kind writer who makes me laugh with her witty phrases and loveable characters. Lady Lit Lovers will not be disappointed with this latest book."

—Tracey Bateman, ACFW President, author of
Leave it to Claire and *Claire Knows Best*

"*RV There Yet?* is a sassy, hilarious story of friendships that last a lifetime—with a little help from chocolate. I laughed all the way through, but it was more than a humorous story—it was a welcome reminder that we baby boomers aren't getting older, we're just hitting our stride. Buy this book for yourself and your best friends. And some DeBrand truffles to eat while you read."

—Colleen Coble, author of *Alaska Twilight*,
a Women of Faith selection

"From the get-go, Diann Hunt makes copious use of feminine humor to pad the emotional potholes that cannot be avoided on this journey to spiritual healing. *RV There Yet?* is definitely 'a girl thing,' that will leave you light-hearted, and grateful for lifelong friends who know you and like you anyway."

—Kathy Herman, author of the Seaport Suspense Novels,
the Baxter Series, and *Poor Mrs. Rigsby*

"Friendship, chocolate, a motor home that's seen better days . . . and God. Jump on board and enjoy the fun and adventure, with many a surprise and inspiration along the way!"

—Lorena McCourtney, author of The Ivy Malone Mysteries, *Invisible*,
In Plain Sight, and *On the Run*

"*RV There Yet?* is like a best friend whose witty words lift your spirits. The characters of DeDe, Millie, and Lydia are so real, I felt like a fourth friend tagging along on their RV journey. Diann Hunt has an incredible knack for finding the humor in life and a rare talent for expressing it in writing!"

—Denise Hunter, author of *Finding Faith*

"Diann Hunt scores again in her latest book where her trademark humor shines on every page. A delightful cross-country romp, *RV There Yet?* kept me laughing while it affirmed the value of friendship and reminded me it's never too late to find new meaning in our lives."

—Carol Cox, author of *Ticket to Tomorrow*

"*RV There Yet?* is a delight. Diann Hunt tickles our funny bone while she touches our heart. Hitch a ride and enjoy every mile."

—Kathryn Mackel, author of *The Hidden*

rv there yet?

DiAnn Hunt

WestBow
PRESS
A Division of Thomas Nelson Publishers
Since 1798

visit us at www.westbowpress.com

Published in Nashville, Tennessee, by WestBow Press, a division of Thomas Nelson, Inc.

Scripture quotations are from the King James Version of the Bible and from HOLY BIBLE, NEW INTERNATIONAL VERSION®. Copyright © 1973, 1978, 1984 by International Bible Society. Used by permission of Zondervan. All rights reserved.

Publisher's Note: This novel is a work of fiction. Names, characters, places, and incidents are either products of the author's imagination or used fictitiously. All characters are fictional, and any similarity to people living or dead is purely coincidental.

ISBN: 978-0-7394-6998-9

Printed in the United States of America

To my sister, Shelia Dawson,

for our memorable trip

to Mackinac Island.

To my sisters-in-law Julie Hunt,

Patti Hunt, and Beth Wallace,

for a fun vacation in Florida.

Anybody want to go RV next time?

Prologue

We're talking three women living in an RV—with one bathroom—and you're okay with this?" My voice rises with every word across the phone wires of our three-way call.

"It's only for a few weeks, DeDe. You can handle it. We have faith in you. Right, Lydia?" Millie says.

"Sure we do. Come on, Dee, you can do it!" Lydia agrees with all the eagerness of a junior-high cheerleader.

"Shall I mention that whole hookup process thing?"

"Don't be so dramatic. This will be great. You and I can fly in to Maine and meet at Lydia's house. We'll load up the RV and set off to Colorado. How fun is that?"

"I have an opinion, but I'll keep it to myself." Kicking off my shoes, I stretch my legs and lift them onto the kitchen chair across from me. Tiny red spider veins are gathered at my ankles like a church family at a potluck. Ah, the joys of growing old. I remember when I had not a blemish on my skin. Then again, one day I'll be lucky to remember anything, so I guess it all evens out.

"It's better that way," Millie says. "Besides, what's a little discomfort when we're trying to save Aspen Creek Bible Camp?"

"Can I answer that?"

"No," Millie snaps.

She can be so rude.

A bleep sounds across my phone line, and the caller ID says Rob's calling again. My heart pauses, the familiar ache for this traitor I thought I loved growing more intense. Why can't he leave me alone?

"For Aspen Creek!" Lydia quotes the words like a sacred mantra, pulling me from the place where my heart keeps going but my mind tries so carefully to avoid.

"Okay, so I'm slime." A speck of lint dots my black chino shorts. I flip it off.

"You're not slime," Lydia defends.

"Not slime, just opinionated," Millie argues. "Come on, DeDe, regardless of our personal discomfort, who doesn't want to save our teenage haven from being closed for all time?"

"Um, that would be me," I say.

"Why don't you tell us how you really feel?" Millie banters.

We all laugh.

"Besides, why wouldn't you want to go? You had every guy in camp after you," Millie says with a slightly bitter edge to her voice.

"Oh, I like the sound of that. Things were pretty good back in the day. Let's see, there was David, George, Ralph, Tony—"

"Spare us the gory details," Millie says, bitter tone still in place.

Lydia laughs. "Well, her popularity with the guys didn't hurt us any, Mil. Remember Terry and Russ?"

"Oh yeah," Millie says wistfully. I can almost see the stars in her eyes. She liked Russ a lot. "Wonder if he'll be there?" She quickly adds, "Not that it matters. I'm not ready for another relationship. Still, it would be fun to see him." Her voices escalates. "Truthfully, Dee, can't you set aside your fancy hotel rooms to save the camp?"

"I don't do RVs. Claustrophobia and all that. Wait." My legs drop to the floor, and I sit up straight. "Did I just see my kitchen walls move toward me? I'm pretty sure I saw that."

"You want to be with us, right?" Millie asks.

It takes me a moment before I'm convinced the walls didn't move. "Not that much. You snore." Legs back on the chair.

Lydia laughs.

Millie doesn't. "Come on. This will be great, and you know it. A little R&R, work on the camp with old friends—"

"*Old* being the key word here."

"David, Tony, George, Ralph—any or all of them could be there." She hangs each name before me like a dangling carrot. "What do you think, Lydia?" Millie pushes.

"Well, it would be really fun to connect with our old friends, but I'm a little worried about driving Waldo."

Waldo? She's named her RV Waldo? Okay, this just scares me.

"Oh, it's a piece of cake. Bruce and I rented one once," Millie says, referring to her ex-husband.

"Well, I suppose if we all take turns," Lydia says.

"All of us drive? Need I remind you that I can get lost in a parking garage?" They just don't get it.

"We'll have a map," Lydia offers.

"I had a map for the parking garage."

They are stunned to silence.

"I'm kidding."

Lydia lets out an audible sigh. Millie snorts.

"We have to empty our Porta Potti somewhere, Millie. Does that mean anything to you?" I ask.

"It means we have to find a hole and get busy," Millie quips.

"And you're my friend, why?"

"Because I make you stretch, DeDe. I'm telling you, we can do this, girls. We must do this for Aspen Creek!" Millie says this as if she's leading a demonstration in front of the White House.

"For Aspen Creek!" Lydia joins in.

"DeDe?" Millie just can't leave me alone.

Thoughts of my caller ID come to mind. George, Tony, David, Ralph come to mind. Might not be a bad idea after all. Besides, I need a break. From work. From Rob. From everything. "All right, all right. For Aspen Creek."

3

Millie and Lydia whoop and holler like a couple of seniors on graduation day.

"It's all set then. Beverly Hamilton has heard from lots of the alumni already," Millie says, referring to our longtime friend who took over the position of camp manager when her parents retired. "Most are sending money, but a few are coming to work. What fun to be part of a bigger cause."

This should make me feel noble, but I'm not there yet. I'm still stuck on the Porta Potti thing. Well, not literally . . . at least, not yet.

"Look out, gang! The girls are back in town!" Lydia blurts out of nowhere, practically heaving between breaths. She sounds like a fifty-year-old at a Donny Osmond concert.

Okay, I'm growing used to the idea. Still, there's something I just can't get past.

You know how you feel when you think there's a storm a-brewin' somewhere?

Yeah, it's kind of like that.

Remind me again. I left a shop full of chocolates behind, why?

Okay, that's lame. I mean, as a chocolatier I'm surrounded by chocolates every day. Truffles, caramel pecan patties, cherry cordials, chocolate-covered pretzels, mints. A myriad of textures and tastes. One would think I'd be sick of the rich, decadent scent that greets me every morning and causes me to drool like an old lady after a George Clooney sighting. Truth be told, I could use a break. Besides, friends mean more than chocolate.

And why is that again?

When I see Lydia Brady running out of her house dressed in jean shorts and a plain pink pullover, the breeze blowing her wavy, shoulder-length hair away from her green eyes and flour-speckled face, I remember.

Chocolate comforts me for a moment, but friends encourage me for a lifetime. Close friends. Friends like Lydia Brady and Millie Carter.

We've stayed in touch since our camp days over thirty-some years ago. It's true that at one point we dwindled down to a Christmas card, but we reconnected at the camp reunion six years ago and have stayed in touch through phone calls and e-mail ever since.

Since Lydia's husband, Greg, died last November, our bond has been even tighter. We're determined to see one another through the worst and the best of life. In the last six years, our friendship has seen us through divorce, job changes, kids, and now death. Nothing can separate us.

Well, except maybe this RV thing.

After paying the cabdriver, I push open the taxi door, causing it to squawk in protest. Lydia rushes to my side and hugs me fiercely.

"Oh, sorry," she says with a laugh, "I got flour on your pretty silk blouse."

"No problem," I say, brushing it off.

"Silver looks great on you, DeDe, makes your dark eyes stand out. Looks nice with those black pants too." Lydia looks down at her own top, then touches her hair. "I should have dressed better to meet you girls."

"You look wonderful," I say, giving her one more hug.

She brightens.

In spite of all she's been through, Lydia does look good. She's put on a little weight since the last time we were together, but then, haven't we all? It surprises me to see that she's let her hair go gray, but she still looks pretty. Older, but pretty.

'Course, who am I to talk? I have a few more wrinkles—er, uh, laugh lines—than I did in November. But, hey, I laugh a lot.

My luggage rollers squeak as I pull them over a sidewalk bumpy with age and littered with stubborn weeds that have pushed through the cracks.

"Millie should be here shortly," Lydia says, her words coming out in short bursts of air. "I can hardly believe it's been a month already since we talked about this, and here we are."

"Speaking of which, are we sure we want to do this? Could I entice you with a little gourmet chocolate, perhaps, to give up the idea?" Our gazes collide. "I'm teasing here, but then again, maybe not. You, me, Millie, packed in an RV. For endless days?"

Picture sardines in a can. Speaking of which, I've never appreciated sardines. Yet here I am feeling sorry for them. All crammed together in those little metal cans.

"You don't mind, do you, DeDe? I mean, you want to do this, right?" We step inside Lydia's home, and I set the luggage aside. The wrinkles between her eyebrows deepen at the question.

My heart constricts. Lydia, ever the peacemaker. "Of course I want to do this. Would I miss the chance to get together with my best friends?" Well, maybe I considered it, but she doesn't need to know that. And just for the record, David, Tony, Ralph, and George had nothing to do with it. Well, okay, maybe Tony, but only a little.

Her face softens. "I was afraid, you know, because of the RV and all."

"What? Just because my idea of roughing it consists of a hotel room without a view?"

Lydia laughs and leads the way toward the kitchen. "That would be it."

When we step close to the room, we are greeted by a glorious aroma. "Something smells delicious and vaguely familiar."

"I'm not surprised. There's chocolate in the air," Lydia says with a chuckle. "Cappuccino cheesecake with fudge sauce. We'll have some after dinner."

My mouth waters. Closing my eyes, I lift my nose in the air, take a deep breath, then practically start to purr. It's my natural Pavlovian response to chocolate. "I owe you my firstborn," I say.

"You don't have a firstborn," she says with a laugh.

"Well, if I ever get one, you're down for first dibs."

Another grin.

"No, wait. At my age if I ever get one, medical science will want first dibs."

"Oh, you!" Lydia playfully hits my arm. "That's why you're so good at running your business, you know. You're passionate about chocolate."

"How pathetic is that, Lydia? I mean, some people are passionate about world peace, some want to rid the world of poverty,

7

others strive to wipe out disease. Me? My life is devoted to chocolate."

Lydia grabs some glasses from the cupboard, fills them with ice cubes and tea. "There's a place in this world for chocolate connoisseurs."

"Yeah, it's called a kitchen." The wooden chair at the table scrapes against the ceramic-tiled floor as I pull it out and sit down. Lydia laughs and shakes her head.

"All kidding aside, chocolate is a serious business," I say in defense of my profession. "Why, did you know that the Aztecs and Mayans were the first to discover the value of the cocoa plant? That's only because *I* wasn't born yet, mind you, but still."

Lydia chuckles, and I hurry on.

"It was brought into the United States in the 1700s. So it's been around for a while. Lucky for me, or I'd be out of a job." I'm totally enjoying my little wealth of knowledge until I notice that Lydia isn't really paying attention to me. With a glance out her kitchen window, she points.

"You can see Waldo from here," she says.

I walk over to the window to see my new home for the next few weeks. One glance and I suddenly understand that "bucket of bolts" concept. Her RV looks tired. It could spring a leak. It needs assisted living. The tan-colored motor home has taupe and blue horizontal stripes around its midsection. Can we say stretch marks?

Maybe I'll just visit a day or two and go home.

"I know he doesn't look like much," Lydia says, seeming to read my mind. "He is, after all, fifteen years old, but, hey, I'm no spring chicken and I do okay," she says with a laugh. We both look out the window once more.

It surprises me to see Lydia's RV sitting in a pile of weeds. Her lawn would normally qualify for a magazine photo shoot.

"I need to work on the lawn," she says. "Just haven't had the time."

I'm wondering what she does with all her time now that the boys are out of the house and her husband is gone.

Lydia picks up a glass and hands it to me. Then she grabs one for herself. "Let's sit down at the table."

The wooden chairs creak as we settle into them at the bare oak dining room table that used to be laden with tablecloths and candles.

"You doing okay, Lydia?"

Her eyes lock with mine. "I'm fine, really. Greg has provided well for me. My church activities and friends keep me busy. Oh, and did I tell you I joined the Red Hat Society?"

"Is that one of those groups where the ladies are fifty and up and they wear red hats?" I ask.

"That's the one." Lydia laughs. "I'm telling you, those girls know how to party! They even go on cruises together."

"Sounds enticing, but since I'm only forty-nine, I'm not eligible," I say with a wink.

Lydia's left eyebrow arches. "Not a problem. They accept women younger than fifty, but instead of red hats, they wear pink ones."

"Well, there you are," I say, thumping back against my seat. "Won't happen. Pink washes me out."

"You don't know what you're missing." Lydia says the words like a jingle for a commercial.

"Actually, there is a group near my area that I've been thinking of joining. They buy a lot of chocolate from my store. That tells me they're a fun group with good taste. By the time I get back, I'll be fifty, and I can wear a red hat."

"That's right. You were always the birthday girl at camp."

I nod, and we grow quiet, each sipping our iced tea, remembering. The ticking clock on the wall echoes through the room. Lydia studies the cuticle on her index finger. "I still miss him, you know." She lifts a hesitant smile. "Things are so different now."

"I'm sure that's something one never gets over. I mean, losing the one you love."

She waits a moment, as though she's had to mentally pull herself up by the bootstraps. "Well, one thing I know for sure—Greg would want me to do this trip. He always wanted me to go out with my girlfriends." Her eyes take on a faraway look. "Sometimes I wonder if he knew I would have to go on without him one day." She glances toward me, eyes shining again. "You remember Greg. He continually fussed over me. Like he thought I was too fragile or something." She goes to the refrigerator for the pitcher and adds more tea to her almost-full glass.

My heart aches for Lydia. She and Greg had a wonderful marriage, a model family. Now she's alone. True, I live alone, but then, that's all I've ever known. You don't miss what you've never had. Oh, there was the dream of that once . . .

The doorbell rings.

"It's Millie!" Lydia says, barely sitting down before she hops up again. We both rush for the front door. Once it opens, a bright flash greets us.

We're stunned with blindness for a moment.

"Sorry, but I wanted to get your expressions on our first meeting of this trip," Millie says, clicking off the camera that's dangling from her neck.

The door frame helps me maintain my balance. Lydia steps aside and lets Millie stagger through the door with her luggage.

"Wow, you look great!" Lydia says, hugging her sideways to steer clear of the camera.

"How can you tell? All I can see is a blaze of light." My fingers continue to grip the door frame for support.

"Same old DeDe," Millie says, laughing and pulling me into a hug.

The light dissipates, and I see that Millie does look great. In fact, there's something different about her. I know what it is. She's not dressed in her usual beige polyester. Woo-hoo, the old Millie is back! She's smiling. Millie hasn't smiled since—well, for a very long time, that I can remember.

"Oh my goodness, it's true! You really do have teeth!" I say.

She laughs in spite of herself. "Well, don't get used to seeing them. I show them sparingly."

She chuckles again and reaches up to touch the blonde fringe at the base of her neck, running her fingers through the hair at the side of her face. Wispy bangs fall just above shapely eyebrows that top wide blue eyes. With a handkerchief, she blots her forehead, revealing faint lines where smooth skin used to be. Dark-framed eyeglasses are perched upon her head the way some people wear sunglasses.

Millie sees us looking at them, and her fingers reach up to pull them off her head. "I always forget I have these things up there. But it sure comes in handy to have them when I need to read something." She pulls an eyeglass case from her handbag and stuffs the spectacles inside. "Plus, you know how I'm always losing them. If I stick them on my head, I can usually find them."

Though Millie is one of the most organized people I know, she has a flaw that just doesn't match up. She has a problem with losing glasses the way most people misplace pens. When non-prescription glasses appeared on the scene, she thought she'd died and gone to heaven. Cheap glasses have relieved her of the heavy guilt she once carried for losing prescription glasses. Now if she forgets where she put her glasses, she can afford to go out and buy a new pair—especially if she finds a sale where they go for a dollar a pair. She says she keeps a pair in every room of her house.

"So good to see you, Millie. You've lost weight," I say, stepping back to look at her.

She takes a minute to catch her breath. "It's easy to drop forty pounds after a divorce." She shrugs.

"I'm glad we have God to help us through these things," Lydia says, placing her arm around Millie and ushering her into the next room.

I haven't talked to God in years. Wouldn't know His voice if I heard it—though I'm pretty sure I would suspect something was amiss if He sounded like George Burns.

"Oh my, that smells good, Lydia," Millie says once we arrive in the warm and delicious-smelling kitchen.

"It is good, if I do say so myself. But you have to eat your dinner first," she admonishes like the mother she is.

"No problem there. I'm starved," says Millie. "Those peanuts on the airplane just don't cut it for me anymore."

Lydia says a prayer for our food, then Millie gets up and snaps a picture. "Just wanted to record our first meal together."

We laugh and settle into light conversation over a dinner of grilled chicken, potatoes, broccoli sautéed in butter and spices, homemade dinner rolls, and crisp salad heavy with tomatoes, cheese, and all the fixings.

"Have you girls entered the hot flashes and cold-cream phase yet?" Millie asks, wiping her face again with the handkerchief.

"I've got the cold cream down but haven't had the hot flashes. What are they exactly?" I ask, buttering another roll.

"It's where your head heats up pretty much the same as a block of charcoal in a grill," Millie says, continuing to pat her face. "What about you, Lydia—do you get them?" she asks.

"Yes, I get them. My internal temperature seems to always be running several degrees hotter than everyone else's."

"That would explain why I've been freezing since I arrived. Of course, being from Florida, I just figured it was a climate adjustment—that whole going from south to north thing."

"I also struggle with sleeping at night and sometimes concentrating on things. I'm so forgetful," Lydia adds.

No doubt losing Greg has something to do with the sleeping and concentration problems. "Maybe you should try some chocolate. Chocolate can get you through anything, you know. Especially the smooth, rich Belgian chocolate we buy." I've never been one to linger on heavy issues.

"You always did think chocolate was a cure-all." Millie digs through her handbag, pulls out her glasses, and places them on the bridge of her nose to look at the recipe card for Lydia's dessert. She stops a moment and looks at me. "You don't make the chocolate at your place, do you?"

"See, the thing is, we don't have cacao trees where I live. You know, those tall plants out in the yard that produce cocoa beans? Those would be the ones. Don't have any. Zero. Zip. Nada. The best my tree can do is produce leaves."

Millie stares at me. "That's a shame. You'd have been so good at it, sorting the beans and all," she says with eyes twinkling.

"Could you, by any chance, be referring to my punishment at the camp where Tony and I had to sort through the mounds of green beans simply because Tony put a pine beetle in the green bean tray and I laughed?"

"That would be the one." Millie winks at Lydia.

"To this day I hate green beans."

We all laugh. Only they laugh harder than I do.

"Hey, I brought you both a box of my signature truffles."

"Oh, you're a doll," Lydia says. "Mocha?"

"Of course. Would I bring you anything else?"

Lydia grins. "My emotions thank you. I won't tell you what my hips say."

"It's better that way." I stop and enjoy another bite of Lydia's homemade dinner rolls. "These are absolutely fabulous, Lydia."

"Don't forget to save room for dessert."

"You're kidding, right?" Millie says. "Like she would ever pass up chocolate?" She puts the card aside, shoves her glasses back into the case, and drops it into her handbag.

With a shrug I say, "It's good for the hormones."

"But of course, since you're younger than us, you wouldn't really have a problem with that, right?" Millie teases.

"Right."

"Hey, won't you celebrate a birthday while we're at camp?" Millie asks.

"I'm not doing birthdays this year."

"Can't say that I blame you. Fifty isn't fun."

"Thanks for the encouragement, Millie."

"Fifty is great!" Lydia says. "We should have a party!"

"No party," I say emphatically, cutting off Martha Stewart before the invitations can be addressed and sent.

"Why not?"

"My party self will be bingeing that day. If anything, it should be declared a day of mourning." Millie nods her head in agreement— which I'm not sure I like—while Lydia gapes at me.

"You're no fun."

"Sorry to burst your bubble, Lydia. I'm just not into the attention this year, okay?"

She struggles to agree. It goes against everything in her nature to ignore a birthday event, but her aversion to arguments wins out. She finally nods.

"Well, now that that's settled," Millie says, as if brushing her hands of the matter, "I've told you, Beverly says they received a great response with donations from alumni for the camp restoration." Her eyes spark with excitement. "This is going to be so awesome. I can hardly wait."

"To tell the truth, girls, if I didn't feel such loyalty to Aspen Creek, I would be afraid to try this trip," Lydia says.

Millie and I pause to look at her.

"It makes me a little nervous to take Waldo out. I'm not comfortable with that. Greg always managed Waldo. I just went along for the ride."

Millie pats her hand. "We'll help you, Lydia. This will be an adventure, you'll see."

I try not to gape here. Lydia's staring at her too.

"Have you been sucking on helium balloons again?" I ask, referring to the time I coerced her into doing that with my birthday balloons at camp. The director had walked into our room and asked us why we weren't at the afternoon session, and Millie said—in her Mickey Mouse voice—"I'm not feeling very well." With her mouth dangling, Mrs. Woodriff just stared at Millie. If she hadn't spotted the balloon, I'm sure she would have whisked Millie off to the hospital in a heartbeat.

"No helium." She grins. "Just rediscovering who I really am." Before we can say anything, she goes on. "Oh my goodness, I forgot to tell you girls. Guess who Beverly said is coming to help at the camp?"

Lydia and I stop our forks midair. "Who?"

"Eric Melton!" Millie's eyes are wide, and she's smiling as she thumps back into her chair.

"Really?" Lydia's right hand reaches up to straighten her hair.

"Eric Melton, aka Mr. Egomaniac? That Eric Melton?" I ask.

"As I live and breathe." Millie wipes her mouth with a napkin. "I couldn't believe it when Beverly told me. Wonder what he looks like after all these years."

"Oh, that's right. He didn't make it to the reunion," I say, noticing that Lydia's face has turned a curious shade of pink.

"He's probably still a jerk," Millie says with a grunt. "Remember how he always used to run the palms of his hands along the sides of his head to smooth his hair when girls were looking? It's a wonder he didn't rub his head bald."

Millie has a way of saying things.

"Hopefully his ego has toned down a bit," she continues before finishing off the last of her broccoli. She turns to Lydia. "Didn't you date him a couple of times?"

Lydia lifts her glass of tea and without looking at us says, "Yes, I did." Ice clinks against the side of the glass before she takes a drink. "If you hadn't been going steady with Tony, he would have asked you out, Dee."

"He was pretty cute," I say. "But I did have it bad for Tony," I add in a dreamy voice.

"Yeah, lasted for all of, what, two weeks?" Millie laughs.

"Don't knock it. That was a record for me back then." *'Course, I beat that record when Rob came along. Rob, the guy I thought might finally be the one . . .*

"Eric really liked you, Lydia; I remember that," Millie says, pulling me back from my memories.

Lydia says nothing. She gathers dessert dishes and teacups, then serves us cheesecake and coffee.

I fill my glass with a swallow of warm water from the tap to clear my palate, then sip it until it's gone. Once I'm seated, I take a small bite of the cheesecake, close my eyes, and move it slowly over my tongue, savoring the moment. When I open my eyes, Lydia and Millie are staring at me.

"What? Don't you know there is a correct way to experience chocolate?"

Lydia and Millie shake their heads.

"Oh my, yes." I sit up in my seat. "You should eat it at room temperature. Don't drink something cold before tasting it, because a warm mouth is important for the chocolate to melt quickly."

Lydia and Millie continue to stare, their mouths wide open, resembling baby birds at mealtime. I'm enjoying this immensely.

"A glossy surface is a must if it's a well-made bar," I continue like a professor at a French cooking school. "You will notice that all my chocolates qualify." Getting up from the table, I say, "Be right back." My luggage is by the door, so I rush to it and pull out a couple of boxes, then run back to the kitchen and take my seat. "Mocha for you, Millie. Lydia, since you don't seem to have a preference, I brought a good mixture of praline, peanut butter, raspberry, and mocha."

They each grab a truffle and lift it to their noses. I do the same. "See, you break the chocolate into pieces so you can smell the aroma." Once I break off a piece, we each take turns smelling it.

"Oh yeah, then when I take a bite, I allow the aroma to fill the nasal passage at the back of my mouth, engaging my senses of smell and taste." Taking a bite, I pause. "Bliss, sheer bliss."

Millie and Lydia exchange glances.

"Wow, chocolate is serious business," Lydia says with utmost reverence.

Raising my eyebrows and my chin, I pull my hand to my chest (picture Napoléon Bonaparte here). "A chocolate connoisseur has trained senses to discover the very best chocolate." My head tips in a slight bow. Then I grin.

Millie doesn't look all that impressed. She shrugs and goes back to her cheesecake.

I put my chocolate away—well, not the broken pieces. Those go on my plate with my cheesecake, and I take another bite. "Didn't you say this was cappuccino cheesecake?"

Lydia nods.

"For some reason, I don't taste the coffee part. 'Course, I like my coffee a little strong, so maybe that's why I can't taste it." Lifting my napkin, I wipe my mouth.

Lydia blinks. "Oh dear." She rises and walks over to the counter.

"What's wrong?" Millie asks.

Lydia turns to look at us. "I forgot to add the coffee."

"It's still delicious," I say with a shrug.

Lydia rejoins us at the table and shakes her head. "See, I forget everything."

Millie shrugs. "It happens. Now what were we talking about?"

"Let's see, we were talking about you dating Eric, I think," I say to Lydia.

"Eric liked me, but he liked himself even more," she says. "He wasn't the type to stick with one girl."

"Besides, if I remember right, Greg showed up at camp and swept you off your feet about that time, didn't he?" Millie asks, innocently enough, but suddenly everything gets quiet.

Lydia stares at her with a sort of dazed look. "Yeah, he did." Her voice is upbeat, but she stares in the distance to a place I suspect she visits often.

Things suddenly feel very awkward.

"Remember how we called Mrs. Woodriff 'The Warden'?" Lydia asks, changing the subject.

"Ethel Belle Woodriff, The Warden," Millie and I echo together with a laugh.

"Oh boy, we were so in trouble for breaking curfew with her around," I say.

"Because she knew we were always up to something." Millie turns to me. "Especially you. How I let you talk me into such things, I'll never know. I'm telling you, books are safer than friends."

"Oh, come on, it's much more fun *doing* something than just reading about it. Besides, it's not like you didn't want any part of spraying her bed with sugar water. If I remember correctly, you were all too eager to participate."

Millie brightens with the memory. Just as quickly a frown appears. "Well, how were we to know it would attract every mosquito and ant within a twenty-mile radius?"

We burst into laughter.

"For putting up with us, the woman probably is wearing a huge crown in heaven as we speak," I say.

Hand over her chest, Lydia says, "She was a saint."

"Amen," Millie and I say together.

We talk awhile longer, reminiscing about our camp days. Lydia lets us know her motor home has had a recent checkup and should be as good as new when we start our trip. That makes me feel better—slightly—but I still don't understand why we can't all pitch in for Hiltons along the way. At least they leave chocolate mints on your pillows.

Finally, we all grow tired and climb the stairs to our rooms.

"Now, I want one of you to stay in my room." Lydia raises her hand before anyone can protest. "Don't argue with me about it, because it will do you no good. When someone visits, I give up my bed. It's the most comfortable bed in the house."

Millie and I both fudge here. We're a bit uncomfortable with the idea of taking Lydia's bed. It just doesn't seem right. Besides, we know there isn't a bed in her house that is uncomfortable.

"Where will you sleep?" I ask.

"In one of the boys' rooms. One of you will be in the guest room."

No one says anything.

Lydia pulls a coin from her pants pocket. "Heads or tails," she says, flipping it in the air and catching it. She turns to me. "DeDe?"

"Heads."

"Heads it is," she announces.

Just then my cell phone rings. Slipping the phone from my purse, I see Rob's name on the screen. I toss Lydia and Millie a smile, then tuck my ringing phone back into my purse.

"Aren't you going to answer that?" Millie asks.

"I'll call them back," I say.

"Okay, well, put your things in there," Lydia says, pointing.

Once we settle into our respective rooms, I pull out my phone. Why does he keep calling me? Can't he get it through his head that it's over? With a deep breath, I shove the unwanted feelings away from my heart like a mess of clothes behind a closet door.

I glance around Lydia's bedroom. While the rest of her house and yard looks a bit unkempt, this room appears immaculate. Books, magazines, and forgotten projects clutter my bedroom back home. To make matters worse, I'm almost sure every disease known to humankind lurks beneath my bed.

The funny thing is, this room smells a little musty. Not like Lydia at all. Maybe she hasn't opened her windows in a while. Hauling my squeaky luggage across the hardwood floor, I heave it onto a chair, pull out my pajamas, then put them on. I plop on the bed and stretch out. It is heavenly, but how can I sleep without a book? The one in my suitcase is too emotionally draining right now. Glancing at the nightstand, I figure Lydia might have some reading material, so I open the drawer. It's empty. How odd.

Shame on me for being so nosy, but I walk over to the dresser and peek inside. Sweaters line the drawers. Clothes for the fall and winter. It suddenly occurs to me.

Lydia doesn't sleep in here.

She appears as upbeat as always, but now I'm wondering if it's all a front. We'll have to help her through this. Walking over to the bed, I climb between the satin sheets. My thoughts drift from Lydia's grief to her RV sitting in a pile of weeds.

I'll turn fifty on this trip. Fortunately, I haven't slowed down long enough to think about that. But here in this house, seeing my friends, seeing the RV, well, things are changing, that's all.

Scrambling out of bed, I pull the cold cream from my suitcase and smear it on.

Unfortunately, there are some things even chocolate can't fix.

2

Just after breakfast, the three of us take our coffee, paper, and pens into the family room, ready to make our lists for the trip. While Lydia and I settle into our seats, Millie snaps a picture of the moment, then joins us. Same old Millie.

Steam curls and lifts the aroma of hazelnut from my cup, and I take a deep whiff as I glance around the family room. Lydia's boys used to have such fun in this room. Back when they were younger, it was more of a game room, complete with table hockey, big-screen TV, board games, and in one corner, darts. The games are gone now, and an extended sofa sits in their places, along with a twenty-six-inch standard TV and a wide area of open, hollow space that emphasizes something is missing. It lacks warmth and shows little evidence of the family noise and fun that used to take place within these walls.

"You look good in red," Millie says, pointing to Lydia's shorts outfit.

"That's why she joined the Red Hat Society, you know," I say with a grin.

"You did? I've thought about doing that, but I'm too chicken to wear a hat in public." Millie takes a drink from her mug. "I just don't have the face for it."

"Oh, I would love to jump on that one," I say with a chuckle.

Millie's left eyebrow rises.

We discuss the advantages of belonging to a Red Hat group, and Lydia convinces us to check it out when we get back home. Which, of course, I was planning to do anyway.

Breaking the silence that follows, someone starts whistling *The Andy Griffith Show* theme song. Millie and I look around.

Lydia laughs. "It's Cobbler," she says, pointing to her blue and white parakeet perched in the birdcage that is situated on a stand in the corner of the room.

"Your bird whistles *The Andy Griffith Show* song?" Millie asks with wide-eyed wonder.

"Cobbler is a Mayberry groupie," Lydia responds with all the admiration of a proud mother. "She has to have her fix every day."

"How do you mean?" I walk over and peer into the cage. Tiny birdseed hulls litter the paper-lined floor, covering the ad for an upcoming George Clooney movie. Only half of George's face is showing. That is just wrong. Leaning toward the bottom, I blow a teensy bit in hopes of clearing George of this disgrace, but the hulls scatter about, some settling outside the cage and onto the carpet. I sneeze three times, causing more hulls to scatter. "I'll deal with you later." I won't rest until George Clooney's dignity is restored.

Lydia places coasters for our mugs on the coffee table. Millie and I sit on the sofa, and Lydia sits across from us in a rocking chair. "If I don't turn *The Andy Griffith Show* on for Cobbler every day, she throws a fit. Dumps the hulls from her seeds all over the floor, squawks up a storm. She has a thing for Barney."

I can't imagine how the bird—or any species for that matter—could pick Barney on TV over George Clooney, who is right in her cage—well, his image anyway. This bird needs help.

"What makes you think Cobbler has a thing for Barney?" I ask.

"After the episode where Barney was caught kissing Thelma Lou, Cobbler didn't eat for two days."

First a motor home named Waldo, and now this? "Anyone know the number for Dr. Phil? *Someone* has some serious issues."

Lydia puts her index finger to her lips. "Shh, or she'll hear you."

"Actually, I was talking about you."

Lydia stops and looks at me to see if I'm serious. Only after I laugh does she join me. "Well, Cobbler is a tad bit different too," Lydia whispers.

All righty then. Do I really want to take this trip? Just how well do I know these people? I mean, really?

Lydia takes a drink of coffee, then places the mug in a coaster. "Okay, you girls ready?" she asks, pen and paper in hand.

"Armed and dangerous," Millie answers, pen poised over the paper. She takes over. "How about you make the grocery list, Lydia? DeDe, you write down the miscellaneous kind of stuff we need, like paper towels, batteries, that kind of thing. I'll make sure the map I printed off the Internet jibes with this atlas; will that work?"

Lydia and I stare at Millie.

"What?" she asks.

"Just admiring your leadership abilities," Lydia says.

"Actually, my thoughts took a different direction."

"Ha-ha," Millie says. Her gaze flits to Lydia. "What can I say? It's my gift."

"I have a different name for it," I mumble under my hand.

"I heard that," Millie says.

"Girls," Lydia warns.

Millie and I exchange friendly growls, then move on. "Now, girls, do we want to travel the most direct route or the most scenic?" Millie pauses here, but before we can say anything, she hurries on. "Beverly said everyone else was making the effort to get there within two weeks. That gives us a little leeway. It's roughly a twenty-one-hundred-mile trip. We could probably make it in a week if we drove straight through, but around two weeks would give us time to do a little sightseeing and just have fun on the way. I vote for the most scenic route. What do you think?"

"Sounds good to me," Lydia says. "It will be good to get some time away," she says, looking around the room.

While I hate to be gone too long from my business, my partner has assured me things will be fine and has told me to go enjoy this time with my friends. Rob won't leave me alone, and my feelings for him scare me. It's better if I get away—before I do something really stupid. "Sounds good to me too," I say with a grin. "Let's make this a memorable vacation!" *Though something tells me traveling in an RV will be memorable enough.*

Lydia and Millie catch my enthusiasm. "That's more like it," Millie says. "To our trip." She lifts her coffee cup toward us. Lydia and I join in, and we carefully tap our cups together.

"I have another idea. After we get the things we need, how about we pack everything into Waldo, then go to the beach this afternoon?" Lydia says.

"The beach sounds great," I say. "Will it take long to get there?"

"Not at all. It's just about twenty-five miles east of here."

Millie claps her hands together. "Great! Let's do it. I've got a new book I'm ready to *dive* into."

We set to work, and by morning's end we've made a list of everything we need to pick up at the store, and Millie has mapped out our trip's route.

Soon we wander the aisles of the grocery store, picking up the necessary supplies, and I have to admit I'm getting a little excited. The "brewing storm" feeling has subsided, and I'm actually getting into this whole save-the-camp idea. Not only that, but Rob, the love-of-my-life-turned-traitor, has only entered my brain a couple of times today. Baby steps.

"I'll unlock Waldo so we can load everything inside," Lydia says when we arrive back at her house.

Though I'm not into motor homes, I have to admit the RV looks all right. Large windows flank the home, giving it an airy feel. Lydia opens the various compartments on the outside, revealing storage, the sewer hose, hookup compartments, and such.

An ammonia scent greets us when we enter the blue and light gray interior. Just behind the driver's seat, a blue sofa hugs the wall. On the opposite side is a matching love seat.

"That pulls out into a bed," Lydia says, pointing to the sofa. "This is our kitchen," she says after we take two steps forward.

"Nice touch." I nod toward the bouquet of yellow, red, purple, and pink flowers erupting from a blue ceramic pitcher on the table.

"Thanks. They're from my flower garden." There's a smidgen of pride in Lydia's voice. "We'll have to store them under the sink once we start moving. Here's the sink, stove, microwave, and refrigerator," Lydia says, touching each one with her hand as we stroll by—okay, we can stand still and touch everything. Yes, they really are that close.

"It's very nice, Lydia," Millie and I assure her. And it really is. I mean, as far as motor homes go.

Oak storage bins border the tops of the walls as we edge down the hallway. And I do mean *edge* down the hallway. I'm thinking if I overdo it on dessert, I'll be wedged between the refrigerator and the bathroom for the duration of the trip.

The door on my right leads to the bathroom. A shower, stool, and sink. All the comforts of home—in a frightening sort of way.

Straight ahead is the bedroom area that encases two twin-sized beds and a nightstand. Lydia lifts the bed mattresses to reveal more storage beneath them. Cabinets border the bedroom walls. Plump pink and blue throw pillows give the matching quilts on the beds a cozy feel. *Cozy* is the polite word for "cramped."

"Tiny but quaint," Lydia says with a smile.

"I think it's great," Millie says.

They both turn to me. "Quaint," I say, grabbing Lydia's word. I'm wondering how I will describe it after two weeks. Two days. Two hours.

"I'll let you girls have the beds, and I'll sleep on the sofa bed," Lydia offers.

Millie and I emphatically refuse. This is her motor home, and she will sleep in a real bed.

"Well, I think you're being ridiculous, but you're both head-strong, so I'll have to concede." Lydia looks at the beds and then back to us. "All the beds are comfortable, but we can toss a coin to see who sleeps in the actual beds and who sleeps on the sofa bed."

"No need to do that. I've slept on sofa beds before, and I'm fine with that," Millie says.

"You don't need—"

Millie holds up her hand, cutting me off. "My mind is made up. Besides, I like sleeping near the door where I can keep an eye on things."

One thing I've learned over the years, you don't want to mess with Millie when she hasn't had her beauty sleep. She could tear the hide off a grizzly.

We store our clothes and toiletries away. With horror I watch as Millie stores a familiar case. "Is that your trumpet?" *Please, oh please, say no.*

"Yes." A proud smile lifts the corners of her mouth.

An inward groan. "You're planning to play on our trip?" I ask nonchalantly, though every neuron in my brain is standing at attention.

"Hopefully at the camp." The tone of her voice tells me she thinks she's doing us a favor. "It relaxes me when I play."

Can we talk about what it does to everyone else? My gaze collides with Lydia's. The panic I see on her face matches what I'm feeling. She shakes her head slightly.

"That's nice," Lydia says with a sweet smile.

Nice? She thinks that's nice? A Girl Scout helping a little old lady cross to the other side of the street, *that's* nice. A vase of roses? Nice. Millie playing her trumpet? That's just wrong.

Lydia shoots me a "behave yourself" look, so I keep silent—on the outside. But inside I'm screaming to beat the band.

We step outside the motor home, and Millie snaps a picture. She's going to get on my nerves during this trip; I can feel it. To calm myself, I take a deep breath of fresh air and a sweeping view of the late sky. Fortunately, it's not late enough to stop true beach lovers such as ourselves from going on a little jaunt to the sea.

After packing the RV, we make our way to the house, put our bathing suits on beneath our street clothes, and grab the suntan oil, beach towels, and snacks; then off we go like college girls on spring break.

The wind whips against the motor home's side, causing it to groan like an old man with arthritis. And this hunk of metal is carrying us twenty-one hundred miles? I can only hope we have enough Bengay.

On the way to the beach, the oldies station crackles from the radio speakers, and we crack right along with it, totally charged by the time we arrive.

With the long hours I put in at Le Diva Chocolates, this break will do me good. Away from work and, well, other distractions. It will give me time to sort out what I want to do with my future, besides work. Funny how different my future appeared less than a year ago when Rob Grant was in my life. We did everything together. Well, on the weekends, since that was the only time we could be together. Like an idiot, I dropped my church, my friends, everything and everyone, to keep my weekends free for him. How could I have been so stupid?

"Hey, you gonna sit there all day like a bump on a log, or are you coming?" Millie asks with a wide grin.

Climbing out of the motor home, I take a big whiff, allowing the salty sea air to fill my lungs. Cupping my hands over my eyes, I gaze at the water. The ocean seems such a contradiction to me.

One minute it inspires me to soar; the next minute it calms my heart to a whisper. How can that be?

Seagulls caw overhead, swooping here and there for dry crusts of bread or soggy chips left on the sand. An old man with scraggly gray hair, tattered pants, and a dirty white T-shirt combs the beach with a metal contraption, looking for hidden treasures. A smattering of kids splash and squeal at the water's edge while frazzled mothers look after them. A few bikini-clad teenagers bake in the sun, and a makeshift volleyball net stands in the distance while buff young men spike a ball back and forth.

"Where is everyone?" I ask Lydia as we unfold our lounging chairs.

She turns to me with a smile. "This beach is Maine's best-kept secret."

"Last one in is a rotten egg," I squeal, running toward the water.

Lydia and Millie laugh, running behind me.

I plunge into the water with gusto, and a scream escapes me. Not quite Janet Leigh in *Psycho*, but close.

Lydia laughs and braces herself for the cold. "You forget Maine is not Florida. Our water is cold."

"Cold? You call this cold? Polar bears could come here in search of food." I scan the horizon for icebergs headed our way.

"Don't be such a wimp, Dee," Millie says as soon as we're all waist-deep in the water. Millie cups her hands and lifts water to her face and neck.

Just watching her causes me to shiver uncontrollably.

Lydia points to my face. "Your lips are blue, Dee."

"No, I'd say purple. Definitely purple," Millie says with an evil laugh.

"Are you kidding? You could leave me here, and I wouldn't age a day in three years."

"Now there's an idea," Millie says. She continues to splash the water over herself. "This is wonderful. I should move near the ocean. Then if I'd get a hot flash, it would be no big deal. I'd just go skinny dippin'."

Lydia turns and gasps.

"What?" Millie looks offended. "You can't imagine me being so bold?" A smile lights her face.

Excuse me? That's a vision my stomach just can't handle. "It will cause all aquatic life within ten square miles to scatter," I say.

Millie's grin disappears.

"I'm just kidding." Well, sort of.

"You know, girls, I'm thankful we met each other all those years ago." Lydia splashes water in the air at nothing in particular.

"Yeah, it's good we got something out of that leadership camp. I sure haven't done much with what I learned there," I say between shivers.

"You're a leader, or you wouldn't have your own candy shop," Millie says, now splashing water over her head.

"I guess that's true." She must have missed the whole point of our being there to learn how to be leaders for Christ.

"I'm not sure it was fair that they let the three of us keep coming all through high school. I mean, seems like others should have gotten the chance," Lydia says.

"Well, we weren't the only ones. Besides, it takes more than one week to train leaders, and they knew that," says Millie, ever the practical one.

"Well, I'm glad we did meet, and I'm glad that God has brought us together yet again."

I agree with Lydia. My relationship skills aren't what they used to be.

"You know, for me camp was a reprieve from my parents' constant arguing."

Lydia and I look at Millie with a start.

"Don't you remember me talking about how my parents fought all the time?"

As the memory unfolds, I slowly nod. "That's why you loved your books, right?"

"Exactly. I could escape my 'real' world. Maybe it's just as well I didn't have children. Probably wouldn't know how to behave in a real family setting."

"You'd make a great mother," Lydia interjects. "You'd introduce them to the world of reading. They'd have a thirst for knowledge, I have no doubt." She punctuates her sentence with a charming smile.

"Mine would have a craving for chocolate."

We all laugh.

"Well, I've had enough," I say, dragging my freezing self out of the water. The others follow suit, and we soon dry off and settle into our chairs.

Pulling the suntan oil from her beach bag, Lydia unscrews the cap, pours some on her arm, then rubs it in. The sweet, buttery aroma reminds me of when I was a kid and would go to the swimming pool with my mom. She would slather me with suntan lotion like a greased pig at the county fair. I sure miss her. My loss is heaven's gain.

Millie pulls a gray contraption from her bag and holds it near her face.

Lydia has one too and is doing the same thing.

"What is that?" I ask, wondering what they have that I don't.

"A lifesaver," Lydia says with a smile, wind blowing in her face, her bangs lifting with the breeze.

Millie's hair is blowing too.

"Are those fans?" I'm still thawing out, and they're hot? I'm thinking these wimps would never make it in the Florida sun.

"You'll understand when you have hot flashes." Millie lifts her chin and tilts the fan toward her neck.

"We're on the beach, Millie. Everyone gets hot on the beach. It's part of the whole tanning process."

"You'll find out," Millie says as though she can hardly wait. She bends over and grabs a book from her bag.

I don't mean to be rude here, but as I watch Millie and Lydia, I'm seeing that the three of us aren't what we used to be. My gaze travels to their swimsuits and then to my own. The truth is, we're not overweight exactly—well, maybe a little—but it's more like our skin zigs where it used to zag. Unlike the stud-boys down the beach playing volleyball, the only thing that's firm on my body now is the callus on my right pinkie toe.

Once we've all rubbed in a fair amount of lotion, we settle into our reading material and just relax to the sounds of the tide as it makes its way to the shoreline and then back out to sea.

After a while, Millie fidgets around in her as if like she just can't get comfortable.

"You all right, Millie?" I ask.

She sighs, closes her book, and pulls off her glasses. "The truth is, I need to tell you girls something."

The tone of her voice makes me take off my sunglasses. Don't ask me why, but I just hear better with my sunglasses off. Weird, I know, but, hey, I don't have an RV named Waldo.

"Well, I've put off telling you, but Bruce remarried six months ago," she says, referring to her ex-husband.

"I'm sorry, Millie," I say.

"Me too, Millie. I know how hard it is to lose someone you love."

"But you had no choice, Lydia. If only I had—"

"We all have regrets," I say. "We have to move on, learn from past mistakes, and do better next time." Yeah, I'm one to talk. Will there ever be a *next time* for me? Maybe I should tell them about Rob. Maybe not.

"You're right." For a moment we sit in the silence while Millie gazes at the ocean. "You know, it's funny. It was the little things about Bruce that used to drive me crazy. Like how he would iron a shirt and then when he put the iron back in its slot on the wall, he would just let the cord dangle instead of wrapping it tightly into the slot made for it. I should have been happy that he ironed his own shirts." She looks at us, gives a sad smile, then looks back out to sea. "Now the cord is perfectly in place."

My heart stings from her last sentence. Millie has always seemed so in control. It surprises me to see her vulnerable. If only we could fix it for her.

"I wish my story had a different ending, but I'm happy for Bruce. Really. He's a good man, and I hope his second wife is able—well, that they are happy."

Lydia is sitting closest to Millie. She reaches her hand out and places it on Millie's arm. "You're on a new path now."

Millie turns with a bright smile. "Yes, that's why saving the camp is so important to me. My marriage failed for many reasons. But after my divorce, I decided to stop making mistakes and start making a difference."

There's a lot of good in what Millie says. Still, no matter how hard I try, sometimes I still mess things up. How could I have known about Rob? The familiar churning comes back to my stomach. How could I have been that gullible? If only I could stop thinking about it. About him.

By the time the sun dips over the horizon, most of the beach dwellers are gone, along with our snacks. We bring our afternoon of reading and catching up to an end, fold up our chairs, and gather our things, then head back to the RV (I refuse to call it Waldo). Once we settle into our seats, Lydia starts the engine. The motor home *grrrs* twice, shivers, then goes completely mute. She turns the key again. *Click.* Once more. Nothing. Nada. Zip. Zilch.

Now, call me paranoid, but I'm thinking this is where that whole storm-brewing thing comes in . . .

3

After some persistence, Lydia is able to get the RV up and running again. And this thing is carrying us twenty-one hundred miles? Okeydokey.

By the time we get to her house, we're all tired, so we eat a light snack and go to bed.

The next morning we take our time over coffee, double-check that we've packed everything, and manage to get on the road just after lunch.

Lydia is driving. Millie is sitting in the passenger's seat, studying the map of Maine that's sprawled out on her lap.

With a glance at Millie's printed map, I notice she has roads going north highlighted in blue, south roads highlighted in green, and west roads in orange. She's so organized, and I'm, well, not.

"Could someone get me a pillow for my back?" Lydia asks.

Running the six feet to the "bedroom," I grab a pillow. "Here you go." She leans forward, and I stuff it between her and the seat back.

"Thanks, DeDe. Um, could you get me a bottled water from the fridge?" she asks. "Should have gotten one before I started driving. Sorry."

"Oh, grab me one too, Dee, will you?" Millie calls out.

Something tells me I'm going to have the hardest job here. Okay, so I walk all of four steps to go from their chairs to the refrigerator, but still.

"We're planning to travel four or five hours a day to allow for any problems and to give us time to relax, so this should be a pretty easy trip," Millie says.

"Where will we end up today?" I ask, handing them both their bottled waters.

"Thanks." Millie looks at her map. "We'll be going a little ways through New Hampshire, then heading south into Massachusetts. From there we'll hit New York State and finally stop around Albany, New York."

"How far is that?" I ask.

"I'd say roughly two hundred fifty miles."

"Oh, look at those sweet little high school boys," Lydia says as a school bus comes alongside us. She smiles and waves.

"They're hoodlums; don't encourage them," Millie grouses.

"Oh, for goodness' sake, they're a friendly high school football team. Probably just won a game or something," Lydia says, still waving.

The bus finally passes and pulls in front of us. Lydia's scream splits through the air, the RV wobbles, and I fall off my seat.

"Well, that is the most disgusting thing—pull alongside that bus right this minute, Lydia, and tell their coach," Millie barks, her snapping fingers punctuating the statement.

By the time I pull myself off the floor and hobble up to the front, the objects of their distress are fading farther down the highway.

Still, I can't help but giggle when I see the bare rumps of two high schoolers shining in all their glory from the back window of the bus.

"I can't believe you're laughing," Millie says. "They're mooning us!"

"Shame on them," I say with an appropriate amount of reprimand in my voice. I try to stop laughing, but for the life of me, I can't.

Millie snorts. "And you're letting them get away, Lydia?"

"Waldo can't keep up, Millie," she says.

"Besides, if we stop them, it will take up too much time, and we'll get *behind* in our trip," I say, laughing harder.

"Yeah, and if we're the last ones to arrive at Aspen Creek, we'll be the *butt* of everyone's jokes." Now Lydia is laughing too, so hard I'm afraid she's going to pop a rib.

Millie huffs—or is she trying to cover up a chuckle?—then cracks open another book. "I thought it would be fun if we brushed up on some trivia along the way about Rocky Mountain National Park, since we visited there so long ago."

"Now there's a thrill a minute. You're forgetting that geography is not my forte? It's linked right up there with the getting-lost-in-the-parking-garage thing."

"That's why I'm helping you. Once you learn geography, you might actually notice, oh, I don't know, exit signs, road signs, tree scars, you know, the typical things that help you get where you need to go." Millie flashes a smile.

I pop open my water bottle and pause to look at Millie. "Bottoms up," I say with a grin before taking a drink.

She ignores me completely. Still, Lydia giggles, so I'm satisfied.

"Besides, it will be fun to see how much we remember from being in Colorado as teens," Millie says.

"Oh dear," Lydia says. "I'm doing good to remember things I did five minutes ago."

Not one to be deterred, Millie sits up in her chair and clears her throat. "We'll start with wildlife in Rocky Mountain National Park. What type of wildlife does one find in Rocky Mountain National Park?" she asks with all the eloquence of a game-show host.

Strains of the *Jeopardy* theme song swirl in my head, and for the life of me, I can't help feeling that I need to slam my hand against a buzzer. "What is elk?" I say in my most intellectual voice.

"Very funny," Millie says without smiling.

"Party pooper."

"What else besides elk?"

Lydia jumps in. "Bighorn sheep."

"Coyotes, beavers," I say, feeling the spirit of competition. "Mountain lions, moose, great horned owls—"

"Okay, this is too easy. Let's try something else," Millie says, thumbing through the pages of her book. She just can't stand it when I'm right.

"What's the name of the colorful orange and red flowers one finds in the mountains? Sometimes they're yellow too."

Lydia's arm shoots straight up. "Oh, oh, I know!" I half-expect her to say, "Mr. Kotter, Mr. Kotter!"

"Lydia?" Millie nods.

"Indian paintbrush."

"Right!" Before Millie goes on, she looks up at the sign. "Oh, you have to exit here."

I'm thankful for the reprieve. My brain can handle only so many questions. Okay, two's pretty much my limit. But? I know my chocolates, so that should count for something. Speaking of which, I haven't had any in a while. Reaching into my cloth bag of essentials, I pull out a mocha truffle. This creamy milk chocolate is heavenly. Though I admit I always pluck the coffee bean from the top. Too bitter for my taste.

Suddenly a low rumble sounds beneath my feet—coming from the RV's underbelly.

I stuff the truffle into my mouth, all thoughts of savoring now gone. I admit it: I eat for comfort. I like comfort. It's a good thing, unlike the noise that this bucket-of-tin-on-wheels is now making . . .

If I didn't know better, I'd say somebody laced the RV's oil with bean dip. It's jerking like a wild bronco, and the smell that's shooting out its back side—well, it ain't healthy, that's all.

The metal contraption sputters and spasms until Lydia exits the ramp and pulls into a combined convenience store and filling station. Maybe it's emotionally distraught. Carrying around two menopausal women—hey, *I'm* still normal—could do that.

Millie looks at Lydia. "Everything okay?"

Lydia doesn't look troubled in the least. "Everything is fine. Waldo just needs a fill-up. Gas goes through him a lot faster these days."

"You're saying Waldo can't hold his gas?" I pipe up.

Lydia chuckles, and Millie laughs right out loud. Mark it on the calendar! It's a rare event when Millie cuts loose—you know, like the appearance of the seventeen-year cicadas.

Lydia sets to work at the pump.

"I've never even driven a van," I say, peeking over the driver's seat and staring at the panel on the dashboard.

"These things aren't all that hard to drive, really," Millie says. "Why don't you sit up here a minute and get a feel for it?"

"Really?"

"Sure."

I climb into the driver's seat. "Wow, this is so high up. Gives you that king-of-the-road feeling. You know, all-powerful and everything."

Millie chuckles. "Much more than a convertible, that's for sure."

With my hands clamped on the large steering wheel, I turn it slightly back and forth. "I could get into this. It's kind of fun."

"You'll have to tell Lydia you want to try it."

Lydia pops her head in the door. "Hey, I'm going to go inside for a minute to get a bag of chips. You guys want anything?"

"No thanks," we say.

"You want to drive next?" Lydia asks me.

Gulp. "I'm not sure I'm ready for that just yet."

"You can try it out by moving straight ahead, away from the

pumps, so other people can get their fuel." Lydia motions to an empty spot.

"Really? You want me to try it?"

"Sure." Lydia closes the door.

Starting the engine, I carefully edge forward. My queenly perch lifts me above the masses, and I sense this whole power thing could get the better of me. Okay, so I only moved forward a couple of feet, but still.

"You're blocking those cars," Millie graciously points out.

I turn to face Madame Librarian. "Well, if the drivers come back before Lydia, I'll move. No use worrying about it now."

Lydia steps up to the store's door as if she hasn't a care in the world. Just goes to prove you never can know what's going on in the heart of another person. A man holds the door open for her.

"Now that's just nice," I say, pointing to the man, who is dressed in a crumpled white T-shirt, black jacket, tattered jeans, and dark, scuffed boots. Gray stubble shadows his chin. "Not much to look at, but nice."

Millie turns to see what I'm talking about. "Yeah, you don't see many men doing that nowadays. If you're not a babe around twentysomething, the men don't even notice."

"Babe? Did you just say 'babe'? In all the years I've known you, I've never heard you use that word." You think you know a person.

"Hey, I'm hip," she says, thereby proving she's not.

We look back toward the guy holding the door open for Lydia. "That guy reminds me of Bruce when he lost all that weight before they found out he had diabetes," Millie says. "He probably weighs all of, what, eighty pounds?"

"Um, I'd say he'd tip the scales at a hundred five, at least." We both chuckle.

"Here he's doing something nice, and we're making fun of him," Millie says, spoiling everything.

"Just like we used to make fun of the boys at camp when we

were fifteen," I reminisce. I pull out a magazine and read an article on the latest breakup in Hollywood. When I look up, Lydia is exiting the store.

"You know, a bowl of grapes sounds pretty good to me right about now," Millie says, getting up from her chair and heading for the refrigerator. "You want some?"

"No thanks."

Lydia walks toward a trash can at the side of the store, still in view. I notice a teenage boy walking behind her, a little too close to suit me. Lydia must sense it too. Just as she attempts to turn around, his hands reach out to grab her. Lydia struggles to break free and takes off running toward the open field at the side of the store.

"Millie, he's after Lydia!" I scream.

"What?" Millie asks, semichoking on a grape.

A driver is waiting in a nearby car with its engine running. In case he's in cahoots with that kid, I kick the RV into reverse so I can block him. Millie loses her balance and drops her bowl, sending grapes rolling all over.

The RV's side is too close to the car, so getting out on the driver's side is not an option. Springing into action, I scramble to the other door. "Come on, we've got to help Lydia!"

I shove the door open and run toward that teenager in full middle-age fury. He trips when he sees me coming and falls forward, hitting his forehead on the ground. "Lydia, run!" I scream. My legs and arms spread like those of a flying ninja, and I lunge at the criminal for all I'm worth. A Bruce Lee scream pierces the air. In one swoop I fall hard on the perpetrator, most likely taking years off his life.

Footsteps race toward us, and I turn just in time to see Millie take a high jump. I open my mouth to scream, but in one giant free fall, Millie's derriere comes crashing down upon us, snuffing out my cries and pushing my spleen to the other side of my body.

The kid groans. I don't have the strength. Lydia is nearby, her mouth hanging open in shock—whether from being grabbed or from the sight of Millie and me sprawled on top of this kid, I'm not sure.

Now, call me pessimistic, but something tells me this trip is just wrong.

4

By the time the policeman arrives and sorts through everything, we find out that the kid thought Lydia was his mom's friend, and he was trying to scare her just for fun.

Well, Lydia wasn't his mom's friend, he did scare her, and it wasn't fun. Still, we don't press charges. We figure Millie's free fall was enough punishment to last him a lifetime.

Millie takes a group snapshot of the policeman, the kid, and the three of us before we part ways. For a reward, I go back into the store and buy a bag of assorted candy.

Once we get back into the RV, I step over the grapes on the floor—hey, Millie spilled them, and she's the neat freak—and pull open my sack of junk. Though I normally snub my nose at store-bought chocolate, that little episode with Lydia begs for it. Besides, I like to keep tabs on the competition.

Millie bends down to pick up the scattered grapes and tosses them in the wastebasket.

My hand stops digging through the bag for a moment. "You missed one," I say, pointing.

Millie glares at me. "Thanks." All sincerity is gone from her voice, but I enjoy our little exchange just the same.

Glancing out the window, I have no idea where we are, not that it matters. As I root once more through the sack, it occurs to me that Lydia is not saying a whole lot. "You okay, Lydia?"

"Yeah, I'm fine. Just a little shaken." She gives a nervous laugh.

"I'm sorry. I'm sure that was scary for you. It was scary for me, and I wasn't the one being chased," I say. Lydia will no doubt have nightmares after this. Like I said, too many cop shows.

"Well, it's not every day that a teenage boy pays attention to me," she says with a chuckle.

"That kind of attention we can do without," Millie joins in.

"That's the truth," Lydia says like the benediction of a prayer.

Lydia's handling it better than I thought. "Well, that kid will think twice before he messes with a couple of middle-aged *babes*," I say, winking at Millie.

"I see why you didn't want to drive," Millie says, pointing to the sack. "You wanted to stay back there with the junk food."

"You're quick, Millie, I'll give you that." I continue to dig through the bag like a bargain shopper at an after-Thanksgiving sale. "You guys want anything?"

"No thanks, not now. Maybe later," Lydia says, as in save me some.

Millie shakes her head. "Hey, have you guys seen my glasses?" She looks around her seat area.

"You didn't have them on when you tackled that kid, did you?" I ask, my eye on a Snickers in the bag.

"No, I had gotten up to get some grapes."

"It takes real talent to lose glasses in a motor home, Millie." I decide to wait on the chocolate, pull out a bag of Twizzlers instead, and rip it open.

"What can I say? I'm gifted." Her fingers reach under her seat.

"Try your head," I say dryly, taking a bite of red licorice. The Twizzlers are good, but they're not Le Diva's.

Millie's fingers tap against her head until she touches her glasses. "Oh good. See, I told you this was a great place to keep them so I don't lose them."

"Yeah, too bad you don't remember that's where you keep them." I get up and grab a bottled water from the refrigerator.

"You know, we laugh about what happened at the store, but that was pretty scary. Even once we saw that it was only a kid, I was afraid," Millie says.

"You sure didn't show it with your determined free fall," I say. We chuckle.

"You should talk, Miss Ninja," Millie says.

Lydia stays serious. "I wasn't sure whether that kid had a gun or what. Made me think how fragile life can be."

A somber moment passes between us.

"I'm telling you, just the sight of you and Millie running after us. I mean, the look on your face, Millie—" Lydia starts laughing. "And, DeDe, that Bruce Lee scream, the whole ninja thing—" Tears are running down her cheeks now. Her words are indiscernible, and I'm wondering if she should pull over to the side of the road. She's guffawing, and Millie soon starts in with her trademark chipmunk laugh. Think Alvin. It's a little frightening, but still I join in.

Despite the RV's problem starting at the beach and that prank-gone-sour deal, I think we're having a good time after all. Maybe the worst is behind us.

When we finally calm down, Lydia says, "Hey, DeDe, would you mind checking on Cobbler? She's awfully quiet, and I just want to make sure she's okay. All the commotion probably scared her to death."

"Sure," I say after taking a drink of my water. We risk our lives, and Lydia's worried about the bird. Hello? I could have had a heart attack. After finishing my water, I throw it away and walk to the bedroom. Cobbler's cage is hanging from the ceiling in a corner so she can see out the window. Her cage is swinging as our metal home on wheels creaks down the highway. I'm wondering how Cobbler keeps from getting carsick. Now that I look at her more closely, she does look a little, well, frightened. Her eyes have that sort of deer-in-the-headlights look, and her feathers are all fluffed out. Not to mention the fact that several feathers are lining the floor. I sneeze twice. Her feathers and I just don't mix.

"You all right?" As if she's going to answer me. I'm telling you, Lydia's messing with my mind. First an RV dubbed "Waldo," and now I'm talking to a bird.

I stagger back to my seat at the table. "She appears to be all right, but can birds get carsick?" My teeth vibrate with the dishes in the cabinet.

"Well, I suppose so, but I'm sure she's fine. She's traveled with us before. It's actually a blessing when she travels. She's not nearly as vocal." Lydia gives a slight chuckle.

I'm thinking if I were hanging in midair in unfamiliar surroundings feeling nauseated and frightened, I'd be quiet too.

"What about when it's time for *The Andy Griffith Show*?" I ask.

"Oh, we'll hear from her then, believe me. She won't want to miss Barney."

It scares me to even think about that.

"Speaking of which, I brought some videotapes of the show. Would you mind putting one in for her so she can watch it?" Lydia asks.

"You buy Cobbler videos of *The Andy Griffith Show*? You're kidding, right?" My friends never cease to amaze me.

"No, why? I have my favorite shows; why shouldn't she?" Lydia asks with a broad smile that I can see in the rearview mirror.

"The fact that she's a *bird* comes to mind, but then, maybe that's just me," I say.

Lydia ignores me. "The tapes are in the stand beside the bed."

Trudging to the bedroom, I pull out a tape. "I suppose she'll squawk if I put in an episode she's already seen?" I call out.

"Of course not, silly," Lydia says. "She's seen them all before and loves every one."

Right. Sticking a tape in the VCR, I set the channel. Lydia has placed a small portable TV and video player on the nightstand in the bedroom specifically for Cobbler. We also have a small television set anchored in the ceiling just behind the driver area. At least that ensures the driver won't be watching and driving.

Cobbler starts walking sideways back and forth on her perch. She shivers once, ruffling her feathers, and then settles down. The tape needs to be rewound, so I hit the rewind button.

Our feathered friend whistles. First she just does a couple of notes, similar to the vocal exercises one would expect from a professional singer on the opening night of a concert. A kind of warming-up thing.

Then Cobbler breaks into a full rendition of *The Andy Griffith Show* theme song. Okay, maybe it's not the full rendition, but it's the first few bars over and over. And over. And over.

Upon hearing her whistle the tune for the second time, I'm totally convinced it wasn't a fluke. "Wow! She really can sing that," I say, totally amazed.

"Told you," Lydia says.

Though this bird is weird, I have to admit it's pretty cool that she can whistle this tune. In my opinion, that takes some brains— or at the very least a good set of pipes. The video stops. Once the show is on, Cobbler bobs her head and scampers back and forth on her perch. She says something, and I'm almost sure it's "Barney," then she wolf whistles.

Okay, that creeps me out a little.

"Hey, DeDe, come here," Millie says.

I go back to join Lydia and Millie. "Are we there yet?"

"Not quite," Millie says. "We don't see a listing for an RV campground in Albany. Lydia and I were thinking we could stay at a Wal-Mart. I could get my film developed while we're there too. What do you think?"

"Do people camp at Wal-Mart?" I ask, totally oblivious to the camping world.

"Yes, they allow people to park their campers for an overnight stay."

"Sounds all right to me," I say.

"There are several; we'll pick the one closest to where we're ready to stop."

"Waldo won't have any problems finding one. I am, after all, his owner." Lydia reaches for the radio knob. "Do you mind if I turn on the radio?"

Millie and I agree. I'm feeling a little tired from our late-night talk and the excitement at the convenience store. Okay, the truth is, my body aches from head to toe where Millie pounced on us with all the grace of an elephant.

"Aren't you tired, Lydia?" I'm amazed she's still holding it together since she was up late too. She has to be emotionally drained after all she's been through.

"I'm doing fine. I'm too keyed up to sleep now." She turns the radio knob and comes upon an easy-listening station.

I no sooner fall asleep on the sofa than we stop at Wal-Mart and call it a day.

"If you want dinner and you don't want to wake up in the middle of the night, you'd better get up," Millie says.

I yawn. "What time is it?"

"It's about six thirty," Millie says.

We decide to eat at a Chinese place that's in the same shopping complex as Wal-Mart. Asian spices greet us the moment we enter. I haven't eaten Chinese food in a while—actually, not since I was with Rob. We loved to eat Chinese together. I miss him.

About halfway through the meal, my cell phone vibrates. Thankfully, Lydia and Millie are sitting across from me and don't seem to notice anything. I discreetly pull it from my pocket and look under the table to see that it's Rob. If Millie and Lydia weren't here, I think I'd answer it. He must sense that I'm eating

Chinese. We connect on a deep level. Wonder if that's a sign? The phone stops vibrating, and Rob is gone—again.

"Boy, we must be tired," I say before I finish the last bite of my orange chicken. "We've hardly said three words here."

"I know I am." Lydia touches the corner of her mouth with a napkin.

With the snap of my fortune cookie, I pull out the paper and read it silently. When I look up, Lydia and Millie are staring at me. "What?"

"Aren't you going to read it?" Millie asks.

"Um, no."

"And why not?"

Millie again. This woman never gives up, I tell you.

"Well?" Millie pushes.

With a long sigh, I pull out the paper. "It says, 'A long-lost friend will come into your life soon.'" I look up in time to see Millie's eyebrows shoot up and Lydia smile.

"Wonder if his name is Tony, George, David, or—who was the other one—oh yeah, Ralph?"

My eyebrows wiggle playfully, and I have to admit there's a teensy bit of hope lifting inside me. Maybe this little journey will help me forget Rob. Not that I need someone else in my life to forget him. I just wonder if there ever will be someone else in my life.

"Just remember to save a couple for us," Millie says as if she's half-serious, though I don't think she is. She doesn't seem ready for another relationship. Still, I could be wrong.

Tossing my paper aside, I slurp the last of my iced tea. The server brings back our receipts and thanks us for coming in.

"You girls ready to go?" Lydia asks, rising from our booth. Millie follows her, and they start walking away.

"Aren't you forgetting something, Millie?" I call out to her.

She turns around.

I'm waving her glasses. "I think you used them to read your fortune cookie—which you failed to read to us, by the way."

Millie walks over and snatches the glasses from my hand. When she turns around, Lydia stands in the way, arms folded across her chest.

"We made DeDe tell us," Lydia says.

"It said something about losing my glasses," Millie comments dryly, pushing past Lydia.

※

A wet sensation on my cheeks lures me slowly to consciousness. My hand wipes across my face.

Drip, drip, drip.

Working through my sleepy haze, it takes me a moment to get my bearings. Something drips onto my face again. My eyes squint to see the ceiling through the darkness. Another plop hits my eyelid, making my lashes wet.

My fingers work the blanket as though I'm reading Braille. The top cover is wet. Okay, either we have a roof leak, or I'm dealing with night sweats that could get me on the Oprah show.

Throwing off the damp covers, I climb out of bed. It's not until I hear the thunder boom and the lightning crack that I realize what's happening. Cobbler's cage is moving, but she isn't making a sound. I peek through the cover. Feathers litter the bottom of her cage. Still, she flutters a moment, so at least I know she's alive.

Carefully I tiptoe into the living room, trying not to wake Millie, when I step on a few more wet spots. My eyes have finally adjusted to the dark. Security lights from the parking lot seep through the cracks in the blinds and front curtains, revealing roof leaks in the hallway and kitchen. With a glance back at the bedroom, I see there's a leak over my bed.

I groan. Lydia will not be happy about this. Her poor motor home. It's showing its age just like the rest of us. Well, anyway, Millie and Lydia are dealing with age issues. I'm just getting started with that whole perimenopausal deal. Makes me feel sort of young. This is a terrible thing to say, but there's just a teensy bit of pride going on in the deepest corners of my heart. I hate to admit that, but there you are.

Of course, now that I've reveled in this thought, I'll probably sprout two new wrinkles by daylight.

Thunder splits through the air, and I jump. The rain is coming down with a vengeance. Quickly I pull pans and kettles from the cupboard and place them on the floor to catch the water. Though I try to keep still, the pots and pans clang against one another and the cabinet.

Unbelievably, I manage to set everything in place without waking Lydia or Millie. The rhythmic *tap, tap, tap* in the pan as the water drips from the ceiling doesn't even wake them.

By the way, Millie's mouth is wide open here. I'm thinking if I could strategically place her mouth under one of those leaks . . .

Stepping closer to the bedroom, I peek in at Lydia. Out cold. She really was stressed about driving. Maybe I should take a turn driving. Then she would realize, yes, it is possible to feel worse.

The rain pelts the motor home, and I turn to see that the pans are rapidly filling up. One by one, I empty the water from the pans into the sink.

Wal-Mart stays open all night. Maybe I should go pick up some buckets. Better still, something for the leaky roof would be good, but I have no idea about that kind of stuff. I'm the kind of gal who would stick gum on a leak.

A damp chill fills the motor home, and I shiver beneath my pajamas. The angry night sky roars and jumps with lightning. A flash of light causes the white polka dots on my blue pajama bottoms to glow in the dark. Suddenly a childhood ghost story plays in my mind. It has to do with a ghoul scratching the top of a car. My heart zips to my throat. I can't think about it. Did I just hear something on the roof? I have goose bumps. Definite goose bumps—and heart palpitations.

If I have a heart attack, heads will roll. Wait. I don't mean heads will roll. My breath crouches in my throat, refusing to leave, while my gaze shoots back and forth in the darkness. I huddle against the refrigerator. More lightning and thunder. The hair on my neck bristles. Think porcupine.

I want to go home. Now.

Something touches my arm. A scream pierces the air. I could be wrong, but I think it came from me. Lightning flashes, and I see Lydia's face, ghostly white. If she lifts a candle, I'm *so* outta here.

Millie stirs in her bed, but a second later, her mouth sags open again. I blink. Hard. Twice.

"Are you all right?" Lydia asks while tightening the belt on her white terry robe.

"Ask me after they insert the pacemaker."

Lydia giggles, then tugs on my arm to lead me back to the bedroom. "We have to get something for these leaks. I'm afraid if we wait, Waldo's interior will be ruined."

I have no idea why she's whispering. We couldn't wake Millie with a Mack truck.

Lydia walks over to Cobbler's cage, peeks under the towel, then turns to me. "She seems to be keeping warm enough."

She obviously hasn't noticed that I'm quivering like the leaves on an aspen tree. "My interior isn't exactly toasty warm," I say.

Lydia's eyes twinkle. I'm relieved to see that the ghoul is gone. I much prefer Lydia's twinkle self over her ghoul self. Though her eyes are still a little weird-looking. Just how well do I know her, anyway?

She coughs, then sneezes.

"Are you getting sick?"

She shakes her head. "Allergies. Damp, musty smells make my throat itch, and I sneeze."

"Oh, I'm sorry. So you think we need to get something for the roof?"

She nods and wipes the tears from her eyes. "I hate to ask you, I really do—"

Suddenly I know what it means to turn a deaf ear, because although her lips are moving, I hear nothing.

"I wouldn't ask you to go if I could do it myself"—sneeze, cough—"but as you can see, I'm a mess." Lydia smiles sweetly.

My mother always said it was the nice ones you had to watch out for.

"Okay, I'll go." My voice betrays me. Reluctantly I shrug on jeans and a sweatshirt. Then, before I can blink, Lydia is shoving a raincoat and umbrella my way.

"What's going on?" Millie cracks open her eyes.

"Millie, you could sleep through a flood," I say with my hand on the door. She should be doing this instead of me. My grumpy self turns from Millie to peek out the door. Oh well, at least the rain has slowed to a light sprinkle. "See you guys later." My fingers shove on the knob, then I stop and turn back. "Oh, I forgot to ask—what am I getting?"

Lydia squeezes her lips together and thinks a moment. "Just something to fix leaky roofs?"

"Okay, that pretty much narrows it down." I turn and shove open the door. Without looking down, my leg plops to the first step outside our door and causes a splash. An icy chill runs up my skin, causing me to gasp.

"What is it?" Lydia asks behind me.

With a shiver, I turn to them. "Anybody receive a divine message about an ark lately?"

5

"What's the matter, Dee?" Lydia says, trying to see past me out to the Wal-Mart parking lot. She looks confused. Join the club.

"Grab me a towel," I say over my shoulder.

Lydia scrambles for one and brings it to me. She hovers near the doorway and peers outside. "Oh my goodness, Millie, come see this." Lydia steps out of my way while I lift my sopping pant leg from the rainwater. Paint me pink and I could be a flamingo lawn ornament.

Millie peers around me to get a view of the parking lot. "Oh my, the lot is flooded," she says.

"Like I've always said, you're quick."

Lightning sparks again, giving me a good glimpse of Millie's pajamas. "Whoa, Gloria Swanson sighting!" I yell. "As in silent film star. Call the paparazzi." Peals of laughter make my balance waver slightly. Millie's pj's resemble a black-and-white-striped bathing suit from, well, let's just say way before Esther Williams was ever born. Wisely I stay just out of reach so she can't push me into the water.

"They're comfortable," Millie says, making a face at me.

Millie rushes over to grab her camera and snaps a picture of the flooded lot.

My eyes lock on her camera.

"Don't even think about it," she warns.

In that fraction of an instant, I snatch the camera from Millie's hands before she knows what hit her. Her arms flail about as the flash goes off, catching her in full pajama drama.

"DeDe Veihl, you give that back to me this minute," Millie barks.

"Millie, I'm thinking that picture could win us ten thousand dollars on *America's Funniest Home Videos*," I say, laughing uncontrollably. Like the poor sport she is, Millie grabs the camera out of my hands.

"The fun is over," she says.

"Okay, you two," Lydia says between chuckles, "we need to figure out this problem."

"What's to think about? Unless we have a canoe, I ain't going out there," I say, pointing to the lake outside our door.

Millie and Lydia give me a hard stare.

"We don't have a canoe, do we?" Millie asks. I'm picturing canoes, Indians, beaver skins. She's probably going to quiz us on the Lewis and Clark expedition.

Lydia shakes her head, then sneezes. "But I do have some galoshes."

"Oh goodie," I say, but they ignore me.

Lydia tromps back to the bedroom and comes out with a smile and a pair of what must be size 30 green rain boots.

"Oh, you do have a canoe," I say, staring at the boots. "Two of them."

"These were Greg's. I know they're a little big, but they'll get you to the store." Cough, sneeze. "You sure you don't mind, DeDe?"

I stare at her. Did I say I didn't mind? Um, I don't think so. Those words did not come from these lips. That would be her interpretation. Which is, by the way, just wrong. Reluctantly I reach for the boots, and Lydia looks relieved. No wonder. She doesn't have to go out in the rain. And why is that? "Are you punishing me because I'm younger?"

Millie snorts. "You'll be fifty in a matter of days," she says, her eyes shining with pure evil.

"At our age, every day counts," I say.

Millie shrugs. "I don't know, DeDe. There might be lines down or something. Maybe you shouldn't go out there."

"Excuse me? Did I just hear words of compassion coming from your mouth?" I wag my finger in front of Millie's face. "We want Millie back, and we want her now."

"Oh, that's cute," she says. "If you want to fry out there, suit yourself." She steps out of the way. She's far too accommodating. "But who knows what kind of bugs lurk in those muddy waters," she calls behind her.

Gulp. I hate bugs, and Millie knows it.

"No, don't go. I hadn't thought of that," Lydia says, biting her fingernail.

"The bugs?" Millie wants to know.

"We have to get these leaks fixed, don't we?" And I ask that, why?

"No. We'll wait until the water recedes," Lydia says. "Remember, this trip is not about being in a hurry. We will not risk you getting hurt." Wow, Lydia's taking charge. I like that. Especially when it means I don't have to go outside.

With a glance at Millie, I smile. "Lydia has spoken." I pull off my raincoat, and we set to tidying the RV as best we can around the rain-filled pans.

By the time we finish breakfast, the water has found its way to the area drains, and I can see the pavement well enough to walk up to the store without fear of electrical wires or bugs.

It doesn't take me long to pick out a product since I have no idea what works and what doesn't. I also get Millie's film developed, plucking out the pajama picture before she can throw it away.

"Did you find something?" Lydia asks when I step back into the motor home.

Smiling, I hold up my purchase. "Considering I'm clueless as to what we should use on leaks, I thought it best to buy duct tape. Dad always said it works on just about anything." Lydia helps me take off my coat. "That should hold it until we get to camp and someone can tell us what to buy."

"Hmm, I guess that's okay," Lydia says as if we have a choice.

It doesn't take long for the three of us to slap on the duct tape where appropriate, and soon we're on the road again. I resist the urge to play tic-tac-toe on the ceiling.

How curious that Lydia hasn't sneezed once since I've returned. Not wanting to allow bitterness to take root, I brush off the thought. "So where we off to today?" I figure it's always good to be "in the know."

Millie looks at the map, then at the sheet she printed off from the Internet. "We're stopping in Erie, Pennsylvania, today."

"Oh, I hear that's a pretty area," Lydia says.

"Yeah, it is." Millie opens her Rocky Mountain National Park book. "All right, girls, time for Rocky Mountain trivia."

"Wait. I forgot to give you the pictures Wal-Mart developed," I say, handing her the package.

Millie snatches them from me and carefully pulls open the envelope. I hold my breath to see if she'll notice the missing pajama picture. She doesn't. We laugh and talk through each photo. She dates each one, then goes to one of her bins and pulls out a box the size of a shoe box titled "Trip to Aspen Creek," complete with dividers in it, where she promptly deposits each photo behind the proper date. She brushes her hands together. "Thanks for getting those for me, Dee," she says with a smile. "Now we're ready for the Rocky Mountain trivia," she says, opening her book.

My eyes start to roll back in my head.

"Pay attention," Millie snaps at me before flipping through the pages.

She can get her own film developed from now on.

"Okay, here we are," she says, running her fingers down the

crease in the book so the pages will stay open. "Little mounds of discarded cone fragments called middens are left near Bear Lake by what kind of animal?"

"Um, what would be a bear?" I say, laughing.

Millie glares at me.

"Get it. Bear Lake, *bear*?"

Still glaring.

"Um, I'm guessing that's wrong?"

"You guessed right. Finally."

"Oh, I know," Lydia says with far too much enthusiasm. "A chickaree."

"Correct!" Millie says.

I cross my arms in front of me. "Oh sure, play favorites."

"Don't be a sore loser, DeDe." Millie turns the page.

"What's a chickaree?" I ask, further proving my ignorance.

"A red squirrel." Lydia nails it before Millie can take a breath. "Derrick did a report on mountain wildlife for school," she says, referring to her oldest son.

"*Somebody* needs to get out more."

Lydia shrugs.

"Here's one," Millie continues.

"Didn't you say we were going through *one* piece of trivia per day? All this knowledge is making my head hurt."

Millie peers at me over the rims of her glasses. "It's good for you." She sits taller in her chair as though she's part of a debate team on competition day. "Besides, I feel inspired today."

"Now there's one for the books."

"Oh, you're funny," Millie says without cracking a smile. She pushes her glasses back up her nose. "What lives in rotting logs?"

"Excuse me, do we want to know this?"

"Yes, you do. Now, what's the answer?" Millie sounds suspiciously like a librarian.

"Hmm." Lydia is really thinking here. I can tell, because she's not noticing that every other car on the freeway is passing us. "Well, there are bacteria in those logs."

Millie's eyes are sparkling over the thought of bacteria. She so scares me.

"Fungi?" Lydia asks.

"Yes! Bacteria and fungi contribute to the decay. The cycle of life is just so amazing," Millie says.

"Who knew?"

"Lydia did," Millie says dryly.

"Does she win a star? 'Cause if she wins a star, I'm so mad."

Lydia giggles.

"All right, I'm done. We don't want DeDe's brain to blow a circuit," Millie says, closing her book. She pulls off her glasses.

"Okay, smarty-pants, what is the name for the chocolate mixture that is made by combining semisweet chocolate and boiling cream, stirring until smooth?"

"I have no idea," Lydia admits, still playing along.

Millie tries to act disinterested, but I can tell she's trying to figure it out.

"Give up, Millie?"

"I'm too tired to think of it right now," she says. Still, I imagine the neurons in her brain are stretching and jumping around like participants in an aerobics class.

"Ganache," I announce before she can think of it.

She frowns.

"I didn't want you to strain your brain," I say with a sweet smile.

Millie shrugs. She's a good sport, really—a little weird, but a good sport.

We travel a ways and finally come upon a road sign that says, "The Chocolate Dessert Bar." "Oh, can we stop there?" I ask, pointing to the sign.

"Absolutely. We're enjoying the journey, remember?" Lydia says.

"Are we there yet?" I tease.

"Where?" Lydia asks. Obviously her mind is somewhere else.

"You said we're on a journey. I said—oh, never mind." It's just not worth it if I have to explain myself.

Lydia pulls the motor home off the interstate, and we travel a little ways down the road until we spot a white wooden sign with the name "The Chocolate Dessert Bar" scrolled across it in fancy gold letters. A profusion of colorful flowers lines the front of the white aluminum-sided structure, complete with a picket fence. Millie takes a picture of Lydia and me in front of the sign. Then I take one of Lydia and Millie.

Candles flicker from linen-clad tables around the room once we step inside. The walls resemble milk chocolate, and all the trimmings are in gold.

"Oh my, this is lovely," Lydia says. "My Red Hat group would love this."

An elegant light fixture with four cream-colored globes hangs from the ceiling's center. Spotted with creamy flecks, a cocoa-shaded Oriental rug in the shape of a truffle hugs the hardwood floor and muffles our footsteps as we follow the hostess to our table. She seats us across from a brick fireplace that has fake logs burning in the hearth.

"I feel underdressed," Lydia whispers.

"Too bad we don't have some white gloves," Millie says with a grin.

We all laugh as loud as is proper for society ladies—which is a good thing considering Millie's Alvin laugh and all.

In no time we finish our rich chocolate cake and hot coffee, then head back to the RV—after I buy a truffle for each of us.

"These aren't as good as yours," Lydia says after taking a bite.

"You can tell the difference?" I'm feeling proud that Lydia noticed.

"Sure can. I must be learning something about this chocolate business."

Millie takes a bite. "You know, I believe I can tell too. This chocolate is slightly more bitter and almost has a fruity taste—which is odd since there's no fruit in it."

"True. It depends on the beans. Researchers are still trying to find out why some beans have hints of fruits, raisins, and numerous other flavors while others do not. Some beans make great chocolate; others don't."

"It is interesting," Millie admits. "Hey, it's my turn to drive," she says upon seeing Lydia head for the driver's door. "I won't take no for an answer, Lydia."

Lydia shrugs. "Just remember, you offered."

Funny that no one asks me to take a turn. I'm okay with that. We climb back into the motor home with Millie behind the wheel.

"Boy, I'm stuffed, but that sure was good cake," I say, settling into the sofa for a snooze.

"Wasn't it, though?" Lydia says.

Millie looks over the map before pulling out. In the quiet of the moment, Cobbler suddenly breaks out in his Andy Griffith number.

Lydia looks at me. "Sounds like Cobbler is ready for her Barney fix."

"I'll take care of it." I feel like a slave to this creature. She whistles, I jump. "Still, I have to wonder how healthy it is for a parakeet to be addicted to Barney Fife," I call over my shoulder.

Why do they always ignore me?

"Here you go, Cobbler." Shoving *The Andy Griffith Show* video into the VCR, I trudge back to the front.

"Thanks, DeDe," Lydia says.

"No problem." Stretching my legs out in front of me, I lean back on the sofa. My eyes no sooner drift to a close than a cell phone rings.

We dive for our handbags. Well, Lydia and I do, anyway. Millie's driving.

"It's mine." The caller ID reveals that it's not Rob—phew!—but my business partner, Shelley Cooper, who is holding Le Diva together while I'm gone. "Hi, Shelley. How's it going?"

"Sorry to bother you while you're on vacation, Dee, but I wanted to check in with you."

"I'm glad you did. I've tried to call you a couple of times but couldn't reach you. So what's up?"

"Things are going well here," she says. Silence.

"Is everything all right?"

"Now, don't worry. I'm sure everything will be fine," she blurts.

"Houston, we have a problem."

"No, no, I'm sure it's not a big deal."

"What's not a big deal?"

"Well, it's just that—um, you remember that new structure they were building down the road?"

"Yeah."

"It just opened."

"And?"

"And it's a candy store."

"Our town is big enough for two candy stores."

"On the same block?"

"All right, so?"

"Two candy stores that specialize in chocolates."

"Oh."

"Actually, they offer chocolates and gourmet coffee."

"Okay, we were talking about doing that." My mood is inching southward.

"We shouldn't be too worried, though. The owner has to be all of fifteen," Shelley says as if she's adding a bright spot to my day.

"Fifteen?"

"Okay, twenty-five, tops."

Audible gulp here. Mine. "Twenty-five?"

"Uh-huh. A mere baby. What would she know about running a business?"

"Exactly." I'm thankful Shelley is forty-two. We understand each other.

"I just didn't know if you would want to run a special or anything."

"Let me give it some thought."

"Okay. Oh, and one more thing," Shelley says.

I'm wondering if I want to hear this. "Yes?"

"Rob called." Pause. "He said to tell you that he loves you, can't live without you; he's taking care of everything and will see you soon."

Another pause.

"You still there?"

"I'm here."

"I hope I haven't ruined your day," Shelley says.

"No, just given me food for thought."

Shelley doesn't press me to discuss Rob. Instead, we talk about my trip and finally say good-bye. *Thanks for the mood swing, Shelley.*

"Everything okay?" Lydia asks.

I shake off thoughts of Rob. "Uh, yeah. Shelley told me there's a new gourmet chocolate shop that just opened down the road." Placing my cell phone back in my handbag, I go up to sit on the floor between Millie and Lydia so I can hear them better.

"Uh-oh, that doesn't sound good," Millie says, checking her rearview mirror before she makes a lane change to pass someone who is, unbelievably, going slower than we are.

"Well, I don't know that it's such a big deal," Lydia counters. "Competition is the name of the game."

"And that should make me feel better?"

"Do they offer the same services?" Millie asks.

I explain the deal about the gourmet coffee.

Millie shakes her head. "You may have to rethink your business strategies."

"Well, Millie, I don't know why you're saying that. I'm confident that Le Diva Chocolates has made its niche in our town."

Millie shrugs. "I hope you're right. It's just that—well, never mind."

"No, go ahead. Say what's on your mind."

"Is it a woman owner?"

"Yes."

"How old is she?"

"I don't know. Why?"

"I have a friend who got her job knocked right out from under her."

"What does that have to do with it?"

"A younger woman, fresh out of college with new ideas, enthusiasm, zest for her job, that kind of thing." Millie pauses here. "No inkling of how old she is?"

"As I said, I don't know." I'm almost sure I can hear Millie clicking her tongue.

"Come on, DeDe, spill it."

"Doggone it, Millie, I didn't ask her name, rank, and serial number."

She continues to stare. Sweat forms on my forehead. The pressure gets to me. I crack. "Okay, Shelley thinks she's about twenty-five."

Millie's eyebrows lift to her hairline (which, by the way, is heading farther north with every passing year). I wait for her to say something.

She doesn't.

"I hate it when you do that."

"Do what?" Millie asks as if she's so innocent.

My head swivels to Lydia. "If I hurt her, can I plead menopausal insanity?"

"This from Miss I'm Still in the *Peri*menopausal Stage?" Millie jeers.

"That does it. After you go to bed tonight, I'm scrambling the canned goods you organized."

"You do, and I'm swiping your chocolate," Millie shoots back.

"I'm gonna give you both a good thrashing if you don't stop this arguing," Lydia says, surprising us both.

Millie takes a deep breath. "Look, I'm merely saying you'd better keep an eye on things, that's all."

"Oh, come on, Millie. It's not necessarily a bad thing," Lydia says.

"Did I say it was bad? Just keep an eye on things. That's all."

Lydia changes the subject, for which I'm grateful, but if I'm awake at midnight, those canned goods are so gonna get mixed up . . .

6

"*Are we there yet?*" *I ask for the hundredth time just to annoy* Millie. I'm also wondering if Millie has noticed that I not only scrambled the canned goods but also made a mess of her sock drawer, putting brown socks with white ones, black ones with brown ones. I can't remember when I've had such fun.

"Oh, this is it; turn in here," Millie says, pointing to the campground. She handed the driver's seat back to Lydia a few miles back so she could rest.

Lydia turns the motor home, gravel crunching beneath the tires as we make our way down a wooded lane. About a half mile down, the trees give way to an open section of land lined with RVs and campers.

"There's the office." I point to a rustic log cabin building not much bigger than an outhouse. Lydia pulls into a parking spot, leaving little room for anyone else.

Once we get everything squared away with the campground owners, we make our way to the lot. Dusk has settled upon us, and a variety of lights can be seen from the various campsites.

One camper has bulb-illuminated beer cans hanging from his awning. Another has birds with rhinestones. Others are adorned with elk, bears, fish, lanterns, and the list goes on. Whirligigs, pink flamingos, and ceramic children litter sparse lawns. People sit around campfires laughing and talking with their neighbors, children run and play between RVs, guys huddle in front of decks of cards. It's a small community bound by their appreciation for camping life.

Minimal accommodations and dirt. Yeah, that's the life for me, uh-huh.

Have I mentioned it's exhausting to pull into our lot and get hooked up to everything? I don't know where Lydia finds the patience to do all this stuff. Causes me to shiver just thinking about it.

When we step outside, the scent of hamburgers on the grill reaches me, and I'm reminded of my teenage years at camp. Despite my prejudice against camping, those were good days. After all, they brought Lydia and Millie into my life. Well, I'm glad about Lydia anyway. Oh, all right, Millie too.

Lydia shows us how to help her with the hookups and get situated in our new yard for the night. The good news is, we don't have to use a community bathroom. I just can't handle that idea.

Once everything is in place and we've pulled out the awning, Millie takes a couple of pictures of our campsite while Lydia and I gather things from the cupboards for dinner.

"Anything else we need to do?" I ask.

"Well, there is one more thing. I have some lights I'd like to put up around the awning," Lydia says.

"Oh, let me do that," Millie pipes up. "DeDe can help you with the dinner."

I'm positively speechless. Never in a million years would I have guessed Millie to be a lights-putter-upper sort of person. There's a mysterious side to Millie, you know?

Lydia and Millie go outside, where Lydia pulls a box of string lights from one of the storage bins. Millie sets to work hanging strings of bird lights around the awning, while Lydia and I finish the meal of fried chicken, mashed potatoes, corn on the cob, salad, and apple pie.

The amber-colored bird lights offer a warm glow as we sit at the picnic table and enjoy our dinner together. Nice ambience, but the dim lights make it hard for me to see if a bug lands on my food. And I'm not buying that whole "extra protein" thing.

"This is delicious," Millie says, scooping a forkful of mashed potatoes. She takes a bite and looks at us.

"What's wrong?" I ask.

"Um, the potatoes; do they have any butter in them?"

Lydia looks up, wide-eyed. "Oh dear."

"Did you forget to add the butter, Lydia?" Millie asks.

Lydia nods. "I meant to. I even got it out of the refrigerator, but when I saw it, I was thinking it was for the corn." She laughs it off good-naturedly. "I'll just go plunk some butter in this and stick it in the microwave. Be right back," she says.

"You're sure that's a menopausal thing?" I whisper to Millie.

She nods. "I do that now and then too. We get busy and just forget."

"I hope I don't do that while I'm making chocolates."

"You might want to start delegating," Millie says with a laugh.

Lydia no sooner returns with the potatoes and sits down than someone calls out to us.

"Millicent Carter, is that you?"

We all turn at the sound of a very male voice. A man about five feet eight inches tall with shaggy brown hair, gray eyes, and a scraggly beard stands in jeans and a tattered T-shirt with a beer logo on it. A petite woman in a red top with cap sleeves, jean shorts, and multicolored sandals of red, green, and yellow joins him. She's looking at the ground, so I can't see her eyes.

Completing the trio, dressed in full Gap wear, is a teenage girl with long blonde hair and a cute figure that she's all too happy to reveal to the world.

Millie's face is stripped of all color. "Doug?" She stands as they walk over to our picnic table.

"Guilty as charged," he says. "How ya doin'?"

They exchange some chitchat, and Millie introduces the family to us. We learn that Doug is a friend of Bruce's. Great, just what Millie needs right now.

"Yeah, I guess you heard about the wedding?" Doug asks.

"Yes, I did," Millie says. "I hope things go well for Bruce."

"Oh, I think they'll go well all right," he says with a laugh and a poke to his wife's side. "He married a pretty little thing. Not much older than Melanie here." He nods to his daughter.

Melanie smirks. "She's cool too. She might let me borrow some of her clothes."

"That's nice," Millie says.

Seeing how uncomfortable Millie is, I quickly direct the conversation toward camping. They talk about how they're on vacation headed toward some place in New York to visit his wife's family. The man talks ad nauseam about his past experiences of living out in the wild. When they leave, Millie goes into the motor home.

Cupping my hand near my mouth, I whisper to Lydia, "I expected him to beat his chest and swing on a tree branch back to his RV."

She laughs. "Oh my, DeDe, how do you come up with that stuff?"

"I'm not trying to be funny."

Lydia wipes tears from her eyes.

Crickets chirp, a dog barks in the distance, and cute little girls giggle as they walk down the lane with two older women.

"Do you think she's all right?" Lydia asks with a glance toward the motor home.

"I'll go check on her," I say, rising from the chair. When I step inside, Millie is standing at the refrigerator. With her mouth wide open, she's aiming the nozzle of a whipped cream can toward her tongue.

"Don't do it, Millie. He's not worth it!" I say with a heavy dose of drama, attempting humor to ease the tension.

She glares at me, then squirts the cream for all she's worth, filling her mouth with a vengeance.

When Millie resorts to the whipped cream, she's seriously upset. I step toward her and put my arm around her.

"Don't take it to heart, Millie."

She wipes her mouth with her hand. "I'm fine." Opening the refrigerator door, she slips the can back inside as though she hasn't a care in the world.

"You know that whipped cream is not the answer."

"Maybe not, but it helps."

Who am I to talk? I have my chocolate issues.

"I'll be all right. Just seeing Doug and hearing about Bruce's new wife—"

I cut her off so she doesn't have to explain. "I know. Want to go back outside?"

Millie takes a deep breath, hesitates a moment, then lifts her chin. "Why should I let what Bruce does bother me?"

"That's the spirit," I say.

"Let's go."

We no sooner step outside than a woman leaves her camper across from us and heads our way.

"How are you folks tonight?" she says with a friendly smile. "I'm Sara Lee Gentry."

"Sara Lee, as in desserts?" I ask.

"No, my mom just liked the name."

"DeDe is a chocolate connoisseur, so she automatically thinks of desserts when she hears a name like that," Millie explains.

The woman smiles. "Never acquired a taste for chocolate myself, though you probably find that hard to believe," she says, patting her ample midsection.

"Have you seen anyone about this problem?" I struggle not to back away as though she has a contagious disease.

She stumbles a moment, then laughs. She tries to tell me how much better her life is without it, but her words are like a foreign language. "Blah-blah, blah-blah, blah, blah."

We spend some time getting acquainted with our new neighbor, and before the woman can leave, Lydia has her sitting down to sample a piece of apple pie. The next thing we know, her husband wants some, as do the three kids and the mother-in-law. The dog tries to get in on the action, but they make him go home. Another neighbor and husband soon join in, and Lydia passes out tomorrow night's apple pie to them too. She doesn't seem to mind, though. Lydia is in her element when she's entertaining. She's a regular Betty Crocker. But if she offers my truffles, I *will* strip off her apron and close up shop.

After our guests finish their pie, Millie takes several pictures of our new friends, and we settle around the fire pit. Above the flames, I glance at Millie. She seems to feel better now. She has more color in her face. 'Course, she could be having another hot flash, so it's hard to tell.

One of the neighbors shares a story of how someone backed a rig and car into a bathroom facility.

"Oh, that's a frightening tale," I say. "Stephen King?"

It takes a minute, but he finally laughs.

"Any of you do this full-time?" the man with salt-and-pepper hair asks.

Surely my ears deceive me. "People do that?"

He laughs. "Yep. All the time. That's what we do," he says, pointing to his wife beside him. They barely look old enough to drive.

"How do you support yourself?" *Sell baseball cards, bubble gum wrappers, lemonade?*

"We have some real estate investments that provide monthly income, and we also work in camps along the way," he says.

"How do you mean?" Lydia asks.

"We belong to a group where we find out about camps that

hire full-time RVers like us. Some places you work at to make some money; other places you work at because they're on your way to where you want to go, and you get free camping in exchange. It's really a great setup."

"Uh-huh, loads of fun."

Everyone looks at me. "Did I say that out loud?"

They nod.

"Sorry. I don't mean to be rude, but I just can't imagine it."

"Oh, I see, we have a non-RVer in our midst, huh?" the man teases.

"Afraid so. She's a hotel woman all the way," Millie tattles.

The man's wife laughs. "I was the same way until we got our motor home. They're really quite nice."

"Has all the comforts of home," he says.

Sure, if your home is no bigger than a tree house.

"Why don't you come over and see it?" He rises from the chair and takes two steps.

"Oh, Rick, they don't care about that," his wife says. "By the way, my name is Cyndi Pointer, and this is my husband, Rick."

"Nice to meet you, and sures we do." I have to see for myself what kind of home away from home they can stand to live in full-time.

We all walk a little ways down the road and come to their home. Okay, by the looks of their RV, I'm thinking this is *so* not a motor home. It can't be. Can we say mansion on wheels? When we step into the tile entryway, my breath catches in my throat. If I didn't know I was in a motor home, I would never believe it. Leather furniture, cherrywood, ceiling fans, side-by-side refrigerator, expensive countertops, washer and dryer, Bose surround-sound stereo system. Two televisions. Satellite dish. King-size bed and ceiling fan in the bedroom.

"This is way nicer than my home. Want to trade?" I say.

The wife laughs. "It is nice, isn't it?"

Nice? Did she say nice? I'm thinking it must take a lot to really wow this lady.

"And you know, DeDe," the woman says as if we're old friends, "if it's hotel service you want, there are some campsites that offer maid and butler services."

"Something tells me I'm in the wrong line of work for that."

"Yeah, it's your wallet," Millie says with a laugh. This time, I ignore *her*.

We sit down on a leather sofa that is so soft, I'm afraid I will slip into the folds and never be found again.

"Oh, what do you do?" she asks.

Before she decides that I wear a colored vest and clean trash from the highways, I explain about my work as a chocolatier.

"That is fascinating. You know, one thing I've always been curious about is why chocolate doesn't spoil. Do you know? Or maybe I should ask if you can tell me in layman's terms?" She laughs.

"Sure. Tiny seed bits from the cocoa beans called 'nibs' are crushed to the point that the heat generated liquefies the nibs into a thick paste called chocolate liquor. This liquid is then placed in a huge press that squeezes out the cocoa butter." Quickly I look around to make sure no one is sleeping before I continue. "This butter keeps the chocolate solid at room temperature. That's why it doesn't spoil—yet it melts in the warmth of your mouth."

"How fascinating," the woman says, practically breathless.

Another connoisseur of fine living *and* fine chocolates. I'm in good company.

"Do you have a business card or Web site? I'm always looking for exceptional gourmet chocolates to send for special occasions. I assume you carry an assortment?"

"Yes, we offer truffles, a fruit and nut collection, caramel pecan patties, cherry cordials, a whole list of things. You can sign up for a catalog on our Web site." I hand her my card with the information.

"Splendid. Once I place my order, you could ship it out for me, I assume?"

"Absolutely." I'm feeling quite proud that I've managed to get some business while on vacation.

We talk for a little while, go back to our RV, and prepare for bed.

"That motor home was totally unbelievable." Lydia fills Cobbler's food and water bowls. "They're called land yachts, you know."

"What do you mean?" Millie asks on her way to the bathroom.

"The big fancy motor homes are called land yachts."

"It's easy to see why," I say. "Who could have imagined that people lived in those things full-time? With a home like that, even I could do it." Pulling my covers down, I crawl into bed.

"It would be one way to see the country, that's for sure." Millie's standing in the doorway, scrubbing her face with a washcloth.

I wonder what it would have been like to travel with Rob. I can just imagine him behind the wheel of an RV, laughing at something I've said. His smile teasing me, his eyes flirting. The cry of a child outside interrupts my daydream, reminding me of my cold reality.

"Uh-oh, sounds like somebody is unhappy," Millie says, referring to the crying child.

"Seems like camping would be a lonely life," I say.

"Well, there are plenty of people around at the camps. Greg and I used to love to visit with other campers around the fire in the evening, just like we did tonight. When the boys were little, they would try to catch bugs while we visited with the neighbors." Lydia covers Cobbler's cage with a dark cloth, then turns with a smile. "Those were great days."

"Thanks for reminding me about the bug part."

Lydia chuckles.

"How do the boys like college, Lydia?" I ask.

"Derrick is doing great. He'll be a senior this year—can you believe it?"

I shake my head.

"Drew will be a junior, and I'm afraid he enjoyed last year more than he should have. As in partied more than studied." A shadow covers her smile. "I suppose Greg's death played into that more than any of us care to admit."

"I'm sure it did." We pause a moment. "Where did you say they were this summer?"

"They live in an apartment near campus. They both have good jobs, so I encouraged them to stay there for the summer. They're only a couple of hours away, so I still get to see them."

That's so like Lydia to put their needs above her own. I'm sure she'd much rather have them home, especially now that Greg is gone, but she would never hold them back.

"They check on me every few days."

I feel better knowing that. "I'm glad."

Lydia adjusts the cover on Cobbler's cage.

"You know, I keep meaning to ask you why you cover her cage like that."

"If I didn't do this, Cobbler would talk all night." Lydia takes off her slippers and climbs into her bed. "It lets her know it's time to go to sleep."

I laugh. "Boy, I've sure got a lot to learn about birds."

"I'm going to bed now," Millie announces.

"'Night, Millie."

"Oh, one more thing," she says. "I hope you don't mind, Lydia, but I organized the medicine that we had in the bathroom cabinet, separating each of our meds from the other, clearly labeling them so you can easily see which ones belong to you. The labels will peel off easily after our trip, by the way."

"Thank you, Millie," Lydia says with a smile.

"Thanks, Millie," I say, feeling guilty that I've messed up her sock drawer.

"You're welcome. Well, good night."

"'Night," we answer in unison.

The room grows quiet.

I think a minute about Lydia and Greg doing the RV thing. I hadn't thought about it before, but this trip has to be hard for her, stirring up old memories.

"Lydia, how do you get through it? I mean, without Greg and everything," I ask.

She doesn't answer me right away, and I figure she's already fallen asleep.

"I talk to the Lord about it, and I cry. A lot."

My heart constricts. I wish I could spare her the pain.

"How about you?"

"I cry and then I get mad at myself for being so stupid for falling in love with a—um, jerk."

"We all make mistakes, DeDe. That's what dating is all about, getting to know someone."

"I got to know him all right." More than I want to talk about.

"You can start over. With a clean slate. Like we learned at camp, remember?"

"I remember." I just don't want to talk about it. "'Night, Lydia."

"'Night, Dee."

7

Either I've got the hearing powers of Superwoman or we have paper-thin walls, because I can hear our neighbors clanging around their breakfast pans. In fact, I'm pretty sure I'm smelling bacon and eggs. I wonder if they'd invite me over.

"Woke you up too, huh?" Lydia says with a grin.

"What's the matter with these people? Don't they know that people on vacation are supposed to sleep in?" I yawn and kick off my covers.

"Uh-oh, *somebody* didn't get enough sleep last night," Millie says before she pulls open the bathroom door.

The smell of coffee makes its way to my nose. "You made coffee?"

"I did," she says.

"I don't care what anybody says about you, Millie; I think you're all right." I flash an ornery grin.

"Well, don't get excited. You don't get any. It took me a good half hour to get my socks back in order," she grouses.

Lydia looks at me. I pull the covers back over my head.

"Yeah, I'd hide too if I were you," Millie says.

Down come the covers. "Well, doggone it, Millie. You drive me to distraction. I couldn't help myself."

"DeDe, you didn't," Lydia says.

"Yes, she did," Millie says, hands on her hips. "But then, I guess she wouldn't be DeDe if she didn't do something like that on this trip," Millie says with a tiny chuckle, shocking me to the core.

It takes me a minute to find my tongue. "Are you sick, Millie?"

She smiles. "But I'd watch my backside if I were you," she calls over her shoulder with a hint of orneriness in her voice.

My gaze collides with Lydia's. We're speechless. Positively speechless.

"By the way, have you guys seen my glasses?" Millie calls out.

"Millie, we're living in a two-by-four—" I turn to Lydia. "No offense, Lydia."

She grins. "None taken."

Back to Millie. "It's impossible to lose glasses in a two-by-four."

"And yet here we are," she says, arriving at the bedroom door once again.

"I think I saw them by the kitchen sink last night," Lydia says. "You were reading my friend's recipe for poppy seed bread, remember?"

Millie snaps her fingers. "That's right. Thanks." She steps into the bathroom and closes the door.

"She could lose her glasses in a tent," I say.

"I heard that," Millie calls out.

Lydia and I giggle.

We quickly tidy up the bedroom. And of course when I walk into the kitchen, I see that Millie's sleeping area could pass a military inspection. The woman is a wonder of organizational skills. How do people live like that? It's not healthy.

After breakfast, more snapshots, and good-byes to our neighbors, Lydia climbs back into the driver's seat, and we're on the road again.

"We have to drive a couple of miles along this country road before we'll hit the highway exit," Millie says.

"So where will we stop tonight?" I ask.

"Why is it you always ask where we're going to stop right when we start driving?" Millie wants to know.

"Does that bother you?"

"Typos in books? Those bother me. Dog-eared pages? They bother me. But you? You don't fit into a category."

"I can live with that."

She turns back around and studies her map.

"Now listen, you two, am I going to have to referee you the same as I did in camp?" Lydia asks.

Sometimes that peacemaker thing is way overrated. I shrug.

"You two were always at each other, remember?"

Millie is ignoring Lydia the same as me. It's just better that way.

Lydia sighs. "You two are worse than my boys. I would have thought when Mrs. Woodriff banned you to a cabin together, apart from the rest of us, you would have learned your lesson."

"She never would have gotten that brilliant idea if *someone* hadn't said, 'Hey, DeDe, it's just like that movie *The Parent Trap*.'"

"Well, how was I supposed to know she'd hear me? Besides, we didn't put honey on her feet," Millie snaps.

"Maybe not honey, but hello? Two girls stirring up trouble in a girls' camp? Notice the similarities?"

"You stirred things up. I just happened to be nearby. *And* we're not identical twins."

The very idea makes me shudder. "Everyone thought you were the perfect little bookworm. So quiet and calm. They didn't know that it was you who came up with most of the ideas."

"Well, I didn't know you would actually carry them out."

"No, you just hoped she would," Lydia says.

"Hey, Millie, you're getting your sass back," I say with a grin. "We thought it was gone for good once you got married."

"I've learned that the wallflower gets passed by," Millie says.

"I'm sorry, Millie." Pause. "You want some whipped cream?"

She shakes her head. "It's no big deal. Bruce is happily married, and I'm—well, not." She laughs at herself.

"Look at it this way, if we were married, we probably wouldn't be going on this trip, and look at all the fun we'd miss," I say.

"If *we* were married, one of us would be dead. And I wouldn't marry you anyway," Millie says.

"I can see your point."

We all start laughing.

"Look, there are some wildflowers," Lydia says, pointing to an assortment of colorful flowers along the roadside. To my surprise, she pulls over.

"What are you doing?" I ask.

"Getting some flowers for our pitcher. I just hate not having flowers on the table when we eat." She shoves the motor home into park and eases out her door. Thankfully we're not on a busy street.

"What's wrong with the ones already in there?" Millie asks.

"They're dead," I say.

"Can't she just put salt and pepper shakers out like everybody else?" Millie says.

Millie's a class act all the way.

"You know, I've been thinking I'll talk to Beverly about using my horn to wake people up while we're at camp."

Excitement sparkles in Millie's eyes while dread looms over me. In her teen years, playing the trumpet was one way Millie really expressed herself. Though she showed her true self only to a few people, in front of a crowd she could blare her horn like nobody's business. Notice I didn't say she could "play" her horn. 'Nuff said.

"Don't you think most people will have alarm clocks?" I ask, trying to subtly suggest she might want to reconsider this whole trumpet alarm thing.

"Oh, sure, some people will, but some might not. It's just a creative way to get going in the morning, and it will give us that old camp feeling. Remember how we always used to start our mornings with a trumpet call?"

"Oh, I'd forgotten that," I say. "I think it's called suppressed memory."

"Ha-ha," Millie says.

I don't mention the fact that someone else played the trumpet then, and it was actually on pitch.

Lydia knocks at the side door, and I open it.

"Aren't these gorgeous?" Lydia climbs in quite out of breath.

"Do you want me to take care of those for you?" I ask.

"Oh no, no. I love putting together fresh flowers. I've forgotten how much I enjoy it. Greg and I used to go walking in the country near our home, and we would always pick wildflowers along the way. By the time I'd get home, we would have a beautiful vase of colorful twinflowers, goldenrod, lupine, cosmos, daisies, whatever. They were wonderful."

She stuffs the flowers in her blue pitcher, plucks one flower here, places it there, snips another, rearranges until she's satisfied, then sets the pitcher carefully on the table. "There," she says, brushing her hands together, "that should do it. We'll stick it under the sink for now so it won't fall off the table."

I'm curious as to the names of a couple of the flowers, but if I ask her, she'll spend the next fifteen minutes explaining them to me. She can be as bad as Millie when it comes to explanations—at least with flowers. Can we say information overload? Unless it's about chocolate, I'm not really that interested.

"Hey, you never did answer my question. You know, the one about where we're headed today," I say.

Millie turns around, looks at me, and rolls her eyes.

"You keep doing that, and one of these days your eyes will stick," I say.

Lydia chuckles. "I guess we didn't. We're headed to Indiana. Plan to stop at Pokagon State Park, isn't that right, Millie?"

"Yes." She studies her map a moment.

"Do you guys mind if I turn on the radio? I could use some nice music. Plus, I haven't listened to the news since we started our trip, and I'm feeling out of touch with the rest of the world," Lydia says.

"Great idea. I like to keep up on current affairs too," Millie says.

They're such good citizens. Me? My world consists of chocolate and shopping. If no earthshaking news happens there, I just won't know about it. Okay, so it's my responsibility to be informed, but, well, news equals pain. It's like this. Sometimes the news just depresses me. And when I'm depressed, I eat chocolate. That's why I maintain a regular Pilates workout, so I won't get overweight from all the chocolate, and of course all that exercise leads to pain. So the bottom line is, news equals pain.

My reasoning may be a little off here, but there it is.

Lydia fiddles with the radio knob, but she can't find any news. "I guess we'll just have to wait for it to come on," she says.

"I can turn on the TV to see if there's any news on. I think *Good Morning America* is still on," I say.

"We don't usually get a good reception unless we're in a park," Lydia says.

"You know, if we stumble upon a coffeehouse, I could sure use some decent coffee," Millie says. "Ever since the Starbucks opened beside the library, I've been hooked."

"Well, you all know how I feel about coffeehouses," Lydia says. "I love them. I've been keeping a watch out for one, but no luck yet."

"Yeah, me too," I say. "Did you know I never drank coffee at all until they started with the flavored stuff?"

"It's a conspiracy," Millie says.

"Yeah, coffee beans are rising up to gain control of the world," I say dryly.

"It could happen. The coffee suppliers merely need to get us addicted, and look out," Millie says with conviction.

"I'll take my chances," Lydia says.

"Yeah, me too." Millie shifts on her seat and turns back around. "So if you see a coffeehouse, pull over."

Lydia nods. "Trust me, if I see one, we're there."

My cell phone vibrates in my pocket. One glance tells me it's Rob. My heart sticks in my throat. I rush to the bedroom. Facing the rear window, I keep my back toward Millie and Lydia. With sweaty palms, I hold the vibrating phone. My pulse beats wildly in my ears. My shaking finger reaches up to press the on button.

"Hello?" My voice sounds weak, uncertain.

"Hey, precious, I've missed you—"

"Everything okay?" Millie asks from the doorway.

She so startles me, I drop the phone on the floor. I stoop to pick it up and push the off button. "I was going to call Shelley, but I think I'll wait until later," I say, sticking the phone back into my pocket. My face burns under Millie's scrutiny.

"You sure you don't want to talk about it?"

"About my call to Shelley? Just checking on things, that's all," I say in all innocence. But the look on Millie's face tells me she's not buying it. Still, she leaves me alone and walks back up to the front of the RV.

Sitting on the edge of the bed, I take a deep breath to calm myself. Instead of being thrilled at the sound of Rob's voice, I feel weird. The voice that once made my heart flutter when he called me "precious" now makes me think of Gollum in The Lord of the Rings, and that's just creepy. An involuntary shudder escapes me.

I'm going to have to tell Millie and Lydia sooner or later. They know something's up. Is it so wrong to want to talk to Rob? He told Shelley he had worked everything out, that he would see me soon. Does he know where I am? How did he find out? Shelley wouldn't tell him, would she?

I hate sneaking around like this, not being honest with my friends, but how can I tell them the truth? I just need to let him go. He's not right for me. Hello? Gollum should be a clue. The truth is, there are many things that were wrong with our relationship from the start. But I've overlooked them. Who wants to spend their weekends alone? That wasn't the way I wanted to live the rest of my life. But then, what Rob had to offer wasn't any better.

Is that the only thing holding me to him? I'm afraid of growing old alone?

"Want to stop for a burger, Dee?" Lydia calls out.

"Sure, that would be great," I shout back. Standing, I gather my courage and go to the front to join Millie and Lydia.

Lydia pulls the RV off at the next exit.

"I'm starving," Millie says.

Reaching for my handbag, I pull out my makeup and touch up my face. A darker foundation or a little tanning might do me some good. I'm starting to look like Johnny Depp in *Charlie and the Chocolate Factory.* That phone call didn't exactly do wonders for me.

Once my makeup is applied to my satisfaction, I put my powder away and plop a malted milk ball in my mouth. It's that comfort thing again. I glance out the window. Lydia maneuvers the RV around the corner toward a burger place. My eyes lock on a man on the street who looks just like Rob, and I gasp, pulling the milk ball to the back of my throat like lint to a vacuum.

My arms flail about as I gasp for breath.

"Oh my goodness, she's choking!" Millie yells, rushing back to help me.

Lydia hits the horn by mistake and it locks. People on the crosswalk scatter. Lydia gets so flustered she drives up over the curb. The contents of my makeup bag drop to the floor, spilling in every direction. Millie stumbles over the debris, jostling this way and that, trying to get to me. I gasp for air. Lydia bangs on the horn to try to shut it off.

Once she gets to me, Millie wraps her arms around my midsection with the strength of a sumo wrestler. Grunt one . . . if this thing doesn't come loose, she's going to kill me.

Against all logic, Lydia stops the RV and throws herself over the horn.

Grunt two . . . death by chocolate.

Amazingly, the horn's blare dies down to a whine and fizzles out.

Grunt three, the malted milk ball pops out of my throat, bounces off the window, and rolls to the floor. I gulp in three huge helpings of air through what I am sure are cracked ribs and vow right then and there never to mess with Millie's sock drawer again.

I fall onto the sofa in a heap. Lydia's limp form lies across the horn like a rag doll, and Millie wipes the sweat from her brow, looking as though she hasn't had this much excitement in years.

From the window I can see and hear an angry man shouting obscenities, but the man I thought I recognized has disappeared into the crowd. No man is worth all this.

Especially Rob.

8

Call it an educated guess, but I'm thinking my hair could turn gray before the day's over.

"Are you all right, DeDe?" Lydia asks once she's picked herself off the horn.

"I'm fine."

"I've told you more than once that chocolate would be the death of you, and you came mighty close," Millie says.

Swallowing my sarcasm, I say, "Thank you for your help, Millie. You saved my life."

She stretches two inches beyond her natural height.

"But don't go getting any ideas. I'm not going to walk around and serve you for the rest of my days," I say.

Lydia giggles.

Millie looks disappointed and heads to the fridge, where she pulls out her whipped cream.

I walk over to her, wait for her to swallow the whipped cream, then put my arm around her. "I'm sorry, Millie. That really upset you."

"Well, of course it did." She turns watery eyes my way. "I don't want to lose you, DeDe." Then she quickly adds, "Even if you do mess up my sock drawer."

At this *my* eyes water, and we hug each other. Lydia walks over and joins us, and in that hug we release a multitude of tension between us.

"Well, all's well that ends well," Millie says, clearly uncomfortable with all the sentimentality. Pulling apart, we dry our eyes and settle into our seats once again.

Lydia drives away from the people and farther into the parking lot.

I rush to the back of the motor home to peek out the window. The angry man is walking away, but the man who looked like Rob is nowhere in sight. Was it him?

Turning, I take two steps toward the front and stop when I see that Cobbler's cage has lifted off its hook in the wall bracket and is now resting on the bed. Birdseed is scattered all over my quilt, thank you very much, and Cobbler is hanging on to her perch for all she's worth. As in death grip. As in I couldn't pry her loose if I tried. The poor thing. Another triple sneeze and I'm good. She lost a few more feathers in the whole ordeal, and despite the fact that she's overdue for her Barney fix, she doesn't make a single peep.

Lifting the cage carefully, I hook it back into place, then return to the front. "I've got to clean the mess on my bed," I say, looking for the dustpan and swish broom under the cabinet.

"What's the matter? Did you have an, um, accident?" Millie laughs at her clever self.

"Uh, no. Cobbler did."

"Oh dear, is Cobbler okay?" The frown between Lydia's eyes resembles an exclamation point without the period.

"She's fine. Just a little rattled is all. Her cage landed on my bed in the commotion."

"Poor thing." Lydia could cry here. She's pretty sensitive when it comes to her animals, flowers, whatever. Come to think of it, Lydia can be sensitive over ants. She has a hissy fit if you step on one. Never mind that you can't see it. If she sees it, that's all that matters. Excuse me? But I'm over forty. I'm lucky to see the sidewalk. That little thought rocks my world for a minute, but I remember that I still haven't had hot flashes, so I'm good.

Checking on Cobbler once more, I notice that her food bowl is empty. That's because most of it spilled on my bed. Now, feeding Cobbler is Lydia's job, but she's busy driving at the moment. Since I'm not driving much—okay, try not driving at all because of my lack of directional ability—it seems I ought to do something to help out. Cobbler has perched on my hand before when she was out of her cage. How hard can it be to fill her food bowl?

Walking over to the nightstand in the room, I reach into the bottom drawer where Lydia keeps Cobbler's food, pull out the box, and place it on top of the stand. Then I walk back to Cobbler's cage.

The door of her cage lifts up easily enough.

"Poor Cobbler had a rough time, didn't ya?" I say with a sort of sickening coo in my voice. Holding the door open with my left hand, I reach into the cage with my other one and Cobbler hops onto the back of my hand, causing a little tug in my heart. How cute is that?

Cobbler stays on my hand while I lift the food cup from the cage. The RV isn't exactly helping matters, jostling us around as it hits bumps in the road.

Pulling the cup toward me, I try to tug the bowl out, but Cobbler won't jump off my hand. Twisting my wrist this way and that, I try to drop her off, but she keeps her feet—or whatever those things are called on a bird—fixed on my hand. I'm beginning to feel like a statue.

When I try to wrangle free, Cobbler pokes her head out of the door and squeezes through the opening. Before I can blink, she goes fluttering around me through the bedroom door opening and heads straight toward Lydia. Fortunately, she's had her wings clipped—Cobbler, not Lydia— and doesn't get very far. She flutters to the floor and starts hopping forward.

"You get back here right now, Cobbler."

"What's going on?" Millie turns around, none too happy about being distracted from her book. Her eyes grow wide. "You'd better get her before she causes a wreck, DeDe," Millie says as though I'm sitting down filing my nails.

"Oh no, Cobbler is loose?" Lydia asks.

"It's all right. I've got everything under control," I say as the RV hits a pothole. The refrigerator door swings open—Millie probably forgot to lock it after her whipped cream binge—knocking me into the bathroom before I can regain my balance. Pulling myself together, I step back into the kitchen. Cobbler has flopped down to the first step off the kitchen floor.

Lydia sees Cobbler out of her peripheral vision and screams. "Oh no, get my baby, Dee!"

"I'm not exactly having a pedicure here, Lydia." My voice wobbles with the RV wheels.

Another pothole almost sends Cobbler to her eternal reward as I fall within an inch of her scrawny body. Her round, beady eyes look up at me. Just before she scrambles to get away, I reach over and lightly scoop her into my hand.

Mistake.

Cobbler bores her crusty little beak into my hand as though it's a cuttlebone. She doesn't have to ask me twice. She's set free.

"Haven't you gotten her yet?" Millie asks.

By now I'm sweating, my hand resembles Swiss cheese, and I'm seriously reconsidering my friendship with these two.

Lydia takes the next exit and pulls into a business parking lot. She crawls back to Cobbler and talks sweetly. The parakeet immediately jumps into Lydia's hand and cuddles up to her. *Traitor. How about I just pluck out your little feathers one by one?*

"Poor baby, did you get hurt? I'm so sorry, Cobbler. Mommy's here," Lydia coos.

It's enough to make me puke.

"I'm sorry, Lydia, I was trying to help by putting food in her cage." The warm soap and water in the bathroom make my injured hand burn. If I could just get that hand around that bird's scrawny little neck . . .

"Don't worry about it. But in the future, you'd better let me take care of that. Thanks for trying, though." She places Cobbler back in her cage, plops in the Andy Griffith video, then walks back up to the front.

My gaze collides with Cobbler. I throw her an evil glare. If she bites me again, I'll bite her back.

Lydia climbs back into her seat. "You girls watch for a store. We'll stop there first, and then we'll go out to eat."

"Oh good. I want to develop some more film," Millie says.

"Oh my goodness, look at that!" Lydia says, pointing to a green, life-size model of a Tyrannosaurus rex standing just at the edge of the road. Lydia slows the RV so we can get a good look.

"Oh my, that's a little scary," Millie says, grabbing her camera and snapping away. "Wouldn't want to stumble upon him while walking through the woods. Look at all those teeth."

"Yeah, can you imagine fitting dentures for a mouth like that?" Awe and wonder fill Lydia's voice.

"I read in one of our brochures that there's a 'Prehistoric Forest' in Ohio somewhere. They have a walking tour with dinosaurs scattered throughout the forest," Miss Librarian informs us.

"Boy, I must be out of the loop. I thought dinosaurs were extinct," I say.

Millie rolls her eyes and shakes her head. "Well, if we can have Elvis sightings, there's no reason we shouldn't see dinosaurs," she says in a sudden burst of humor.

"Do you want to stop and check it out?" Lydia asks.

"I'll do whatever you two want," Millie says. "Though I'm not a huge dinosaur fan."

Pulling my hands to my chest, I say with a heavy dose of drama, "Let the heavens rejoice! Millie is passing up an educational opportunity."

Lydia giggles. Millie shrugs.

"How about you, DeDe—do you want to stop?" Lydia presses.

"You're kidding, right? Somehow Dee doesn't strike me as the prehistoric monster type," Millie says.

"Well, unless they're edible and covered in chocolate," I add.

We laugh and continue on our journey for some time until we come upon another Wal-Mart.

Lydia parks the RV and we get out. The warm air hits my face so fast, I'm wondering if that's how a hot flash feels. 'Course, I'm basing that on what Lydia and Millie have told me. I want to cup my hands together, circle them in front of me in a semidance, and say, "Oh yeah, I'm still in my prime. Oh yeah."

What does it mean to be in my prime anyway? As in still able to have children? Those days are over for me. It's not as if I have time for kids anyway. I'm too busy with my business to be a good mom—or so I tell myself.

"Boy, it's hot out here," Millie grumbles. She lifts her hair and waves her hand under it. I've never understood why people do that. I mean, let's be honest here—does our hand really generate enough air to cool us off?

The asphalt is so hot that the tiny heels on my sandals leave imprints behind. We can't get into the store too soon.

Once we're inside, we shop around for a little while. The stupid cart I picked has a wobbly wheel, dipping and squeaking with every rotation, but I try to look cool as I push it along. Aside from the rickety cart thing, I'm wondering if it's even possible to look cool when you're forty-nine. Judging by the stares we're getting now, I'm thinking no.

I place a few cosmetics, some lotion, and a bottle of nail polish in the cart. Millie gets her film developed and picks up another suspense novel and an extra set of glasses. Lydia buys dish soap, flour, sugar, blueberries, bananas, orange juice, some baking chocolate, and a cooking magazine.

"You know, I've been thinking about coloring my gray hair," Lydia says thoughtfully as we walk down the hair color aisle.

"And why not?" I say.

"This is the time of life where we should be having fun," Millie says as if she's all over that. Yeah, right.

"I agree, Lydia. This could be fun."

Now, I could be wrong, but I don't remember learning all these colors in grade school. Yet I have to admit they sure sound pretty. We finally decide upon Saharan Rose strawberry blonde as the color for Lydia. It takes all three of us to pick it out, by the way.

After paying for our purchases, we climb back into the motor home and head to the nearest fast-food restaurant for a quick burger. Following that, we continue down the road in complete silence, but for the sputtering and occasional cough the RV spits out. Wobbly cart, ailing RV. Does everything around me have to be old and falling apart? As if on cue, Lydia turns up the air. Another hot flash.

"Whew, it's hot in here," she says with the vent tilted up toward her face, blowing her hair back as though she's caught in a windstorm.

"You two ever think about upping your hormone meds?"

"I would if I took any," Millie says.

"You're not taking anything? That suffering in silence thing is way overrated, Millie."

"I just don't like to take medicine. I've read a lot on the subject, and I take a few supplements, drink lots of water, exercise, eat right." Millie shrugs.

"Well, something's not doing it for you," I say. "What do you do, Lydia?"

"I'm on bioidentical hormone cream. Just started, so it probably hasn't had enough time to work. If it doesn't get better, I'll either up the medication or try something else. It's hard to know what's safe these days."

"Glad I don't have to think about it yet." I stretch out my legs and lean back on the sofa, thinking life is good.

"Yeah, you're just a spring chicken for a few more days," Millie says with a grunt and a smirk.

"I don't mean to brag, but I still grow hair on *top* of my head and not beneath my chin." Okay, that was harsh.

Millie glares at me. Really glares. As if she could swallow me whole. Then she bends over for something on the floor.

"Boy, I've been slipping," Millie says, flipping through her book on Rocky Mountain National Park.

A groan rises in my throat, but I swallow it. Trivia Millie is totally in her element. She's teaching us, and there's not a thing we can do about it. I mean, where we gonna go? Besides, if I complain, she might break out the trumpet.

I'm envisioning Millie as a military weapon. Picture a weary prisoner dressed in ragged, dirty clothes, white rag stuffed in his mouth, hands and feet bound with a rough rope to a wooden chair in the middle of a deserted warehouse. Dressed in a white uniform, plastic gloves, with her hair pulled back in a tight bun, Millie would make her entrance. In thick-soled shoes, she would pad up to a chair and sit down in front of him, her back ramrod straight. She'd snap the rolled edges of her plastic gloves into place, causing the prisoner to jump. Sliding on a pair of glasses, she would proceed in her monotone to drone on and on with first one fact and then another, until the poor man broke into a cold sweat and finally cracked. By the time she finished with him, he would tell her everything he knew and, in exchange for his freedom, offer her his golf clubs and season tickets to the NBA.

I know this is true, because when she's on a trivia roll, I'm ready to give her my complete chocolate inventory.

Millie perches the new glasses at the tip of her nose. Thumbing through the pages of the book, she finally stops. "Here we go." She peers at me over the rims of her glasses. "This is easy. Even *you* might get this one, DeDe."

"Excuse me? Do I have the word *stupid* on my forehead?"

"What are you complaining about? You still grow hair on *top* of your head," Millie quips. Okay, she's gonna hang on to that comment like a librarian clutching a best seller at a book sale. She gets all situated in her seat and smiles as big as you please. "Name the highest continuous paved road in the United States."

Jeopardy music again. I'm hoping Lydia jumps in here, because I have no idea what the name of the road is that leads up the mountain, and to be perfectly honest, I'm not all that interested. Sad but true. Millie's gaze lands on me, and she gives me one of those teacher looks. You know the one. It says, "You know this. Now cough it up."

"Lydia, feel free to jump in here anytime. I don't know what it is," I say dryly, obviously disappointing Millie, who clucks her tongue and turns to Lydia.

"It has the word *ridge* in it, I think," Lydia says, her brows pulled together in concentration.

I just refuse to strain my brain that much. Life's too short.

Hope springs to Millie's face. "That's right, it does. One more word now." She's practically sitting on the edge of her seat.

For this she's excited? Give me chocolate, give me diamonds, give me *amore*. But "continuous paved road"? No.

Lydia thinks some more. Unwrapping a truffle from my bag, I sink deep into the sofa cushion and kick my feet up. Might as well join in. "Come on, Lydia, you can get it," I say like a cheerleader on the sidelines. Well, minus the flexibility and wad of gum.

Millie's fighting the urge to keep from saying the name, I can tell. Her lips tense up to form a word, then pull tightly together, resembling a kid refusing a forkful of spinach. Eyebrows lifted, Millie waits with bated breath.

Watching this scene is terribly amusing, but I hold my giggle to a mere muffle. Millie has far too much emotion riding on this one. One hot flash from her, and this RV could become a rolling ball of fire.

"I've got it!" Lydia says with a snap of her fingers. "Trail Ridge Road!"

"That's it!" Millie flops back against her chair in a heap. She closes the book with a thump. "That's enough for today," she says, quite out of breath.

Okay, the fact that they're getting this excited over that whole question/answer thing? It just ain't right.

"Hey, did you know that refining the chocolate crumb mixture from the cocoa beans is a risky business?" Why should Millie be the only one to spout off her knowledge? She gives me a look that says she doesn't care, which, of course, fuels my need to tell her more. I sit up straighter and display my half-eaten truffle. "Oh my, yes. If the manufacturers don't crush the mixture enough, the chocolate will be coarse and grainy. But if they blend it too much, the chocolate will be pasty and gummy."

Millie looks surprised.

"My goodness, I take so much for granted," Lydia says as though we're talking about a mission trip to a remote country.

"Well, I have to agree with Lydia on this. DeDe, I had no idea there was so much to learn about chocolate," Millie says.

That wasn't at all the reaction from Millie I had expected. Takes the fun out of everything. Still, if I can talk about chocolate, I'm good.

"Swiss and German chocolates are refined for longer periods. That's why they're smoother and finer than American or English candy. Some people prefer that. Some do not. It's all about texture, you know." With the last bite of my truffle, I realize how true it is.

"I'll never look at a chocolate bar the same again," Millie says dryly.

"Well, you certainly shouldn't. Truffles should never be compared with, say, a vending-machine chocolate bar. There is just no comparison," I say.

"Can we talk about something else? I'm getting hungry," Lydia interjects.

"By the way, mixing up the canned goods was just immature," Millie says, looking at me.

"Took you long enough to find them," I say.

"That's because I was doing other things. You and Lydia have been in charge of meals."

I shrug.

"If you do it again, I'll put locks on the doors," she threatens.

"And you think that could stop me? Have I mentioned how many times I've watched Houdini?"

Millie ignores me and starts talking about the map directions. Their words finally blend with Waldo's engine as I close my eyes.

"Do you want to stop at the outlet mall, girls?" Lydia's voice rouses me from my sleep. All someone has to do is mention shopping, and I'm there.

"Sure," I say, rubbing my eyes.

"What did I tell you?" Millie says to Lydia with a laugh.

With a glance at my watch, I see that I've been napping for about thirty minutes. Quickly I grab my makeup bag—fortunately, I was able to retrieve everything that had spilled on the floor—and touch up my face as best I can.

Lydia pulls the RV into the mall parking lot, and my eyes feast upon endless clothing and shoe shops. My joy knows no bounds.

Just before we climb out of the vehicle, Lydia's phone rings. I spruce up my hair a little while we wait for her to finish the call.

"Derrick, calling to check on me," she says with a smile as she flips her cell phone closed.

"That's so sweet how they keep tabs on you," I say, spraying the last dab of spritz on my hair.

"Would you ladies mind going on ahead, and I'll catch up with you?" Millie asks.

With my hands on my hips, I say, "Don't rearrange my sock drawer while I'm gone, Millie."

"Why would I stoop to your level? Besides, it's your shoes that need the help."

"Nobody messes with my shoes and lives to tell about it."

Lydia gasps.

Millie and I both look at her. "I'm kidding. Sheesh, don't take things so seriously." I lead the way out of the motor home. "Besides, my shoes are meticulously stacked in my storage bin under the bed."

Millie grunts loudly enough for me to hear.

"I *will* know if you move anything," I call over my shoulder.

Lydia laughs. Millie ignores me.

We all know it's not true. I haven't had order in my life since— hmm, it's just not coming to me. All I know is, if I can make a grocery list of four things and actually make it to the store with said list, I'm doing good.

"Join us as soon as you can, Millie," Lydia says.

"Will do."

We close the door behind us and head for the closest dress shop. We browse from rack to rack in one store, then another. After shopping through several stores, Millie calls my cell phone to see where we are. I tell her, and she soon catches up.

"What were you doing all that time?" I ask while sorting through the hangers in search of a red top to go with the jeans I purchased in the last store. Millie fudges here. I stop moving hangers.

Lydia and I both look at her. "What's up?"

"The hair on the bathroom floor bothered me. All that hair-spray DeDe uses"—she throws me a disgusted look, and I shrug—"makes it stick and turns the tile yellow. I had to clean it. No offense intended, Lydia."

I gaze at the ceiling. "Somebody's compulsive behavior is show-ing," I say in singsong fashion.

Lydia pokes me in the side. "No offense taken, Millie. Thank you for your help."

When they passed out the gene for organization and cleanli-ness, I'm guessing I was in the back eating chocolate—either that or shopping.

I can think of worse things.

9

"*Here goes nothing,*" *Lydia says in the RV that night as she* dunks her head into the sink so I can set to work on her hair.

Millie's outside hanging the lights on the awning. Though she won't admit it, I think she's really getting into this camping business. Lydia too. On the other hand, I am here merely because they are my friends. Period. It's all I can do not to jump out of the motor home when we pass a Hilton.

Lydia and I talk while waiting for her hair to dry 'til it's barely damp, then with newspaper spread across the floor, I plunk her in a chair and start parting her hair so I can apply the color, beginning at her roots.

"Now, if the smell of this gets to you, DeDe, you tell me." She's pinching the end of her nose and talking as if she's all stopped up.

"What? The fact that the smell could singe your nose hairs makes you think it will bother me?" I laugh. "I'll be fine. It's not as strong as the solution for permanents. I was kind of worried about Cobbler. Though I don't know why after what she did to my hand." I'm still bitter about that. Might I suggest a punishment to fit the crime, as in ban her from Deputy Fife? Have her debeaked?

Lydia groans. "Oh, I hadn't thought of the fumes bothering Cobbler. Maybe I should set her cage outside."

The evil side of me wants to agree, though I'm wondering just how much pleasure I'd have watching Cobbler keel over beak-first when a squirrel lands on her cage. I'm just not that cruel.

"I don't think I'd do that since there are other animals out there. But maybe we should turn off the air-conditioning for a few minutes and open the door to keep the ventilation going."

"You're right. You want to do that?" Lydia asks.

I'm itching to say, "With pleasure," since most of the time I feel as though I'm living in a meat locker. But I simply agree and walk over and slide open a couple of windows.

"I'm sorry Cobbler hurt your hand, DeDe."

"I'll live," I say. "Just barely, mind you, but I'm a survivor, so I'll pull through." I continue squirting the color on Lydia's hair.

"One more push, and we're good to go." I'm feeling kind of like Picasso here as I squeeze out the final bit of color, though I resist the urge to kiss the tips of my fingers and shout, "Voilà!"

I pile Lydia's hair up on top of her head as best I can. "Boy, we don't want to get any color on the floor. Do you have some plastic wrap?"

"Kitchen drawer, second one down to the left of the stove."

With a quick tug on the drawer, the brass handle comes off. "Uh-oh."

Lydia turns around with a drip of hair color running down her temple. "What's wrong?"

"I think your RV's body parts just aren't what they used to be," I say, waving the handle.

Lydia bites her lip to keep from laughing. "Bless Waldo's heart. We're all getting older. Oh well, we'll replace it later. Just stick it in the drawer so we don't lose it."

Dropping the gold handle and the loose screws from the other side into the drawer, I pull out a box of plastic wrap. After tearing off a large piece, I wrap it securely around Lydia's head so she won't drip all over the place. She's a sight to behold, that's for sure. If Millie sees this, she'll run for her camera, no doubt about it.

"I'll set the timer on the stove for twenty minutes," I say.

"I got the lights all put up," Millie announces when she steps inside. One glance at Lydia and Millie's eyes grow wide.

"I suppose I look as ridiculous as I feel," Lydia says, showing a definite need to be encouraged here.

"Uh, yeah," Millie responds with complete honesty. Her feet stay planted. Not moving even an inch toward her camera. Smart lady. She could bring out Lydia's dark side.

"You're fine, Lydia. Besides, these are the things we women have to go through to be beautiful." I give her a sideways hug and usher her over to the chair at the table. "You sit here, and I'll get you some iced tea."

She sits down. Millie grabs her picture box. After we look at them once more, she files them in the box.

"Oh, could I see that again?" I ask, pointing to the picture of the dinosaur.

"Yes, but be careful that you don't get smudge marks on the print. Hold the picture at the edges."

I stare at her a moment, then look down at the dinosaur. Suddenly their teeth look very much the same. After looking at it again, I hand it back to Millie. She puts everything away, then glances at the cabinets.

"What happened to the handle on the drawer?" Millie asks.

"It fell off," I say, gathering the tea glasses and ice.

"Well, why didn't you put it back on?"

Turning, I stare at her. "I was in the middle of dyeing Lydia's hair, Millie. Kind of hard to reattach the handle when I have on gloves stained with dye."

Millie sighs and gets up. "I'll do it. Is it in the drawer?"

"It's there." I want to comment on her compulsion, but I decide not to since she's been a little sensitive lately.

Millie sets to work on the handle while I get the tea.

"A family has moved in next door. They have two teenage

daughters. I hope that doesn't mean every young buck in the county will be clamoring to get to them," Millie says, making a face as she turns the screw to attach the handle to the drawer.

I laugh and place the glasses of iced tea in front of Millie's and Lydia's places. "Leave it to you to think of that, Millie."

Lydia jumps in. "That's wonderful! I think I'll bake a couple of pies tonight and invite them over," she says, already rising and grabbing the recipe box. Her sudden movement causes more drips to slide down her cheek. She wipes them off with a napkin. "Blueberry. Got it." She pulls the card from the box. "I'm glad I bought the blueberries at the grocery. We're all prepared." Smiling, she sits back down at the table.

"You know, Lydia, it's easy to see where your passion lies. You just sparkle when you're in the kitchen," I say.

Her hands feel her cheeks. "Do I?" She smiles. "I must say I love cooking."

"I understand. That's how I feel about my chocolate. I love mixing the filling, or whatever I happen to be working on, into a syrup over the stove, then transferring it to the machines to strengthen the texture and change in color."

Lydia sits up with excitement. "Oh my goodness, DeDe, what you do with chocolate is pure art in its finest form."

"They taste good too," Millie adds with a grin.

"Okay, if you two are trying to get more truffles, you're on," I say, going to the bedroom and retrieving my box. No use making them take from their own boxes, since I can get all I want back home. "Who wants what? I have raspberry, mocha, cordial, and caramel truffles left."

"You're a doll," Lydia says, reaching for the mocha.

"I could never work around this all day. I'd weigh five hundred pounds," Millie says, grabbing the cordial.

"That's why I have to work out," I say. "Unfortunately, I haven't had the time since we've gotten together. I'd better make time soon, or I'll have to kiss these truffles good-bye. And we know that's not gonna happen."

We all laugh together.

"There was an article at the library that talked about how chocolate is made from cocoa beans. Are all cocoa beans the same?" asks Millie, ever the information gatherer.

"That's a good question, Millie. Actually, they are different. The Dominican Republic cocoa has a low chocolate flavor with bitter and astringent accents. Let's see, Venezuela has lightly colored cocoa with a chocolate and slightly bitter fruity flavor. Ecuador is distinctively fruity. Brazil's cocoa beans have a cocoa flavor accented with a sharp acid taste. And Africa has a gold standard of cocoa, a balanced mix of strong chocolate, sour, and fruity flavors."

"You know, you're smarter than you look," Millie says.

"How badly do you want that truffle?" I ask as she's about to take a bite.

"Kidding. I'm kidding."

The timer on the stove goes off.

"Time's up," I say, giving the towel to Lydia.

"Oh dear, I hope I don't live to regret this," she says.

"You won't, I promise. You're going to look beautiful. Okay, you need to dunk your head into the sink," I say, trying to get her mind off things. With some hesitation, she complies. I test the water, and when it's warm enough, I apply just enough to her hair to work up a good lather. After that, I rinse it thoroughly, making sure all color is washed down the drain, right down to the last tinted bubble.

"Oh, I think you're going to like this, Lydia," I say, noticing how it's lightened her hair a bit.

"I hope so," she says in a muffled tone with her face pressing against a towel.

Grabbing another towel, I wrap it around her head, and she stands upright.

"I'll go blow-dry it so I can get started on these pies." She heads for the scrubbed bathroom—compliments of Millie's compulsion.

After a few minutes, Millie pipes up, "You coming out, Lydia?"

The bathroom door cracks open, and she steps out into the hallway and into the kitchen as though she's afraid of what we might say.

Millie gasps.

I can't believe the difference. "Lydia, you look drop-dead gorgeous," I say, meaning it.

"Really, do you like it?" Her hands absently reach for her hair.

"I can't get over it," I say. "You remind me of Heather Locklear."

Lydia laughs and primps her hair.

"Yeah! It makes you look ten years younger," Millie adds.

Lydia appears genuinely pleased. "Guess I should have done this a long time ago." She touches her hair once more and bites her lip. "You sure it's not too much?"

"No way. It's gorgeous," I say.

"Well, all right, if you two say so," Lydia says.

We quickly eat a light dinner together, and Lydia says, "I'd better get to those pies, or we won't be able to visit with our neighbors tonight."

"I'm going to close these windows," Millie says. "It's way too hot in here."

"Probably a good idea since I have to start the oven." Lydia sticks her head through the hole in her blue-and-white-checkered apron and ties it in back.

"I think I'll just go out and start a fire in the pit." I head out the door. My blood barely starts to move through my veins again, and those two start up with the freezing routine. At this rate, I'll be an ice sculpture before we get to Colorado.

Grabbing the bundle of wood that we bought at the camp store when we arrived, I start the fire. Once I get it going, I sit in a chair and watch the flames build. Not only does the fire keep me warm, but it keeps the bugs at a fairly safe distance.

Night crickets call out, their chirps mingling with the squeals of laughter from children at play. Doors squeak open and closed, people call out to one another, and meat sizzles on nearby grills, the scent of charcoal and steak filling the air. Though I'm not a camper—and trust me, nothing has changed my mind on that—I have to admit it's kind of nice here. Leaning my head back, I stare straight up at the dusky twilight. Not a cloud anywhere. I sigh.

"We'll make a camper out of you yet," Millie says as she descends the steps of the motor home. "Want some s'mores?"

"Aren't we going to eat pie?"

"Yeah, so?" Millie winks. "Don't tell me you've never had more than one dessert in an evening."

"My lips would love it, but my hips would not."

Millie shrugs. "Suit yourself." She stabs a marshmallow onto the end of a deformed hanger and dangles it over the fire.

"Oh, all right." I get up and dig into the bag of marshmallows. "But when I have to go in for liposuction, just remember, I'm holding you and Lydia personally responsible."

Millie and I enjoy the fire, then Millie goes inside to get her book. Thoughts of Le Diva Chocolates and the new competition flit across my mind, and I follow Millie into the RV to get my notebook that holds pictures of the various chocolates we offer. It wouldn't hurt to come up with some new ideas in case that new chocolate shop gives me too much competition.

While we're all inside, someone knocks at the door. Lydia goes over to answer it.

"Hi, my name is Ned, and my wife and I are staying next door with our daughters. Anyway, I was talking to a man down the road, friendly sort, when we got interrupted."

"Oh?" Lydia says.

"I thought I would tell you 'cause he said he was looking for a motor home that matched the description of yours. I wasn't sure how important it might be for you to know someone was looking for you."

He no sooner leaves than the things around me start to spin. My equilibrium goes amuck, and the last thing I remember is the scuffling of feet and Millie saying, "She's going down."

10

They say I was out for less than two seconds, but Millie and Lydia helped me into the bedroom and onto the bed anyway. Millie dampened a washcloth with warm water and placed it on my forehead.

"Are you all right?" Lydia asks. She looks worried. "I've never seen anyone faint before."

"I'm fine. Thanks, Lydia."

Millie settles on the edge of the bed. "It's time you told us what's going on."

My heart skips a beat. "What do you mean?"

"You know exactly what I mean."

"Well, Millie, she might not feel up to talking just now," Lydia says in a motherly voice.

"DeDe?" Millie presses. "Why did you faint? Something that man said? Is someone following us?"

"I don't know for sure."

Lydia gasps and puts her hand to her throat.

"So there *is* someone following us?" Millie studies my face.

"It's nothing bad—well, not for you anyway."

Lydia and Millie stare at me. I blow out a sigh. "All right, I think Rob might be trying to find me."

"Rob? I thought you two broke up," Millie says, her eyes narrow and searching.

"We did." I smooth the covers in front of me. "It's a long story, really."

"Well, we're not going anywhere, and we have plenty of time," Millie says.

"Let her rest, Millie. We can talk later," Lydia says.

Millie makes a face, then looks at me. "All right," she says, wagging a finger, "but we want the story when you're up to it. We can't have him upsetting your trip like this. If you're afraid of him, we'll take action," Millie says, lips pursed.

Lydia turns around. "What are we going to do?"

"Oh, come on, you two. We don't even know that it's him."

Millie puts her fists on her hips. "What are you going to do, DeDe, wait until he comes knocking on your door?"

"Have you ever been in the military?" I ask.

Millie blinks. "What?"

"Never mind. Don't worry. It's probably not him."

Just then someone knocks on the door again. Millie's gaze rams into mine. She rolls up her sleeves. "I'll get it."

"No, you had better let me," I say. I'm afraid Millie will cut him off at the knees, and it could be a junior ranger or something.

"Oh, are you sure you should get up?" Lydia asks, trying to help me walk to the door.

I shrug off the tiny voice asking me what I'm going to do if they're right. With a peek out the kitchen window, I instantly feel better. It's a man, but it's not Rob.

"Yes?"

"Ma'am, I'm sorry to bother you, but when you drove into the park, I noticed your RV was trailing water."

The movement behind me is Millie. A quick glance shows me she's at my side—out of the man's view—holding a baseball bat over her head.

"Millie, put that away," I say in a hushed reprimand.

"Excuse me?" the man says.

I turn back to him. "I mean, yes, yes. I'm sorry, I was talking to someone else. Water, did you say? You saw the motor home leaking water?" Saying the words loud enough for Millie to hear, I turn and glare at her for an instant. She shrugs and walks back to the bedroom with the baseball bat.

"Yes," he says, looking at me as though I'm weird.

I stretch out my hand. "Thank you so much, Mr.—"

"Cornwell. Doug Cornwell."

"Mr. Cornwell, thank you for letting us know. We'll get that looked at right away."

"I'd be happy to look it over for you, if you want. I've worked on plenty of RVs in my time." He throws his chest out and stands taller. If he starts to crow and strut around the yard, I'm closing the door.

"No, don't let him do that." The warden is back. "We don't know him from the man in the moon," Millie warns in a frantic whisper.

"Uh, I appreciate your offer, but I'd need to talk to my, um, *friends*"—can I just say that at this point I use that term loosely?—"about that," I say, hoping he didn't hear Millie.

"Well, if you decide you want me to look at it, I'm about seven RVs down on the opposite side of the road. We're driving a green-and-black Fleetwood motor home."

"Thank you so much, Mr. Cornwell."

"Call me Doug." He smiles. "You camp much?"

I blink.

"Figured you didn't camp much, or you'd know most campers aren't so formal. It's pretty much a first-name basis in the camping community. Everyone's your neighbor. We're all common folks, just enjoying the journey."

I relax—but then Millie returns with the bat in her hand, telling me not to trust him.

"Thank you, Doug."

"Have a good day," he says with a wave, then turns and heads down the road.

Before I can get the door closed, Millie starts in. "You're too trusting, DeDe. Even if he's not associated with your *Rob*, we don't know this man."

"Millie, would you stop? You're scaring Lydia half to death, and there is no reason to suspect that man of anything."

"There's no reason not to."

"Oh, for crying out loud. I'm going outside." I grab my business notebook and slowly head out the door since I'm still feeling a little weak. Those two are driving me crazy.

Before I can open my notebook, our neighbor comes over.

"Well, hello again," he says. A woman walks up beside him. "This is my wife, Gail, and our daughters, Ami and Amanda."

"Hello."

I tell them about the water leak, and Ned says he'd be glad to take a look too. "Had any overheating?"

"Overheating?"

"You know, engine overheating? There's a place on your dashboard that shows you if the engine is overheating, just the same as in your car. The needle will crawl up to the red line."

"Lydia hasn't mentioned it. I'll have to ask her."

"Could be a leak in your radiator if it's overheating."

Before I can answer him, Millie and Lydia step outside and join us.

After introductions, Lydia says she hasn't noticed that the RV has been overheating. She says she'll keep an eye on it, then invites the neighbors for pie. Before long we're engrossed in conversation, each of us filling the others in on our lives. "My boys are both in college," Lydia says, collecting the dirty dessert dishes. "Derrick is in engineering, and Drew hopes to become a dentist like his father."

Lydia's eyes light up, and her face glows. I'm not sure if it's from talking about her boys or if it's because she's hostessing. She is the domestic queen, no doubt about it.

"Where is your husband now?" Gail asks, having no idea she's entered a difficult subject.

Lydia bites the corner of her lip. "Oh, he died in November of last year," she says.

They express their condolences, and an awkward silence follows.

"How about I check out that radiator for you now?" Ned offers.

Millie and I look at Lydia.

"I guess that would be okay," she says.

"Hello, folks." A white-haired lady dressed in capris, a brightly flowered top, and a straw hat walks across the road toward us. "I was wondering if I might join you for a spell?" She smiles sweetly, and Lydia pounces on the opportunity to serve someone else. Before the woman can say another word, Lydia places a piece of pie and coffee before her on the table and sits down beside her.

We soon learn that the woman's name is Greta Mitchell, and she's from Michigan.

"My mom named me after Greta Garbo," she says with a mischievous grin. "There's a resemblance, don't you think?" She turns sideways to show off her wrinkled profile, and I love her instantly. She chuckles and goes back to her pie.

"So what brings you here?" Lydia wants to know.

Greta finishes her bite of pie. "Oh, honey, I travel the countryside."

"Is your husband here?" Lydia presses.

"Oh my, no. He died twenty years ago."

We fall silent.

"Does anyone travel with you?" Gail asks.

"For the love of Pete, what for? I'm too set in my ways. I'm best at traveling alone."

Lydia puts her hand to her throat and gasps. "You travel all by yourself?"

Greta snaps her head. "Sure do. Just because I'm eighty-two years old doesn't mean I need to leave all the fun to the young people." She winks at Ami and Amanda. They smile back at her.

Lydia sits still for a moment with her mouth gaping.

"I can see you're surprised by that," Greta says, her eyes twinkling.

"It's just that, well, what if your motor home breaks down, or someone tries to hurt you or take advantage of your kindness or—"

Greta holds up her hand. "I decided a long time ago I could get killed walking out to my mailbox, but if I worried about it all the time, I'd never get the mail." She thinks a minute. "'Course, on the days it brings me bills, that might not be a bad idea." She slaps her knee and laughs to the count of one, two, three, snort. One, two, three, snort.

"I guess that's true, but still," Lydia says, obviously not convinced.

"Take my advice, young lady"—Greta pats Lydia's hand—"don't spend your life worrying about the what-ifs. That's a narrow approach. Expand your what-ifs to the positives. What if I spent my life living instead of worrying about dying? That kind of thing."

"That's good advice, Greta," Gail says.

"Life's too short to waste it. I'm using up every bit of mine doing what I want to do," Greta says with a wide grin. And I believe her.

Ned rejoins us. "You've got a radiator leak for sure," he says.

"Oh dear." A shadow covers Lydia's expression.

"Well, you can get by a short while by keeping water in it until you can get it fixed," Ned advises. "Just don't wait too long."

Lydia follows him to the front of the RV, and Ned shows her where to fill the radiator.

We finish off the evening in wonderful fellowship outside the motor home with our new neighbors. After Millie gets group pictures, we all go inside, where we go through our nightly routine. We wash for bed, brush our teeth, and smear on the cold cream. Since her cage fell on my bed, Cobbler's been plucking out her feathers. Lydia says that's how her bird handles stress. She decides to let Cobbler out of her cage for about ten minutes, hoping that will help the bird feel better. Cobbler hops around on the bed and flutters from Lydia to the window blind to my head. We laugh at Cobbler's antics, and finally Lydia puts the parakeet to bed for the night, covering her cage with a towel.

"Millie and I are going to have some tea in the kitchen," Lydia says. "You want to join us?"

"No thanks. I'm kind of tired," I say.

She nods and closes the bedroom door behind her, leaving me alone. Maybe I should call Rob and see if he is nearby. Maybe I should meet him somewhere—or at least check to see if he's left a message. I pick up my cell phone. Before I can turn it on, Greta's words come to me: "Life's too short to waste it." I stare at the phone. That's what I've been doing, wasting my life with Rob. There's no future with us, so why would I even consider going back to him? It's wrong to be with him, and I've let him stalk me long enough. It's time I took control of my life—and maybe talk to the One who gave it to me in the first place.

Thanks to Cobbler's squawking all night, I'm pretty tired in the morning. But of course, she's sleeping peacefully on her perch while I have to get ready for church. I have a notion to rattle her cage. That would teach her. But since it's Sunday and I'm going to church, it doesn't seem the thing to do.

After attending a little service in an amphitheater on the campgrounds, we enjoy a great morning of singing and worshipping together. Then after lunch, much to my surprise, I'm able to talk Millie and Lydia into taking a hike into the woods.

"This feels so great," I say. "Without my regular Pilates workout, my legs were turning to pudding."

Lydia laughs. "You work too hard. I think you look great."

"Remember what Greta said—you can't worry about things all the time," Millie says.

"This coming from the baseball bat queen," I say dryly, stepping over a fallen branch in the path.

"Even Girl Scouts know to be prepared. I don't worry about what may happen, but I keep things on hand just in case."

"Guess I'm the only worrywart here," Lydia says with a sigh.

"Don't be so hard on yourself, Lydia. We're all struggling with issues." Rob flits to my mind.

"Even you, Dee?" Millie asks, surprising me. "When are you going to tell us the truth about Rob?"

Millie's not one to beat around the bush. She won't stop nagging me until I throw her something to gnaw on for a while. "I didn't want to break up, okay? Are you happy?"

"So why did you?"

"He—" I stop myself.

"Another woman?" Millie asks.

"Something like that." I can't bring myself to tell them he's married. Not yet. What will they think of me?

"Nothing more painful than being left for someone else." Millie's voice grows soft.

My ego makes me want to defend my position, but there is no way to do it without making me look worse. So I keep silent.

"Want me to hurt him?" Millie asks abruptly.

Lydia gasps. I look up in surprise.

"I will. You just give me the word."

"Millie, I think you're half-serious."

"Can't stand by and do nothing while someone hurts my friend."

Millie's threat of violence truly touches me. Shame on me, but there it is.

"I'll be fine, Millie. It's just everything right now. My business, my—well, everything. I wonder if I will ever know love again."

And I wonder if I have the right to. Guilt washes over me anew. Maybe if I could forget what happened, I could find peace.

"I'll be praying for you, DeDe," Lydia says.

"Thanks." I prayed last night, though I don't know why He would listen to me.

Birdsong echoes throughout the forest. Our steps crunch upon broken sticks and debris in the path. A bluebird swoops overhead and lands on the branch of a shagbark hickory tree. Cupping my hand over my eyes, I snatch a look at him against the bright afternoon sky peeking through the trees.

Though it's hot outside, the air within the forest is bearable. Well, aside from that whole exercise thing.

"One down," Millie shouts.

Lydia's sitting on a decomposed log bordering the path. Millie walks over and joins her. A healthy shine covers them both. That's a nice way of saying they're working up a good sweat.

"Pretty good workout, huh?" I smile. They don't. Popping the top of my bottled water, I take a drink.

"I didn't rest well last night," Lydia says.

"More night sweats?" I ask.

She nods.

"Oh, man, those are the worst," Millie says.

"We can rest awhile, Lydia, if you'd like," I say.

"How much farther is it?" Millie asks.

"Hey, I thought that was my line," I tease.

Millie gets it and smiles.

"Probably half a mile to go." After checking the trail brochure, I look up and nod. "But we're in no hurry. Sit and rest a moment." A soft breeze blows against my face.

"This is nice," Lydia says. "I'm glad you thought of it, DeDe. I needed this. The truth is, I'd rather get a root canal than exercise."

I laugh. "Spoken like the wife of a dentist."

"You know, Greg never could understand why I hated going to

the dentist, especially since he was one. Just never got over that fear, I guess."

"Is anybody else getting hungry besides me?" Millie asks.

"I am," Lydia says.

"Me too. Hey, you want to eat at the Potawatomi Inn?" I ask.

"That might be fun," Lydia says.

"Let's do it," Millie agrees.

Once we get back from our walk, we eat an enjoyable lunch at the inn, then spend the rest of the afternoon sunning beside Lake James. Millie and I go out on the paddleboats, but Lydia doesn't like to go boating since she can't swim. She stays on the beach and looks through a new cookbook she bought at the gift shop.

We have such fun we decide to stay over another night and leave in the morning. Tomorrow we'll stop by the outlet mall that's nearby before we leave.

Since it's Sunday, we weren't able to get the motor home in for repairs on the radiator, but we figure as long as we have water, we should be okay. We can stop at gas stations and rest stops along the way to fill him up if we don't want to use our water supply. That should get us by until we find a repair shop or settle in at Estes Park. Right?

11

Millie gets behind the driver's seat today, giving Lydia a break.

"Want me to drive?" I offer, hoping all the while they don't take me up on it.

"You're not old enough," Millie quips.

"I'm good with that." I settle into my seat and brush a crumb of toast from my mint green shorts.

"But you will be old enough on the way home." Millie smirks and snaps a picture of my outrage.

"I can't get over Greta traveling by herself," Lydia says, waving farewell to our new friend. The motor home creaks and groans as we ease over the gravel to exit the park.

"Yeah, that is something. But they say people do it all the time," I say as if I'm suddenly an RV expert. Turning to wave at Greta, a whiff of the sea wafts from my top, compliments of the ocean-scented potpourri I picked up before leaving Florida. If only I could imagine myself on the beach instead of in this—this—never mind. It's better if I don't work myself into a mood.

Lydia shakes her head. "Not me. I would never be brave enough."

"Well, remember, there are clubs you can get involved in with other campers that help. Towing services, all that kind of stuff," I say.

"Yeah, I guess so."

"You need to take more risks, Lydia." My makeup bag is nearby. Unzipping it, I root around for my foundation.

"That's what Greg used to say. He always wanted to try new things. I'm sure there were other things he wanted to do, but he knew I would be too afraid to try." She thinks a moment. "I've never been the adventurous type." Our eyes lock. "But maybe you've noticed that?"

My gaze shifts toward the ceiling, then back to her. "Maybe a little."

It's time to make Millie's day here. "Hey, Millie, where are we going to stop tonight?" My lips are squeezed tightly together so I won't laugh.

"Are you sure you're not fifty yet? You're beginning to repeat yourself."

"Nope, still in my forties." I'm wearing that little fact like a badge.

"We'll go through some of Illinois and then stop around Davenport, Iowa, tonight," Millie says. "We're a little over halfway to the camp."

"Which reminds me, that's in a different time zone, so we'll have to remember that," Lydia says. She glances at the map. "There's road construction going on between Angola and Fremont, so we may be redirected. We could take Highway 20, which goes over to this Amish area, and we can connect with our main route around Elkhart."

"If you're going off the beaten path, it's a good thing I'm not driving," I say, opening a bag of chips.

"You've got that right," Millie says. "Hey, can I have some of those?"

Getting up, I lean the opening of the bag toward Millie. She grabs a handful. Lydia doesn't want any, so I resume my slug position on the sofa.

"You know, I think I'll call Le Diva and check on things," I say, already punching in the numbers.

"Great," Lydia says. "You can tell us what that new shop is up to."

"Hi, Shelley? This is DeDe. How are things going?"

"You remember Katie Graham, the girl who used to work for us?" Shelley asks.

"Oh yeah. I liked her a lot. Did you run into her or something?"

"You're not going to like her after this."

"Uh-oh, what's wrong?"

"She's going to work at the new chocolate shop."

A gasp catches in my throat. "Is she past the confidentiality time frame?"

"Yep. I checked. It's only for three years."

I had made an appointment with my attorney to change that. He had a last-minute emergency and had to cancel. Then all that happened with Rob and it simply slipped my mind. That slip could cost me my business. *Thanks for ruining my life, Rob.*

"You still there?" Shelley asks.

"I'm here."

"Don't worry, DeDe. You've changed quite a few things since she was here."

"Yeah, maybe. The Belgian chocolate is much better than what we had back then."

"Yes, and you've changed a few of the filling recipes. The cordial and fruit fillings are your best sellers, and you've changed those a little. Definitely improved the taste."

"Listen, Shelley, call Mike's office and let them know we need a new confidentiality agreement drawn up. This time I think we should make it for five years. What do you think?"

"Really? Five years? I don't know."

"Well, Shelley, if we're going to have competition in town, we need to get tough. We can't afford to lose people and have them join up with the competition. That could put us out of business real quick."

"Yeah, I guess you're right." Shelley scribbles something on paper. "I hate to bring this up, but, um, Rob called again." It makes me mad that my heart leaps here. Why can't I control how I feel? I said I wouldn't go back to him. Why do my feelings betray me? How can I even entertain thoughts of him after what he's done?

Quickly I step toward the bedroom so no one can hear me. "What did he say?" I whisper.

"He said you won't answer your cell phone, and he needs to talk to you."

"It's all about him and what *he* needs."

Shelley is quiet here. She knows about as much as Lydia and Millie. Funny how I keep this part of my life from everyone. Just can't bring myself to talk about it.

"He also says to tell you—" She pauses.

"Yes?"

"Again he said to tell you that he's sorry and he still loves you. He said he will do whatever it takes to make it work."

My heart beats wildly. If only that were possible.

"You still there?"

"I'm here. You haven't told him where I am, have you?"

"Just that you're on vacation with friends. Why?"

"Oh, I'm sure it's nothing. I just thought I saw him."

"Well, I didn't tell him."

"Thanks, Shell." After a moment's hesitation, I change the subject. "Hey, listen, once I get to Estes Park, I'm sure there's a place where I can receive a fax. Tell Mike I'll have him fax the document when I can, and I'll sign it for him so we can execute it immediately."

"Okay, will do."

We talk a little longer about the new store that's soon to open. Shelley does her best to relieve my concerns, but let me just say if there are no chocolates in my future, things could get ugly.

We slow to a near stop.

"Oh no, Lydia. You've taken a wrong turn somewhere. We shouldn't be on this road. You'd better not try to go in any farther," Millie warns.

"What's wrong?" I duck my head to look out the front window.

"We took a wrong turn somewhere. Now we're stuck in some kind of old railroad overpass," Millie says.

"I can't believe they still have these." Lydia's upset, and now that I see how tightly we're wedged inside the overpass from top to bottom, I can see why.

"You'll have to back it up," Millie says as though it's not a problem whatsoever.

"I can't back it up! I'll damage something." Lydia's voice is on the verge of hysteria. The color of her face is blending with the purple in her blouse.

"Well, you have to do something, or we'll have to camp out here." Millie just won't let up.

"I'll just go forward," Lydia says. Her chin is definitely hiked here.

She presses on the gas, which produces a loud, screeching noise but not much movement. I'm guessing the RV is getting scalped.

We come to a halt. "We're stuck," Lydia says. Her white-knuckled hands are holding the steering wheel in a death grip.

"Are you sure we can't back out?" I ask.

"I don't want to cause any more damage. I'm afraid to back out."

"Okay, girls, there's got to be a way around this," I say.

"Well, I'd like to know what it is," Millie snaps.

"Take a chill pill, Millie," I say, matching her snarl for snarl, and edge toward the door.

"What are you doing?" Lydia is breathing heavily and looks close to tears.

"I'm just going to assess the situation." I'm trying to maintain calm here, which is more than I can say for my friends.

"Oh, that's going to help," Millie says with definite attitude.

Ignoring her, I push through the door. Graffiti colors the overpass. Big orange letters spell out, "George loves Alice." Yellow paint says, "Suzie loves Bobby," and big red letters spew out a few choice words I can't repeat. Stepping out of the overpass, I edge into the sunshine and see that we're on an old, deserted country road. We'll be lucky if someone stumbles upon us in the next month, and if they do, we can only hope they're friendly. No sooner do I think that than a white van comes down the road toward us. Hopefully it's a model citizen.

When the driver sees our predicament, he steps out of his van. "Hey, lady, you need some help?" A man who is young enough to be my kid walks up to me.

"We're trying to figure out how to get out of here."

"Looks like your air-conditioning unit got stuck under there," he says, pointing at the top of the RV.

"Right. We can't go forward, and if we back up, we'll tear up the unit."

"You know, this happened to a friend of my parents once. They eventually had to deflate the tires so they could get on through."

"Smartest thing I've heard all day," I say with a grin.

His eyes brighten. "You want to try it?"

"Let me check with the owner. Be right back." I go inside and explain the situation to Lydia. She not only agrees; she appears greatly relieved that there actually is a solution—or at least the hope of one.

The young man gets something from his car and brings it over to the RV. Stooping down, he sets to work on the tires. He places the instrument—I think it's called a tire gauge, but then, I'm not exactly *Jeopardy* contestant material—on the tire valve and releases air in short spurts. One by one, he takes care of each tire. By the time he's finished, the motor home is a bit shorter. We thank the man, then inch our way through the overpass. Pulling into the nearest gas station just down the road, we pump air back into the tires, and soon we're on our way.

The air-conditioning is making a strange sound, but it's still working, and that's all that matters as far as Lydia and Millie are concerned.

Me? I'm just wondering once again about the wisdom of taking this trip. Judging by the fact that Millie is stone-faced, staring straight ahead at the road, and Lydia is chewing on her pinkie nail again, I'm thinking they're wondering the same thing.

Millie's driving, and Lydia is on the passenger's side, talking on the phone and looking none too happy. I try to give her some privacy by making small talk with Millie. Lydia finally gets up from the passenger's seat and walks to the bedroom at the back end.

"Is everything all right with her?" I ask Millie.

"She's talking to Derrick. It must have something to do with a girl, because I heard her say she thought he had broken up with her."

"Oh. I was afraid it was something serious."

"Well, college romances can be serious, especially if you're the mother who is unhappy about your son's partner."

"I guess so," I say, having no idea since I've never been a mom. It's odd to think that I never will be a mother. My brother hasn't married yet, either, so I can't even be an aunt. At this rate, my poor dad will never know the joys of being a grandpa. He'd make such a great one too.

Lydia's voice carries from the other room. Millie and I look at each other when we hear the alarm in her voice.

"That doesn't sound good," Millie says.

"I know."

We wait awhile, trying to ignore the muffled sounds coming from the bedroom.

"Be right back. I'm going to check on her," I say. "Will you be okay, or do I need to look at the map for you?"

Millie's eyebrows rise. "If it's all the same to you, I'll pass on that one."

"Suit yourself." I step around the passenger's seat and tiptoe toward the bedroom. Though her voice is muffled, Lydia is talking to someone. Sobs. Then silence. After I'm sure she's off the phone, I knock on the closed door.

"Lydia, are you all right?"

Silence.

"Lydia?"

The door slides open, and a red-eyed Lydia emerges. "I'll just come up and tell you both at the same time," she says.

I turn around, and Lydia follows me to the front. Once we're seated, she waits a minute to catch her breath or gather her courage, I'm not sure which.

"Derrick is seeing this girl. I didn't tell you guys about her because I thought it was a done deal. Now he tells me they've never broken up."

"Is she that bad, Lydia?" I ask.

"She's a very sweet girl, but she and Derrick don't share the same beliefs."

"In what way?" Millie wants to know.

"She's an atheist."

Now, my walk with the Lord hasn't been what it should be over the years. As a matter of fact, right now we're not really on speaking terms, but an atheist? It amazes me that anyone could doubt God's existence—especially since the whole world is drenched with His presence. "I'm sorry, Lydia."

Tears form in her eyes. "Oh, it gets better."

We wait.

"He says I always think the worst of him and his choices but that I act like Drew is perfect. When I tried to convince him that wasn't true, he dropped the bomb."

Grabbing a tissue, I hand it to Lydia. She wipes her nose.

"Is he getting married?" Millie asks, voicing what I was wondering.

"No, it has nothing to do with Derrick. It's Drew."

"Drew? Is he okay?" I ask.

"He won't be when I get through with him. It seems after Greg died in November, Drew failed to show up for his classes or his finals afterward. He dropped out of school second semester, and he's been working ever since. I don't know why I was never notified. Maybe in my grief, I somehow managed to overlook the college mail. I don't know."

"Drew dropped out of school?" Millie asked.

"Yes."

Poor Lydia has enough to deal with, and now this.

"I'm sorry, Lydia. Maybe he just needs time to work through it. I felt the same way when Mom died. My classes that semester were a total bust, and I had to take summer school to make it up. The school worked with me, though, knowing my situation. I'm sure the university would cut him some slack if he talked with his counselor."

"Yeah, that's a good point. How did you get through it? The grief over your mother?" she asks.

"Well, at first I couldn't get over how life went on as usual for everyone after Mom had died. It upset me terribly. I wanted to scream for everyone to stop what they were doing. Things were not the same and never would be again, couldn't they see that? At least, that's what I thought. But somehow I muddled through it. Aspen Creek helped me too, no doubt about it."

Lydia brightens. "That's right! I remember the summer you came, and you made a commitment to the Lord that very week."

Guilt twinges my conscience. "Uh, yeah, that's right."

"Boy, you were on fire too. You couldn't stop talking about Him." Lydia laughs. "I mean, you were still hurting over your mother, but it was like someone had handed you the gift of peace wrapped in paper and a bow."

"Yeah, I remember. My sense of loss was still great, but knowing

I didn't have to go through it alone made all the difference." Funny how I'd forgotten that after all these years.

"Thanks for reminding me of that. It gives me hope for Drew."

"Would you like to have your seat back?" I ask.

"Sure."

We both get up.

"Uh-oh, looks like the RV needs a drink," Millie says.

"How do you know?" Lydia asks, the usual worry line between her brows in place.

"The heat gauge says so."

"I guess you're not the only ones who have hot flashes," I say, laughing at my own joke.

They're not amused.

"There's a gas station right up the road," Lydia says, nodding. "Let's pull in there. And I tell you what, I'll take over since you've been driving for a while."

"You don't need to do that. I haven't been driving that long," Millie protests.

"My mind needs to be occupied with something right now," Lydia says.

"All right then." Millie pulls in to the rest stop. She hands Lydia the keys. We climb out of the RV.

"Oh, I'd better get the container to fill with water," Lydia says, stepping back inside.

Once she returns, we walk into the small station store. "We'll have to wait a little bit 'til the radiator cools so I can get the cap off," Lydia says.

"You know, the first thing you should do is set Drew up with a counselor, someone who can help talk him through the grieving process," Millie advises.

Lydia thinks a moment. "I suppose you're right."

"That does help," I say. When I returned from Aspen Creek, I discovered the counselor at camp had arranged for me to see a counselor back home. It helped a lot to be able to talk about how I was feeling—the denial, anger, all of it.

We enter the no-frills bathroom, complete with graffiti, and I help Lydia get the water she needs. It's kind of tricky because the container is too big for the sink, but somehow we manage.

"The temperature is probably around the low eighties, so it's a near perfect day," I say.

"It is nice. Now if I can just get my boys straightened out."

Lydia is never one to stay down long. She might get in a tiff about something, but she'll talk herself out of it as quickly as it comes. She's one of those who always sees the silver lining in the darkest rain cloud.

"I'm going to grab a snack," I say. "Anybody else want anything?"

They shake their heads, so I go grab my pretzels and come back to join them. When I edge closer, I notice that Millie and Lydia are waiting and they're not getting inside.

"What's wrong?" I ask when I come up alongside them.

"Um, it appears that I've locked the keys inside the RV," Lydia says with a nervous giggle.

This trip just keeps getting better . . .

12

The heat does little to improve our plunging dispositions. Okay, so that's one menopausal symptom I share with Millie. Attitude. 'Course, Millie and I have always had a slight edge to our happy selves. Unfortunately, now we could ride a broom.

The locksmith told us he would be here an hour ago. Yet here we stand, leaning against the RV, waiting at a gas station. The air smells of diesel fuel and overheated engines. Lovely. Lydia digs in her purse, fishes out a hair band, and gathers her hair in a pony-tail. Millie's expression says one word could make her erupt like Mount St. Helen's. Me? I just want more chocolate.

"There he is," Millie says.

We all look toward the red truck coming our way with the words "Joe's Locksmith" on the side in big white letters. He swerves into the parking space and jumps out. He's probably close to fifty years old, dark hair fringed in gray along the border of his face. His skin appears weathered, as if he grew up in Florida rather than the Midwest. His midsection says he's enjoyed one too many potlucks. He pulls his baseball cap off, wipes his forehead, plunks the cap back on his head, and smiles.

"You the ones called for a locksmith?"

Lydia steps forward. "Yes, we are."

He looks at Lydia and smiles, obvious pleasure in his eyes. "Is this the RV?" he asks, walking toward us.

Well, duh, it's the only one in the parking lot. See what I mean? Broom.

"Yes."

"You locked yourself out, huh?" He chuckles.

We don't.

"Well, I think I can get you back in without much trouble," he says, already working his magic with the lock. Joe's the jolly sort. He immediately jokes around and puts us at ease. In no time he pulls open the RV's previously unyielding door, and we're a grateful lot. We make a new friend in Joe, laughing and talking together—until he gives Lydia the bill. She reluctantly pays a premium price for her mistake, though I have a feeling if she'd whipped up a blueberry pie, he would have taken it for payment in a heartbeat.

Before Joe leaves, Lydia asks him where in town she can get a radiator leak fixed, and he gives us the name of a place and directions for how to get there. Millie makes him pose with us for a picture and gets a passerby to take it. She says it will be a good memory of the trip. I think she's losing it in her old age.

We wave and watch him leave. Lydia turns to us. "Well, we've already lost some time; should we just go ahead and have the radiator fixed while we're at it?"

"At this rate, we'll never get out of Indiana," I say.

"I can think of worse things," Millie answers, defending her Hoosier state.

We drive a little ways from the highway, following the directions of Locksmith Joe, and settle into the heart of an Amish community.

"Oh my goodness, look at that," I say, pointing to a black covered buggy.

"It's an Amish buggy." Anytime Millie can impart knowledge, she's in her element.

"Wow, it feels as though we've stepped back into the nineteenth century." Lydia slides open her window so we can hear the clip-clop of the horses' hooves. Do we need a life or what?

"Or we stepped onto the set of *Little House on the Prairie*," I add.

"They have a good-sized Amish community around this area," Millie says.

"Where are we?" I ask.

"We're in Shipshewana right now. Depending on what happens with the RV, we might go into Middlebury and check out Das Dutchman Essenhaus for lunch." Millie glances once more at her map.

"Okay, if you say so. The name sounds very German," I say.

"That's because the Amish are of German descent." I'm almost sure Millie will add, "If you would read more, you would know that," but to my relief, she doesn't.

We pass quilting stores, restaurants advertising Amish cooking, Yoder Department Store, and furniture stores boasting the superior workmanship of the simple people. There's even a flea market.

After making our way through the tourist section of town, we find the shop Locksmith Joe told us about, and the man at the shop tells us he can fit the RV in, which is great news. He says he owns a motor home and his son owns a motor home, so they keep spare parts on hand. Check back around four o'clock.

Lydia turns to us and sighs. "I'm sorry for the inconvenience, girls. But at least we can get it fixed."

"Don't worry about it. We can go shopping," I say, excitement clearly in my voice.

"Guess we'll have to skip lunch at Das Dutchman Essenhaus. But they have nice restaurants here too. We can eat at the Blue Gate Restaurant. You'll certainly get a feel for the Amish community here," Millie says.

I'm excited that Millie is looking at it this way. I lock arms with Millie on one side and Lydia on the other. "We're enjoying the journey, remember?"

Lydia's shoulders relax, and she smiles. "You're right. Now I know why you two are my best friends."

"Excuse me? Are you saying you didn't know why before?" I ask.

"Let's just call it a memory lapse," Lydia teases. A man from the shop drops us off in the middle of the hustle and bustle of town, right in front of the Blue Gate Restaurant. Okay, hustle and bustle here is not the same as in, say, New York City. Just so you know.

We amble down the main drag, waltzing from one store to another. And just for the record, three middle-aged women waltzing into a store look nothing like Fred Astaire and Ginger Rogers have led you to believe.

We admire the colorful quilts and sewing goods, the thick, sturdy oak furniture, grandfather clocks, and cuckoo clocks, then walk back to the Blue Gate Restaurant for lunch.

Once we step into the restaurant, scents of fried chicken and sweet pies mingle and stir overhead, tingling my taste buds. Servers are milling about clad in dark dresses and white aprons. Many have white caps covering their hair.

Muted sounds of silverware clanging against glassware and hushed conversations join the home-cooked smells that hover in the room. After eating a plate of thick chicken and noodles, I can see why these simple chefs have such a following. The noodles are melt-in-your-mouth tasty. The broth is rich and creamy, and the chicken makes me want to start a franchise. 'Course, they ladle these tasty noodles over creamy mashed potatoes. Not exactly diet cuisine, but we only live once, right? It doesn't help that they serve homemade bread with apple butter and Amish peanut butter spread. This stuff tastes as though it's mixed with marshmallow cream, but I'm not sure. I just know it's to die for.

We top it off with a trip to the bakery, where we pick up some peanut butter, and Lydia buys a shoofly pie. Rich with molasses and brown sugar, this pie could almost turn me from chocolate.

Almost.

"That's just about the best meal I've ever eaten," Millie says, patting her stomach.

Lydia and I agree.

"You might have to crank me out of this chair," I say, feeling way too stuffed but convinced I've never had better chicken and noodles in all my born days.

The server drops our bills off to us, and we grab our handbags.

We continue on with our shopping and finally call the repair shop to find out the RV is good to go. They send their driver to pick us up.

All in all, we've had a wonderful time shopping together. Still, I'm a little rattled by Lydia's quiet behavior. It's obvious she's had a good time today. No doubt memories of Greg and their years together have cropped up and pulled her into a place of reflection.

Hopefully she won't allow old memories to stop her from making new ones. Let's just hope I can do the same.

***

"Your motor home seems to be as good as new, doesn't it?" I say, hoping to get Lydia to open up. She simply nods. A sure sign she's lingering in memories. At those times, she always retreats within herself. Millie glances my way. We both know Lydia's hurting.

With Lydia so quiet and Millie reading her latest novel, I'm feeling bored. I rub my arms in an effort to keep warm. I want to turn on the oven and bake something so we'll have some heat in this contraption. Too bad the air-conditioning unit didn't break when we went under that railroad overpass. Oh, the unit mimics the cry of a sick bird, I'll give you that, but it's still working. I look over at Millie and Lydia. The air-conditioning vents are aimed straight at their faces, and their hair is blowing with the breeze.

They need some serious help.

With a sigh, I head for the bedroom. We've traveled a ways since the RV's repair, and I'm so restless the thought of watching an *Andy Griffith* episode sounds exciting to me. I consider hiding Millie's glasses but decide against it. No wonder she gets cranky—she puts up with enough from me. One would think at my age I would give up on pranks. Maybe I'll stop when I turn fifty. Then again, maybe not.

Cobbler and I are bonding. Yes, I've forgiven her for hurting my hand. But if she even *thinks* about doing it again . . . Reaching into the drawer holding the videos, I think a moment. I'll have to stay in here to watch it. How cruel would it be to watch it where Cobbler couldn't see it?

I plop it into the machine. "Though we've had our differences in the past, I figure you'll appreciate this." The tape rewinds as I make my way to Cobbler. She doesn't look right. Her feathers are all plumped out, and she has her head tucked in one wing. Wonder if that means anything.

"Hi, Cobbler, you doing okay?" I ask, leaning toward the cage. Wonder if that scares her. You know, this huge face just peering into her cage. I consider throwing in a "boo" for good measure but decide against it. She looks too fragile for it.

Her eyes turn to me, and she shivers a moment, then sticks her head back under her wing. A glance at her food bowl tells me she hasn't eaten much today. Maybe she was traumatized at the repair shop. Lydia's already so quiet, I hate to bring this up to her, but she'd probably want to know. Cobbler doesn't look quite right.

I edge my way back up to the front. "Um, Lydia, I don't know if this means anything, but Cobbler keeps tucking her head into her wing."

"Oh, sometimes birds do that when they're upset. She probably got riled up at the repair shop with all the machine noises and such," Millie pipes up.

"That's true," Lydia says. "But I'll take a look at her when we get to Davenport. We're about an hour and a half away."

Figuring it must be no big deal, I head back to the bedroom and put in the tape. The music starts, and I turn to Cobbler, expecting her to sing along, but she keeps her head tucked, not once looking up. Okay, I don't know anything but birds, but this behavior is just not normal for this parakeet.

I go back and explain it to Lydia. Millie gives me a dirty look, no doubt for worrying Lydia, but I think she has a right to know. Though I have no idea what we can do about it.

"Maybe I had better take a look at it her. I'm sure it's nothing, but I think I'll check just the same," Lydia says, pulling off at the next exit and parking in the nearest McDonald's.

One glance at Cobbler and Lydia pales. "She's sick, all right. I'll go into McDonald's and see if anyone in there can suggest a reputable veterinarian."

"Why did you have to tell her that?" Millie snaps once Lydia's out of the vehicle.

"She loves that bird. What if something happened because I didn't say anything?"

"She has enough on her mind right now."

"Exactly. That's why we need to get Cobbler well," I argue.

"Shh, here she comes."

"I don't think anyone in this town owns a pet. Either that or they have the healthiest pets around," Lydia says, climbing back inside.

"So what are we going to do?" Millie wants to know.

Lydia stares at the steering wheel. "I don't know." She closes her eyes a moment, and her lips move. Millie and I exchange a glance, both realizing Lydia must be praying.

"Let's just drive into town; maybe someone can help us there," she says, pulling out of the parking lot with tires squealing.

It could be just me, but I'm thinking this RV is in no shape to squeal tires.

"Lydia, um, you'd better slow down. The speed limit is thirty through here," Millie warns.

"I can't slow down, Millie," Lydia says, near panic. "It's close to five o'clock. Businesses will close soon."

Before we can comment further, we hear the roar of a siren behind us.

Uh-oh, busted.

Lydia keeps going.

"Uh, Lydia, I think that siren is for us," I say, thinking the officer speaking through the bullhorn and facing our way is a pretty good indication.

"What?" Lydia looks confused.

"Bullhorn. Policeman. Behind us," Millie says.

"I guess the Lord misunderstood me," Lydia mutters with a sigh, pulling to the side of the road.

"Here comes Barney Fife now," I say. "I can't believe this man has nothing better to do than pull over three middle-aged women in a motor home for going five miles over the speed limit."

"You be still, DeDe; you'll get us into more trouble," Millie says.

Yeah, whatever. I'm feeling a little snappy myself right about now. But I'm still forty-nine, so life is good.

"Ma'am, do you know you were going about eight miles over the speed limit?"

"Yes, sir, I did."

"You did?" He's probably never had anyone be that honest with him before.

"I'm sorry for breaking the law. It's just that—"

"I'm going to have to write you a ticket."

Probably the first chance he's had all day to write one, and he's chomping at the bit, just like Barney.

"People come into this area after being on the highway, and they think they can just race through our streets. Well, we have citizens to protect around here. It's my duty to uphold the law, and that's what I aim to do." He pulls out his ticket holder and starts to write.

Lydia starts crying. "I'm so sorry. I was just worried about Cobbler—"

"You were speeding because of a dessert?" He sounds agitated, to say the least.

"No, sir, Officer—"

He bends farther over to get a glimpse of who's talking.

"—her bird's name is Cobbler. She's sick. We were trying to find a veterinarian before they closed for the day," I say.

His eyes brighten. "A vet? Well, why didn't you say so?" He puts his ticket away. "My sister is a vet. You follow me, and I'll get you there in time. He looks at his watch. I'll call her so she doesn't leave."

We are all speechless as we watch him walk away. He gets in his car, turns on the colored lights, and gives us an escort. "See, you got your feathers all ruffled for nothing," Millie says to me as though she knew all along the policeman was going to help us.

"Great way to put it, Millie," I say dryly.

Millie turns to Lydia. "Guess the Lord heard you after all."

Lydia's smile shows through the rearview mirror. "He always does. Just doesn't necessarily give me the answer I want."

I think about what she says and glance out the window. Dusk has settled upon this small town where the glow from street lamps spills onto front lawns, spotlighting children at play. They pause a moment to wave at Barney Fife as he drives past. I half-expect him to throw candy. I'm thinking he's been in one too many parades.

How frightening is this? Somehow we've managed to end up in Mayberry. I wouldn't be surprised if Aunt Bee was down at the county jail right this very moment, serving evening snacks.

Maybe I should see if they're offering chocolates.

13

I'm guessing the RV is in for a good thaw. Let the heavens rejoice!

Dr. Sherri Johnson advises that Cobbler has a cold and needs a warm environment. The wise veterinarian hands Lydia a bottle and tells her to put two drops into Cobbler's water bowl daily, and she should be as good as new in a few days.

Maybe now I won't have to wear my snowsuit to bed.

We thank the kind pet doctor and head back to the motor home. Her Barney Fife sibling walks with us, giving Lydia one more speech about the dangers of speeding, and off we go— within the speed limit, of course.

"Millie, will you get my fan for me?" Lydia asks. Millie already has her own fan blowing against her face. She reaches into Lydia's bag behind her seat, pulls out the fan, and hands it to Lydia.

I dare not gloat, but I'm actually feeling the blood start to move through my veins once again.

Since Lydia isn't great at night driving, Millie takes over. We haven't taken the time for dinner yet, and we're all starved. We shouldn't be after that big lunch, but there you are. I make turkey sandwiches for everyone and pass out drinks so we can continue driving. Finally, we arrive at a campsite near Davenport, Iowa.

It's fairly late by the time we settle in for the night. While washing my hands at the sink, I spot a goldfinch playing in a nearby oak tree. If the neighbors hadn't turned on their camp light, I never would have seen it. "Millie, Lydia, come here," I say.

They both come and gaze out the window.

"Oh, that's the state bird, DeDe. It's a goldfinch." Millie is a walking encyclopedia.

"How did you know that?" I ask her.

"I research facts about each place we visit."

I roll my eyes.

"You know about chocolate. I know about, well, everything else."

"You certainly are a wealth of information," Lydia says sweetly, cutting me off before I get a chance to give Millie what for. Lydia hooks her arm into Millie's, they walk a few paces, then both of them settle in at the kitchen table.

"You girls want a snack?" Lydia asks, already rising.

"What do we have?" Millie asks.

"I was thinking maybe some cheese, crackers, and pepperoni."

"Sounds great," Millie says.

Lydia gets the snack ready, then she joins Millie at the table. She looks up at me. "Aren't you joining us, DeDe?"

"You know, I think I just need to walk. I've eaten so much in this past week that I feel like I'm going to explode," I say.

They stare at me, mouths gaping.

"Trust me, it wouldn't be a pretty sight." I grab my sweater and walk toward the door.

"You're going out?" Lydia asks, behaving like a mother hen over her chicks.

"I could be wrong, but I'm thinking I'd have to walk up and down this RV for ten years to lose a single pound. Walking outside is my only alternative."

"But it's dark out there."

"I'm not going far. Just walking to the end of the lane and back to get some fresh air, a little exercise."

"I should think you'd be happy now that we've turned the air-conditioning down," Millie grumbles.

"I appreciate it, I really do. 'Course, we all know you did it for Cobbler, but still I'm grateful." With a wink, I turn and push through the door.

The temperature is probably in the low seventies and quite pleasant. A slight breeze stirs the oak leaves. Children laugh and squeal from campfires. People nod and wave. As much as I hate to admit it, campers are nice people. I could get into the friendly atmosphere and the workless days.

Wait. Did I say workless days? What am I saying? It's hard work to camp, and we're not exactly roughing it in a motor home. But when Lydia backs that thing up into our camping site, I'm sure *somebody* will blow a vein.

Wild roses gather along a trellis in front of the office building at the end of the path. I've always loved roses. Rob used to send me roses every month to celebrate the day we met. I shake my head to get rid of the memory. If only it were that easy. As much as I say I'm over him, that I'm not going to think about him any-more, he keeps creeping back into my thoughts—my heart. As weak as I feel tonight, if he called, I'd probably answer.

Stooping down, I pick up a fallen oak leaf. We all have to move on with our lives. Lydia without Greg, Millie without Bruce, and me without Rob. Life can be so unfair. We have lived very differ-ent lives up to this point, and yet we've all arrived at the same place. Now that we're here, I'm not sure any of us know what to do about it.

In my younger days I thought my life would be so different, and I've had plenty of dates along the way. Still, becoming a wife and mother was never my number one goal. Until Rob came along, I had never allowed my heart to get involved with anyone. Business kept my mind and heart pretty much occupied. My dad drilled into me the importance of being able to take care of myself. He wanted me to be self-sufficient, and maybe he pushed a little too hard. A slight breeze rustles through the trees and brushes against my face before moving on, and I can't help thinking how life is just as fleeting.

So here I am, a successful businesswoman at forty-nine—okay, so I'll be fifty in a few days—just what Dad wanted for me. But after being with Rob and seeing what life could be, well, I'm not convinced that this is the only life I want for myself.

In my mental wanderings, I don't pay attention to where I'm going, and I end up walking past the office building toward the street. Lydia and Millie would have a fit if they tried to find me and couldn't. Quickly I turn around and head back for the motor home. Upon hearing a car's motor coming up behind me, I step farther into the shadows so as not to be seen. The driver has his elbow tipped out the window, and I get a brief glimpse of him. Though he doesn't turn my way, he looks familiar.

Please, God, don't let it be Rob.

Somehow I manage to keep Millie and Lydia from lingering at the campsite the next morning. Just in case that man was Rob—and I'm not convinced that it was—what's the point of hanging around?

"Why are you in such a hurry, DeDe?" Millie asks. "Usually you're the last person to get up, and here you are, dressed and ready to go. What's up?" Millie's eyes tell me she knows me all too well.

"My walk last night and my Pilates workout this morning must have done me some good," I say with a big smile.

"Where did you do your Pilates?" Millie asks incredulously.

"On my mat outside. Hardly anyone was up except me and the crickets." Of course, all the while I was looking around to make sure Rob was nowhere in sight.

They both look at me as though they're trying to figure out my brain. Shouldn't take them long. I shift on my feet. Need I mention I'm concerned about the middle-aged spread taking over my body?

"Well, anybody want some breakfast?" I start pulling bowls from the kitchen counter.

Lydia places her hand on my arm. "All right, something is up. You don't eat breakfast, remember?"

Oh, doggone it, that's right. Well, if you don't count the chocolate, anyway. "I guess I'm just anxious to get to the camp," I say brightly.

They still don't look convinced, but Millie's cell phone rings, cutting off further discussion. "Hello? Well, good morning, Bob. You're sure calling bright and early. Oh dear. I'm so sorry to hear that. Oh my."

Lydia and I exchange a glance.

"How wonderful!" Millie says with a full-blown smile. She winks at me, then heads toward the bedroom and pulls the door closed behind her.

"Well, whatever it is, it's good news," I say.

"We could use that after all that's happened with Waldo and Cobbler." Lydia starts the coffeemaker while I put the bowls on the table.

"How is Cobbler this morning?" I ask, settling into my seat at the table.

"She seems a little better today. Not as fluffed up as she was before." Lydia hands me a coffee cup and places the creamer and sugar on the table. "And to think it's all my fault she caught cold." She sits across from me.

"You mean with the air-conditioning?"

She nods and stares at the gray Formica tabletop. "Who could have guessed my hot flashes were that bad?"

Um, me.

"Guess not everyone else felt the same way."

Now there's a news flash. "My woolen mittens and hat should have been a dead giveaway."

She looks up, and we both laugh. The coffeemaker perks and rattles, causing the deep scent of coffee to permeate our home away from home.

"If you owned a pair of mittens, I would worry, you being from Florida and all."

"That's true. It's hard to surf wearing all those clothes." I smile. The coffeemaker plops the last bit of the brew into the carafe. "Let me get our drinks," I say, grabbing both of our mugs when Lydia starts to get up. Pouring coffee into them, I carry them carefully back to the table.

"What do you suppose is keeping Millie so long?" Lydia dumps a pack of cream and sugar into her cup.

"I don't know, but whatever it is, she seemed happy about it."

Just then the bedroom door pulls open. Millie steps into the room to join us. Judging by her expression, her conversation dipped downward. Can we say South Pole?

Without saying a word, Lydia jumps up and pours Millie some coffee.

"Thanks, Lydia," Millie says, joining us at the table. She rests her hands on the table and stares at her palms. "I can't believe this is happening."

I touch her arm. "Millie, what is it?"

Lydia places the coffee in front of her. "After all these years," Millie says, ripping the top off two cream packets. She turns to me, eyes flashing. "After all I've done."

I've seen that look before. If memory serves me, it was when we got into trouble at camp. Picture charging bull.

"What's wrong?" Lydia asks. "You sounded happy when you were talking on the phone."

Millie takes a couple of long, deep breaths. "Gertrude Pendleton, a longtime friend of the library, has passed away. It seems her attorney called Bob Greenley, the president of the library board, and informed him that Mrs. Pendleton has bequeathed a large sum of money to the library."

"Isn't that good?" Lydia asks, both of us clearly confused.

"Well, yes, that part is good."

"And the bad part is?" I press.

She turns to me with wild eyes. "They're calling a board meeting next week to discuss installing a computer system in the library."

So that's what this is about. Poor Millie. She lives in the Dark Ages. She still owns the manual typewriter her parents gave her in high school. Not only that, but she uses it.

"It was bound to happen sooner or later." I mean, hello, her small Indiana town has yet to convert from its card catalog system.

"Well, I say, if it ain't broke, don't fix it," Millie snaps, lips pursed, eyebrows pulled into a sharp frown.

If there was any doubt before, I have none now. Millie is upset, pure and simple. She never uses the word *ain't*. It's like a four-letter word to her. Oh, wait. It *is* a four-letter word.

"I understand how you feel, Millie," Lydia says as if she's tiptoeing through the tulips, "but I'm afraid the world forces us into its way of doing things."

Am I the only one trying to stay current here? "Come on, you guys. It's not the end of the world. The computer is a wonderful invention," I say.

"You don't understand. I'm the head librarian. I will have to oversee this project. Entering all the books into the system, setting up the cataloging, retrieving holds on books that people have placed online. I will have to know how to run the whole thing." Millie's voice is tight. She puts her hand to her forehead. "That Bob Greenley has been pushing for this ever since he visited that fancy-schmancy library over in Cleveland, Tennessee."

Millie gets up, grabs the whipped cream, sprays enough to spill over the top of her coffee cup, walks over to the refrigerator, and puts it away. She sits back down and carefully picks up her cup.

"Millie, you're in your early fifties. Don't act old and set in your ways," I say, bracing myself for the hurricane that's about to hit.

Lydia cuts in. "The computer is not an easy thing to learn. My boys tried to teach me, but I finally gave up."

"Yes, but you don't use it on a regular basis. Millie will work with it every day."

"Not if I can help it," Millie says with a stubborn edge to her voice.

"You surf the Internet once in a while," I remind her.

"Once in a while is key here. I don't have to do everything on that computer," she snaps.

We grow silent.

"Maybe they'll vote against it at the board meeting," Lydia encourages.

"Fat chance. Bob will schmooze everyone with his big computer talk, and I won't be there to counteract it."

"When do you think this technological takeover will happen?" Lydia asks as though we're being invaded by Mars.

"Who knows? Knowing Bob, he'll try to get it in place as soon as possible. Though I'm sure these types of systems take a long time to get them truly up and running online and all that." She shrugs. "But who knows? That computer stuff is beyond me." She fingers the handle on her coffee cup. "I can only imagine how overwhelming it will be."

My heart softens. This really is a big deal to Millie. My personality drives me to keep up to date on things, so this type of attitude is hard for me to understand. "I'm sorry, Millie, that this is difficult for you. I'm not all that familiar with how libraries work, but I'll be happy to help you with computer questions in any way I can. Just e-mail me when we all get home if you need my help."

Millie rolls up the sleeves on her short-sleeved tee and pulls her fan to her face. Her jaw is set, but fear lurks in her eyes. "It's better if we stop talking about it for now so as not to spoil my vacation." Millie pulls a napkin from the holder and blots her face and neck. She pushes her coffee cup away from her. "This is just too hot to drink now."

Lydia and I lock eyes.

"It's hot in here." Millie pushes through the kitchen and steps up to the passenger's seat without saying another word.

Guilt washes over me about that whole air-conditioning thing until I remember they're suffering because of Cobbler, not me. "Why don't you bring Cobbler's cage out here, Lydia? That way you could crank up the air-conditioning a little more and she wouldn't be so enclosed with the cold air. It's more open out here." Well, as open as you get living in a two-by-four. "We could put her cover around the bottom half of her cage to insulate it a bit."

Millie and Lydia both brighten, and I have to wonder what's gotten into me. Just when I've thawed out, I have to go and say something stupid.

"We can't have her in the kitchen, and there's no other open area, but that's a great idea to cover the bottom half of her cage," Lydia says. "Though I must admit I'm surprised that you would make a suggestion so we could turn up the air-conditioning."

"Yeah, what's gotten into you?" Millie chimes in.

"Just had a Pollyanna moment. Don't get used to it, though."

Lydia chuckles. "Guess it's time to get going," she says, picking up the cups. She stops at the counter. "Oh dear. DeDe got the bowls out, but I forgot to offer oatmeal. Is anyone hungry?"

"I'm fine," I say, already making plans to eat some chocolate from my secret stash in the bedroom.

"I lost my appetite," Millie calls over her shoulder while flipping through her book.

Lydia tosses an "oh dear" expression my way.

Something tells me we haven't heard the end of this.

14

"*Sorry to bring this up, but*"—*my eyes turn to Millie since* she's the one who always gets mad when I ask this—"I was wondering—"

"Omaha, Nebraska," Millie interrupts. "We will be at Aspen Bible Camp in a couple of days, right around the time you turn the big five-oh, barring any unforeseen circumstances." She turns to me and throws a head librarian glare.

The sound of that "barring any unforeseen circumstances" thing isn't real comforting, but it's probably better if I don't comment on that—or rise to the birthday bait. "What? Since when is it a crime to want to know where I'm going?" I ask.

She ignores me and turns back around. Lydia switches on the radio, and we're soon on our way. As we head out of town, we stop at a local grocery store to gather some needed items. Just before we leave, I pick up a copy of the local newspaper. The fact that I have no idea who the latest Hollywood couples are tells me that I've lost touch with reality.

We settle into our seats once again and into the familiar whir—okay, clunk, bang, rattle—of the RV's engine.

About an hour into the trip, Millie turns to Lydia, then me. "Do you girls ever wonder what your lives might be like if your choices had taken you down a different path?"

Reluctantly pulling my gaze from the Crabby Road cartoon in the paper, I have to wonder if I'm up to this discussion.

"Oh, I know it's a crazy question," Millie admits. "I just look at my life and realize it's more than half over."

"Excuse me? Can we just skip this little talk for now? You might be old, but I have a little time left, thank you very much." Millie and Lydia exchange a glance and a smirk.

"A few days, Dede," Millie spouts with far too much triumph. "There's no time at all before you'll be old just like the rest of us." She cackles here, reminding me of Grandmama on *The Addams Family*.

"A lot of living can be done in a few days, Millie. Need I remind you all of creation took place in seven days? There's still a little time to kick back, thank you." They're struggling with the fact that I'm the youngest of our group. Still, I glance at the crusty old woman in Crabby Road and realize that's me in a few days.

"Sometimes I wonder what things would have been like for Greg and me if we had traveled more. If we had made more vacation memories," Lydia says.

I'm thinking there is only one direction for this discussion to go—south. I fold the paper and slip over to the floor at the top of the two steps between Lydia's and Millie's seats so I can hear their voices over the motor home's groans. Why I'm listening is beyond me.

"I'm not talking about regrets, Lydia. We all have those. Just in general. For instance, had I gone to a different college, I never would have met Bruce. I might have stayed single, or quite possibly married someone else altogether. Or what if I had gone into teaching music like my dad wanted—how would my life be now?"

Stop the presses! Hold your notes! Millie's dad wanted her to teach music? Is the man tone-deaf? I love Millie. I really do. But anyone who has heard her play the trumpet knows exactly what I'm talking about.

"Remember what Greta said about the words *what if*," Lydia reminds us.

Millie looks at her. "I remember, but I can't help but wonder anyway."

"And I wonder what life would be without chocolate. Men, I can do without, but the dark candy? No."

Lydia laughs. "Just think if things had all been different, we wouldn't be taking this trip now," she says in a burst of pure wisdom.

"Meaning?" I ask.

"It would be a real shame," Lydia says, "not to go on this trip together."

"Oh yeah," I say sorrowfully, attempting an appropriate shudder. Hello? Camping. Closed-in spaces. Getting locked out of the motor home, having the drawer handle come off in my hand, and I won't even mention the radiator problem. Real shame? Forget that burst of pure wisdom thing.

"Sometimes I just wonder about my life, that's all." Millie sighs. "It's probably my age. Don't they say old people spend more time in reflection?" A sharp gaze my way warns me not to comment. "I guess that's what I'm doing." She fidgets in her seat. "I'm not ready to be old yet. I've given my life to my work, and look where that's gotten me. No husband, no children."

What she says strikes a chord in my own heart. All those years I struggled to succeed, refusing romantic entanglements for fear they would get in the way of my career. But when push came to shove in the business, I wanted out. Let the real estate moguls have their way, I had decided. Who needed the pressures associated with selling commercial real estate? Not me.

"Chocolates can do a lot of things, DeDe, but they can't warm a cold bed," Millie says as though reading my thoughts.

Her words get my full attention. She's not fooling me. She's pushing for information.

"We don't have to have a man in our lives to be happy, Millie," I say. "Besides, chocolate is good for you. It contains compounds called flavonoids, which might protect against heart attacks."

"It might have some medicinal qualities, DeDe, but it doesn't cure loneliness."

"We do need people in our lives," Lydia jumps in. "If we shut everyone out, we have no life."

Don't I know it.

"You still have plenty of friends at your church, right?" Lydia asks me.

"Well, honestly, I haven't gone to church in a while." I don't have to tell her I was too ashamed to go back and face my friends after dumping them for Rob. Couldn't face God, either.

We fall silent a moment.

"The people who are really happy have a faith that carries them through the tough times, and they also have a community of friends," Lydia says.

"Like the Red Hat Club?" Millie asks.

"That's one group," Lydia says.

She's right about the friends. Aunt Darcy with her old lady friends, my neighbor Irene Conley, and some others pop into mind. They do have a community of friends and a faith that shines through the worst of circumstances.

"That's what we have," Lydia says, smiling.

"You're right, Lydia." Better to change the subject so I don't have to think about this right now. "I think I'll call the shop and see how things are going." Okay, that was a little abrupt, but it works. With a grunt I push myself up from the floor and head back to the bedroom to get my cell phone, but not before seeing Lydia and Millie exchange a glance.

"Hey, Shelley. How are things?"

"DeDe, good to hear from you. Things are going well," she says. "How's your trip?"

We catch up on the small stuff, and I can't help feeling Shelley is trying to keep me from what we both know is the real reason I'm calling.

"So did she open yet?"

"Who?" Shelley feigns ignorance.

"Come on, Shelley. What's the matter—did she have a huge turnout or something?"

"She opened today, Dee. WFRP came out and covered it. The shop owner dressed in bright polka dots of pink, green, and white, passed out balloons and candy samples. She had a display of gourmet chocolates in a chocolate basket, and people entered a drawing to win it. They're drawing in half an hour."

"How's the crowd there?"

"She's doing a good business. Steady stream of customers."

"How are we doing?"

"Well, of course people will go where there are free giveaways."

"Not much business, huh?"

"Not much," she admits.

"Well, it will pass. Once the novelty wears off, our loyal customers will return, because we have really good chocolates," I say with more confidence than I feel.

"Yeah, I suppose you're right." Shelley plays along.

A moment of hesitation here. "Should I come home?"

"Oh no, no. We'll be fine."

I'm not sure whether she's trying to convince me or herself. We hang up shortly after, and I go back in with Lydia and Millie.

"Everything all right?" Millie asks, then she sees my face. "Whoa, what's wrong?"

After sitting, I explain my conversation with Shelley to Lydia and Millie.

"Everything will be all right, DeDe. Things will die down over at the new shop. It's just the excitement of having a new place, the opening day, all that," Lydia says.

"Yeah, that's what I said too. Hopefully we're right."

"We're right," Millie encourages. "Still, I'd sure hate being ousted by a young kid."

"Who said anything about being ousted?" Watch it, lady, or it's mismatched sock drawer for you tonight!

"Nobody, Dee. She didn't mean anything by that," Lydia pipes up.

"Oh, don't listen to me. I'm still stinging from that whole computer changeover deal. Why do things have to change, anyway? It's like we leave a few days and the world turns upside down," Millie grumbles.

"Hey, there's a coffee shop," Lydia says, pointing to the sign that shows a coffee cup. "It's not Starbucks, but it will do. We could use a little pick-me-up," she says.

Millie and I agree.

Traveling another quarter mile, we turn off on the next exit and soon pull in for our coffee. A blended light mocha with whipped cream is my drink of choice. I know the whipped cream kind of cancels out the "light" part, but I figure it would be worse if I ordered a regular drink. Hey, you do what you gotta do.

Despite Millie's love for whipped cream, she drinks her cappuccino plain. She grabs her drink, Lydia gets her latte, and we take a seat at a nearby table.

"They call that coffee?" Millie asks, looking at my drink.

"You know I'll pick extravagant over plain anytime, Millie. Besides, you had whipped cream in your coffee earlier, if memory serves me, and it does." Hopefully she won't remember that her hot flash kept her from drinking it.

"Yeah, but that was different. I was stressed." She takes a sip of her plain, as in *boring*, cappuccino.

"If you don't mind, I'm going to call Derrick and Drew. I had hoped Drew would call me to talk about the school situation, but he hasn't. Evidently the ball is in my court," Lydia says.

"Do you think Derrick told him about his conversation with you? He might not want Drew to know," I say.

"We have to bring it out in the open sometime. I'll be back shortly." Lydia takes her latte over to a corner by herself and opens her cell phone.

Lydia's comment lingers. "*We have to bring it out in the open sometime.*" If only I could reveal the guilt I'm carrying around. But what would they think of me? The fact that I still think about Rob, still care for him even *after* knowing everything. What kind of person am I?

"This is really nice," Millie says.

"Yeah, I needed it." The hot liquid coats my throat and calms my frayed emotions.

I glance around the room. This is a new coffee shop with cream-colored ceramic tile flooring and matching tables crouched in snug corners. A display of coffee goods such as mugs and coffeemakers shines from one wall, while full windows on the other side release a burst of sunlight into the room. A few customers huddle at their tables in quiet conversation. The whir of the cappuccino machine and the spray of whipped cream sound from the counter area. The scent of rich coffee permeates the air.

"Hey, I was noticing in my book that there's a really neat zoo in Omaha. I think it's called the Henry Doorly Zoo. They have a rain forest and everything," Millie says. "I thought maybe we could go there this afternoon."

After another quick drink, I nod. It does no good whatsoever to buck Millie when she's on a mission. Lydia's voice carries our way, causing Millie and I both to look at her. The frown on her face tells me the conversation isn't going well.

"That doesn't look good," I whisper.

"Yeah, I noticed that. Poor Lydia."

"Well, we'll just have to help her through this. You know, us being her community of friends and all." Millie joins me in a smile.

By the time my coffee cup is empty and Millie and I have discussed the fashions of the '70s, as in bell-bottom trousers and psychedelic shirts, Lydia comes back with swollen eyes and a red nose.

"Why do I try? That boy won't even talk to me. He needs help, that's all there is to it, but he won't hear of it." She plops down in her chair.

"Give it some time, Lydia. He'll come around," I say, hoping it is so.

"He's making a mess of his life. Dropping his goal of becoming a dentist and instead working at an ice-cream factory. What is he thinking?"

"He's got time, Lydia. He's still young. We all make mistakes," Millie says.

Lydia takes a deep breath. "You're right. God can handle it. I have to quit worrying about things."

Millie puts her hand over Lydia's. "You're human, Lydia. It's okay to get frustrated, worry, fear, whatever. The important thing is that you don't stay there," Millie says, and I'm just amazed. That's the most profound statement I've ever heard Millie make without quoting from a book. Then again, maybe it is a quote.

"I know we'll be at the camp soon, but I was just wondering, well, do you girls want to go home early?"

Millie and I lift a surprised look to Lydia. There goes my chance to see one of my old flames.

"It just seems like everything's going wrong on this trip. You both are having struggles with your jobs, Waldo's fighting just to hold it all together, and—oh, I don't know. I just wanted to give you that option and let you know I'd be happy to do that, if that's what you want."

We fall silent again.

"That's what I thought," Lydia says, eyes downcast.

"No, we don't have to go home, Lydia. I'm sure I'm worrying about my business for no reason."

"It's all right, really. With all this going on with my boys, I'm wondering if I shouldn't go back early."

"You can't always fix it. That's how they mature," Millie says, and I'm wondering how she knows so much about kids since she's never had any of her own. She fidgets with her cup.

"What about you, Millie? Do you want to go back early?" Lydia asks.

She shrugs. "I've wondered about going home before Bob has time to stir everyone up with this computer thing. Then another side of me says to let it go and just take what comes. Truthfully, I can hardly stand to think about it."

"Well, why don't we do this: let's go on to the camp, see how things go, and we can make our decision then," Lydia says. "Is that all right with you two?"

"That works for me," I say.

"Me too," Millie adds.

We linger over coffee awhile longer and soon get back on the road. Before long, we enter the fine state of Nebraska, where the Missouri River winds its way through a land of low, rolling hills, creeks, and woodlands thick with cottonwood trees.

"Looks like it might rain," I say, glancing up at the sky.

"Yeah, I noticed that too," Millie says, closing her map once more.

One glance at the ceiling and I note the starting-to-curl duct tape that's been holding the rainwater at bay through the few showers we've happened upon since the flood at Wal-Mart. We still have plenty more tape, so I may need to replace it soon.

"It might not be the best day for going to the zoo," Lydia says with a touch of worry in her voice. "We have umbrellas, though, so maybe we'll be okay."

"We'll be fine. We're nobody's sugar; we won't melt," Millie says.

Thanks for the reminder.

Before we find our campsite, the heavens dump clouds full of rain upon the city. The rain is so thick, Lydia can't see to drive.

She pulls off the interstate and into a parking lot until things subside.

The duct tape pulls farther from the ceiling, curling all the more. Grabbing another roll, I apply fresh tape in hopes of warding off the leaks. Millie and Lydia come back and help me.

"Poor Waldo. He seems to spring a new leak with every rainstorm," Lydia says, stretching tape across some fresh drips.

After the rain slows to a trickle, Millie suggests that we go to the campsite and get settled, maybe even take a taxi to the zoo so we don't have to maneuver the RV around in any more rain in the unfamiliar city.

We decide to do that and head for our new site. Once we've been assigned a lot, Lydia drives to the new place. The ground is wet beneath us, almost marshy in some areas. Pools of water stand in small swales here and there. Not the most ideal conditions for camping.

Lydia is getting pretty good at backing into our camping spots. I hop out of the camper and wave directions as she backs into place. A steady sprinkle starts again, slowly turning my hair into a moppy mess. I brush the drops from my face just as the RV's back tires leave the rocky path and roll into the ground. Way into the ground. The farther Lydia backs into the site, the deeper the motor home sags into the ground.

"Stop!" I scream, flailing my arms like a busy traffic cop.

Lydia is talking to Millie while edging back. Neither is looking my way. With the RV's sinking back side, panic surges through me. This rig could bury me in the mud before Millie's next hot flash.

Millie yells something and turns around. Things inside must be falling backward. Lydia gets it. They both turn to me, my arms still waving. The tires grind to a halt, already deep in mud, flicking specks of mud my way.

My stomach sinks with the tires, and I'm wondering where I might find the closest airport . . .

15

The thought occurs to me that the RV's being stuck in the mud is analogous to my life. I've allowed my past to pull me down further with every passing day. I've had enough. When the opportunity presents itself, I will tell Lydia and Millie the truth. I think.

By the time we get a tow truck to pull the motor home from the pit and find another camper-friendly site that can hold us, we're too pooped to go to the zoo.

Before dinner we grab a cab, go to a Laundromat, and clean our dirty clothes. Then we return to our campsite and settle down to dinner later than usual. We're feeling a little less than friendly. Happily for Lydia and Millie, the air-conditioning still works. They continue to keep it at an even temperature for Cobbler's sake, and the leaks have calmed to a trickle, thanks to the duct tape and the clearing skies. Unfortunately, the air still smells like a stale, musty basement.

With my fork I push the green beans, chicken, and applesauce around on my plate, and I notice Millie doing the same. Lydia takes a bite with all the enthusiasm of a sick puppy.

"This hasn't turned out to be quite the trip of our dreams, has it?" Millie asks.

It's just better if I keep my mouth shut right about now.

"I vote we head back tomorrow," Lydia says, her voice thick with disappointment.

We look at her.

Hope dashes through me, but I refuse to dwell on it. It's true I don't want to fight this whole RV thing anymore. I'm worried about my business, and I want to go home. Still, we've come so far, and we need to do what we can for the camp. "What? I'll have to spend my days wondering if Tony and the others are now fat and bald? I just can't live like that, Lydia."

She smiles in spite of herself.

"That's true, Lydia. That could put Dee right over the edge. Do you want that on your conscience? You know how fragile she is," Millie says.

"Death by chocolate," I say with solemn conviction.

"Oh dear, I would never forgive myself," Lydia joins in.

"Exactly." I fall back against my chair, and we all giggle, causing the tension to flee.

"This trip has been a little crazy," Millie finally says.

"I've never seen anything like it," Lydia agrees.

"I hope I never do it again," I say.

Millie calls Beverly to check on things and to let her know we'll be there the day after tomorrow. Beverly tells Millie that several people have backed out of coming, but they're leaving the campground in the Lord's hands.

Later that night we try to play a game of Scrabble, but we're all pretty much drained and decide to call it a night. Lydia and Millie soon drift off to sleep, but no matter how I try, it escapes me. I finally decide not to fight it. Glancing down at my green-and-white-checkered pajamas, I decide I shouldn't get too cold with long pajama pants on. Still, I grab a sweater to put on over my long-sleeved top, slip on my sandals, and step outside. Crawling onto the bench of the picnic table at our site, I take care to avoid splinters. The night air has cooled off the humidity from earlier in the day. It's a little chilly for me, but Millie and Lydia would love it out here right now.

Thoughts of my business, my time with Millie and Lydia, and the way things have changed for us all consume me. I've never minded growing older. In fact, I'm of the opinion that most things get better with age. Still, I can't deny the fact that a younger woman has moved in on my business territory, and that bothers me. There has to be a way to make it work for both of us. After all, there are enough tourists in our town to support a couple of gourmet chocolate businesses, right? There must be a way to stay competitive.

While sorting through my business problems, Rob's face pops into my mind, and I wonder if I'll ever know love again. Though I have the strong opinion that I don't need a man to enjoy life, the older I get, the more I realize I don't want to be alone forever, either. But a future with him is not possible, unless he makes a major change. Another pang of guilt. It isn't possible. Period.

A mosquito lands on my wrist, and I smack it, totally spoiling his mealtime and adding pain to my arm. Another zooms in, then another. Mosquitoes attempt to prick my exposed skin the way unending questions poke through my safe world.

Since I hate bugs—and right now I'm drawing them in like a bug zapper—I'm thinking it must be a sign. Unfolding my legs from the picnic bench, I walk to the door and tug on it to go inside. It doesn't move. Another shove. Nothing.

I'm locked out. Locked out of the RV. Locked away from my chocolate. I try to stay levelheaded, but the sky is really dark and the campground completely quiet but for a rustling in the grasses behind me, and might I note that just freaks me out a little—What if there's a murderer nearby? Wait. First of all, I used the words *what if*. Second, I'm acting paranoid like Lydia and Millie. Third, all this stress could give me gray hair. And right now, I don't have gray hair. Well, not since I plucked out the six strands this morning.

Okay, eight.

Another rustle in the grass.

A mosquito lands on my face, and fear makes me hit myself a

little too hard, which, by the way, does wonders for my mood. Have I mentioned I have a low patience threshold?

Another knock. Loud knock. "Lydia, Millie, get up," I say as forcefully as I can without waking the neighbors. Between the RV's air-conditioning and Millie's snoring, I'm surprised anyone in the Northern Hemisphere can sleep. "See if I tape up your leaks anymore," I grouse, kicking a muddy tire on the RV as I go. The ground is still wet, though not nearly as bad as at the first site. The mud sucks my shoes, causing a sort of *schlop* sound with every step.

I edge my way to the motor home's back side, but the window is too high for me to get to it. Stepping back to the side, I glance around, my gaze stopping on the picnic table. If I could just heave it over to the side window, I might be able to knock on the window and wake someone.

Rolling up my sleeves, I drag the picnic table toward the window. Grunt, heave, grunt, heave. A few more steps, and I'll make it. With one final grunt, I yank the table toward me. My foot sticks in the mud at the same time a splinter jabs into my index finger. My derriere plops smack-dab into a puddle, splattering flecks of mud everywhere. I let out a tantrum-type squeal and smack the muddy water with my hands—which, I might add, also helps things immensely.

Okay, tantrum over. Brushing a strand of hair from my face, I feel the smudge of mud I've left behind and can only imagine how I must look. A mud facial comes to mind, but I'm just not in the mood. I push up from the puddle and shake myself like Beethoven (the dog, not the musician).

Finally, I get the picnic table close enough to step up to the window. The good news is, Lydia's bed is beside this window. The bad news is, if I have to break in, she will not be a happy camper. Not only that, but I'm guessing my muddy self could pass for the creature from the Black Lagoon.

Now I'm tired, muddy, and mad. I give the window some

heavy-fisted pounding. No thumping of feet as they get out of bed. Nothing. The moonlight would help me see if the blinds weren't down.

The mosquitoes are working their way through my thin pajama bottoms now. I can almost hear the dive-bombers as those suckers head straight for my thighs, where there's enough flesh to get their entire colony through the winter.

They come at me in droves, and I shiver. Swatting furiously, I almost lose my balance and fall on the table. I figure I'll either break something or get a giant-sized splinter in my rump, neither of which will win me the Miss Congeniality Award.

More swatting. I'm working on a real hissy fit. There is no way I am going to stay out here all night and be their main course. Mud is dripping from my clothes. The splinter in my finger is killing me. Attempting to see it better in the moonlight, I lift it like a torch. "ET, go home" comes to mind. I wonder how soon after a mosquito bite malaria kicks in.

Stomping on the table, I give the window a hard knuckle rap, rap, rap. Still nothing. Okay, I want Millie and Lydia out of bed, and I want it now! My knuckles thwack harder against the pane. Not a sound. Biting, itching around my ankles, arms, face. A sliver of panic shoots through me. If I don't think of something quick, these mosquitoes will carry me off for breakfast.

What happened to Lydia's sleepless nights, for crying out loud? Tonight she's a bear in hibernation.

I'm wondering if there's any way to pry the window open without damaging anything. Goodness knows this RV doesn't need any help falling apart, but neither do I want to become bug bait. The blinds are down, but if I break a small hole in the window and put a hole in the screen, I can reach in, unlock the latch, slide the window to the left, and take out the screen. Then I can crawl inside. At this point, I am more than happy to purchase a new window and screen.

The trouble is, how do I make a small hole? It's not like I carry a knife on me, though now I'm thinking it might be a good idea to start doing so. My gaze scans the area. Maybe a jagged rock will do the trick.

The road in front of our site has rocks, so I climb down the table and scrunch around in the gravel in search of the appropriate weapon, all the while slapping at mosquitoes. When I find one "lethal" enough for the job, I head back up the table.

Before performing surgery on poor Waldo, I try one last time to wake someone up inside by knocking on the window. Not a single sound. Not even a peep from Cobbler—at least I can't hear her. With a gulp, I rap lightly against the screen in the area where I hope to stick my hand through. After several raps, I attempt to cut into the screen and then the glass with the jagged edge of the rock. A sick feeling curls in the pit of my stomach. I'm defacing someone's property here. I could get ten years—or at the very least community service at a diabetic camp where no chocolate is allowed. Hopefully Lydia will have mercy. It's freezing cold outside, and the mosquitoes are treating me like a hog on a spit, so I have to get inside.

More tapping, more cutting, until finally, a piece of the pane falls from the window. I keep tapping away at the glass until I've created an opening big enough for my hand to slip through. I make a hole big enough to get my head through the screen so I can see how to unlatch the window and pull the screen away, all the while praying Lydia doesn't hate me for this.

Carefully I reach through the hole and feel around for the lock mechanism at the bottom of the window. Bingo. I unlatch it, scraping my arm against the glass in the process, and I'm home free. A quick shove on the window, and it opens so I'm able to lift out the screen.

Now, if only I could figure out how to get inside without waking Lydia. There's just no great way to get around this. I'm stuck outside, and the only way I can get inside to my soft, warm bed is to cause Lydia a few, um, anxious moments. We can get the window and screen fixed when we arrive at Aspen Creek.

Another mosquito sucks the blood from my ankles. If I hesitate much longer with the window open, the entire mosquito population of Nebraska (which I'm convinced by now are all present, accounted for, and dressed in bibs) will follow me inside.

With the blind above me, I crawl through, allowing a shaft of moonlight to spray upon Lydia's sleeping face. I try like everything not to wake her, but let's be honest here. I'm crawling through a window, and I'm not exactly from Munchkinland. I'm five feet seven inches tall, and just for the record, it's nobody's business how much I weigh. Suffice it to say it isn't easy to squeeze a person of my size through a window. I'm not Gumby.

When I heave forward, the blind rattles, causing Lydia to stir in her bed. For a second, I pause. She settles back in, and I push forward once again. Just as I'm halfway through and towering over Lydia's legs, I glance once more to make sure I'm not waking her. It's too dark to see for sure, but I get the feeling here that she's matching me eyeball-to-eyeball. Because at this moment, she screams loudly enough to wake up the entire town—and don't ask me why, but I scream with her.

Her shriek catapults me into full throttle. In one jerk, I thrust forward and come crashing onto the bed, mud and all. She thrashes about, escapes from the blow, and throws the covers over me before I can catch a breath. I'm wondering if she'll take me to a nearby Laundromat for a thorough washing. With any luck, she'll put me on the permanent-press cycle and smooth out my wrinkles.

Millie's voice calls out from the kitchen, and I hear pots and pans clanging while Lydia cuts off my air supply with her death-grip hold on the covers. Soon copper bottoms are slamming against my backside with a vengeance.

I scream. "It's me! It's DeDe!" I fall onto the bed, facedown, in hopes of keeping their blows to a minimum. With a turn of my neck, I scream again. "Lydia! It's me."

Millie and Lydia jump on me, and I'm thinking somebody told a fib about her weight.

More banging and scrambling about.

"DeDe, come help us! It's a burglar!"

I continue to thrash about, trying to find the end of the doggone blanket before I'm bludgeoned to death.

"Don't knock Cobbler over," Lydia shrieks.

"Well"—bam—"I'm doing the best"—thump, wallop—"I can," Millie says, gasping for breath in between floggings. I have the sick feeling that Millie is enjoying this far more than she should.

More thwacks against my backside and for once I'm thankful for the extra meat on my bones—what's left after the mosquito fest, anyway. Finally, I throw off the corner of the comforter and emerge a muddy, cold, beat-up mess. Lydia has a pot stretched over her head and is about to knock me out cold when Millie screams, "It's DeDe!"

Lydia drops the pan. Only then do I dare breathe.

My best friends tried to beat me to death with shiny copper-bottomed pans. Six months tops before I appear on the Dr. Phil show. My body will not move. Can't even lift my pinkie finger. The worst part of all is, I itch like the dickens. Wait. Can you itch if you're dead? I don't think so. Doggone it. That means I'm still stuck in this stupid motor home.

"DeDe," Lydia says with obvious timidity, "are you feeling okay?"

"Oh sure, I'm fine, aside from the fact I was almost beat to death by my best friends." I attempt to get up from the covers and grimace.

"I'm so sorry, DeDe. I've brought you some coffee," she says in a futile attempt at an apology.

"Don't give it another thought, but the pots and pans are going."

"You shouldn't feel so bad," Millie grouses. "Who wouldn't thump someone upside the head if they were breaking into your motor home?"

"Thanks a lot, Millie." If I had the energy, I'd clobber her one. Besides, with all my scratching, I have no free hands.

"Well, I'm sorry we beat on you, DeDe, but you can't blame us, really. For goodness' sake, you looked like you'd been in a hog pen, and it was dark in the room, after all. Why don't you tell us what happened?" Millie asks.

They help me sit halfway up in my bed so I can take a few sips of coffee. "My lips are the only thing that doesn't hurt," I say. There are welts on my body the size of Texas—not from the beating but from the mosquito bites.

Lydia winces.

"It's not your fault, Lydia." I explain what happened. Then I tell Millie to pull back the blind so they can see the damage I did to the window. "I'm sorry, Lydia. I'll repair it as soon as we get to the camp," I say.

"I forgot about the window," Millie says. "We'd better get some duct tape on that to hold it until we get there."

"That's true. We sure don't want a real burglar getting in here," Lydia says, making chills crawl up my bumpy arms.

Though I try, it's a struggle to find a comfortable position on the bed. My face itches and I scratch it, realizing the mosquitoes must have nibbled there too.

"What are all those welts from, Dee? We didn't hit you in the face, did we?" Millie asks.

I shake my head. "Let me just say I now know how a turkey feels."

"What?" Lydia looks confused.

"I was the main course for a mosquito feast."

Lydia tries to cover her chuckles behind her hand. Millie doesn't bother. She laughs out loud.

See if I give them any more truffles. "You wouldn't think it was so funny if it happened to you," I say, scratching my cheek.

Lydia sits at the foot of my bed while Millie applies duct tape to the holes in the screen and window.

"We're sorry, DeDe. It just seems ironic that this would happen to you. I mean, you hating bugs, camping, and all," Lydia says sweetly.

"Yeah, real ironic. As in a joke with poor taste."

Millie glances at me, and I glare back. "Well, don't look at me. I didn't call out the mosquitoes or lock you out of the RV," she says.

"Yeah, whatever." I stretch. "What time are we leaving?"

"We've already left." Lydia laughs. "We've been on the road for three hours. We just pulled off at a rest stop to check on you."

It's hard to believe I slept through everything. "I'm sorry, you guys. I didn't mean to make a mess of things and sleep in to boot."

"No problem. Just use the door the next time," Millie says, sticking on the last strip of tape.

"Remember, I tried that. We'd better get it looked at so it doesn't stick on us in the future."

"Yeah, I guess you're right. We'll be okay until we get to the camp," Lydia says, nibbling at her pinkie finger.

"We'll be fine," Millie says, but something in her voice tells me she's not so sure. Roll of tape in hand, she starts to leave the room. "We'd better get back on the road."

"Where will we—"

"We'll still be in Nebraska tonight," she says. "Some small lake area. Supposed to be really nice."

Lydia follows Millie and closes the door behind them so I can get showered and dressed.

Every bone in my body hurts when I attempt to get up. You would think Pilates would make me a little more flexible, but no. Come to think of it, I was the main course for bloodsucking parasites, to say nothing of the fact I was pulverized with pots and pans by two old women bent on hurting someone. That's enough to make anyone sore.

Maybe this was the reason for that whole storm-brewing feeling I had. I can only hope it's not the calm before the storm.

Okay, that thought *so* does not make me feel better.

16

"*All right, girls, time for our Rocky Mountain National Park trivia,*" Millie says, settling into the passenger's seat and opening her book.

Things could be worse. She could be playing her trumpet.

She stops turning pages, and her finger runs along a line of words. "Okay, when do bull elk and buck deer shed their antlers, and what happens almost immediately afterward?" Millie turns to me with a smile.

"Um, late winter?" I say.

"Early spring?" Lydia chimes in.

"You're both right," Millie says with a snap of her head. "In late winter and early spring." She reads a moment, then looks back up. "What happens almost immediately afterward?"

"They buy a hat?" I ask dryly.

Millie glares at me a moment, then turns away. "Lydia?"

"Don't they start growing their next year's rack?"

"Right again," Millie says, rewarding Lydia with a smile. I half-expect her to pass out gold stars. "Anyone know what new-growth antlers are covered with?"

"A sort of velvet type texture?" Lydia says.

"Right!" Millie's so excited, she's about to jump off her seat.

"Brownnose," I grouse.

"What? I'm sorry, DeDe," Lydia says.

"You should read more, DeDe. You might learn something," Millie says, closing her book with a snap.

"I'd rather make chocolate."

"Which is why you don't know the answers to these questions," Millie quips. "Knowledge equals power."

"Then I guess I'm weak. But I make good chocolate."

Millie humphs, but I ignore her.

"Those motorcycles are driving me crazy," Lydia says.

With a glance out the window, I see a group of four or five cycles riding beside us. All of the guys but one are wearing red kerchiefs around their heads, black leather jackets (can't they be a bit more creative?) with silver studs, the whole bit. But they're not young; they look fiftyish.

"Why are they driving you crazy?" Millie asks.

"They just keep weaving in and out. I mean, why don't they pick a lane and stick with it? I finally passed them, and now they're beside us, no doubt getting ready to pass again."

"And no helmets. I'm telling you, why cyclists don't wear helmets is beyond me. It's so unsafe," Millie says.

"It kills the hairdo," I say.

"That man without the kerchief doesn't have any hair," Lydia says, pointing. "Well, if you don't count that lone patch of gray that's pulled into a braid down his back. Why on earth do men do that?" she says.

Right then the bald man—aka Willie Nelson wannabe—with the mere wisp of a braid starting at the base of his head and running a couple of inches down his back, waves at Lydia. She gasps and jerks, causing the motor home to swerve.

"That man waved at you," Millie says in disbelief. "You're turning red."

Lydia's right hand touches her face. "I am not."

"Yes, you are. You're blushing." Millie just can't leave her alone.

"Do you know him, Lydia?" I ask.

"Why, no."

"He must think you're cute," I say, trying to make her feel better. "It's the hair. I told you that color is good for you."

"Oh, for goodness' sake, I'm not cute. I'm old. Besides, that's probably just his way of saying, 'Ha-ha, I've passed you,'" Lydia says, absently fingering her hair.

"We're not old. We're in our prime," I argue.

"Oh, that's right. *You're* forty-nine—but not for long." There is a definite sneer to Millie's voice here.

"Can I help it if I'm younger than you?" I ask, rubbing it in more than I should, but time is running out.

Millie belts out the final blow. "You'll be getting AARP material by the time you return home."

"You win," I say, thinking all the while that I'll take the handles off the cupboards—maybe even hide them. Just call me vicious.

"Growing older isn't so bad," Lydia says, switching on her handheld fan and lifting it to her face. "I mean, we're smarter—"

"Well, most of the time," Millie says, throwing a glance my way.

"That does it. I'm switching your blouses to your underwear drawer and putting your underwear in with your jeans. We'll see who has the last laugh."

"All right, you two. That's enough. Besides, we are smarter. *All* of us." She emphasizes the word "all" to include me, I'm sure. I stick out my tongue at Millie. "We're not only smarter we're more carefree. Don't worry about the things that used to bother us." She passes the guys on the motorcycles again.

"That's true. But I can't believe you're saying that, Lydia," Millie says.

"Although I'm still struggling with that one, I'm working on it," she says cheerfully. "You and DeDe have inspired me with your own victory over fear."

If you don't count that fear-of-failure thing, sure. "Don't be so hard on yourself. You've done really well considering all you've been through," I say.

"Still, I admire how you aren't afraid to try new things, Dee. You decided to follow your dream, come what may, and look at you. You're running your own business! It took me months to color my hair."

She has me there.

"And, Millie, you've had a divorce to deal with, and instead of allowing it to make you bitter, you're better. You're always so together. Organized and in control. I want to be like that when I grow up," Lydia says.

"I can't believe you're saying all that, Lydia. You've managed to run a home with two energetic boys and then hold the family together knowing you were losing your husband. Well, I just don't know how you've managed," I say.

"That's right, Lydia. I never could have coped with it all," Millie adds.

"Well, I couldn't have done it without the Lord, that's for sure," Lydia says.

So far, Millie and I have managed to steer Lydia's conversation away from the Lord, but I'm wondering how much longer we can keep the subject at arm's length. Her compassionate heart just won't let us go that easily.

"Why are we slowing down?" Millie asks in regard to the obvious change in our speed.

"I don't know. I'm pushing on the gas, but Waldo's slowing." Lydia's worry lines deepen.

"Do you think we can make it to the next rest stop?" I ask.

"I'm maintaining a speed of forty-five, so we'll get there eventually."

Just then the motorcyclists pass us again. This time they holler out and wave toward Lydia.

"Good grief," she says.

"They are totally taken with you, Lydia," Millie says with a chuckle.

"Well, they weren't just looking at me. They were checking out you and DeDe too." There's no denying the twinkle in Millie's eyes because the men are fussing over us. She and Lydia are glowing like schoolgirls. It's probably good for them. Me? I just want to go home.

It's embarrassing the way everyone is passing us as if we're standing still. As if we didn't look old enough riding in an outdated model RV, now we're cruising at the pace of a turtle. I'm telling you, this is the trip of a lifetime, no doubt about it.

We finally crawl to the next rest stop. Once we get there, Lydia lifts the hood of the RV as though she knows what she's looking for, which of course, she doesn't.

"What are you doing?" I ask.

Lydia chews on her pinkie nail. "Um, I don't know. I was hoping something obvious would show itself."

"Like a two-inch little man standing on the engine pointing to a part and telling us what's wrong?" I ask.

"That would be it," Lydia says, laughing.

"You ladies need some help?" The bald motorcycle man with the tiny braided ponytail slips up beside us.

"What? Oh no, we're fine," Lydia says, keeping her head turned away from him while slamming the hood down.

The man backs away, arms up. "No harm intended, ma'am," he says. "Just trying to be neighborly."

Lydia reminds me of a little girl who's lost.

"You got some trouble?" An old man comes up to us now. He's thin and gaunt, a bit stooped over, but has a kind face.

Lydia turns to the older guy. "Well, we were having a little trouble," she whispers to the man before raising the RV's hood once again.

Ponytail Man shrugs and joins his friends back at his motorcycle. The old man tinkers around the area a little bit, then turns to

Lydia. "Sounds to me as though you might have a problem in the fuel system somewhere. Might need to replace the fuel pump," the old man says, closing the hood. "You got far to go?"

"We're headed for the next town," Millie says.

"You should make it there. May have to pull over and let the engine cool off, then start traveling again. But I'd get it looked at once I got there, or it could freeze up on you and leave you stranded somewhere."

Lydia gasps.

"Just take it easy. Of course, you won't be able to go very fast," he says.

We thank him, and soon we all go on our merry ways. There is one thing that bothers me, though. Why did we trust that old guy and not Ponytail Man? I mean, how can you really know who to trust?

"I don't think that's right, Millie," Lydia says. "We got off on that exit, but I'm thinking we should have stayed on the highway until here," she says, pointing.

"I don't know. That detour got me all messed up," Millie says, exasperation in her voice. "We're lost."

"Welcome to my world."

"Well, I'm not a man, so I'm going to pull over and ask someone." Lydia pulls into the next gas station.

She jumps out, leaving Millie and me behind. Millie is beside herself. "We're an hour over schedule. We've wasted all kinds of gas trying to find that stupid campsite," she says. "Not to mention we have to be careful with this fuel system problem. I think we messed up a half hour ago, but Lydia seemed to think she knew where she was going."

I'm not about to touch that one. She and Lydia will have to hash this one out all by themselves. Millie gets up and goes into the bathroom. She's straightening things in the medicine cabinet.

"Well, that's not great news," Lydia says, slamming her door shut. "We've missed a couple of turns. It will take us another hour to get there."

"I told you we should have turned back there."

"It doesn't help to cast the blame, Millie. It is what it is, so let's just not say another word about it," Lydia says.

Millie and Lydia are having "words." Part of me rejoices that there's a ruckus and I'm not involved, and the other part of me hopes we're all still friends by the journey's end.

Hopefully the RV will make it another hour before it gets attention. Most likely, that's on all our minds. It's barely chugging along in between our stops to cool it off. Lydia's and Millie's hot flashes were bound to rub off.

Lydia has switched off the radio, and the only sound in the RV is the grinding of the air-conditioning and occasional grunts and groans. I'm not sure if they're coming from the motor home or Millie.

We're a half hour into our trip when a police siren blares behind us. What? Is there a target on our back side?

"Oh, not again," Lydia says. She pulls to the side of the road.

This guy is nothing like Barney Fife. He means serious business. I can almost hear the squeak of his holster and jingle of his keys when he walks. He tells us that driving too slow can be as hazardous as going too fast. Lydia explains the RV's problem and that we hope to get it in for repairs at the next town. The officer nods and turns to leave, then he swivels back to Lydia.

"By the way, women traveling alone shouldn't have broken windows in this day and age," he says with all the authority of Marshal Dillon in a *Gunsmoke* episode. At which time I slink farther down into my seat. The good news is, we got away with another warning, but our luck may be wearing thin.

After wasting too much time and precious gas getting lost, we manage to find the place. The office attendant tells us where we can get the motor home checked, so we call the place and they fit the RV in for repair. We soon find out that, yes, the motor home has a fuel pump relay problem.

Okay, so the old guy was on the up-and-up; still, one can't be too careful.

The repair shop is able to fix the problem, and we're back at camp just as twilight settles upon the town.

"I think I'll check out the lake area," I say once the awning is rolled out and the lights are in place. I'm barely a few steps away from the RV when my phone rings. It's Rob. Millie and Lydia are still in the RV. My heart pounds wildly. A rush of adrenaline shoots through me. I shouldn't do this. I know I shouldn't do this. "Hello?"

"Hey, DeDe, how about we all go?" Lydia calls out behind me.

Nervously I disconnect the call and punch off my phone. "That would be great," I say, hiding my cell phone and trying to calm my nerves.

Lydia locks up things, and we head off for the lake. "Listen, girls, I'm sorry about my attitude earlier. I was just tired and frustrated," Lydia says.

"It's no problem. I was too," Millie admits.

The walk to the lake is filled with thick, shady trees, shrubs, and wildflowers. Soon we step into the clearing. A partial moon sails from a star-studded sky, its light reflecting upon the water below. Lydia takes a deep breath. "Oh, this is nice."

"Yeah, it is." Though I'm still trembling, I can feel myself start to relax. We needed to stop at a place like this. "How far are we from Estes Park, did you say?"

Staring at the lake, Lydia answers, "Between four and five

hours." She turns to us. "We're almost there. Aspen Creek. Our youth camp. I'm so excited, I can hardly stand it. Doesn't that seem a lifetime ago?"

"It sure does," Millie agrees.

"Hey, you guys remember when we had that lip sync contest where we acted out 'Stop! in the Name of Love'?" I ask.

"I still can't believe we let you talk us into that, DeDe," Millie grumbles.

"Oh, you survived. Besides, you really enjoyed yourself, if I remember correctly—and I do."

We laugh.

"And how you ever came up with all the choreography, DeDe, I'll never know. Genius. Pure genius," Lydia says.

"Yeah, that was pretty neat. Though I kept turning left when I was supposed to turn right, and I used the wrong hand at the wrong time. I was so uncoordinated," Millie says with a sigh.

"Was?"

"Well, at least I'm organized. Coordination isn't all that big of a deal unless you walk a tightrope or something."

"Good point," Lydia says. "Those sure were fun times," she adds, all dreamy-eyed. No doubt her thoughts are filled with Greg.

We hear some guys clowning around and look to our left to see some men roughhousing just across the lake from us. It takes a moment for us to realize it's Ponytail Man and his cohorts.

"What are they doing here?" Lydia asks, fear in her eyes.

"Now don't get yourself all stirred up. It's a free country," Millie says.

Right then Ponytail Man sees us and waves. The other guys stop goofing around and look our way.

No one else is around the lake, which is a little disconcerting. Hopefully these guys won't get overly friendly.

"You guys ready to go?" Millie asks. I'm thinking she's as uncomfortable as I am.

"Yeah, I'm ready," Lydia says.

"Me too."

Quickly we turn and start back for the motor home.

"You don't think they're following us, do you?" Lydia asks in a nervous voice.

"Goodness, no," Millie says in a way that suggests she's trying to convince herself. "Just happen to be going the same way, that's all. They'll be gone by tomorrow."

Millie and Lydia must be getting to me. I'm never nervous about these kinds of things, but I have to admit, right now I'm hoping Millie is right.

By the time I settle into bed, my mind reels with thoughts of our journey. The sights, the laughs, the fears, the struggles. Being with my old camp friends has made the Lord seem closer somehow. More approachable. I've allowed my guilt to keep me away far too long. I need Him. He's the only One who can help me through this mess with Rob. I don't trust myself. I'm weak and lonely. My thoughts of God tangle with thoughts of Rob, and in the whisper of nightfall, I talk it all over with the God who made me. Rob. My future. My fears. Everything.

And I hope deep in my heart that this time—in spite of my guilt—He hears me.

17

When we get back to the motor home, Lydia decides to bake. I'm thrilled. It might get rid of the RV's "old man" smell. Millie goes through the outer storage bins, one by one, and straightens them.

Since I can never refuse Lydia's desserts, I pass on the chocolate truffle in my drawer. Instead, I get out my Pilates mat and go through my routine.

The air is unusually cool for this time of year, so to save on our problematic air-conditioning, Lydia and Millie have turned it off and opened the windows. Lydia's clanging around in the kitchen, and before long, the smell of chocolate wafts through the screens just as my Pilates workout is finished.

"Boy, something sure smells good." A woman's voice pulls me from my bottled water. I look up to see her and a man coming toward me. Great. Now we'll have to share our dessert.

"Howdy, we're the Camerons." The man stretches out his hand, grabs mine, and gives it a hearty shake. "We're from Tennessee. My name is Roy, and this here is my wife, Betty."

"Hello. My name is DeDe. I'm from Florida." *And just for the record, we're not sharing.*

"And I'm Lydia from Maine," Lydia says on her way out of the motor home.

And I'm John-Boy from Walton's Mountain—okay, bad attitude.

Lydia shakes their hands. "I'm waiting for the brownies to cool, but you're welcome to join us when they're ready to eat."

Doggone it. No chocolate binge tonight.

"That would be great," Roy says, rubbing his hands together. "Honey, I'll go get our chairs and be right back." Betty nods and smiles.

I'm dying to call out, "Don't tell your friends about the brownies, okay?" but I don't want to face Lydia's wrath.

"Millie, come outside; we want you to meet a new neighbor," Lydia says. After cleaning the outer bins, Millie went inside to straighten who knows what. Millie would hide in the motor home all evening if we didn't force her to come out when people are visiting. Besides, she's straightened the RV so much, it resembles a ruler.

She pushes through the door and is obviously fighting everything in her not to throw us a dirty look. I smile sweetly, and she tosses a glance that says she'll deal with me later.

"Hello," she says.

"Howdy. My name is Betty Cameron," the woman says to Millie. She's a fairly thin woman, about five foot four, and appears to be in her early sixties with gray hair cropped at the nape of her neck. Delicate laugh lines bunch at the corners of her eyes when she smiles. She's dressed in jeans, a comfortable pink top, and sensible sneakers. She looks pretty hip for a woman her age.

"I'm Millicent Carter. Millie for short."

"Where you from, Millie?"

"Indiana."

Roy's boots crunch the pebbles on the roadway. "Howdy." He pulls his Stetson from his head, runs his hand through his hair, then extends it to Millie. "The name's Roy."

I hide my giggle when Millie stares at his hand a moment before shaking it.

Roy unfolds the chairs for himself and his wife, and they sit down.

"Are you folks on vacation?" Lydia asks pleasantly.

"Oh my, no. This is what we do. This is our home," Roy says.

It amazes me to find so many people doing this RV thing full-time. I can't imagine the draw.

"Yeah, that's right. We sold our home back in Tennessee, and now the United States is our home," Betty says with outstretched arms.

"Do you have any children?" Lydia wants to know.

"Sure do. Two daughters. They each have two children of their own," Betty says. "We sure love to spoil those grandkids."

Lydia frowns. "But don't you miss them? The children and grandkids, I mean?"

"Sometimes. But we see them on a pretty regular basis. One lives in Tennessee, the other in Michigan. We head home anytime they need us or if something special is going on in the kids' lives, like important events, birthdays, celebrations of any kind, that sort of thing."

"You do that?" Lydia presses.

"Absolutely. Nothing more important than family," Roy says, leaning back in his chair. "And with our motor home, we can pretty much go whenever and wherever we please."

Lydia studies them a moment. "I hadn't thought of that."

"People are always thinking about what they think you have to give up, and they don't consider all the things you gain by having a portable lifestyle."

"I suppose." Lydia nips at her nail. It's a wonder she has a nail left at all with the way she's always doing that. "What about emergencies, though?"

"See, the thing is, most kids move away from home anyway. It might take us a little longer to get to them this way, but we'll get there. They know we're never too far to come help them if they need us," Roy says.

"And sometimes we take the grandkids, when they aren't in

school. They've traveled out west with us, and it's opened plenty of discussion on geography and history. They're richer for it."

"That's really neat," I say, smiling at them and then at Lydia, who appears to be feeling better about the idea.

"It has to be freeing to live that way. Nothing really holding you down, doing what you want to every day," Millie says.

Roy stretches out his legs and puts his hands behind his head. "There's nothing like it, I'm telling you. Smartest thing we ever did, ain't it, babe?"

"Sure is," Betty agrees.

"Mind if I start a fire?" Roy asks.

"That would be great," I say eagerly. I've rarely been warm since I left Florida.

We talk about the area and the fact that we are headed on to Colorado. While Roy gets the fire started, our conversation ventures on to Aspen Creek and our antics at youth camp.

"Oh, that's great," I say, warming up to the fire. Lydia and Millie scoot away from the flames.

"Hey, do you guys remember the time we sneaked into Mr. Baldwin's room and decorated it for a surprise birthday party?" I ask.

"Yeah, and we got into trouble for it. Remember?" Millie glares at me as though everything is *my* fault.

"Try to be nice and what do you get? Heartache," I say.

Millie and Lydia groan appropriately with me.

"It wouldn't have been so bad if you hadn't used his deodorant stick to write on the mirror. That's why he got mad. Remember? He said it was too personal," Millie says.

"Yeah, but later he told us he thought it was funny. They just didn't want the other kids to get any ideas or the whole camp would be in chaos," I say.

"Uh-oh, sounds like you gals are a little on the ornery side," Roy says with a chuckle.

"You know, Millie, I'd forgotten that ornery side of you. After you got married, you were much more subdued."

A shadow crosses Millie's face. "Marriage has a way of maturing us."

"Oh, so that's my problem," I say with a laugh, attempting to keep things light. "I'm not married, so I haven't matured."

"You said it; I didn't," Millie comments with all the warmth of an ice cube.

Roy laughs. "It hasn't matured us all that much, has it; Betty Girl?"

She giggles and shakes her head. "Maybe someday we'll act our age."

"Do you remember when Mrs. Woodriff was trying to teach us the basics of swimming, and she almost drowned?" Lydia asks, her eyes wide.

"Oh boy, do I ever. I thought she was a goner for sure," Millie says. "Wasn't it Eric Melton who jumped in to save her?"

We think a moment. "Yeah, I believe it was Eric," I say. "It was the one and only time I saw him put someone else above himself."

"He did struggle with that, didn't he?" Millie says with a chuckle.

"I think deep down there was good in him, though," Lydia says, and we look at her. "Well, he did save Mrs. Woodriff, after all," she says a bit defensively.

I want to press her about how she truly felt about Eric back then, but with strangers sitting here, it just doesn't seem right.

"How are you folks tonight?" A woman in her early forties stops on the road beside us. A lacy white tie holds her dark brown hair in a friendly ponytail and knots into a fine bow at the top. Fringy bangs fall just above her perfectly arched eyebrows. Cranberry red colors her full lips. She's dressed in sporty jeans, a navy sweatshirt with a white border at the neck, and sparkling white sneakers with froufrou sequins and white laces.

"We're fine. Would you like to join us?" Before the woman can answer, Lydia is already grabbing our extra chair from the storage bin.

"Thank you." The woman situates her slight frame in the chair. "I'm Eloise Beamer," she says.

We all exchange greetings while Lydia goes into the motor home to retrieve the brownies. I wonder if she made a double batch. I'm thinking seconds are out.

"Oh my goodness, what is in this?" Eloise asks. "Is it pudding?"

"Chocolate syrup," Lydia answers.

Eloise closes her eyes to chew. "Delicious."

Another chocolate connoisseur. The world just can't have too many.

"So where are you from, Eloise?" Roy asks. I'm wondering if he's keeping a log.

"Well, I was born and raised in Colorado, but I travel all over. Live in my motor home."

"Is that a fact? We were just telling these lovely ladies that we do the same—live full-time in our motor home," Roy says.

"But you're so young. How do you provide for yourself?" Betty asks.

"I'm a writer." She closes her eyes and takes another bite of brownie. We allow her a moment of silence. She must have a regular exercise regimen to love chocolate that way and still maintain her figure.

"What do you write?" Now she has Millie's attention.

"Suspense," she says.

Millie thinks a moment and then suddenly slaps her knee. "Eloise Beamer! I've read a couple of your books!" Millie is wide-eyed and breathless. She stands to her feet. "This is a real treat," she says, walking over to shake the woman's hand.

"Oh good. Somebody other than my mother *is* reading them." She laughs. "I hope that means you liked them?"

"Loved them. Couldn't put them down," Millie says. "Caused me a few sleepless nights, I tell you."

"Great. Always good to keep the reader up at night."

"I don't know how you write that stuff without getting spooked out," Lydia says.

"Sometimes I get a little creeped out," she says. "Especially if I'm camping in a secluded spot up in the mountains. One never knows when a bear will come knockin'." She finishes the last of her brownie and gives her paper plate to Lydia, who is already collecting everyone's trash.

"I should have asked sooner, but is anyone up for coffee?"

"We'd better not. Caffeine keeps us up at night," Betty says. " 'Course, if we had one of your books, it would be all right," she adds, looking at Eloise.

"I just happen to have a couple of extras in my home. If you all want one, I'd be glad to give them to you," she says.

This woman's presence sure has kicked Millie's adrenaline up a notch. She's practically salivating. Picture mad dog here.

"You want to walk with me, Millie?" Eloise asks with a wide grin. That request alone could send Millie to her heavenly reward, but she's tough. I'll give her that. She eagerly agrees and pretty much floats alongside Eloise as they head for her RV.

We decide on coffee after all, and I help Lydia prepare it. By the time we have the mugs in place, Millie and Eloise are back with books. They pass a couple of copies to each of us. *Mediterranean Nights, An Eerie Cruise,* and *Death by Chocolate.* Okay, I don't think I want the third one. It just hits too close to home.

We ooh and aah appropriately over every book and settle in to our coffee and the warmth of the crackling fire. The mosquitoes are a little bothersome, but nothing like I experienced before. Besides, tonight the only skin exposed is my face. By the time I get to Aspen Creek, I'll be utterly unrecognizable if the mosquitoes have anything to say about the matter.

We talk a little more about the full-time RV life, which, by the way, I still fail to see in a positive light, but I'm obviously becoming a minority as I look at Millie's and Lydia's expressions in the soft glow of firelight. They're being won over, no doubt about it.

Okay, I admit I feel better about the whole RV experience than I did when I left home, but you won't see me running out to buy one. Instead, I hold fast to the hotel-room-with-a-view thing. If you throw in a coffeemaker, the Internet, and a complimentary breakfast, I'll sign a lease.

Finally, as the evening winds to a close, we say our good-byes, put away the chairs, and turn to go inside. By the looks of things, we're doing so in the nick of time. Loud engines rev and snarl just down the road. We look up.

The moon and camp lights cast enough beam to tell us more than we care to know. It's the Biker Boys, and they're headed our way.

"Hurry up, get the blinds down," Lydia says, her voice in a panic. She rushes up the steps to the driver's seat and yanks the curtains shut.

"What's wrong, Lydia? They're not going to bother us," I say, trying to get her to see how paranoid she's acting. "Some guys on vacation, just like us. No big deal."

Pulling the blinds down at the kitchen window, she turns to me. "It may be no big deal to you, but I'm not comfortable with it, DeDe."

"I've pulled the ones in the bedroom," Millie says like a military sergeant on secret maneuvers.

"I don't get you two. You can't live in fear all your lives," I insist.

"No, but you don't have to be stupid, either," Millie quips.

"Oh, good grief."

"Shh, they're almost up to Waldo," Lydia says, peeking through the side blind at the door.

We can hear them laughing and carrying on outside, and for a fraction of a heartbeat, I feel a little tense. Those two are getting to me, that's all there is to it. Pulling open my work notebook, I try to concentrate on some things I can do to improve my Le Diva candy, but Millie and Lydia are scampering around up front, whispering, and peeking out the blinds. It's ridiculous.

"DeDe, come here!" Lydia says barely above a whisper.

With all the energy and grace of Igor, I haul my body out of the bed and drag myself out into the kitchen. "What is it?" I'm in a foul mood, and it shows.

"Look at this guy. There's something familiar about him, but I can't put my finger on it," Lydia says.

"To me he looks like every other old geezer who refuses to grow up," Millie says.

She has such a way with words.

With a heavy sigh, I pull back the blind and peek out, feeling silly for doing so. "Do you mean the man with the short braid down his back?"

"Yeah, that's the one," Lydia says.

He's turned around, and I can't see his face. One of them drops something, and they stop while he picks it up. Then they move on. Braid Man never turns back around. "They're gone," I say, dropping the blind back in place.

Lydia and Millie heave a sigh of relief. Their shoulders drop, and they instantly relax.

"Are you kidding me—were you two really that worried?"

"Listen, DeDe, you never know. We are three women traveling alone, after all," Millie chides. "And we do have a broken window," she throws in to make me feel guilty.

"I wonder if Eloise worries about those things," I say, taking a seat at the table.

Lydia and Millie grab a chair too, but they say nothing.

"Yeah, I don't think she does, either. Otherwise, she wouldn't be traveling the countryside by herself. You need to lighten up. Life is too short to spend it worrying about every little thing." I get up and pull a cup from the cupboard to pour myself a drink of water.

"You should talk. It's not like you don't fear some things," Millie challenges.

"Such as?"

"How about love?"

"What?"

"Come on, DeDe. We all know you're afraid to fall for someone for fear you'll get your heart broken again." As soon as Millie says the words, I can tell she wishes she hadn't.

That makes two of us.

Her voice gets softer. "It's just that we all have things to work through. Fear is always an issue for women. I mean, what woman walking down a dark street doesn't look over her shoulder to make sure she's not being followed?"

"I understand that, but we can't let it paralyze us." My own words ring in my ears, and I wish I could shut them out. Is that what I've done? Allowed my fears and guilt to paralyze me?

"We're here to listen, if you ever want to talk about it," Millie says.

"You don't understand. It's complicated."

"We can do complicated, can't we, Lydia?"

Lydia gives a shy nod.

Knowing that what I'm about to say could change our friendship, I take a deep breath. "Rob and I broke up because"—pausing a moment here to gather courage—"he was married."

Lydia gasps. Millie's eyes grow as wide as coconuts.

"It never entered my brain that he was married." I stare at my fingers. "Still, all the signs were there. He was only available at certain times. Said he didn't have a land line, only a cell phone."

"Well, that's true for a lot of people," Lydia says in my defense.

"Yes, but there were other signs, and I ignored them."

"Did you have an inkling?" Millie wants to know. Maybe she sees me as "the other woman."

"No—I don't know. Sometimes I thought things weren't quite right, but I never considered that he was married. I thought maybe he was losing interest in me, you know?"

"So how did you find out?" Millie prods.

"His wife called me while I was with him at dinner."

"Oh no," Lydia says.

"But I didn't tell him she called. I met with her the next day. She showed me pictures of him with their family."

"They have children?"

"Yes, two girls."

"How do you know this wasn't an ex-wife?" Lydia asks, trying to excuse me.

"Because they were recent pictures." For a moment, I just stare at the table and say nothing. "As soon as I knew for sure, I broke it off."

Lydia puts her hand over mine. "I'm sorry, DeDe. That had to be very painful. But you shouldn't blame yourself. He lied to you."

"Yes, then I kept it from both of you." They don't say anything, but Lydia just keeps patting my hand. "There's more. He's been calling my cell phone and my store."

"Well, he'd better not call you while I'm around, that's all I can say. I'll make him wish he hadn't! Besides, he'll get the idea soon enough if you just ignore him," Millie says.

"See, there's the problem. Though I'm convinced now that it isn't love that holds me to him, I still struggle with the temptation to hang on to him." Tears fill my eyes and spill onto my cheeks. "How could I be tempted by that? I know it's wrong."

"Everyone is tempted by something or other," Millie says with a rare show of compassion. "It's what we do with that temptation that matters, Dee."

We have quite a lengthy conversation about how I need to let him go. As much as it pains me to hear that, I know they're right. If only my heart will obey . . .

"Thanks for letting me talk it out."

"This is what being a friend is all about. Getting each other through the hard times," Millie says. "I know I don't always communicate sweetly like Lydia does—"

"Not even close," I say with a laugh while wiping away my tears.

A smile breaks out on Millie's face. "Guilty as charged. Still, I want you to know there is nothing I wouldn't do to help you in any way I could with whatever you needed. And right now you need to get away from that slime bucket."

We laugh, exchange hugs, and talk a little while longer. Finally, we go to bed. Eventually, Lydia's rhythmic breathing whispers into the night air, while the sound of Millie's snoring drifts into our room. When I close my eyes to sleep, our conversation plagues me. My honesty, my fears that they'll think less of me, thoughts of Rob, his wife and family. If only I could make it all go away.

No matter how I twist and shift about, I can't seem to get comfortable. A night walk would do me good, but I stay planted in bed. There's no way I'm going to let this RV lock me out again.

And just for the record, I'm not afraid.

18

Something rouses me from my sleep, and my eyes crack open. It is boiling hot inside the motor home. If I'm dead, I'm *so* in trouble. My feet kick off the covers, leaving only a thin bedsheet over me.

"Welcome to my world," Lydia says, sitting upright on the edge of the bed, holding the fan up to her red face. She lifts her hair with one hand and holds the fan at the base of her neck with the other. "It's unanimous, Millie," she shouts, "Even DeDe is hot."

Millie shrugs down the hall to our bedroom. "Well, you know it's hot if she says so. We're going to have to open some windows." Millie's face is the color of undercooked pork.

Lydia sighs and rises from her bed. "What time is it?"

"It's four thirty," Millie says, patting her face with a wet cloth.

"Four thirty as in a.m.?" I ask incredulously. "Hello? I don't do 4:30 a.m."

"You do now," Millie calls over her shoulder.

"Quick, somebody whack Millie with a happy stick," I yell back.

"Now don't you two start," Lydia interjects.

Millie and Lydia shove the windows open even farther, and I'm not about to remind them that the grandpa bikers are lurking out there somewhere. Just not gonna go there.

"The air still isn't working right?" I ask.

Lydia shakes her head. "It's blowing out hot air." She runs the palm of her hand across her forehead. "Hey, you guys, why don't we go ahead and get started? We're already up, so we might as well."

We're already up? Um, anybody noticing my lumpy self beneath the sheet?

"Sounds good to me. I'm anxious to get there," Millie says, her face aglow with a morning shine. Somebody needs to pull her plug.

Okay, so *I* need the happy stick.

Majority rules, so Lydia and Millie get their way. Before I can adjust to the morning's light, we're on the road again. After making my bed and cleaning my side of the room, I shower for the day.

Now let me tell you, you haven't lived until you've tried showering while traveling down the road. And I thought I had bruises from Lydia and Millie's beating. I had no idea how hard it would be to clean between my toes, in a stork stance, while being jostled about like a piece of chicken in a bag of Shake 'n Bake. Let me just say the dirt between my toes isn't worth the effort.

By the time I dress and finish breakfast, we're a couple of hours into our trip. The breeze blowing in the windows helps keep the heat at bay, but I'm a little worried about Lydia and Millie. By the looks of them, *they're* having radiator problems.

"There's a good breeze by the window above the sofa, Lydia. Why don't you sit back here for a while? It might help," I say.

Lydia turns a red face my way. The little fan blows hair from her face, but a few stubborn strays stick to the sides of her cheeks and forehead. "Maybe I will," she says, pulling over. She climbs back toward me. "You sure you don't mind driving, Millie?"

"I'm fine," Millie calls out, but we all know it wouldn't matter. Lydia is settled into her seat with her face turned to the window's breeze, while her fan continues to blow against her neck.

"We might have to go into a restaurant just to find some relief," Millie says, blotting her face with a cloth. "Would you wet this for me again, DeDe?"

"Sure." I get up and take the cloth, soak it with cold water, wring it out, then return it to Millie, who sighs with pleasure once it's on the back of her neck.

It's then that we notice the sound of motorcycle engines coming up beside us. It's the Biker Boys again, with the wannabe Willie Nelson leading the way.

While we're watching them, they shout and wave, rev up their motors, charge ahead, and cut in front of us. Millie has to brake. The guys wave and speed on ahead.

"What in the world!" Millie says. "Now that just makes me mad!"

Suddenly we zoom forward. Lydia falls to the left, and I fall against Lydia.

"What's wrong, Millie?" Lydia asks while pushing herself back upright on the sofa.

"I have one nerve left, and these old goats are gettin' on it!" Millie grinds out each word through clenched teeth. She's hunched forward, hands tight against the steering wheel. Her lips are squeezed together, jaw set, eyes narrow and beady. I can almost picture her in a black helmet. Think Indianapolis 500.

I sit up straighter, alert and ready for some fun. "It's Menopausal Millie coming through! Woo-hoo!" I say, feeling ten years younger. Apprehension covers Lydia's face, but I'm charged. This is the most fun I've had in days. The breeze kicks up a notch, causing our hair to blow about every which way.

The RV engine sounds as though it might cough up a spark plug.

"You'd better slow down, Millie, or you'll get us killed," Lydia says, trying to ruin all our fun.

"I'm tired of them pestering us," she shouts back.

"Now this is the Millie I know and love," I say despite Lydia's frown. "This is the same Millie who joined me in stirring up trouble at camp. A real rabble-rouser." I grin and rub my hands together with gusto.

Though the motor home is choking and sputtering, we

somehow manage to pull just behind the bikers. Willie turns his face toward us and smiles with surprise. Playing Millie, I snap his picture, which probably wasn't a good idea since he almost runs into us. I didn't think about the flash blinding him.

Millie's lips are still scrunched together, and she's not looking at all friendly.

"You'd better slow down, Millie. You might hurt those men," Lydia says, her own legs stretched into full braking position.

"Exactly." The rearview mirror shows the evil intent lurking in Millie's narrowed eyes. I smell fear, and it's coming from the Biker Boys.

Millie edges closer.

Ponytail Man waves and leads the pack onto the next exit ramp. Only then does Lydia take a breath.

And by the look on her face, I'm thinking she's thankful that it wasn't her last one.

We drive awhile in silence. I'm still pumped from the whole Biker Boys thing, but obviously Lydia and Millie didn't enjoy it as much as I did. That little crisis, along with the RV's faulty air-conditioning, has done little to cool off Lydia and Millie. Though the windows are open, we're still trying to run the air-conditioning to see if we can get it circulating cool air. Unfortunately, it's only blowing hot air. We must be rubbing off on it.

"I think you'd better let me drive awhile," Lydia says.

"Figured that was coming," Millie says. "Want me to get off at the next exit?"

"Yeah, since we left those guys way back there, I think it's safe. This breeze feels wonderful," Lydia says, poking her head out the window.

I stick my arm out.

"What are you doing?" Lydia asks.

"Trying to get a feel for the temperature."

Lydia smiles. "What do you think the temperature is?"

"Hot."

We laugh.

"The RV's engine is getting a tad overheated," Millie says. "I'm sorry, Lydia. I just don't know what got into me with those guys." She eases the motor home off the next exit ramp, and we pull into a McDonald's parking lot.

Once we switch seats, Lydia says, "You're right. Waldo is hot. You overworked him, Millie."

Millie wisely keeps silent.

"We might as well go inside and get a bite to eat since we're here taking up space," Lydia says. "That will give Waldo a chance to cool off."

I'm guessing the RV hasn't worked this hard in years. For that matter, probably ever.

After I run to the bathroom to fix my hair, I step into the hallway just as my cell phone rings. Millie and I lock eyes. She's a foot from my phone, and she lunges for it. I rush toward it too. Not that I want to talk to Rob—if that's who it is—but neither do I want Millie to be my "mother."

"Hello?" Millie says, looking very cross.

"Give it back, Millie," I say, trying to wrestle it from her, but she twists and jerks, keeping it away from me.

"It doesn't matter who I am. You leave her alone, do you hear me? She wants nothing to do with you, you stalker! Go home to your wife and kids! If you call her again, she's going to notify the police." With that, Millie clicks off.

Lydia steps inside, looking as shocked as I feel.

"I'm sorry, DeDe, but you need help getting rid of that jerk. You're too good for him, and I refuse to let him hurt you anymore."

Something about the tenderness in Millie's voice, the way she rescued me from Rob, shatters my anger and brings tears to my eyes. Millie walks over and hugs me. "Please don't be mad at me, Dee. I was only trying to help."

"I know," I whisper. "Thanks. It's just hard."

We talk through it a moment so I can recover from the incident. Then Millie's usual self kicks back into place. "Well, let's go eat breakfast. I'm starved."

Lydia and I smile, and we all lock arms and head for the restaurant.

A few minutes later, I'm one bite into my sandwich when my heart stops as I look out the window. The Biker Boys are back, and they're headed our way.

"Oh my goodness," Lydia says with a shaky voice, "it's those—those men again." It takes three swallows before her bite of muffin goes down her throat.

"Turn your heads," Lydia says. Fear makes her voice crack. "Maybe they won't see us."

If she throws a napkin over her face, I'll be so embarrassed.

"I don't care if they do see us. I'm not backin' down," Millie says, chin jutted outward, eyes flashing.

The five men climb off their bikes and head toward the restaurant. They're old, but they've got the macho walk down; I'll give them that. Think *Mod Squad.*

"Now, Millie, don't you start anything." Lydia is practically crawling under the table.

I glance toward the bikers, and they spot us.

"Busted," I whisper, shrinking into my shirt.

They come our way. "Well, look here, guys, it's our lady friends," Ponytail Man, aka Willie, says.

"We are not your lady friends," Millie snaps.

"Whoa," one of them says. Willie looks back at them, and they all laugh. I'm thinking Millie will lift her handbag and thwack 'em a good one. Instead, she lifts it and takes out her camera, warning the men that she will use the picture to identify them to the police if she has to.

"Just leave us alone." Lydia's voice shakes, and her eyes are wide and droopy.

Willie's jaw drops. "Lydia? Lydia Thornton, is that you?" the man asks, referring to Lydia's maiden name.

Lydia squeaks, and I'm almost sure surprise has sucked the air from her lungs.

"Who are you?" Millie demands more than asks as the flash goes off right in the man's face.

Willie blinks and runs his hand along the side of his hair. I've seen that gesture before . . .

"Why, I'm Eric. Eric Melton."

At this our jaws drop simultaneously. Eric the Ego Melton. From Aspen Creek Camp. Who knew?

"Eric Melton?" I say.

He practically rocks on his heels here. His self-esteem is obviously still intact. I'm wondering if he's looked in the mirror lately.

Lydia lifts a weak smile. "Hello, um, Eric."

Millie is speechless. No doubt trying to get her adrenaline under control.

I'm just having the best morning. I've decided this trip is great after all. I'm so glad I came along.

Willie—I mean, Eric—introduces the other guys, but their names are already a blur to me. "We hang out together back home," he says. "Okay if we get our food and join you?"

I look to Lydia, hopeful. Now, Lydia's a lot of things, but rude isn't one of them. "Sure," she says, looking as though she has no idea how to handle this situation.

Eric flashes a grin and a wink to Millie, who in turn harrumphs. Such a fiftyish thing to do. Once they get their food, the boys take off their jackets and scoot a table up to our booth to settle in for a good visit. I can't believe what I'm seeing. The looks on Millie's and Lydia's faces tell me they can't believe it either. The Biker Boys are actually the Looney Tunes. That's right. Beneath their jackets they're wearing T-shirts with Looney Tunes characters. Let's see, Eric is the Tasmanian Devil (big surprise), whose friends around the table are Elmer Fudd, Porky Pig, Daffy Duck, and Yosemite Sam.

I lean into Millie and whisper, "For cartoons you almost killed us?"

She chuckles. Lydia hears me, and she laughs too.

Eric looks over at us. "Yeah, we get that reaction just about everywhere we go. We may look rough, but we're really harmless." He shrugs. "We like *The Looney Tunes*, what can we say?" The guys laugh, and we join them.

"Just goes to show you can't judge a book by its cover," I say, looking at Millie, who makes a face back at me.

"Lydia Thornton," Eric says, shaking his head. "Still as pretty as ever." He smiles, then chomps into his sausage biscuit.

Lydia blushes but says nothing.

"What's it been, thirty years?"

"Right around there," she says.

"And who could forget DeDe Veihl—well, that was your maiden name, right?"

Oh sure, let's rub it in that I'm still not married. "Still the same name," I say. Maybe he'll think I'm liberated and took it back after a failed marriage or something.

"Boy, DeDe sure kept the guys hopping at camp," he says to his buds. "Everyone tried to get her attention at one time or another."

My face feels warm, but I don't think it's a hot flash. They're probably freaking over what thirty years has done to me.

"No doubt you'll get 'em all stirred up again," Eric adds, making me feel better. He looks over at Millie. "Let's see, you and DeDe always used to get into trouble."

Millie starts to open her mouth.

"No, no, don't tell me. Let me guess." He thinks a moment. "Millipede!" he says, referring to the camp nickname for Millie. I had totally forgotten about that.

Millie's not impressed. "Millie will do," she says, as in thank you very much. "By the way, what was the big idea cutting us off in traffic?"

Somehow I knew Millie wasn't going to let this die.

"Oh, we were just having some fun." He takes a swallow of coffee.

Millie stares at him. "I expected that when you were sixteen, Eric."

"Same old Millipede," he says. "Did you join the service or anything? You know, become a marine sergeant, run a home for juvenile delinquents, work a crack house?" He winks and grins at Lydia.

Though I'm enjoying this banter immensely, I figure I'd better change the subject. "What brings you out this way?" I ask before taking a bite of my fruit.

"Oh, I figured we were headed to the same place." His eyes register disappointment as he looks at Lydia. "We're headed over to Aspen Creek."

Millie drops her fork, and Lydia spills her water.

"Oh, good grief," Lydia says, scrambling to grab all the nearby napkins and mop up the mess.

Eric takes on a studly look. "I still get you all riled, eh, Lydia?" He winks.

With our gazes fixed on him, we freeze, as in nobody moves.

He holds up his palms. "Just kidding." He nudges the guy next to him, and they laugh. "Where are you headed?"

Millie pipes up. "Well, we're going to—"

"Out west," Lydia interrupts. "We're going out west to see some old friends."

Millie and I shoot her a look. She avoids our gaze.

Eric's expression drops. "That's too bad. Aspen Creek could use your help." He explains the dire circumstances of the camp, and

I'm wondering what Lydia's planning to do. After all, this is the reason we came.

"Well, I guess we'd better get going," Lydia says abruptly. She starts to scoot out, causing all the guys to have to get up and move the table out of the way. "Nice to see you again, Eric," she says, and we're back in the motor home before Eric knows what hit him.

Once inside, Lydia's white-knuckled fingers grip the steering wheel as she stares straight ahead.

"Are you all right?" I ask.

"I'm fine." She pulls her hands to her face. "What are we going to do?"

"We're going to go to Aspen Creek and not worry about it. We have as much right to be there as he does, Lydia," Millie says. "Why didn't you tell him we were going there?"

"I don't know. It just came out that way." Lydia pulls her hands to her face for a second. "What was I thinking?" she asks, dropping her hands. "I don't know what came over me. I felt all flustered like I was sixteen again." She takes a deep breath and releases her grip from the wheel.

"It's understandable, Lydia. Seeing Eric again was sort of a blast from the past," I say.

Millie climbs into the passenger's seat. "Well, get used to it. 'Cause we're going to see a lot of him at Aspen Creek."

By the look on Lydia's face, I'm thinking Millie could have gone all day without saying that.

19

A beautiful pine forest surrounds us as we climb the mountain toward Aspen Creek Camp. Though the RV's fuel pump is fixed, it's still struggling with the climb, but come to think of it, I don't do stairs as well as I used to, either.

The Rocky Mountain National Park is a stone's throw away from the camp. As we inch upward, John Denver's voice croons the lyrics of "Rocky Mountain High" over the radio, and we all bellow along.

"I can't believe we're finally here," I say, looking at familiar sights I haven't seen in years.

"Me either," Lydia says. Silence takes over the motor home as we make our way toward Aspen Creek in awe. Up ahead two tree logs stand parallel, and one log is stretched horizontally on top of them, forming the entrance that's marked Aspen Creek Bible Camp. Millie hops out and goes to work with her camera.

Upon seeing a shady nook a short distance away, I remember Lydia and Greg carved their initials on one of those logs and got suspended from the activities one night for defacing property.

"Do you remember—"

"Don't remind me," Lydia says. "I missed out on the Nerd Dance thanks to Greg's bright idea," she says, pulling into the parking lot near the camp's office and shutting off the engine.

"Aspen Creek. It seems like we've only blinked, and now here we are all these years later," Millie says.

"Something about being at this place makes me want to pull out my bell-bottom jeans and psychedelic tees," I say.

Millie laughs. "Oh my goodness, you wore some of the craziest concoctions, DeDe."

My nose lifts in defiance. "Fashion, Millie. It's called fashion."

"Yeah, well, I think you made up your own *fashions* as you went along."

Lydia turns around and looks at us. "You know, with it being a little cooler up here in the mountains, I think we could get by opening the windows. What do you think?"

"Sounds good to me," I say.

The three of us quickly slide open the windows, and once we're finished, Lydia turns to us with a smile. "Well, are we ready to go?"

We nod, and she leads the way through the door. Gravel grinds and twigs snap beneath our shoes as we walk toward the office. My palms feel moist, and my heart is racing with the reality of where I am.

"Do you smell that?" I ask after taking a deep breath. Lydia inhales.

"What are you two doing?" Millie asks.

"Taking a whiff of our youth," I say.

"Eew," Millie says. "Don't you remember how the guys smelled after a day of hiking?"

"Thanks for the reminder, Millie," I say.

We step through the office door into a rustic setting where three desks flank the room. I smile at the young receptionist. "Hello, we're here to see—"

"DeDe, Millie, Lydia!" a voice squeals, and soon Beverly Hamilton comes running with arms outstretched. Before I can take a breath, she pulls me into a hard squeeze. "How are you?" She gives me no time to answer and moves on to hug Millie and

Lydia. "Oh my goodness, how long has it been?" She barely pauses to catch her breath. "We are going to have such fun." She releases her hug and claps her hands together. "I can hardly wait. It's so great to see you." Her jawline is all but nonexistent, and her chubby cheeks radiate a happy shade of pink while fine lines gather at the sides of her sparkling blue eyes. Still, Beverly has never looked more endearing than right at this moment.

"It's been too long," Lydia says. "Same sweet, smiling Beverly."

"And why shouldn't I smile? I'm having a good life," she says, and we all know that's not true. She lost her husband to an aneurysm three years ago, and she has to be worried about the camp. It's closed this year, and we can only hope it will open again one day. But Beverly is not one to complain. Ever. Well, all except for that time Carolyn Newfeld shorted her bedsheets. Beverly tried to get into her sheets for a good half hour before she finally gave up.

"So are there very many alumni here?" Millie asks.

A shadow flitters across Beverly's plump face. "It turns out more have had to back out than I anticipated. Work problems, health issues, family trouble." She tips her head and smiles. "But it's okay. We've received lots of donations, and we have a few people coming. Plus the Aspen Creek Community Church ladies are helping out." She shrugs. "I figure this camp is in the Lord's hands. It's up to Him if it survives or not."

"So have you heard from Tony—"

Millie cuts me off. "George, David, Ralph?" She grins, embarrassing me.

The light of remembrance comes to Beverly's eyes, then she frowns. "I'm sorry, DeDe, none of them can make it. But they sent their best wishes along with photos of their families. Let me just say things turned out for the better." She walks over to her desk.

We all laugh, but I can't deny the twinge of disappointment I feel.

Beverly walks back to us and shows us pictures of the guys. "Oh my," I say upon seeing Tony's family.

"Yeah, that's what I thought. Tony didn't strike me as the type to want twelve kids," Beverly says.

"That could have been you, Dee," Lydia says.

I feel as though I've barely escaped death.

Photos of George, Ralph, and David follow. Let me just say I'm happy in my singleness.

Just then the door shoves open behind us, and we turn to see who it is.

Beverly squeals again and scoots past us to pull the guy into her trademark bear hug. He towers over her five-foot-two-inch frame. He's dressed in chinos and a crisp, blue, freshly laundered button-down shirt that's open at the neck. His muscular arms enfold Beverly in a friendly hug, and finally she turns to us.

"You remember who this is?" she asks, eyes shining.

Millie and Lydia nod, but it's all I can do to close my mouth short of drooling.

"You don't remember me, do you, DeDe?" he asks, his keen blue eyes glistening. Gray strands work through his thick dark hair, giving it a light frost. He stares into my eyes, causing my heart to give a little leap. Okay, it leaps as though I've just been goosed.

"I'm sorry. I'm terrible with names." But how could I forget those eyes?

"I thought maybe you'd remember the nerd who took you to camp prom. You didn't care what other people said; you allowed me to take you anyway." His gaze stays glued to mine. There's a definite zip in my adrenaline here. Reality hits me like a splash of cold water, causing my jaw to drop.

"Steve Knight?" My voice cracks as I remember the night I got mad at the guys in the camp for fighting over me, so I opted to go with Steve instead. Let me just say here and now that this man in no way, shape, or form resembles the gangly, ruddy-faced kid who took me to prom.

"That's me," he says almost sheepishly.

"You've really, um, changed," I say, resisting the urge to squeeze his biceps.

"I hope that's good."

"It's good," I blurt before he can blink. My heart is banging against my chest like a woman shoving her way to a blue-light special. That's it. No more caffeine.

He shrugs. "I've been working out a little to shake that nerd image."

Oh, trust me, you've shaken it way off.

His eyes twinkle. "Anyway, it's great to see you again. And I'm glad you remember me."

"I remember." Wish I had put on my other jeans. The ones I'm wearing make my hips look too big. I tell myself not to squirm or mess with my hair. My hair! The wind has wreaked havoc with it. It's probably standing up like the crest of a cockatoo. *Don't touch it. Whatever you do, don't touch it right now.*

A smile lifts the corners of Millie's mouth ever so slightly. What's that all about?

"Well, change looks good on you," Beverly says in her happy-go-lucky voice, breaking the tension. Without any hesitation whatsoever, she claps her hands again. "Shall we tour the camp?" She turns to the door, and we follow close behind her.

Steve looks away, and my fingers quickly work through my hair, smoothing down the strays, making sure I'm not a total slob. A quick pinch of my cheeks should help with the pasty look of death too. I mean, hello, everyone wants to look their best when they see old friends, right?

Harley engines vroom outside, causing us all to look up. It's Eric Melton and his entourage. They pull into the parking lot and climb off their metal horses. Millie, Lydia, and I lock eyes. Lydia will have some explaining to do.

"Well, Beverly, how are you?" Before Beverly can answer, Eric scans the crowd and his eyes stop at Lydia. He walks over to us. "You mean my little speech was so convincing, you decided to come after all?" He exchanges a glance with his cronies and nods as if to say, "I'm da man."

"Excuse me. I believe it was *my* little speech that convinced them to come," Beverly says, grabbing Lydia's arm to pull her away. She stops a moment and looks back at Eric. "By the way, who are you?" Suspicion sparks from her eyes as she holds Lydia's arm protectively.

Eric runs the palm of his hand above his ear to smooth his hair. All five of them. Okay, ten. Tops.

Beverly's eyes grow wide. She drops her hand from Lydia's arm. "Eric Melton?"

"One and the same," he answers as big as you please. It's obvious to me that Eric doesn't mind in the least that his appearance has changed. He's comfortable in his skin. Actually, he's downright pleased with his skin. I think we'll just leave him in his delirium.

We make the necessary introductions, then Eric and the Biker Boys, er, uh, the Looney Tunes, join us on a tour of the camp.

Beverly turns around. "Oh, before I forget. I've set up a concert for us all. It's another way to generate more money. I don't know what kind of talent we have between us, but I know Eric and the boys play guitars, Steve and DeDe sing, I can play the keyboard, Millie plays the trumpet, and Lydia can provide refreshments."

Whoa, rewind. Did she say, "Millie plays the trumpet"? I'm thinking that whole memory loss thing is catching.

She smiles here. "Whatever we lack, the Aspen Creek church ladies will help by gathering up their church's talented and bringing them over to join us. They will also provide us with instruments, so I was hoping each of you could work up a number or two."

Hope sparkles in her eyes. How can we say no to that? We smile and nod.

"Great." She claps her hands and turns to lead the way through the camp. I'm still thinking she might want to reconsider Millie's trumpet number, or we might have to refund some tickets.

"Oh, look!" Lydia points toward an open meadow where a herd of elk is grazing on sagebrush and bitterbrush.

Beverly lifts a proud smile as though she has something to do with it. "They come here often. I never get used to it." Beverly turns toward the forest. "I don't know if you remember, but we have subalpine fir, aspen, and limber pines through the forests."

I never could remember all the names, but I love the smell of pine circling us with the breeze. I look back toward the elk and notice the colorful wildflowers that dot the open meadow. I think the Colorado columbine is one of my favorite wildflowers.

"Oh, look!" I say, pointing toward a red squirrel that scurries across the road in front of us. "Isn't that a pine squirrel?"

"Yes, or a chickaree," answers Millie, ever the librarian.

Watching the chickaree scamper up a tree, I remember why I loved this place as a kid.

Beverly smiles. "We have all kinds of critters around here. Let's see, the birds are Clark's nutcrackers, ruby-crowned kinglets, gray and Steller's jays. You might see a snowshoe hare and, yes, even a black bear."

Behind me, Lydia gasps. "Don't remind me."

"No need to worry, Lydia. As long as you're smart about keeping food picked up, they're not going to bother you."

Lydia doesn't look convinced.

"As you can see, we have some trees down that need to be cleared out, underbrush that needs to be removed, that sort of thing. Over there are the dorms." Beverly points in the direction of a couple of brown wooden buildings. "They are in a bad state. Leaky roofs, loose floorboards. They're too old. The church folks do what they can to volunteer their services, but, well, there's just so much work to do and so few workers. The good news is, we have updated our kitchen to meet the new state regulations, and we've added air-conditioning in the dining area," she says, looking proud. "Still, as you can see, there's plenty to do." She turns to the guys. "I sure hope you all know something about building repair."

"I'm pretty good with a paintbrush, and I've been guilty of using a hammer and a saw," Steve says with a grin.

The Biker Boys throw out their chests, nod, and grunt, assuring Beverly they know all about building repair. Eric tugs at his belt buckle, yanks his pants up, and lifts his chin. "I know about that stuff, Bev. You don't need to worry; we'll get it fixed up." He glances at Lydia and winks.

Beverly just glows with his comment. 'Course, I could be wrong. She might be working up a sweat. I mentally calculate that she should be right around her early fifties, so I'm guessing she's doing that whole hot flash thing too.

We walk through the dorms, taking in the chipped and faded paint on the walls, rusty nails and door hinges, loose floorboards, and leak stains on the ceilings. We evaluate the needed work and continue on through the cafeteria and chapel. The work appears almost daunting, but the guys insist we can do it.

I don't mean to be a downer here, but with the amount of people who have turned up to help, I have my doubts.

"What was with that Steve Knight thing?" I ask Millie once we get back to the RV.

Millie lifts her chin. "I don't know what you're talking about." She bats her eyelashes as though she's a Southern belle. And let me just say she wouldn't qualify as a Southern belle if she clanged from a steeple in Georgia.

"You know what I mean. Smiling and looking at me when Steve was talking." I pull my sweatshirt from the dresser drawer to prepare for our campfire with the others in ten minutes. I mean, if I'm interested in him, it's one thing, but I don't need Millie pushing me. After that thing with Rob, I'm not ready to rush into anything. 'Course, if I was ready, Steve would definitely have my interest.

"Excuse me. I didn't know it was a crime to smile." Millie feigns innocence while I stare at her. "Oh, come on, DeDe, no one missed the sparks flying between you two," she says matter-of-factly while applying white shoe polish to her sneakers.

My heart somersaults here. Either she's right, and I am attracted to him, or I need to see a doctor as soon as I get home.

Lydia, who just finished throwing a bag of marshmallows, chocolate bars, and graham crackers into a paper sack to take with us to the campfire, stops in her tracks at Millie's words.

"Now, you see? You're making Lydia think something that just isn't there. I don't know how many times I've told you two—I'm not interested in another relationship." *Maybe I've changed my mind, but you don't need to know that.*

"No one is saying you have to have that kind of a relationship, DeDe," Lydia says. "Just enjoy the journey. You could miss out on a good friend if you shut him out." Her cell phone rings. She steps outside to answer it while I stare after her.

Closing my mouth, I look back at Millie, who smiles and goes through the door behind Lydia.

Jerking on my sweatshirt, I reluctantly follow. My heart is telling me to give it a try, but I'm not ready to be that vulnerable again. So what if Steve's eyes crank up my blood pressure a notch and his smile, well, could melt me down to a puddle? Who cares if he could pick me up with one arm behind his back? Can I quickly forget what I've been through with Rob? My heart screams yes. My mind says no.

I wonder which one will win.

Millie snaps candid pictures of our little group as each one searches the surrounding area for pine needles and wood branches for kindling. We're soon sitting on logs and hay bales around a crackling fire that shoots tiny sparks into the night air. Millie and Lydia scoot their log a little farther from the fire than the rest of us. Lydia's eyes are red, so I'm guessing her phone call was from one of her boys and the conversation didn't go well.

Not wanting to draw attention to Lydia, I look back toward the fire. It's a good thing I have on my sweatshirt. I'm sitting close enough to the flames to singe the hair on my arms, but I don't care. I love warmth.

A slight breeze stirs through the alpine forest, causing the leaves to rustle and the pine scent to meander our way.

"Isn't this the most wonderful place in the world?" Beverly asks between bites of s'mores.

I close my eyes and breathe deeply. "It really is heavenly."

"Well, we're close enough to heaven, that's for sure," Millie says. "I'm surprised I haven't had a nosebleed yet."

"The stars are so beautiful. Greg used to tell me he would reach up and get one for me." Lydia lifts a sad smile, and suddenly things turn a bit somber.

"I was really sorry to hear about Greg, Lydia," Steve says, sitting down beside me on the log. Goose bumps crawl up my arms. The temperature must be dropping.

"Thank you for your card. It meant a lot, Steve, really."

Steve sent her a card? She never mentioned that—at least, I don't remember if she did. That was thoughtful of him. Too bad all men aren't like that. Then again, who knows what lurks beneath his manners? I mean, what drives him to do the things he does? No one would have guessed Rob's hypocrisy. Least of all me.

"So what do you do for a living, Steve?" If I ask enough questions, we'll eventually find what he's made of.

"I own a boat business in Florida."

My heart skips to my throat. "You live in Fl—Florida?"

"Yeah, why?" He pops a marshmallow in his mouth and looks at me.

"Um, I just didn't know that."

"DeDe lives in Florida," Millie offers.

Attempting an evil glare, I send it her way, but she returns a sweet smile. I have half a notion to pulverize her with a bag of marshmallows.

Steve's eyes study me, and I try not to squirm. Let me just point out that he's sitting so close to me that if he was a magnet and I was a paper clip—well, we'd be inseparable, that's all.

We discuss where we live and the fact that we're about four hours from each other. I'm not going to analyze how I feel about that right now. With his magnetism, I'm having enough trouble just staying on my side of the log.

"Do you remember Ethel Belle?" Steve asks with a laugh.

"Oh, you mean the camp warden?" Eric takes an ambitious bite of his hot dog, dropping a blob of ketchup onto his paper plate.

"That's the one," Steve says. "Boy, you girls could sure get her stirred up."

"Now, why are you looking straight at me when you say that?" I'm acting all offended here.

Steve quirks an eyebrow. "Well, let's just say you have a reputation."

"No, let's say I have a life," I correct him.

Steve lets out a hearty laugh, and something about that makes me feel warm all over. My dad laughs a lot. Probably makes me think of him.

While moonlight sprays over the camp, we talk about our camp days, the good, the bad, and the ugly. We also discuss the concert and make a rough schedule of the program. Darkness and night sounds surround us.

Lydia's gaze keeps shooting toward the forest.

"Are you all right, Lydia?" Beverly asks.

The question appears to startle Lydia. "What? Oh, I'm fine, really." Her hand reaches for her throat. "I was just wondering about, well, bears." Once again she looks toward the forest.

Eric laughs. "Oh, you don't need to worry, honey. I'll protect you." He wiggles his eyebrows, and Lydia looks as though someone has thrown cold water on her face. Eric doesn't seem to notice in the least.

"Well, bears do come up here, but I've never seen them come while we're still out here. We do have to make sure we clean the area thoroughly, though. We can't leave any trace of food, or they'll trash the place before morning, tearing up anything standing in their way of a snack," Beverly says.

"It's the same with DeDe and her chocolate. Get in her way, and she'll hurt you without blinking an eye," Millie says before throwing me another innocent smile.

Everyone laughs but me.

"Well, I don't want to be in their way," Lydia says in a small voice, her eyes still fixed on the forest.

"It's probably a good time to go to bed. We have a big day tomorrow. I'll be passing out work assignments in the morning. Plan to be at breakfast at seven thirty," Beverly says.

Millie nods.

"Oh yes. Millie has agreed to wake us with her trumpet in the morning." Beverly smiles as though she's doing us a favor.

Millie sits taller in her seat.

I groan. "Okay, tell me one more time, why did I come here?"

Everyone laughs. No, wait. Millie isn't laughing. Oh, but that's okay, because I wasn't trying to be funny. I flash a sweet smile to Millie. If looks could kill . . .

We all set to work clearing the area and go back to our places. Lydia continues to speak of bears and her fears. Eric's face pops into my mind. I'm thinking Lydia has more to worry about than bears. She has a wolf on her tail.

That's enough to scare anybody.

20

A loud, annoying sound jerks me from a deep sleep. In my fog, I reach up to thump off the alarm clock, but the noise continues. The trumpeter blares a bad version of "When the Saints Go Marching In," giving me a headache. That can only mean one thing.

Millie.

Suddenly everything becomes clear. I am stuck in an RV, at Aspen Creek Bible Camp, with two women who used to be my best friends, while a metal rooster crows outside my window. Need I mention that our windows are *open*?

Lydia yawns. "Is it that time already?"

"If, by that, you mean time to hurt Millie, the answer is yes," I growl, yanking off my covers.

A retreat to the bathroom sounds like a good idea until I can get my attitude under control. Once I've finished washing my face and combing my hair, blessed quiet fills the air.

Millie clambers into the RV and snaps open her trumpet case, putting her treasured instrument inside. She looks up and smiles as big as you please. "Guess I was loud enough. At least I got you up," she says, wearing a proud expression.

I look her square in the face. "Millie, all of Colorado is stumbling out of bed right this minute because of you."

I've always had a problem with speaking my mind, and, well, today is no exception.

"May as well get used to it, DeDe. I'm gonna be the first thing you hear every morning and the last thing you see at night." She grins savagely, sucking all the joy from the room. The woman is evil personified.

Lydia rolls her eyes. "I don't know what I'm going to do with you two."

"Give it up, Lydia. We can't be helped." For some reason, my own comment makes me sober. Am I beyond help? Does God think so? I'm the one who turned away from Him, but I hope He hasn't given up on me.

Now that the *music*—and believe me, I use the term loosely—is over, I go outside and run through my memorized Pilates routine and then head back inside.

After my shower, we all hustle around the kitchen—bumping into one another in the process—pulling together a meager breakfast of oatmeal, toast, juice, and coffee. At last, we sit down.

"It's cool that we're parked near a bird feeder," Lydia says, scooping some sugar into her cereal bowl. "I noticed Cobbler watching the birds eat. I think she enjoys it."

That sounds as exciting as waiting for a chicken to hatch.

"You want to tell us about your phone call?" Millie asks Lydia without so much as blinking.

Lydia looks at her and hesitates.

"If you'd rather not, Lydia, we understand." Did I say that? My lips betrayed me. I want to hear what happened.

"No, it's okay," Lydia says. "It was Drew. He has no intention of going back to school." She lets out a long breath and shakes her head. "He's so angry. Blames God for Greg's death."

"I'm sorry, Lydia," I say.

"There's not much you can do if his mind is made up." Millie takes a bite of toast.

"I know." Lydia cradles her coffee cup between her hands. "If only I could make him see."

"He'll wake up one day. But it won't happen overnight. Believe me, I know," I say. Lydia's hand pats my own.

"Well, at least I didn't just overlook the school notices. His girlfriend worked at the college, and she intercepted those mailings so I wouldn't know what was going on. Fortunately, they broke up later," Lydia says, now twisting a napkin in her hands.

Silence hovers between us as we search for words of comfort to help Lydia.

"Millie, I've been meaning to ask you how you got so much time off work," Lydia says, changing the subject.

"Oh, I thought you heard me tell DeDe. I've been with the library for twenty-five years, and I had accumulated four weeks' vacation. They threw a party for me before I left and gave me an additional two weeks. So I have a total of six weeks. Wasn't that nice?"

"That's really nice. Too bad they can't have the new computer system in place before you get back. Then you could miss the chaos," Lydia says, taking a drink of coffee.

Millie's face goes from pink to a color pretty much akin to milk toast.

"What's wrong?" I ask.

She waits a moment. "What if they sent me away so they could train someone else on the new computer? What if they are already making plans to replace me? What if—"

"Millie!" The sternness of Lydia's voice catches our attention. "I told you not to say 'what if.' Besides, they wouldn't do that."

Millie makes a face. "I'm not so convinced."

"Have you ever played the trumpet for them?" I ask.

"No." Millie looks confused.

"You should be safe."

She glares at me, but at least some of the tension is gone.

"Well, how about you, Miss Chocolatier? Any news on how your business is going?"

"Okay, that's just ugly," I say.

She tosses a smug smile.

"Oh, come on, Millie. The library wouldn't do that to you. They appreciate the job you've done for them over the years. There is no one more organized than you. I mean, color-coded underwear, Millie. Who does that?"

"I do," she says defensively.

"Exactly. You're the organization queen." I toss her a smile and hope she can't read on my face that I think the color-coded thing is just plain weird.

"Thanks, DeDe."

Whoa. Hold everything. Millie and I are having a bonding moment.

Lydia stands and washes out her coffee cup. "I guess we'd better get going."

"Yeah, you're right." I pull my reluctant self from the kitchen chair and make a mental note to contact Shelley later today.

❋

"Lydia, I've assigned you the task of chief cook and bottle washer," Beverly says with a huge grin. "You're such a great cook—"

"Pretty and she can cook too," Eric says with a wink. He's dressed in ripped jeans and a T-shirt that quotes Shakespeare: "Though I look old, yet I am strong and lusty." Somehow Eric doesn't strike me as the Shakespeare type.

Lydia ignores him. "That will be fine, Beverly."

"I'll take you to the kitchen when we leave here, show you where the supplies are, and help you set up. You will be providing the meals for all of us. A couple of the church ladies will help you as needed."

"Sounds good," Lydia says.

"Oh yeah, and I called the RV place to order your new window and screen. Should be here before you have to leave," Beverly says.

Millie throws me a look, but Lydia keeps her eyes on Beverly. "Thank you."

Beverly looks at her chart. "Organization is not my forte, so I was hoping, Millie, that you would oversee the work and be the manager, so to speak. I will be busy in the office, making a list of all our contacts once the camp opens again. Would you mind that job?"

Millie looks as though she's been awarded an Oscar. "I'd love it. You know how I enjoy order."

"DeDe, I thought you could help with the painting, starting in dorm one. Will that work?"

"Sure," I say. "I'm glad to do whatever." The fact that painting alone sounds very boring to me is probably better left unsaid. "Do we get chocolate breaks?" I ask, ever hopeful.

"If you'll provide the chocolate, I'll provide the breaks," Beverly answers with a giggle.

She then goes over a list of to-dos with the Biker Boys, Eric, and Steve. No one can deny it's very admirable that the Biker Boys came along to help Eric, even though they have no real ties to the camp.

"I know it looks a little overwhelming," Beverly says.

That's the understatement of the year.

"But I don't think it will be all that bad. We'll be up and running again in no time."

Someone is in denial.

"Okay, that's it." Beverly closes her notebook with a snap. "Oh, Steve?"

Dressed in jeans, a short-sleeved T-shirt the color of a mocha truffle, and a smile, he turns around.

Another heart blip here. Hey, whose heart wouldn't blip at the thought of a mocha truffle?

"I have you painting with DeDe, is that all right?"

A choke cuts off my air supply.

An ornery glint touches his eyes. "That's just fine, Beverly," he says with his eyes fixed on me.

Somebody just gulped, and I think it was me.

Beverly tells us where to pick up our supplies, and we head out of the building together, along with everyone else. I'm hoping I don't look too tacky in my work clothes. The jeans are a little scruffy and old. My dingy white T-shirt has a faded red-and-blue design on it, but these are work clothes, after all. I'm having a good hair day, though, so that's good.

"So how do you like RV life with Herb Alpert?" Steve asks as we walk together.

It takes me a minute to get what he means. "Oh, you mean Millie?"

He laughs. "She's the one."

"Have you heard Herb Alpert?"

"Yes. I have some of his old records."

And when was the last time I heard someone talk about *records*? "Okay, have you heard Millie?"

He winces. "Point taken."

I laugh. "Millie's a good friend, though I admit her trumpet playing does take some getting used to. Bottom line? Despite Millie's faults, I love her." *After all, she loves me in spite of my faults. 'Course, I don't play the trumpet.*

"One thing for sure, she takes her job seriously," Steve says.

"That she does. Millie's always worked hard. Actually to her detriment. Sort of a workaholic."

"I can relate to that," Steve says. "I suppose that's why my first wife ran off with someone else." He picks up a twig in our path, throws it, then turns to me. "That's the way it goes."

"I'm sorry, Steve."

"It's old news."

"How long ago did this happen?"

"She left around five years ago. We tried counseling a couple of times, but it didn't work. I was willing to do whatever it took to pull our marriage back together. Guess I just didn't try soon enough, though. She ran off with another guy." Pause. "Oh well, ancient history. How about you? Pretty as you are, I know you've been married, probably a couple of times?"

Hold everything. Did he just say, "Pretty as you are"? Mr. Biceps himself just said that to *me*? A vision of Rob is trying to break through here, but it's just not coming.

"No, never did."

"Just didn't find the right one?"

"Work got in the way, and then when I found someone—well, it just didn't work out."

"I'm sorry."

"Thanks."

We step inside the dorm into the first bedroom. In big black letters stretched across one wall are the words "Elaine was here." Another wall has "Melody loves Ed." Another says, "Mrs. Woodriff wears grandma underwear." I try not to laugh. Looking at the cracked paint and gouges on the walls, I can almost hear Millie, Lydia, and me giggling as we talk about boys and camp life. Visions come to mind of me painting my toenails while lounging on the bed, Millie glancing through a magazine, and Lydia staring at the class ring Greg gave her. It was a lifetime ago, and yet it was only yesterday.

"Looks as though this could use a good paint job," Steve says, surveying the room.

"Sure does." In the middle of the room stand wooden bunk beds, scarred, splintered, and faded with age. The stained, sagging mattresses have seen better days, but then, haven't we all?

"Well, I see you've found where to start," Millie's voice breaks into the room. We turn around to see her standing in the doorway; glasses perched on the tip of her nose, camera aimed at the walls, taking the "before" pictures so we can document our progress, no doubt. "First thing you need to do is sand the walls, taking off any peeled paint. Then we'll wash them down to prepare them for painting. I've got sandpaper, buckets, and rags just down the hall for you." She's so happy one would think she'd just won the Publisher's Clearing House Sweepstakes. "Any questions?"

"I think you've covered it all," Steve says good-naturedly.

"Great. I'll check on you in a little while." With that, she turns on her heels and prances off to her next assignment.

"She's enjoying this entirely too much," I say.

"You noticed that too?" Steve laughs. "Well, I guess we'd better get started before Attila—er, uh, Millie, comes back." He winks at me, and we both laugh as we head down the hallway.

"Oh, come on, Millipede," Eric says just outside the dorm building door. "Let me repair some drawers or cupboards or something. Please?"

"Eric, you are not going to work in the kitchen with Lydia, and that's final." Millie's voice snaps with every word.

Steve turns to me and raises his brows. We grab our buckets of soapy water and the sandpaper and head back to the room.

"Sounds like Millie will have her hands full with this job." I grab the sandpaper and pick a corner to start working.

"Something tells me she can handle it," Steve says with a gut laugh.

"Here's something I thought you might like while you're working," Beverly says as she enters, placing a jam box in the middle of the room and pushing a button to start an old Andrae Crouch tape.

"Wow, I haven't heard him since—"

"Camp?" Steve asks with a grin.

"Right." I smile back. "Thanks, Bev. You're the greatest," I call over my shoulder amid the scratchy sound of sandpaper against drywall.

"Let me know if you need anything." Beverly calls back, her footsteps fading down the hallway.

"So tell me about you, DeDe. What's going on in your life?"

With a pause, I turn and look into Steve's twinkling blue eyes. Everything in me says to run, but my feet just refuse to obey.

21

Lunch is over, and I still could eat a moose. Don't get me wrong. Lydia's chicken-salad sandwiches, chips, and apple slices were great—if you weigh, say, five pounds. But for adults? Think hors d'oeuvre.

And the fact that I refused seconds had nothing whatsoever to do with Steve sitting beside me. Counting the church help, there are almost twenty people in our group, after all. I didn't want to be a pig. Even I have my limits—well, except where chocolate is concerned.

After lunch, Steve and I go back to the dorm and finish preparing the walls for painting. The sanding part is done, and now we're washing the walls. I heave the bucket of warm, sudsy water up the ladder with me. My back aches a tad, and I have a feeling this is only the beginning.

The building is definitely not soundproof. Eric and his cronies are working in the bathrooms downstairs, and though the radio is on in our room, I can still hear every word the Biker Boys are saying. They obviously are unaware that their voices are carrying, because a couple of their crude comments make me blush down to my toes. As long as I keep my eyes turned toward the wall, I'm good.

"Same old Eric," Steve says, shaking his head.

"I don't remember that side of him. He was always on his best behavior around me, because I was usually with Lydia." My right arm feels shaky from scrubbing the walls. I'm praying Mr. Biceps doesn't notice that flab-under-my-arm thing. 'Course, this workout should help firm me up.

"Boy, was he mad when Greg horned in," Steve says.

"Greg sure did sweep Lydia off her feet." I dump my rag in the water, wring it out, and start washing the wall again.

"It was such a shock to hear of his death. He was a good man. It's always hard to let them go."

"Did you and Greg stay in touch through the years?" A chunk of plaster falls from the wall.

"Uh-oh, looks like we'll have to fill some places in," Steve says. "I have a couple of those myself." He points to some glaring holes, then continues to wipe his wall, the muscles in his biceps twitching and bulging. Feeling the blush creep into my cheeks, I turn away. "Yeah, Greg and I kept in touch. He was sort of my spiritual mentor through the years. He helped me a lot while I was going through the divorce."

"I didn't know you two were such good friends."

"When other kids made fun of me, Greg was always there to defend me. I'll never forget that." Steve stops wiping the wall and looks at me. "You were the same way."

I scrub the wall hard with my cloth. If Steve knew the truth about me, he wouldn't be so kind. I'm no different than the man who stole his wife.

"Is Lydia doing all right? I mean, really?"

My arm feels as if it's going to fall off. "Seems to be. She misses him, of course, but she's adjusting. The only thing that bothers me is she doesn't talk about it much. I'm guessing there's just too much pain."

"Maybe."

"What do you mean?"

"I hope it's not deeper than that," he says.

"You think she's not dealing with it?"

"Could be. We'll keep an eye on her. It's never good to allow poison like that to grow. I know all about that."

Steve and I grow quiet, each lost in our work, our thoughts. I think about how my own life has been poisoned.

My throat feels as though it will crack and break off if I swallow. Climbing down the ladder, I say, "I'm going to get a bottled water; do you want one?"

"Sure, that would be great."

Just then someone downstairs complains about being thirsty. I smile. "I guess I'd better ask the guys if they want one too."

Steve nods.

The stairs creak and groan as I step on them. It's either because they're old or because I'm—okay, no chocolate break tonight. The smell of mildew hits me once I get downstairs. My throat tickles, causing me to cough.

The Biker Boys are joking with one another when I step into the room. The scene is amusing, if I do say so myself. These big, burly guys, dressed in Looney Tune shirts (I think they have a different one for each day of the week—at least I'm hoping they're not wearing the same ones), are cleaning the toilets. Hey, it's a dirty job, but somebody has to do it. And might I add that it just does my heart good to see men doing that?

"You guys want a bottled water?" They're talking and laughing so loudly that they can't hear me. Deciding to look for Eric, I step past each stall until I come to one where Eric is sandwiched between the toilet and the stall. His back is to me. Now there's a picture. Too bad Millie isn't here. I have an overwhelming urge to shout, "Fire!" but I refrain. Edging my way closer, I bend toward him while he continues to use a rag to clean the outside of the pipe. "Eric, do you want a bottled water?"

My voice startles him, and in his attempt to turn around, he bumps against the rusted pipe, causing it to burst open and let go for all it's worth. Water shoots straight at me, soaking my face and shirt.

"Shut off the water!" he yells, trying to pull himself from his crouched position.

The Biker Boys scurry about the room. Dashing away from the vomiting pipe, I struggle to keep my dignity intact. The water soon stops gushing. The Biker Boys come over to gawk at me as though I'm some sideshow at the fair. I'm not feeling very charitable at the moment.

One of the guys stares at me. Clearly he is amused.

"Does the term *swirly* mean anything to you, big guy? You know, as in *me* dunking *your* head in the toilet bowl and flushing?" I don't care if he does resemble John Bunyan. There is enough adrenaline shooting through my veins to take him on. He knows it too. With palms up in front of him, he backs away. Slowly.

Eric's mouth lifts at the corners.

"Something funny to you, Eric?" I growl. "You want to laugh, do you?" I shake my hair like a wet dog.

"I don't have a death wish, DeDe."

Stopping, I look at him. "Smart man." With that, I turn, lift my chin, and stalk toward the stairs. They can get their own bottled water.

"What happened to you?" Millie asks when she sees me outside the dorm.

"I went for a swim. What does it look like?" I say as I tromp past her. Abruptly I turn back around. "And don't you dare take a picture!"

Millie puts her palms in front of her and backs away. "I won't.

I promise. By the way, did you happen to see my glasses in the dorm where you're painting?"

"I'm dripping wet, Millie—and freezing—have I mentioned that?"

"So is that a 'no'?"

"Grrr! Try your head!" I turn around and stomp off toward the motor home. Okay, maybe I'm being a little harsh, but I can't help myself, for crying out loud. Shoving through the door of my room, I rummage through the dresser drawer. "Why I ever agreed to this stupid trip, I'll never know. What was I thinking?" I yank a fresh shirt from the drawer.

"That you might help save the camp and enjoy being with your friends?" Lydia's standing in the doorway, her expression hopeful.

Her presence so startles me, it takes me a moment to catch my breath. "I'm sorry, Lydia."

She closes the door behind her, and I change into my dry top.

"What happened?"

First, I tell her everything. Then without warning, I start to laugh. My anger has subsided, and I realize how ridiculous the whole thing must appear to onlookers. Lydia hesitates at first, then laughs with me. "All I wanted to do was get a drink of water."

"You got your wish," Lydia says through peals of laughter.

Both of us are letting off some tension. When we finally calm down, and my clothes are changed, we head back toward the dorm. We talk about how things are going and part ways once I reach the dorm. Steve is gone. Grabbing my bucket, I climb the ladder once more, and Steve walks in.

"Where did you put my water?"

I smack my forehead with my hand and look at him. "Did you ever have one of those days?"

"So what do you do back home, DeDe?" Steve asks, steadying the paint can on his ladder.

Thick paint covers my roller, and I lift it to the walls. "I co-own a chocolate company, Le Diva Chocolates."

"Really?" He chuckles. "Somehow that doesn't surprise me."

"Why is that?" Fresh paint lifts from my roller as I push it across the faded walls. Have I mentioned that my arm feels like putty?

"Well, I remember how you loved chocolate, and you've always been a take-charge type of gal."

For a moment, I stop painting and look at him. "You think so?" For some reason that comment surprises and pleases me.

"You helped organize a few things back in the day. Of course, it was usually something that got us all into trouble."

Back to painting. "You're right. I do have a reputation." I laugh. "I need to do something different in my business."

"Oh?"

"There's a new shop down the road from us, a chocolate shop, as a matter of fact, and, well, I'm a little worried." Sopping my roller with more paint, I glance at him.

"You afraid it will hurt your business?"

I shrug. "You never know."

"How are the shops different?" His strong arm pulls his roller across the wall, and I struggle not to stare.

"We both offer gourmet chocolates, though Shelley—my co-partner—says ours are better. The other shop owner offers coffee too."

"Why don't you expand in some way? Offer a different twist."

While my paint roller rubs the wall, I think about that. My

234

thoughts flit to the dessert bar we stopped at on our way to the camp. "I suppose I could offer a dessert bar or something."

"Now you're talking. Always improving, keeping up with the times; that makes all the difference." He steps off his ladder and pours more paint into his pan. "It's a challenge, that's for sure. I'm always looking for ways to set my business apart from the competition." He lifts his pan and glances at me. "Hey, you could offer a free giveaway once a month. Something that would keep customers coming in to sign up." He climbs the ladder again.

"That's a great idea!" My mind is already clicking. Creating chocolate boxes and baskets for special events is such fun. They are such a huge hit. Smaller ones could be made for giveaways. "Thanks for your help, Steve." I'm so excited, I can hardly wait to get back and call Shelley.

"You're welcome. We businesspeople have to stick together," he says with a wink.

Something about this whole conversation makes me feel better. I'm thinking it has to do with more than just his suggestions. I'm enjoying working alongside Steve. Lydia was right. Why should I miss out on a good friendship? I think that's what we have here. A nice friendship.

*

We're all a little quiet as we gather around the crackling fire tonight. Everyone has worked hard today. Steve comes over carrying a hot dog and chips on a paper plate and sits on the bale of hay beside me. Before I have time to feel uncomfortable, he bows his head to pray over his food. It takes a strong man to be a man of faith in this world. *What a rare find.* Why would a woman leave a guy like this?

"Did you get in touch with Shelley today?" Steve interrupts my thoughts.

"Oh, uh, no. She was out. I'll call her in the morning."

"Speaking of the morning, rumor has it that tomorrow is your birthday," he teases before taking a bite of hot dog.

"I don't do birthdays anymore."

"Fifty, huh?" He grins.

"Yeah."

"You'll get used to the idea. It took some time for me too."

I stare at him, wondering how this could be the same kid I knew in camp. I remember Steve being very sweet back then, but let's face it, he was a nerd. High-water polyester pants, dark glasses—I just can't believe this is him. He turns and catches me staring at him.

"What? Is there something in my teeth?" he asks.

I laugh. "You're clear. I was just thinking how different you are."

He laughs out loud, causing the others to glance at us a moment before going back to their own discussions. "When Dad died, Mom remarried. My dad was a science geek. Loved him fiercely, but, well, he was too busy experimenting to worry about style and fashions. That's all I had ever known. My stepdad helped me with those things. Changed my life, really. My ex-wife helped me too. She wouldn't put up with the old me at all."

I nod and move a couple of pretzels around on my plate. "So did you drive straight here or fly?"

"I drove my motor home."

My head jerks around to him. "You have a motor home?" What is it with people and these motor homes?

"Yeah." He looks proud. "I just bought it a month ago and figured this would be a good time to try it out. I'm just a couple of homes over from you. There's your motor home, then two homes that belong to the camp for workers, and then mine."

"That big fancy one?"

He laughs. "That's the one."

"Wow, that looks really nice." Talk about a big motor home!

"Would you like to see it?"

"Well, I—sure. I'll ask Millie and Lydia if they would like to come along." Twinkling eyes again. If he keeps this up, I'm going to put him at the top of my Christmas tree.

After dinner, Millie and Lydia come along, and we follow Steve to his motor home. Eric sees Lydia leaving, so he promptly plants himself in the entourage. I don't see chemistry between the two, but Lydia seems comfortable with his friendship.

We step into Steve's motor home, and my breath lingers somewhere between my chest and my throat. We all gather inside on the ceramic tile and stop short of the plush white carpet.

"Nuh-uh. This is *so* not a motor home," I say. "No offense, Lydia."

"None taken."

Steve laughs. "Yeah, it is. Just don't call it a *camper*. We tend to frown on that."

"This is unbelievable," I say, slipping off my sneakers at the door. Those behind me do the same.

"You don't need to do that," Steve insists.

"Oh, yes, we do. This is absolutely marvelous." Taking in the spacious slide-out units, I can hardly believe how roomy everything appears. The posh white-leather seats in the driver's area momentarily make me want to take a ride. The thick carpet squishes between my toes as I step over to sink into the passenger's seat. I swivel back and forth like a kid in a barber chair. The living room consists of a soft, velvety sofa in white and blue-gray tones and a white recliner on the opposite side of the room. Ample windows are at every turn, giving a gracious view of the subalpine forest surrounding us. A large flat-screen TV is perched near the ceiling just before the driver's station, for viewing from the living room.

The kitchen area is just beyond the living room. Fine sturdy oak cabinets grace the kitchen area, along with a fashionable table and chairs. Ceramic tile surrounds the area in front of the sink and cabinetry. The bathroom boasts a shower with glass doors, a large tub, ceramic tile, and all the conveniences of home. Now, for this, I could pass up a Hilton.

As we step into the bedroom, we see a queen-size bed, hidden washer and dryer, and another large flat-screen TV in one corner, along with a full wall of mirrored closets with ample room for clothing and such.

"If I hadn't seen it, I never would have believed it," I say, smiling.

Steve seems pleased with our reactions. "Thanks. It's just stuff, though. I try not to get too attached."

I stare at him. How can he say that? This is fabulous. "I'm actually surprised you don't have a houseboat," I say, teasing.

"I do." He almost looks embarrassed.

Gulp here. Millie nudges me, though I'm not sure why.

"But I can't travel everywhere by boat. I needed something to take me places inland."

"A land yacht," Millie says, nodding.

We look at her.

"Remember, that's what they call the nicer places like this one, a land yacht."

"I don't know that I would call it a land yacht, but that's nice," Steve says.

"How do you have time to travel when you own a boating business?" I ask.

"I've had it for thirty years. Built up a modest business, and my son helps me run it."

"Your son?" For some reason it surprises me that he has children.

"Yeah. My wife and I have one son. Aaron is twenty-five, and we're close. I was thrilled he wanted to help me with the business. I'm grooming him to take it over one day."

"Well, obviously you've done well for yourself," I say, looking around.

"You know, it is nice, and I'm thankful for it, but honestly I used to own a clunker motor home, and I can tell you, one is just as good as another as long as it's home. You know, traveling and sharing the beautiful sights of the United States with the people you care about." His gaze holds my heart perfectly still.

Someone coughs, breaking the spell of whatever that was. We all visit awhile in Steve's home and finally call it a night. Energized by the evening, Millie, Lydia, and I head back to our home away from home.

"Well, this is it, DeDe," Millie says. "Your last fling with youth. Tomorrow you'll be old like the rest of us."

"You just had to remind me, didn't you?" I step on a pebble and resist the urge to grind it to powder.

"That's what friends are for," Millie says, her eyebrows shifting up and down for emphasis.

Lydia locks her arm through mine. "Fifty is good, DeDe. You'll see."

"Tomorrow I qualify for issues of the AARP magazine, Lydia. What's good about that?"

She thinks a moment. "Well, you don't qualify for the senior-citizen discount yet."

Okay, she's got a point. I'm good.

By the time we step inside Lydia's RV, I'm feeling a little better. And let me just say here that I'm not buying that whole one-motor-home-is-as-good-as-another thing.

22

*The next morning the smell of chocolate tickles my nose, caus-*ing my eyes to flutter open. Who can sleep with chocolate lurking about? Millie and Lydia walk in, wearing smiles and singing "Happy Birthday to You." Lydia is carrying a chocolate cake complete with burning candles. And can I just add that if we're not careful, we could start a forest fire. I scoot myself up in bed and attempt to straighten my hair.

They sing "Happy Birthday," inserting "Happy fiftieth birthday, dear DeDe." Millie sings the "fiftieth" part very loudly, and I've never seen such a huge smile on her face. She's enjoying this birthday more than I am, doggone her.

"Chocolate cake for breakfast?" Okay, I'll take the good with the bad.

"It's your fiftieth birthday. You deserve it," Lydia says, leaning the cake toward me.

"No Pilates today?" I ask, hopeful.

"None."

"True friends. Though you could have gone all day without reminding me that I'm fifty."

Millie snaps a picture. So much for that true friends business.

"Oh, Millie, not now. I'm a mess."

"Trust me, you look great. And so much better than you will ten years from now."

241

"Oh, that helps. You really should go into counseling."

Millie's nose hikes. "Because it's your birthday, I've resolved not to argue with you today."

"Now, Millie, I ask you, what kind of birthday is that?" I wink at her, and she grins.

"Boring?" Millie says candidly.

"Exactly."

"Hurry up. You'd better make a wish before the candles melt." Lydia still acts as if we're kids.

"Or burn up your RV—is that what you're thinking?" I ask.

"That does come to mind," Millie says.

"What in the world can I wish for? I have everything I want. I'm surrounded by my best friends at our summer youth camp in a beautiful setting." I have to say Steve's motor home has changed my outlook on the RV life. And just for the record, this change in my outlook has nothing whatsoever to do with his biceps.

"Quick. Call 911. She's delirious," Millie says.

"Ha-ha." Closing my eyes, I make a wish that I'll have many more birthdays to celebrate with my good friends.

Sucking in a deep breath, I blow it out for all I'm worth, extinguishing the flame of every candle and practically stripping the sheets off the bed.

Millie and Lydia clap.

"Thanks, you guys."

Lydia smiles. "You know, DeDe, now that you're fifty, you should try something you've never done before." She thinks for a moment. "Like driving an RV or something."

"And why would I want to do that?"

"No kidding. You think she could handle this thing? Remember, DeDe almost flunked out of driver's ed," Millie so graciously reminds us.

"How was I to know that old woman was going to step off the

curb?" I say in my defense. "Besides, I didn't hit her. That should count for something."

We laugh, but I have to admit I'm a little miffed that Millie brought that up. Besides, I could drive a motor home if I wanted to. I just don't want to.

Millie sits down on my bed. "Do you know you slept right through 'When the Saints Go Marching In' this morning?"

How is that possible? Millie's playing could blast the snow off Longs Peak. "Wow. I must have been tired."

"Listen, DeDe, I know we like to banter and all, but, well, I just want you to know, I'm so thankful—"

Boy, this is serious. Millie must think fifty is synonymous with death. She rarely expresses herself this way. We used to call her Spock. After I glance to make sure her ears aren't pointy, I put my hand on hers. "I know. I feel the same way."

She brightens. "Thanks." She stands, and I start to get up.

"No, no. You have to stay in bed. We're serving you cake and coffee in bed."

My eyebrow lifts. "Who am I to argue?" I settle back in and smile, plumping the covers around me. "Just be warned, I could get used to this."

"Well, don't. It won't last. Cinderella's coach will turn into an RV at midnight tonight," Millie says.

I groan. "Thanks for the reality check."

"I'll go cut your cake," Lydia calls over her shoulder. "I'm sorry to say we're almost out of milk, so you'll only get half a glass until we get to the store."

Every birthday has its glitches.

Lydia and Millie spoil me through breakfast—and let me just say you haven't lived until you've had chocolate cake and icing for breakfast—and we're soon reporting for duty.

Everyone wishes me happy birthday as I make my way to the dorm. Steve and I have finished the first bedroom, and now we've moved on to the next one. We're already at the painting stage in the second bedroom.

When I step inside, my eyes immediately are drawn to the far wall and to the outline of a bright red butterfly with the words "DeDe's New Beginnings" beneath it.

I stare at it, then turn to Steve. "Did you do this?"

"I'm not much of an artist, but the butterfly represents a new beginning. Remember one of our camp verses, 2 Corinthians 5:17: 'If any man be in Christ, he is a new creature: old things are passed away; behold, all things are become new'? It seems to fit our birthdays these days."

"I—"

"This is a new season of your life. You're not getting older, remember; you're getting better." He winks.

Warmth shoots through me.

He walks over to the wall and points to the wings. "I've given you the wings to fly, DeDe Veihl." He turns to me and lifts a wide grin. "So fly."

Without warning, tears spring to my eyes.

He walks over to me, puts his hand on my shoulder, and looks me in the eyes. "I'm sorry, Dee. Did I upset you?"

"No, no. That's just really sweet." He's standing so close to me, I feel a little unsettled. The scent of soap and pine fills the space between us. My shoulder warms to his gentle touch. A tear slips down my cheek, and I look back at him. "Thank you."

His finger reaches up and tenderly lifts the tear from my face. "The best is yet to come, DeDe." Something in the way he says that makes me think he just might be right.

"Well, I'd better hurry up," I say, pulling my gaze from him.

He nods.

An hour goes by, and I reluctantly paint over the butterfly, but the memory of it burns in my heart. Things seem to be changing for me. My friends gave me love and chocolate cake. Steve has given me hope.

When we break for lunch, I head back to the RV to grab some pain reliever. No doubt that cake for breakfast gave me the headache. Oh well, it was worth it. As I approach the motor home, I see a bird on our bird feeder. But the weird thing is, the bird seems to be chirping toward our bedroom window. I stop in my tracks to listen. When his birdsong stops, I hear another tune, but it's coming from inside the motor home. It's Cobbler!

Stepping inside, I tiptoe back to the bedroom and listen as Cobbler continues to "talk" to her new friend. When I poke my head around the corner, the mountain bird sees me and flies away. Cobbler flutters around in her cage, clearly agitated that I've broken up the little rendezvous.

"Well, well, I'm thinking Barney has some serious competition." Once I take some pain reliever, I start to head back out when my cell phone rings. For a moment, I expect it to be Rob wishing me happy birthday. It's Shelley instead, and I'm surprised to find that I don't feel the slightest bit of disappointment.

"Hi, Shelley."

"Happy birthday."

"Thanks."

"I was hoping I'd catch you. I've been trying to call you, but evidently you're out of range."

"Yeah, it's on again, off again up here in the mountains. Depends on where I'm standing at the time. So what's up?"

"Well, you remember that property we had our hearts set on awhile back that the owners decided not to sell?"

"Yeah."

"They've changed their minds."

"You're kidding."

"No. They called me a little while ago."

Is this where that whole spread-your-wings thing comes in?

"Are you still there?"

"I'm here."

"Well, what do you think? Are you interested?"

"I love the property location, but now that we have competition, I'm wondering if we'll have the business to pay for it."

"I think the fact we'll be on a busier street will help us, DeDe."

I share with her what I talked about with Steve and the ideas for a dessert bar and a monthly giveaway. The longer we talk, the more excited we get.

"Tell you what, let me talk it over with Steve, and I'll call you back tonight."

"Talk it over with Steve? Steve, the guy you just told me you reconnected with after all these years? This sounds serious."

"No, no, it's nothing like that. He's just really smart when it comes to business. I'm telling you, Shelley, you should see his motor home."

"Motor home? You've seen a motor home you actually like?"

"I know! Can you believe it?"

"No. What's going on with you, girl? I think this trip is changing you."

The verse Steve quoted about being a new creation comes to mind.

"Maybe it is."

"Well, I'd better go. Things are getting busy here, Dee. I'll look forward to your call tonight. We'd better get on it if we decide we're interested. That property won't last long."

"Okay. Thanks, Shelley. Talk to you soon."

"Have a great birthday, girl!"

We hang up, and I can't help feeling this day is more than just a milestone in my life. It's a turning point.

While everyone eats lunch in the cafeteria, I sneak back to the RV. Millie's comments have bothered me all morning. I'm not one to cower in the face of a challenge, and doggone her, she's put one out there that I just can't ignore.

With one glance out the window to make sure no one is out and about, I dig in the kitchen drawer for Lydia's keys. I probably shouldn't do this, but I don't think Lydia will mind. I'll just run into town, pick up a gallon of milk so I can prove I took the RV for a spin, and then come back. That will show Madame Librarian a thing or two! Just because I'm fifty doesn't mean I'm not up to the challenge.

After unhooking everything as Lydia has taught us, I settle into the driver's seat, put the key into the ignition, and slowly drive down the path, being careful to avoid trees and buildings along the way. Something tells me Lydia would prefer that. With everyone still in the cafeteria, it's a cinch to edge out of the campgrounds. Now I have to drive a little ways down the mountain, and the fact that I can see the wide expanse of trees and boulders over the cliffs does little to encourage me. Panic rides on the fringes of my mind, but so does Millie's voice. It's that voice that pushes me forward. And just in case anyone wants to know, if I die here, it's Millie's fault.

Confidence sets in once I get about halfway down the mountain. As a matter of fact, I'm feeling like I'm king of the road. Get out of my way, I'm coming through. Yeehaw!

Though I'm directionally challenged, the town is nearby, so there shouldn't be a problem. 'Course, with me, you never know.

Waldo and I are bonding. Wait. Did I just call him "Waldo"? Okay, that's a little freaky. Still, I can't deny the seat feels pretty good, the RV is keeping its groans to a minimum, and I am in control. Turning the radio knob, I stumble upon "Respect" by Aretha Franklin and start singing with her at the top of my lungs, "R-E-S-P-E-C-T"—I mumble the rest because I never did learn the words. Still, I'm thinking Waldo and I could conquer anything today.

Seeing a wide-open space available up near the store doors, I carefully pull into a free spot. "How lucky is that?" I say, giving Waldo a playful tap on the dashboard. Once Waldo is parked, I get out and notice that he's straddling two parking places. Still, I didn't hit anyone, so that's a good sign.

There's a spring in my step as I go into the store, pick up the gallon of milk, and climb back into the motor home. This has been such a quick trip, no one will even know I've left. Yes sirree, I'm feeling mighty fine.

Starting the engine, I put the gear into reverse. Easing up on the brake, I start to back out when a knock on my driver's window stops me and nearly gives me a heart attack. There stands a uniformed policeman. Goodness, what could he want?

Rolling down the window, I look at him and offer my best fifty-year-old birthday smile. "Yes?"

A not-so-pleasant expression looks back at me. "Ma'am, are you aware you're parked in a handicapped zone?"

Gulp. I look in front of Waldo, and sure enough, there's a post with the little handicapped emblem. "Well, how do you like that? They sneaked that one in on me while I was doing my shopping," I say with a chuckle.

"I need to see your driver's license," he says in his most professional police voice.

"Oh, sure." What's the big deal? I didn't mean to park in a handicapped space. I'm normally very careful about all that, but I was so concerned about parking Waldo, I just didn't notice. Oh well, this little matter shouldn't take long to clear up. At least, I hope not, or the group will start to wonder where I am, then they'll notice Waldo is gone, and—

"Do you realize your license is expired?"

An icky taste starts to crawl up my throat. "What? Listen, Officer, I'm sure we can fix this little matter. You see, today is my birthday—"

"Are you suggesting a bribe, ma'am?"

Okay, now he's scaring me.

"No, no, of course not." My voice sounds weak and old. Definitely old.

"Let me see your registration." His frown deepens, and his voice does not sound neighborly at all.

This little outing isn't going at all the way I had planned. "Registration?" My voice cracks like a brittle leaf.

"Ma'am, do you have a hearing problem?"

Another gulp here. Reaching above the visor, I pray that Lydia's registration is there. It is. With a triumphant smile, I hand it to the officer.

The expression on his face makes me nervous. "This is not your motor home?" His question slices through my birthday self. He looks cross. As if he might have to call my dad.

Quickly I explain everything to him, about this being Lydia's vehicle, about our trip, and about our efforts to save our camp—hey, it doesn't hurt for him to see my charitable side.

"Unfortunately, I can't check out your story since the computer in my car is on the blitz, so you'll need to come with me to the station."

"To the station? The police station? Where criminals are hauled off in handcuffs?" My voice is a near shriek, but I just can't help it.

"That's the one," he says with nary a smile. "Park your RV over there," he says, pointing, "and I'll take you down to the station."

I consider making a break for it, but let's get real. Waldo just couldn't handle it. "Am I under arrest?"

"Not yet." He follows me in his car while I park Waldo away from the handicapped zone. Once I stumble out, the officer opens the door of his car for me to get inside. In the back. Like a criminal. I wonder if it would help if I pointed out that he's stripping the joy right out of my birthday self?

After some time at the station, Steve brings Lydia and Millie down, and we get the matter cleared up. And let me just say it makes me downright mad when Millie takes a picture of me with the police officer.

"Well, I'll say one thing for you, DeDe, when you set out to try something different, you do it with gusto," Millie says with a laugh on the way back to pick up Waldo.

"Don't start with me, Millie. I'm not in the mood."

Not another word is uttered all the way back to the camp. So much for my birthday. I hope this is not an indication of my life in the old lane . . .

Millie and Lydia go on ahead to the campfire gathering while I change from my paint clothes. Everything in me balks at going tonight. By now everyone knows about my little incident today. I'm sure I've been the object of all kinds of jokes. Steve pictured me as a butterfly. Instead, I'm a jailbird. Well, it's not the first time I've had a little trouble, and it certainly won't be the last. With stubborn determination, I pull on my jacket and yank the RV door shut before I lose my resolve to join the others.

The air smells woodsy and tart from the burning branches. I see everyone sitting around the circle, drenched in firelight, laughing, eating together, but when I step into view, everything grows quiet. Okay, that makes me feel stupid.

"Hey, there's the birthday girl," Steve calls out. Everyone starts to clap.

That's not exactly what I had expected. All right, I can do this. "I'm surprised you all aren't wearing black," I say, laughing.

"We thought about wearing handcuffs," Eric says.

"You've probably had plenty of experience with that, haven't you, Eric?" I snap.

"Whoa," the Biker Boys say in unison with a laugh.

"Here, Dee, why don't you come over and get something to eat," Beverly says, throwing a look at Eric. He laughs.

"Next thing we know they'll have your mug shot up at the county library," Eric continues.

"Speaking of which, who did yours last time, Eric? Maybe I can use the same photographer."

"Just ignore him, DeDe," Lydia says with a nervous laugh.

"Come on, DeDe, it's all in good fun. You have to admit what happened today was pretty funny," Eric says.

Blowing out a sigh, I feel a slight smile playing on my lips.

"See there, that's better." Eric lets out a gut laugh. "I mean, it was such a DeDe thing to do! Only you could start out on such an innocent adventure and end up in jail."

Chuckles softly ripple around the group, and once I grin, everyone cuts loose, and pretty soon I'm surrounded by DeDe stories.

"Oh my goodness, do you remember the time you got us thrown out of the sock hop because you snuck in a forbidden record?" Lydia says.

"That was George—whatever his last name was—it was his fault, because he gave it to me for my birthday as a joke, and I didn't know what it was!" Kids can be so cruel.

"Yeah, but what about the time you put a worm in Bob's soda and told him it was tequila!" Millie pipes up.

"Did I do that?"

Everyone in the group who was at camp when we were teenagers nods.

"So I have a reputation."

"I'll say," Eric says. "Doesn't seem to have changed all that much. You're still getting into trouble."

My gaze darts over to Steve, and I wonder what he's thinking of all this. He smiles and winks. I'm feeling better.

"I won't even tell you how she broke into Lydia's RV on our way here," Millie says. And then of course she follows up by telling them how I fell headfirst into the motor home through Lydia's window.

"Oh, by the way, Shelley sent something for you," Lydia says, pulling a box from behind her. True to her peacemaker self, she's trying to change the subject for me. She hands me Shelley's package.

"Truffles!" I scream.

"She said something about it not being safe for anyone if you're without your chocolate," Millie adds.

"Oh, that's cute," I say. "Real cute."

"She sent enough for everyone," Lydia says, pulling out another box of twelve.

"Actually, she sent one for all of us, two boxes for you. Now that's a good friend," Beverly says.

"She's the best." I look up at Millie and Lydia. "Next to you guys, of course."

"We all have a little something for you too, DeDe," Beverly says, bringing out a chocolate cake with candles.

Millie, Lydia, and I lock eyes.

"We didn't plan the party, honest," Lydia says, crossing her heart with her finger. "It was all Beverly's idea."

Beverly smiles as big as you please. "And why not? This is a special occasion."

No point in fighting it. Besides, I never argue over chocolate cake—unless it's for a bigger piece.

The group sings to me, and it's very nice—well, okay, there are a couple of people singing off-key, putting me in mind of *The Gong Show*—but still, it's nice. I make a wish and blow out the candles, and everyone laughs.

"I'll cut the cake while you open your presents," Beverly says, walking away with the cake. I'm wondering if I can trust her with that.

Looking to my friends' smiling faces, I'm warmed by their generosity. "How did you have time to get anything?" I ask, totally confused.

"Well, you made it easy on us. We went shopping in Estes Park while you were in jail," Millie says. Then she snaps more pictures. The woman should join the paparazzi.

"While I languished in a dirty cell, you were out shopping?" Do my ears deceive me? "I wondered what took you so long to get there."

"Kind of you to help us out that way," Millie says with an ornery smile.

Lydia hands me a package. When I open it, I find a Pilates CD with a note of apology for making all the desserts during our trip.

"Guess it's my turn," Millie says, handing me a gift. I pull off the wrap and uncover a book titled *The Joys of Turning Fifty*. I can't help noticing it's a thin book.

"Thank you, Lydia, Millie."

Eric acts almost bashful as he walks over to me and hands me his package. "It's from me and the boys," he says, pointing to the Biker Boys.

"Thanks, guys." Inside the box is a Looney Tunes shirt with Tweety Bird on the front. I laugh. "Does this make me an official member of your Looney Tunes group?"

"It does," Eric and the boys agree.

"All I need now is a Harley."

A shadow crosses Lydia's face.

"Don't worry, Lydia. That's not going to happen anytime soon."
She relaxes.

"Aw, come on, Lydia, they're not so bad," Eric says.

Everyone laughs. Lydia ignores him.

"It sure doesn't seem right without your parents here, Beverly,"
Lydia says, referring to Mr. and Mrs. Vandenplas, who used to run
the camp when we were kids.

"Yeah, I miss 'em. Especially now that Will's gone."

"It amazes me that you shoulder the responsibility of this
place," I say.

"It's not as much fun as it used to be. After living around this
camp most of my life, I'm itching to get out and see the country,"
Beverly says.

"Really?" Lydia looks at her curiously.

Beverly shrugs. "Not that I have a chance of doing that. "Oh
well, I'm happy to have a job—at least, I think I do." She smiles
bravely.

"We'll see that you do, Beverly," Steve says. "Or die trying."

Excuse me? Do I want to go that far? I'd rather take Beverly
home with me and plunk her in my chocolate shop.

"I would think this job would be heaven," Millie says. "Summer
camps in-season and off-season, the only intruders being nature's
creatures." Millie looks dreamy.

"Yeah, as in bears," Lydia says.

"What's a bear here or there? I could read all the books I
wanted."

"As with any job, it has its good and bad points," Beverly says.
She passes out the instruments from the church folks as Eric and
his guys begin to play their acoustical guitars around the fire, and
we sing some songs together. Steve's rich tenor voice envelops me
like a cloud.

And then we do the ultimate camp thing. We sing "Kumbaya"
around the campfire. Millie offers to go get her trumpet, but

everyone quickly mumbles something about the fact that we have an early day tomorrow and need to get to bed. Something rustles in the trees, and the guys run to investigate but find nothing. I wonder if someone threw a rock so they could avert Millie's attention. Lydia's still worried about the woods and the fluttering leaves, so she makes it back to Waldo in record speed.

Steve walks me back to the RV, and we discuss the new business property idea. I decide to call Shelley before going inside. I hate to make snap decisions, but we thought long and hard about the property before when we made an offer on it. Unfortunately, we had to give it all up when the owners had a death in the family and decided to stay awhile longer. This time it looks as though we might have a chance. Shelley and I talk about the price we're willing to offer and decide she will send a copy of the Offer to Purchase via fax to Beverly's office. The whole thing gets us excited. If it falls through this time, we'll give up the idea of moving and make the best of our current business location.

Clicking off my phone, I stand just before the RV door and linger beneath a star-studded sky. A day filled with friends and truffles. It doesn't get any better than that.

I step inside to find balloons and crepe paper hanging from every nook and cranny of the ceiling. In big red letters, "Happy Birthday, DeDe" sprawls across our kitchen cabinets.

"Oh dear. I'm sorry, Millie. This is quite a mess," I say, though I can't hide the fact that it thrills me that my friends went to all this trouble.

"What are you sorry about? It was Millie's idea," Lydia says with a laugh.

"It was?" I'm truly shocked. Reaching over, I give both of the girls a hug.

"Just so you know, though, everyone had a part in it, so who knows what you'll find," Millie warns.

"I don't like the sound of that," I say, feeling a little nervous.

Millie shrugs.

"Shall we take everything down?" I ask.

"Leave it up 'til tomorrow," Millie says, surprising me.

We each get ready to turn in, and after no major disaster befalls us, I pull off the covers to slip between the sheets but pause to whisper a "thank you" heavenward. Afterward, I climb into the bed, and it suddenly occurs to me that my feet are stuck midway.

Somebody has short-sheeted my bed.

23

Millie's horn-blowing rouses me from sleep the next morning, and I'm ready to tell her to put a cork in it. I mean, she's experimenting with her notes this morning, and that's just wrong. Something else is bothering me, though. I'm hot. Really hot. From the neck up.

I rush out of bed and go to the bathroom. My face is red. Think match head. I'm sweating. I rip off my top and throw cold water on my face as fast as I can. Fifty years and one day old, and I'm experiencing my first hot flash.

Before I can work up a good hormonal fit, I hear a big commotion in the living room. Millie is near hysterics. Quickly shrugging my top back on, I step out of the bathroom. "What is it, Millie?"

Lydia joins us, and we both stare at Millie, who, by the way, has all the color of a white gourd.

"Three elk came out of the woods and were coming straight at me," she answers between short breaths. Carefully she peeks out the window blinds. "They're still milling around out there."

"Do you think they meant you harm?" Lydia asks, hand touching her throat.

"Well, they didn't come to talk about life in the Rockies, I can tell you that." She peeks out again.

"How curious. Usually animals stay away from noise out of

fear. What were you doing when they came into view? Did you have food out there?" Lydia asks.

"No, I was play—wait!" Millie says, snapping her fingers.

"What is it?" Lydia wants to know.

"I was playing my horn. You know what that means?" Her eyes are wide.

"The noise was getting on their nerves too?" Millie glares at me, and I shrug.

"What?" Lydia asks.

"I'll bet they thought I was a male."

"Really? Your horn doesn't sound like that," Lydia says.

"Sound like what?" I'm totally clueless here.

"Well, I don't know how else to explain it. Stranger things have happened." Millie glances out the window again.

"Stranger things than what?" Everyone is ignoring me.

"Oh my goodness, that's hilarious," Lydia says, laughing.

Millie's laughing with her, and I'm still clueless. I mean, Millie's not model material, mind you, but she hardly passes for a bull.

Millie glances at me. "If you'd visit your local library once in a while, Dee, you might learn something." Her chipmunk laugh is back, and I'm worried about Chip and Dale's extended family showing up.

They continue laughing, and I'm feeling a little out of the loop. Opening the bread wrapper, I plunk a slice into the toaster. Irritated, I turn to them. "Okay, fill me in."

"The female elk are drawn to males by their bugle, or mating call." Lydia's words are splattered with giggles.

Now my jaw drops, and I look at Millie. "You're bugling the elk mating call?" Did I not say her playing is weird?

"Well, not on purpose. But God's creatures know good music when they hear it," Millie says.

"You sound like a bull, Millie. You have an elk following, and you're okay with this?" I ask.

Millie lifts a smug face.

"Okay, I can see the advantage of that." I form a phone receiver with my hand and bring it to my ear. "Hello? Carnegie Hall? My name is Millie Carter, and I thought you'd like to know that I can mimic the bull elk's mating call on my trumpet.' 'Why, Ms. Carter, how fabulous! When can we schedule you for an event?'" Lydia and I bust up with laughter.

"Oh, why do I bother," Millie says, brushing me away with her hand. Briefly she peeks out the window once again. "They're gone." She turns and breathes a sigh of relief. "They were big."

"You'd better get out of that brown," I say, pointing to her blouse. "It makes you look, well, sort of elkish." I laugh. "And just for the record, if you start growing antlers, I'm outta here."

Millie makes a face. I giggle.

Just in case the elk are still hoping to get a glimpse of Millie, I decide to skip my Pilates routine this morning. Instead, I head for the shower. "Only you, Millie. Only you."

"What, can I help it if I have the magic touch?"

This woman is definitely in denial.

Later in the morning we gather on the wooden pews in the white clapboard chapel, and the Aspen Creek Community Church ladies lead our little gathering in a worship service. Though some of the men have helped us, the women have been unable to help us up to now, and this is their way of getting acquainted before they "rub elbows" (their words) with us next week.

These older women could charm the antlers off a bull. Think Proverbs 31 woman times five. There ought to be a law against it, but there you are.

They lead us through choruses in the dog-eared pages of faded music books sitting in the pews, give a few announcements about the area, and take an offering. To my surprise, when it's time for the morning message, Steve Knight steps up to the front.

He talks about, of all things, starting over. Brings up that same verse in 2 Corinthians and shares with us how God makes everything new in our lives when we turn everything over to Him. Our circumstances may not change, but God helps us to see things through different eyes. The things we used to care about don't matter as much, and things we didn't care about before suddenly become important.

"A personal relationship with a living God makes all the difference," he says. And I believe with my whole heart that he means it.

Steve looks so alive, content, happy. I had that kind of relationship with God when I was younger. I've been praying, but I can't deny something still gets in the way. I think it's guilt.

The message is soon over, and we go our separate ways to eat lunch so Lydia can have Sunday off.

"Hey, how about we all go into Estes Park to eat lunch?" Eric says, walking up behind us.

Lydia looks as though she's about to say no, but Eric cuts her off.

"Come on, Lydia, just as friends."

"My motor home is all hooked up; I don't want to drive anywhere," she says.

" 'Course not. We'll take you women on our bikes."

Her eyebrows shoot up and quiver beneath her bangs.

"Come on, Lydia, this might be fun," Millie says, sounding every inch the biker woman. "Besides, after we shopped for DeDe's birthday, you said you wanted to go back into Estes Park and look around. And I need to get some film developed."

My shock must register, because Millie looks at me.

"What? I have my moments," she says.

"Obviously," I say.

"Now you're talking, Millipede," Eric says, nudging Millie's arm.

"You want to go with us, DeDe?" Millie asks me.

"Wait, I haven't said I would go," Lydia says. This is all happening far too fast for her. Millie pins her with a stare. "Oh, all right," Lydia says, then they both turn to me.

"No thanks," I say. "I need some think time this afternoon. Do you two mind?"

Lydia and Millie shake their heads.

"Still, I don't know about this," Lydia says, nibbling her fingernail.

Eric leans toward her. "Remember, they have a Starbucks."

Everyone knows Lydia's penchant for Starbucks. She weakens. Eric moves in for the kill.

"I've got a helmet in my storage bin, and you can wear that. I promise to drive as safely as I would if my grandma were on the back." He winks.

Lydia stiffens a moment. "I'm hardly your grandmother."

"Trust me, I can see that," Eric says with a grin.

She gives him a "don't go there" look, then dares a glance at Millie, whose eyes are pleading with her to go. She finally says, "Okay."

"Great. We'll be by here in a few minutes." Eric and the Biker Boys race off before she can change her mind. Beverly runs up to tell me the fax came through from Shelley, so I go over to the office to sign the offer and fax it back to her.

Afterward, Millie, Lydia, and I go inside the motor home to freshen up and get some money. Lydia wants to rethink the whole thing, but Millie isn't about to let her. I think this fresh mountain air is doing something to Millie's brain. As in causing dead cells to spring to life. It definitely agrees with her.

It is a sight to behold to see a black-helmeted Lydia flanked on the back of Eric's bike, in a setting of silver and black, holding Eric in a death grip—which I suspect is what he hoped for all along. Donned in a red helmet, Millie is on the back of Elmer Fudd's cycle, looking for all she's worth as though she hasn't had this much fun in a month of Sundays—which I suspect is true. The burly cyclist says something to her, and with one jolt, they're outta here.

Eric trails behind at a pace that would get him kicked out of any self-respecting motorcycle group.

A slight breeze wafts through the window screens and gives our home on wheels a fresh mountain scent. The broken air conditioner hasn't bothered me, though I've had to rethink that after experiencing my first hot flash. By the way, I haven't told the girls yet, nor do I plan to at this point. Maybe I can sneak into town with Steve and look for a small fan. Slipping on the shoes I bought for walking trails in the mountains, I'm ready to go. My walking stick is perched in a corner of the bedroom, so I grab it and head out the door.

Since Rocky Mountain National Park is within walking distance, I head that way, glancing once more at the brochure that lists the trails. There is a trail marked "easy to moderate" fairly close to our campsite, and I decide to take it. The altitude hasn't bothered me. I've been drinking lots of water, which is one thing they tell you to do when you're in high altitudes. Once I spot the trail, I head in that direction.

The afternoon sun attempts to poke through occasional gaps in the pine branches that canopy overhead, but the pines stand firm in their grasp to keep the path below dark and otherworldly. The trail looks beaten and worn by the many trailblazers who have gone before me; an earthy path littered with pinecones, sticks, and leaves. The tips of leafy shrubs stir with the mountain air. Aspens quiver, their trunks scarred and chipped away by wildlife. Ponderosa pine and assorted spruce trees reach for the sky while shedding a thin layer of pine needles on the ground below.

A short distance into my trek, I enter a clearing, with ragged mountain peaks looming tall and intimidating before me. Then the trail takes me back into the forest where the echo of my footsteps magnifies my isolation.

Alone. I am alone with my guilt.

A mountain bird mocks me from a nearby tree. Another joins in. "Look at her! She dated a married man. Look at her! Look at her!" I fear they will swoop down and start pecking at me.

Staring at the path inches in front of me, I shake my head. Lately I've been praying, but my prayers can't penetrate my shame and my guilt to get to Him. I look toward the heavens. "What if I fail again?"

"Apart from Me you can do nothing."

My thoughts wrestle within me as I try desperately to shake myself free. Fallen trees litter the forest. Bruised, battered. Dying.

Dying so that others might live. That's what Jesus did for me.

I was a kid when I made my commitment to Him so long ago. How can I blame Rob for my mistakes? I've been deceiving myself, just as Rob deceived me. Saying I loved God, I would serve Him, live for Him, all the while ignoring Him and going my own way.

Two clusters of columbine poke through the soil bordering the path. Heavy weeds have sneaked from behind and attached around one plant, causing it to wither to shades of brown, while the other plant has one lone bloom forging upward, petals leaning toward a spray of sunlight.

Still it survives.

Stooping down for a closer look at the plant, I'm amazed by the little bloom's persistence. A lost petal lies beside it, revealing the challenges of the forest. Scarred and weary, this small flower refuses to die. In a world of fierce winds, shadows, and predators, this tiny bloom looks to the sun for strength. The sun pushes through the thick branches and bathes the columbine with new life it could not obtain on its own.

My fingers reach for the flower, but I stop short. Wrapped in the sun's embrace, it begs to be left alone. Tears slip down my cheeks. I look to the dying plant. It is me. Choked off, shriveling. I've stepped into the shadows, away from the Son. Oh, how I need Him! I can't survive the journey through this life on my own. The temptations are too great without His help.

The tiny columbine survives, but it too has scars. My fingers lift the fallen petal, then I look back to the flower basking in the sunlight. The fragile bloom is far from perfect, but its strength comes from the sun. Just as mine comes from the Son. I can't erase my shame. What's done is done. But I can start over. From here. In the whisper of the forest, I surrender the shame and my guilt to the One who sees all my flaws and loves me still.

How long I stay beside the flower, I'm not sure, but it doesn't matter. God has heard my prayer, and that's enough.

My aching legs push me up, and I walk forward with a new spring in my step. Another clearing appears, and I ease into the warmth of the sunshine. My gaze rests upon an open meadow washed clean by the sun's rays.

That's me. I'm clean. The butterfly drawing comes to mind. What's that Steve said? A new beginning. This is my new beginning. A short distance to my right, the water of Aspen Creek bubbles and foams as it glides swiftly over rocks and boulders toward its destination.

My gaze scans the horizon, where majestic peaks topped with a glaze of snow stand proud and strong. In the mountain quiet, Psalm 121:1 comes to me: "I lift up my eyes to the hills—where does my help come from? My help comes from the LORD, the Maker of heaven and earth."

I can't do this alone, but I can do this through You; You give me the strength. I will not move away again. I will stay by Your side and trust You, come what may, for I now remember the truth that I had long ago forgotten.

"I am never alone."

24

"*How was lunch—better still, how was your cycle ride?*" *I* tease Lydia and Millie when they step inside the motor home.

Lydia's cheeks are pink, her eyes wide and vibrant. "It was magnificent."

"Really?"

"I told you that you would like it," Millie says, her face matching Lydia's flush for flush.

"We went to the nicest shops, Dee. Jewelry, clothing, books, you name it. What a wonderful town," Lydia says.

"You should see the Stanley Hotel," Millie says, breathless.

Sounds as though the Biker Boys treated Lydia and Millie well. "The guys took you up there?"

Lydia nods. "That's where we went to lunch."

"Wow, that's really nice. I've heard about that place."

"There was a Red Hat group having lunch together there," Lydia says, eyes twinkling.

"They were having a great time, I can tell you," Millie adds.

"I told you they're a fun group to be in." Lydia turns to Millie. "Oh, we forgot to tell DeDe about the hauntings."

I laugh. "What?"

Lydia swivels to me. "I don't believe it, though."

"Believe what?" I ask.

"Don't be too quick to discount it, Lydia. Those testimonies sounded pretty convincing," Millie says before turning to me. "They say the Stanley Hotel is haunted. They even have books about it." Millie reaches into a package and pulls out a book. We browse through it together.

Lydia looks up at me. "How about you, Dee—did you have a nice walk?"

Settling onto the love seat, I look at her. "It was life-changing."

"Whoa." Millie stops her walk toward the bedroom and turns back around to join us. "This I've got to hear."

I tell them about my walk, my talk with God, everything.

Lydia comes over and hugs me. "That's wonderful news, DeDe. I'm so happy for you." Tears fill her eyes.

Millie lifts a tentative smile. "Hey, I got your birthday pictures developed." She pulls them out of the package, and we carefully go through them, laughing and talking about them along the way. Once Millie files them, we decide to walk around the camp and see how everything looks before the district board comes tomorrow.

A fresh wave of pine scent hits me the moment we step outside. I have to admit it's been great to be here again.

"I sure hope the powers that be give this place another chance. So many memories," Millie says as we glance around the camp. "I can't bear to lose it."

"We'll just keep praying," I say, feeling wonderful that I can mean it this time.

Millie and Lydia head toward the kitchen while I walk to the dorm. I'll just push the rags and paint things over to one corner so it doesn't look quite so unkempt when the board comes. When I step inside, Steve is already in the room straightening the area.

"I'm sorry, Steve. I didn't mean for you to do that."

"It's no big deal. Just straightening a little," he says with a smile.

Picking up one of the rags, I toss it in with the rest of the pile. "I enjoyed your message this morning, Steve."

He brushes his hands together and turns to me. "Thanks."

"Um, in fact, I thought about it a lot on my walk." I look up at him, wondering if I should tell him what happened.

He waits a minute. "New beginnings?"

Smiling, I nod, thinking of the butterfly.

"I thought so. I could see it on your face when you walked in."

We talk about what happened to me on the trail, and before I know it, an hour has passed. A deep friendship is forming between us, and I'm enjoying it.

A lot.

After dinner we go back to the motor home to prepare for our evening gathering around the campfire.

"I just don't know what to wear. None of my clothes fit," Millie complains. "I've put on too much weight out here."

"Tell me about it," I say.

"Sorry, girls," Lydia says, obviously meaning it. "I don't mean to mess up everyone's diets."

"Oh well, it's a great way to go. Besides, we can go back to our diets and exercise routines when we get home." I smile at Millie, who doesn't smile back.

"My things are in such disarray," she says, lifting clothes from her storage compartment. "How can I find anything in this mess?" She dumps everything from her bin and starts refolding.

"Millie, what's wrong?" I ask.

"Nothing is wrong," she says in clipped tones.

"Oh, yes, there is, Millie," Lydia joins in. "When you go on an organizational binge, we know something is amiss."

She stops folding and looks up, tears pooling in her eyes. "I called the library. I think they've replaced me."

Lydia gasps. "Replaced you? Not possible."

"Why would you think that, Millie?" I ask.

"They've hired a new lady to help out. We don't need anyone else. What other reason would they have for doing that?"

"Maybe she's there to help with the computer transitioning," I encourage.

"So they say. I don't buy it. They think I can't handle the computer, that's what. They've hired some young thing to take my place."

My thoughts flit to one new chocolatier in town, and I feel Millie's pain.

"I'm sure you're mistaken," Lydia says. "You've been there too long."

"Precisely," Millie says.

"No, no. I mean, you're valuable to them." Lydia dabs on some perfume.

I smile.

"What? Just because I'm not interested in anyone doesn't mean I have to smell like a moose," Lydia says.

"Agreed." It's great to see Lydia enjoying herself. This trip has been good for her.

"I don't think they care a twit about me," Millie says, bringing us back to our discussion.

"Do you think you need to go home so you can check things out at the library?" Lydia asks, looking worried.

Millie's back stiffens. "I will not do that. I don't bail out of a job once I've committed myself to it. I will see the camp through to completion."

"One thing for sure, now is not the time to think about it. You have enough on your mind just managing this project. You can deal with the library when you get home. For now, enjoy your time at the camp. Tomorrow will take care of itself," I say, smiling inwardly at my sudden burst of wisdom.

Lydia and Millie must notice it too, because they both stare at me.

"What?"

"Since when did you get so smart?" Millie wants to know.

"Some things we don't learn through books, Millie. We can also learn by experience."

Twigs snap and pop in the campfire as we enjoy another great time of bonding over hot chocolate and coffee.

"Did you know that researchers have decided that the special sense of well-being that comes from eating or drinking chocolate has more to do with the experience itself rather than anything actually in the chocolate?" I take another drink of my chocolate. "Isn't that interesting?" When I look at the others, they're staring at me. "Okay, maybe not."

A couple of comments are made about my candy addiction, but I ignore them and change the subject to our progress at the camp. Our enthusiasm is almost electric as we discuss the improvements we've made so far and the things we hope to do.

Beverly joins us, and we finally get down to business.

"I'm afraid I need to talk to you about something," she says.

"What is it, Beverly?" I say.

"I've been going through our finances, and it's taking far too much of the donation money just to keep things afloat." She flips through her notebook. "We had to repair the plumbing—"

Eric clears his throat.

"We've had to buy supplies, food. The list goes on. I just don't know how much longer the funds will last." She looks up at us.

"It's all right, Bev," Steve says. "If the Lord wants the camp to survive, it will. All we can do is offer our best. The rest is up to Him."

"I know that's true, but it's so hard not to worry," she says. "This is not only my job, but it's been my home for years."

Lydia nods.

"I know." Steve reaches for my hand and Beverly's hand on the other side of him. "Let's join hands and pray," he says.

We all grab hands, and Steve leads us in a wonderful prayer of thanksgiving and surrender.

By the time we finish, we're all a little teary-eyed and much lighter than before. I don't know what the future holds for any of us, including the camp, but one thing is sure—after going through this adventure together, our little group will never be the same.

About four o'clock the next morning, the storm raging outside my window wakes me up. I'm thankful that last night before we went to bed we closed the windows enough to keep the rain out of the motor home and that the duct tape is still holding. I look over at Lydia's bed and see that it's empty. Soft voices sound from the front room.

"You couldn't sleep either?" I ask, dragging my sleepy self into the living room.

"Who could sleep with all that racket going on?" Millie wants to know.

"Anyone want some tea?" Lydia is up and fixing it before Millie and I get our "yes" out.

A sharp crack of thunder sounds close enough to split Waldo in two, then a loud crash causes us to shiver right along with Waldo.

"What was that?" Lydia asks, her eyes wide, her breathing shallow.

"I don't know, but it doesn't sound good." Though I'm not given to fear, I have to admit that right now "a dark and stormy night" conjures up more than Snoopy's attempt to write novels.

"Should we check it out?" Millie asks.

Separating the blinds, I peek out the window. "We'd better wait until the storm settles down a little."

When our tea is ready, we settle down to drink it and talk awhile, waiting for the storm to subside. Once the rain slows to a steady fall, we put on raincoats and step outside. Others from the camp are already surveying the area.

Beverly is wringing her hands when we find her.

"What's happened, Bev?" I ask.

"A tree has fallen over dorm one. The trunk missed the building, but branches have broken through a couple of windows."

I put my arm around her. "It will be all right."

"That's not all."

"What else?" Lydia asks.

"Bears have broken through the back door of the cafeteria, made a mess of the kitchen." Beverly lifts her hands to her face and breaks out in heavy sobs. "We may as well give up. It's a lost cause."

Everyone has gathered around her by now.

"If you think I've come all this way, at the risk of losing my job, just to turn tail and run, you are sadly mistaken, missy," Millie says, her nose hiked. "We knew it wouldn't be easy when we started this venture, and we were right. But nothing worth having is easy. The way I figure it, we have a few hours before the board gets here. I aim to get to work." With that, Millie turns on her heels and goes back to the motor home to get dressed.

By the look on everyone's face, I'd say her little speech has encouraged the hearts of all of us. We quickly set to work, not knowing if it will do any good or not.

Beverly sure knew what she was doing when she put Millie in charge.

By the time the board comes, some of the mess the bears made has been cleaned up, but it's obvious the toaster, blender, and bread machine will have to be replaced. The bears swatted them across the floor and sent them reeling.

The guys had to wait for someone from the church to bring saws, and now everyone is working together to cut the fallen tree into chunks of firewood.

Beverly placed orders for two new windows, and soon the world is set right on its axis once again.

The only problem is, the concert is tomorrow night and the electricity is out.

25

The next afternoon is a buzz of activity, everyone frantically working on their concert pieces. Church guys are trying to get the electricity up and running for our microphones and keyboard.

Some of the men heave a wooden platform over to the open meadow, then Steve and I work around the endless cords, setting up microphones and stands. In hopes that the electricity will be back on for tonight, the sound guys from the church put together some sort of PA deal, and one glance at the stage screams preschool program. An avalanche around seven o'clock tonight might be a good thing.

Lydia brings a lovely brass kettle stuffed with wildflowers to the platform and sets it to one side. Okay, that's as helpful as putting a dirty kid in clean clothes.

"That's nice, Lydia." I mean, it is nice. Well, if you don't count the fact that it's sitting a little whopper-jawed on the boards. But, hey, who's going to notice?

She brushes her hands together. "Good. I'm going to bring another one out for the other side. It will give the place a little more warmth." She looks once again at the flowers, then walks away.

We're surrounded by an alpine forest and majestic mountains, and she's thinking we need wildflowers for warmth. Okeydokey.

Millie's horn blares from a nearby dorm. She's been going from place to place to practice in hopes of keeping the elk away. Just call her the "Pied Piper." Millie plays, the elk follow.

Truthfully, they've been hovering at the edge of the woods, though they're not coming too close since there are so many of us milling around.

Beverly is darting around the camp here and there, trying to get things ready for the concert. She has assigned teams from the church to help. Once the microphones are in place, several of us begin to set up folding chairs, facing the platform.

The weatherman promises a pleasant evening, and hopefully he'll be right. I glance up. A few tiny wisps of cloud sail along the azure sky. Enormous mountains sweep down upon a sun-washed meadow.

"DeDe, will you come here for a minute?" Steve calls me over to the keyboard that the guys have just placed on the stage. "Can you grab that microphone and say something?"

"Testing one-two-three," I say just as Steve pushes on the keyboard. My words and his note lift with the breeze. We all turn toward the volunteer electricians and clap. Beverly's shoulders relax. One less thing to worry about.

For now.

Lydia places the second bunch of flowers on the stage and calls out to everyone that dinner is ready. We all head to the cafeteria and soon devour Lydia's offering of sandwiches and homemade vegetable soup. Some people talk excitedly while eating; others sit in quiet. All of us handling stress in our own way. I figure, what's to worry? It can't be a sellout crowd. Not that I don't want to sell a lot of tickets, mind you. We need the money, that's certain. But, well, there's something to be said for keeping one's dignity intact, and I'm thinking our reputations could be on the line here. On the other hand, the crowd knows we're not professionals, so why not enjoy ourselves?

Dinner is soon over; we're all dressed and ready for the concert.

We make our way onto the open field where about fifty people have gathered for the event.

I have to admit I'm surprised to see so many. I might add here that most attendees are in their twilight years—as in this concert could last past their bedtime. Okay, my bedtime too. The frightening thing about it all? The program is forty-five minutes long. An hour, tops.

Beverly interrupts my thoughts by welcoming everyone. Her microphone sends a sharp echo through the crowd, causing Beverly to step back. "Guess my voice is more powerful than I thought," she says with a chuckle. Smiles light the crowd.

Nice audience. That's a good sign.

One by one we perform our numbers. We get through the first half and midway through the second half, and now it's Millie's turn. If the people go home now, they've seen a fair share of the program.

Millie's face is flushed as she walks up to the stage. She smiles at the audience, pulls her trumpet to her lips, opens a valve, blows, and spit falls onto the stage. Nice touch.

She pulls the horn to her mouth once more and begins to blow. One of Eric's buddies pulls out a trombone, and another belts out a second trumpet. Millie turns to them, looking as surprised as I am. The fellows turn this little number into a jazz ensemble, giving "When the Saints Go Marching In" a New Orleans type of sound. Finally, they come to the chorus the third time around, and the fellows drop out, leaving Millie to finish the number alone.

By now her confidence is in full swing. I half-expect her to bebop through the crowd, moving her horn up and down with the rhythm of the music, but to her credit, she stays planted, merely lifting her horn heavenward as her notes climb higher and louder with every blow, bouncing from one mountain to the next until a strange bugle and grunting sound join the mix.

I look past Millie at the guys to see who's joined her this time, but they are looking around too. The strange bugling continues. Other people crane their necks, looking for the source of the sound. It's then that I notice a group of elk, peeking just at the edge of the trees.

Then out of the woods on the opposite side comes a bull elk. And let me just say that sucker is huge, with antlers that could serve as a coatrack for Goliath. He's headed straight for Millie, who by now is so absorbed in her music, she has entered the heavenlies. People scream and scatter about while the men on the stage rush to Millie's side and yank on her arm. She looks as though she's ready to bop someone for interrupting her moment of glory until her eyes lock with Mr. Bull. This is where Millie's legs kick into gear and carry her off like a hungry cheetah chasing his lunch.

You can say what you will about Millie, but she's no slacker.

In a flash the entire meadow is cleared out. Mr. Bull reclaims his females, and off they go into the woods, leaving me, and most likely others, thankful that we opted not to take instrumental instruction.

"Boy, I hope it's all right that we left everything set up in the meadow tonight," I say once we're safely inside Waldo.

"The guys were going back to tear down," Lydia says. "They wanted to wait and make sure the elk were gone."

"Well, don't expect me to go back," Millie argues. "I'm not about to take on a seven-hundred-pound bull elk, thank you very much." She plunks down on the sofa. "It was bad enough duking it out with my husband, and he was a scrawny man."

She glances up at us, and we all start to laugh.

Millie's cell phone rings. Lydia and I make sure the way is clear, then we head back outside to help the guys clean up.

"Well, that wasn't quite the grand finale we had planned, but it worked," Beverly says as we pick up litter around the concert area.

"Poor Millie. Is she all right?" Beverly's face shows nothing but concern, but Lydia and I both bust up laughing. She joins in, though I can see she feels bad doing so.

"Millie is fine," I say. "Though I don't suspect she'll take home any elk souvenirs."

Others join us in our efforts, and finally the concert area is clean. When we get back to the motor home, Millie is still sitting on the sofa, only now her eyes are red and puffy.

"Millie, what's wrong?" Lydia asks when we step inside.

She waits a moment. "That phone call before you left?"

We nod.

"It was my mother."

Lydia gasps. "Is she sick?"

"She's fine. She called to tell me that Bruce's wife"—fresh tears fall, and she wipes her nose with a tissue—"is pregnant."

"Pregnant? Isn't he a little old for that?" I say, incredulous that a man in his fifties would become a father for the first time.

"Do you know why Bruce and I never had children?" Millie asks as if she never heard my comment at all.

Lydia and I shake our heads.

"I have a tipped uterus. Did I ever tell you that?"

Well, it's not like that comes up in regular conversation. "So how's the family?" "Why, they're fine, thank you. By the way, I have a tipped uterus."

"Um, no," I say.

She nods. "That's what made it so hard for us to get pregnant. It can happen; it just didn't happen for me." She looks up, tears swimming in her eyes. "Oh well, now he'll get that baby he's always wanted."

I want to say, "You've got a lot of elk admirers," but this doesn't seem to be the time.

Lydia sets to work making tea. That's a cure-all as far as Lydia is concerned. Millie cries some more until her tears are spent, while we sit beside her, saying nothing, hoping our presence is enough.

"I've been as narrow as this motor home," Millie says with disgust. "No offense, Lydia."

"None taken."

"When I couldn't have a baby, I just threw myself into my work. At the library, I could control my environment. At home, I couldn't control anything."

She stares at the wad of tissue in her hands. "And now I can't even do my job." Millie looks up at us and shrugs.

We grab her arm, saying nothing, just being her support while she cries the last of her tears.

Afterward we sit down to tea. "I guess we've all been narrow, Millie. I had my sights set on my career too. Now what do I have to show for it? A business whose very survival is threatened by someone younger, more energetic, more creative." I look out the window, then back at Lydia and Millie. "I always thought that by the time we reached this age, we would have arrived at the place of contentment, the place where we would finally feel settled, as though we had fulfilled our God-given purpose."

They nod.

"Are we there yet?" I ask with a sly grin.

"I don't think so. I'm not sure we ever 'arrive.' We just keep traveling, growing, learning." Millie cleans her eyeglasses with the edge of her blouse. Guess she does learn something from her books.

No one says anything for a few minutes.

"Well, I didn't put a career first, but I haven't done so great myself. Talk about narrow. My world was my husband, my kids." Lydia cradles her hands around her teacup. "I'm not saying that I'm sorry I put them first. Still, I should have reached out more to others as well. Expanded my world. The only world I have ever known is gone." She looks up at us. "Where do I go from here? What now?"

"Trust our future to the Lord and take one day at a time. The older we get, the more precious each day becomes," I say, feeling strangely solemn all at once. Extending my hands to each of them, I grab hold of theirs. "In case I haven't told you lately, I love you both, and I cherish your friendship. Thank you for getting me through the hard places."

Lydia and Millie say the same, and soon we're all bawling and hugging each other.

"But no matter how much I love you, Millie, I still can't get used to your horn-blowing," I say. "So try to be kind if you decide to play in the morning." I wink at Lydia before I turn and head off to the bathroom to smear on some cold cream—praying all the while that Millie won't take a picture.

A piercing scream zings through Waldo's interior, alerting every nerve in my body. Either Millie's trumpet is rebelling, or somebody's in trouble. Could be both.

Lydia and I scramble out of bed and run to the front room. Millie is frozen in place. She is standing in front of the sofa, trumpet case in hand, staring at the driver's window like a statue—as in Lot's wife has nothing on her. My gaze goes from Millie to the window. What I see there causes my heart to attempt a fast escape from my chest.

We are staring into the face of the biggest moose I have ever seen in my life. Okay, so I've never seen a moose, but can I just say here that Bullwinkle never prepared me for this. I'm wondering if the moose got a glimpse of Millie's trumpet case and decided enough was enough. I mean, even animals have their limits, right?

Go, Bullwinkle!

I'm just glad he's outside and we're, well, not.

"What do we do?" The words squeeze out of the side of my mouth toward Lydia, who has also turned to stone.

"I would say run, but that doesn't seem to be an option." You know how Lydia handles that fear thing? Well, if I placed her in the forest right now, we'd be hard-pressed to tell the difference between her and a quaking aspen. Does that tell you anything?

"I sure wish I could get a picture. But we dare not move," Millie says with all the talent of a ventriloquist.

"Lydia's shaking—does that count?" I'm tattling here, but nerves do that to me.

"Just keep it to a minimum, Lydia," Millie whispers.

"I'm doing the best I can." Lydia's voice sounds old. Think Whistler's mother.

Bullwinkle's eyes glance around the home. Frankly, I don't think he's all that impressed. He snorts and grunts a couple of times. Yes, we can hear him. It's as though we're on the set of *The Lost World: Jurassic Park*, only we're not pretending. As far as instruments of torture, Millie's trumpet is looking better all the time.

Then again, maybe not.

Just as I'm beginning to think we're going to be stuck in this Mexican standoff all day, Bullwinkle gets bored and moves on. It's only as he ambles back toward the woods that Lydia, Millie, and I collectively let out our breath. Then Millie runs for her camera and gets a shot of Bullwinkle's backside.

Now there's one for the album.

"Well, that was exciting," I say. They both turn and stare at me.

"That type of excitement, I can do without," Lydia says. She's never been all that adventurous.

"I'm half-afraid to play my horn this morning," Millie says, wavering with indecision.

Hope rises inside me. "Yeah, I don't blame you. It might bring the moose back, or maybe even get that bull elk all stirred up."

Millie thinks a moment and nods. "You're right. I'd better not risk it." She puts her trumpet back in the storage bin.

My insides are singing, "Let the heavens rejoice!" but I dare not let my face show it.

After we eat breakfast, we show up for duty around the campfire, which is now just a heap of ashes, and find out that one of Eric's buddies (Porky Pig) sprained his arm last night. It seems the guys had a rope and were trying to swing from a tree. Maybe somebody should tell them that Tarzan didn't do trees once he hit midlife.

Evidently he lost his grip on the rope and fell on his right arm. It takes real talent. Poor guy. The worst part about it is, he was helping with the roofing, so that will slow down things on that end.

Beverly makes her rounds, telling us that we have some urgent matters to discuss around the campfire tonight.

Everyone seems a little on edge today. Steve and I have almost finished painting the dorm rooms. He's exceptionally quiet today too. I tell him about our moose incident, but he doesn't comment much. He's evidently preoccupied. So I throw myself into the work and keep quiet—well, as much as I'm able.

"Appears to be time for lunch," Steve says, climbing down his ladder. "You ready to go?"

"Sure." I put my brush and paint aside for now. We go to our respective bathrooms and clean up, then meet on the porch to walk over to the cafeteria together.

"You doing all right today, Steve?"

He turns a heart-melting grin my way. "Yeah. Just kind of solemn about everything coming to a close."

His words surprise me.

"What? Do you think that's weird for a guy to act a little sappy?"

"Well, I'll admit it's not every day a guy will open up and show his true feelings, you know."

Another grin. "Yeah, I know." He picks up a twig, snaps it, and then tosses it aside. "Listen, DeDe, I was wondering—well, we live only four hours from each other and all, and I thought maybe we—that is, you and I—we, uh, could get together once in a while." He keeps his eyes focused straight ahead.

He looks so cute, I want to melt down to a puddle, but the reality is, he won't be interested in me when I tell him the truth. "There's something you should know about me before you ask me that, Steve."

Now he stops walking and turns to me. Fortunately, we're still a little ways from the others, so we have privacy.

"I'm not sure this is the place to talk about it, but since we don't have much time left, well, I just want you to know I have a past I'm not real proud of. I—"

Steve holds up his hand and places his fingers against my lips. "None of that matters now. Your past is just that. Past. We're both starting over, remember?"

"It's not as easy as all that," I argue.

"As far as the east is from the west, so far has He removed our transgressions from us." Steve steps closer to me and looks down into my face. Brushing a curl from my brow, he says, "He forgives you, Dee. That's good enough for me." His gaze holds me for a heartbeat, and I scarcely can breathe. Still, his smile seems to lift the weight of a huge boulder from my shoulders.

"Thank you, Steve."

"So is that a yes, you will agree to see me?" Twinkling eyes again—his. Another heart blip—mine.

I smile and nod.

He squeezes my hand, and we continue our walk to the cafeteria, though we've both picked up the pace. We no sooner step inside the cafeteria than we realize something is wrong.

"What's going on?" Steve asks Eric.

"It's Lydia. We can't find her anywhere. Lunch isn't prepared." Worry lines his face.

A pain slices through my heart. "Who saw her last? Where

would she go? What could have happened?" My questions are stumbling over one another as panic rises.

Millie comes over and touches my arm. "I think she went looking for wildflowers, Dee." She points to the counter where Lydia displays her flowers, and I see that the basket is gone.

A cell phone rings nearby. One of the Biker Boys answers it. "She's lost," he tells the person on the other end of the cell phone line. "We're going to look for her now." He hangs up and looks at us.

"Who was that?" I ask. How could anyone possibly know about Lydia already?

"Drew somebody, I think he said."

"That was Lydia's phone and you told her son that she's lost?" I ask in disbelief. Leave it to a man to get things stirred up.

Everyone looks at him. "Well, I didn't know it was a secret," the guy says, completely clueless. His shirt says "Daffy Duck." Somehow that fits him.

I pick up Lydia's phone to see if she has caller ID. She doesn't. Her redial doesn't work. I go through the list of numbers on her phone to see if I can call Drew back so he won't worry. When I finally find it and call the number, he's gone. There's no time to worry about it. There's nothing I can do about it now.

Eric takes charge. "Okay, guys, we're going to look for her. She obviously went searching for flowers and got farther into the woods than she had intended."

"Hold everything. You can't just take off like that," Beverly says. "You need water bottles, snacks in case you're delayed for whatever reason, flashlights." She continues on, but her words are lost on me.

God, please keep her safe. We can't lose Lydia. We just can't.

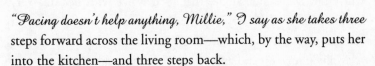

26

"*Pacing doesn't help anything, Millie,*" *I say as she takes three* steps forward across the living room—which, by the way, puts her into the kitchen—and three steps back.

"Well, it helps me. I've already organized everything I can in this place." Three steps, turn, three steps. Millie runs her fingers through her hair. "I don't know how Lydia stands it here. The walls are so close, things are falling apart, if one thing is left out, the whole place looks a mess—"

I walk over and put my arm around Millie. She pulls her hands to her face. "What are we going to do, Dee? What will we do without Lydia?"

"Wait a minute. No one said we had to do anything without Lydia. They are going to find her, Millie, do you hear me? They're going to find her."

"It's been three hours, Dee!"

"I know. God knows where she is, Millie."

"So what? That doesn't mean she's safe. He knew where her husband was too, but he still died."

"Let's sit down, Millie." She wipes her face and reluctantly allows me to walk her over to the sofa.

"We don't know how this will all turn out, but no matter what, we know that Lydia is in God's hands. He loves her even more than we do. And we know that Lydia loves Him too. That's all that matters."

"How can you say that?"

"Because this life isn't what it's all about. We're just passing through."

"I think I've heard that somewhere before. Like here a thousand years ago, remember?"

"I remember." *I could use a little help here, Lord; she's just not listening.* "Why don't we pray for her together?"

"You go ahead. I'll listen."

I lead us in a prayer for Lydia's safety, but most of all that she will know she is not alone, that God walks with her this very minute. Millie and I cry together, and before we can wipe our faces, someone knocks at the door.

Millie jumps up and answers it. I'm right behind her.

"Hi, girls." Lydia's face is dirty, her pants and top are scuffed up, but she's never looked more beautiful.

She steps inside, and soon we're all a tangle of hugs and tears.

"I'm sorry I worried everyone. It seemed like a good idea to go out and pick some more wildflowers. Unfortunately, I forgot to mark my trail as I went along, and soon I was lost. I told you I'm forgetful. I should have dropped bread crumbs." She laughs.

"Right. Then you would have had a bear following you," Millie says dryly.

Lydia stops laughing.

"Well, we're just glad you're back and you're safe," I say.

"That makes two of us." Lydia falls onto the sofa and stretches out her legs in front of her. "But you know, I learned something while I was out there."

"What's that?" Millie asks.

"It doesn't do a bit of good to worry about things. Every fear I've ever had followed me out to that trail, and I almost folded beneath the weight. Then I prayed, and God helped me to get a grip. I let Him know then and there, my future belonged to Him, and come what may, I would trust Him with it."

"That's awesome, Lydia," I say.

"I learned something else too."

"Yes?"

"Don't wear sneakers when you're hiking in the mountains." Lydia pulls off her sneakers and winces when she sees how red her feet are, no doubt from walking over jagged rocks.

Later that evening, we're a grateful lot when we settle around the campfire. The logs crackle and spark, shooting puffs of pine scent through the air. We talk awhile about Lydia's trip into the woods, and we tease her a bit, though there's no denying the relief we all feel that she's safe and with us tonight.

"I need to talk to you all," Beverly says once the group gets quiet. "This has been quite a day. In fact, we've had a struggle from the moment we started this project."

I shift my weight on the hay to get comfortable. Firelight and shadows dance upon the faces of my friends, and with one glance around the group, I realize my life has changed because of these people. This place.

Beverly clears her throat. The expression on her face tells us something's wrong. A weak smile tugs at the corners of her mouth. "First off, I want to thank you for coming here. It's been wonderful to reconnect with all my old friends." Smiles return to her. "I never could have accomplished all this by myself. And because we have put up the effort, I believe none of us will leave here the same as when we came."

"That's sure true for me." The words come out before I can stop them. Everyone looks at me, and I share with them my recommitment to the Lord. Some smile knowingly, and others look at the ground. They might be searching too.

"I've done the same thing, DeDe," Eric says. "My life has been, well, quite frankly, a mess. I'd forgotten the things I learned here. When we arrived at camp, the memories slowly returned."

"It's easy to get caught up in our daily lives and forget what's important. God, family"—Steve looks at me—"and friends." Heat climbs my face.

One by one, the others share what the camp has meant to them over the years and how it has helped them.

Millie keeps silent, and I whisper a prayer for her.

Our conversation dies down. We each stare into the flames in the fire pit, lost in thought.

"Well, I want you to know how much I appreciate all you have done to fix up the camp. The place looks so much better than it did before you came, and I was very hopeful. But I'm afraid I have some bad news—well, maybe not bad, but just not what I was expecting."

We all look to Beverly. Tears pool in her eyes, and my heart squeezes. Lydia puts her hand on Beverly's arm. "What is it, Bev?"

She swallows hard. "I got a call this evening that the denomination has decided to change its district boundaries. As you know, the Red River Church Camp is not all that far away, and since our camp is the smaller of the two, they've decided to close Aspen Creek and put money into their Red River Church Camp."

A collective gasp comes from the women.

"After all we've done? That's just not fair," Millie says in a huff.

Beverly looks at her. "Unfortunately, life isn't always fair."

"When is this going to take place?" Lydia wants to know.

"I believe immediately. They're going to send a Realtor out here sometime next week." A brave smile shines from her lips and eyes. "Though I wish things were different, I know the Lord is in control, so I just have to trust Him."

A twig in the fire snaps while we keep silent. A soft breeze catches a tuft of Beverly's hair, lifts it, and drops it back into place.

"Not enough money from the alumni to buy it, is there?" Millie asks.

"Not even close." Beverly rubs her neck. "Even if we had enough for a down payment, what then? It just won't work."

"So do we pack up and leave tomorrow?" Eric asks.

"Not much point in working any further. It might bring a better price for the camp, but I know you all have families and jobs to get back to."

"It's a real shame. This camp has so much potential," says the man we call Elmer Fudd.

"Well, I think we should stay one more day together," Steve says. "Only let's spend it having some fun. Make one last memory as a group."

"What do you have in mind?" Beverly asks, her perk back in place.

"Walking trails, sightseeing, you know, the normal tourist things."

"I'd be glad to take someone along on my bike," Eric says, eyes fixed on Lydia. She blushes and looks away.

The other bikers nod their willingness to do the same—well, all except Porky Pig, who sprained his arm.

"People are welcome to ride with me in my rental car," Steve says, smiling at the others, his gaze stopping at me.

Beverly claps. "Sounds great. No reason to sit around and mope. Might as well make the best of it."

After talking awhile longer, we head back to our places for the night. As sad as the idea of closing the camp is, we all seem to feel better knowing we have one more day together before we say good-bye.

Just before we turn to leave, I remember Lydia's cell phone. "Did you call Drew back?" I ask her.

Lydia's hand flies to her mouth. "In all the excitement, I forgot and left my cell phone in the cafeteria."

"I'll go with you to get it," I say.

Once Lydia finds her phone, she immediately calls Drew's number. I motion for her to go ahead, and I lag behind so she can have some privacy while they talk. This seems the perfect opportunity to pray for Lydia, Derrick, and Drew.

Now that I've experienced my first hot flash, I'm thinking I need to remind Lydia to get Waldo's air-conditioning fixed before we hit the road again. Funny how perspectives change.

"Good morning," Lydia says from her bed, trying her best to stifle a yawn.

"Hi." I stretch. "Did you have a nice talk with Drew last night?"

"Yeah, it was really good. My little adventure in the woods really scared him. He's rethinking some things."

"That's wonderful, Lydia."

"He also told me that Derrick and his girlfriend are having some pretty deep discussions these days about what they really believe. They have even been studying the Scriptures in search of answers. I know God will give them the answers they're searching for."

We look up to see Millie standing in the bedroom doorway. "Steve's already stopped by this morning."

I rub my eyes. "Really? What did he want?"

Millie's right eyebrow spikes upward. "You." She grins.

"Oh, that sounds exciting," Lydia joins in, her elbow resting on the bed, head leaning in her hand.

"You can't talk. Eric's checked in for you too."

Lydia's eyes grow wide.

"Looks to me like you're in for another motorcycle ride today," I say.

Lydia shrugs. "Might be fun." She shoots a look at us. "But don't get any ideas. Eric is a friend, nothing more. Nor will he ever be. But I have to admit I enjoy his bike." An ornery grin lights her face.

"Friendship is good." I pull my covers off.

"Is that what you have with Steve?" Millie asks.

"Am I on *Sixty Minutes*?"

"Inquiring minds want to know."

"The answer is yes. Steve is my friend."

"Anything more?" Lydia asks.

"Barbara Walters, right?"

Lydia smiles.

"At this point, we're just friends."

"Any chance of that changing?" Millie darts back.

"Good grief, are you guys reporters for *People* magazine or what?"

"Something like that," Millie teases. "We have an interest in you, you know?"

"Let's put it this way. I care about Steve as a friend. As for the future, all that is in the Lord's hands."

"But you think he's cute?" Millie presses.

"I'd have to be blind not to think that, Millie."

Lydia and Millie agree.

"Okay, okay. No more pressure." Millie walks away. "At least for now," she calls back.

I laugh and head for the shower, wondering what my day will hold, let alone my future.

※

Eric's motorcycle vrooms just outside the window of our place. Wait. Did I say "our" place? Please don't tell me that I'm truly bonding with Waldo.

"My ride is here; guess I'll see you at lunch," Lydia says, referring to our group plans to meet for lunch at a restaurant in Estes Park.

"Okay, have a good time," I call out.

"I'm leaving too," Millie says. "Elmer's taking me."

I'm surprised.

"Hey, it's better than calling the cab. Besides, I'm shedding my stuffy image. Who knows? I may be the next Evel Knievel."

"Change is good, Millie, but maybe you should start with a skateboard." I wave good-bye just as my cell phone rings. It's Shelley.

"They accepted our offer to purchase," she blubbers before I barely get out my hello.

"Oh my goodness, Shelley, we're really going to do this!"

"Just call us businesswomen extraordinaire."

We talk awhile about our ideas and the next step in this purchase process. By the time we hang up, I can hardly wait to tell Steve.

Once my shoes are tied, I look over at Cobbler, who is staring out the window, most likely looking for her friend. "You're gonna have a hard time saying good-bye to your friend too, aren't you?" I'm hoping Cobbler doesn't pluck her feathers if she gets upset this time. She could be naked by the time we get back to Lydia's house.

Cobbler looks to me and scampers back and forth on her bar. I feel a little sappy toward my new feathered friend. It won't be easy for her to leave this place. She hasn't even squawked for her Barney fix since we've arrived here. Come to think of it, it will be hard for all of us to leave.

Okay, now I'm scaring myself. First I bond with Waldo, now Cobbler?

A car pulls up just outside. Peeking through the blinds, I see that it's Steve in his rental car. My heart blips—again. That's something I don't want to analyze just now, but I know my feelings for Steve are growing. And Rob what's-his-name? Well, I can't even remember what he looks like!

I am *so* changing.

Steve and I have fun shopping in Estes Park and visiting with our friends at lunch. We stop by a Starbucks on the main drag in town and carry our coffee outside, where the Big Thompson River bubbles over boulders and rocks, offering a restful ambience to those strolling along the Riverwalk. Customers sitting outside Starbucks and other nearby restaurants settle in intimate groups around patio tables or on isolated benches in hope of snatching a moment of peace in the middle of a busy day. We sip our drinks and talk. Steve's eyes sparkle as he talks about his son and their relationship.

"You know, there's still plenty of time. I spotted a movie theater back a little ways—how about we go watch a movie?" Steve asks.

Feeling as giddy as a teenager, I quickly answer, "Sure, why not?"

When we arrive at the concession area of the theater, Steve turns to me. "I know we just had lunch, but how about we grab some popcorn and drinks?"

I'm full, but can I turn down his offer? No.

So with a bag of buttery popcorn in one hand and a bulging drink in the other, we head to the appropriate theater and take our seats.

"I'm having a great time, Steve. Thank you." I stick a kernel of popcorn in my mouth.

"That makes two of us." He throws a couple of kernels into his own mouth. "I had to make up for the short sheets," he says with a laugh.

"It was you!" I slug him, then laugh.

He grabs his arm and holds it as if he's really in pain, but we both know those biceps didn't feel a thing. "The others made me do it."

"Yeah, right." I take a drink of pop. "Oh well, I deserved it for all the trouble I've caused over the years."

He grins. "Am I forgiven?" Those eyes penetrate my heart.

"Forgiven."

The set of his jaw, his muscular frame, the hearty laugh remind me nothing of the lanky boy I knew at camp so long ago. Could I actually consider another relationship? I want to say no, but my heart's telling me yes.

Our eyes stay locked for the span of a heartbeat. I think he might kiss me, but just then previews start playing on the screen and the moment is lost.

After the movie, we head back for Steve's car and pass a jewelry store along the way. "Hey, let's go in here for a minute," Steve says, grabbing my arm.

My spirits dip. What if he has a lady friend back home for whom he wants to buy jewelry? After all, those kinds of gifts are reserved for the special people in our lives.

"May I help you?" A tall woman approaches us. Her hair is pulled back in an elegant but simple style with a pearl-studded comb. Dressed in a silky black shift, she is wearing a thin necklace of pearls and looking very much as though she's about to attend a banquet rather than work in a sales job.

Steve steps up to her. "Yes, I saw a necklace in the window that I'd like to see, please."

Not wanting to intrude on his purchase—and not necessarily wanting to spoil my day—I meander around the room, enjoying the glimmer of diamonds, rubies, and other precious jewels along the way.

Rob took me to a jeweler once. Built my hopes on what could be, all the while knowing it was impossible.

"DeDe, could you come here, please?"

Steve's voice shakes me free from the painful memories. Hopefully we're not adding another one here. As if in slow motion, he lifts a delicate silver chain off the counter. From the center of it dangles a silver butterfly with ruby red wings, the color of my birthstone.

A tiny diamond glistens from its body. My breath catches in my throat. The saleswoman smiles and slips into a back room.

"This is for you," he says in a throaty whisper. Before I can comment, he lifts the chain to my neck and clasps it in the back. His fingers brush through the back of my hair, lifting it from the necklace and sending sparks clear through me. "New beginnings." His whispered words brush against my ear, causing my knees to wobble. I turn to him.

"Steve, this is too much, I shouldn't—"

His fingers press against my lips as his eyes lock with mine. "Me thinks thou doth protest too much." He smiles and leans closer to me. "New beginnings, remember?"

"I remember." Tears swell in my eyes, but I dare not drop them for fear they will break the spell. "Thank you," I manage in a whisper.

My heart pounds hard against my chest as Steve's gaze moves to my lips and he dips his head toward me. Tenderly his lips claim my own in a sweet moment of surrender that I'm sure has set angels' wings to fluttering.

Afterward my cell phone rings. I reach into my pocket and glance at the screen.

Steve smiles. "Important call?"

"Not important at all," I say, stuffing the phone back into my pocket and knowing that all ties to Rob are gone forever.

"The best is yet to come, DeDe Veihl." He tucks a strand of hair behind my ear, his eyes never leaving mine. "The best is yet to come." Right now, looking into his eyes, I believe him with my whole heart.

We spend the late afternoon getting things in order for our trip home. The guys come over and coat the roof with some weird rubberized RV roof treatment that will hopefully help Waldo make it home with few leaks. They also give us some stuff that will help us remove leak stains inside. Beverly manages to get Waldo scheduled to have his air-conditioning looked at the next day, and she tells us the window and screen we ordered are now at the shop and ready to be installed, so we plan to stay over one more day with Beverly and have the RV fixed before we go.

By the time we gather at the fire pit, Beverly pulls out all the stops, insisting that everyone indulge in s'mores. She unpacks bags of marshmallows, graham crackers, and candy bars. Millie passes around the photographs she's taken of our trip up to now, only freaking out slightly when someone forgets to hold them by the edges or mixes them out of order.

When they come my way, I manage to slip in her pajama picture with the rest. Hey, it's too good not to share.

As people start to snicker, Millie gets suspicious. Her gaze locks with mine, and understanding dawns. She dashes over to Eric, who is laughing and pointing at a picture. Upon seeing the photo, she snatches it from his hand.

"That's not funny, DeDe," she says, ripping it to tiny shreds and tossing the pieces into the fire.

"Oh, come on, Millie, it's a great shot—well, all except for your swinging arms got in the way."

The others laugh out loud, and despite herself Millie finally grins and laughs along.

The guys bring their instruments—though they wisely encourage Millie to leave her horn behind—and we enjoy more singing around the campfire. Millie snaps more pictures, and finally the instruments are laid to rest and our time together winds down.

"Though it's hard for everyone to go home, I'm sure you all will be glad to get back to your regular routines," Beverly says.

"I admit I've missed playing my nightly game of basketball." Eric takes on an all-American jock look here.

"You should have told me—I would have taken you on," Steve teases.

"And where would we do that?" Eric wants to know.

Steve looks around. "Oh, I don't know. Right when you come in, just past the office, there's an open space. Sure would have been nice to have a cement slab there." At this he stops, his eyes grow wide, and I can almost see a "think bubble" pop over his head.

"What?" Eric asks.

"That's what's missing."

Beverly scratches her head.

"Sports!" Steve practically comes out of his seat. "What if we make this place into a sports-mountain-adventure-type place? You know, with basketball—"

"Yeah, and football—"

"Soccer—"

"Lacrosse—"

"Waterskiing—"

"Batting cages—"

The guys toss out one idea after another, while the women sit openmouthed.

"Excuse me, I hate to rain on your parade, but are we forgetting something?" Millie cuts in.

Steve looks at her. "What?"

"Money. We need money to prepare a football and soccer field. We need money for tennis and volleyball courts, sports equipment, batting cages. We need money to buy the campground. Those things don't just magically appear."

"I know." Steve rubs his jaw.

"We could form a corporation," Millie says matter-of-factly.

"What did you say?" Steve looks at her as though she's announced a major rise in the stock market.

"I said we could form a corporation."

Steve smacks his hands together. "That it!" He scoots to the edge of his hay bale. "We all want to see this place survive, right?"

We nod.

"Millie's right. We could form a corporation. Those of us who want to participate could be shareholders. We could share in the cost according to our capabilities and go from there. I'd be willing to handle the lion's share of the investment, if need be. I totally believe in this sports concept, and I think it would be an awesome way to draw kids in to hear the gospel message."

"You know, I've been wanting to get involved in something that could make a difference. I mean, all my life I've been living for myself. This would be contributing to the future," Eric says.

It's really cool to see Eric getting focused on something other than his hair. Besides, that will soon be gone, and then what will he have?

"Dude, I feel the same way," one Biker Boy says. "It's like you hit forty, man, and you start asking yourself, what am I doin' here? Will anybody even care when I'm gone?"

"Right, that's it," Millie joins in. "I mean, you work and work, and where does it get you? Who cares that I've cataloged thousands of books in my lifetime? No one. But if I could contribute toward a camp that would change the future of a kid's life, well, then it's all worthwhile."

One comment after another shoots through the night air, hope sparking everyone to life. We'll let other alumni know and see if they want to help in the cause. The quiet biker, Yosemite Sam, pipes up and tells us that he's an attorney. I almost fall off my hay bale. He talks to us about the ins and outs of incorporating, and before the evening is over, we've elected a president, vice president, secretary, and treasurer and made up our minds to make an offer on the camp.

Later when we're back dressing for bed, the three of us are so excited, we can hardly sleep.

Lydia's hair is wrapped in a white terry towel, and she's sitting cross-legged, pretzel-style, on her bed. "Who would have thought things could turn around like this?" She unscrews the lid of her cold-cream jar, dips her fingers inside, and starts applying the cream to her face and neck. "It's just wonderful. I love the idea of contributing to such a worthy venture, playing a small part in helping kids."

"I know, me too," I say, shrugging on my pajamas. "I just hope my business survives our move and things work out so that I'm able to continue helping."

Millie grabs her things in the other room and goes to the bathroom without saying a word. Lydia and I exchange a glance.

"Wonder what's wrong with her," Lydia whispers.

"I don't know. She seemed excited out at the campfire."

Lydia nods.

"I'm going to make some popcorn—you want some?"

"Sure," Lydia says.

Grabbing a bag of popcorn out of the cupboard, I place it in the microwave. Next, Lydia joins me in gathering ice cubes from the freezer, and we plunk them into glasses for iced tea. Soon Millie joins us, and we settle at the table over bowls of popcorn.

"You all right, Millie?" I venture.

"Yeah. Just thinking about the library and all that I have to go back to. I'm not even sure I want to go back anymore."

"What are you saying, Millie?" Lydia asks incredulously.

"I'm saying this trip has made me see I'm ready for a change." She looks at our wide eyes. "Yes, Ms. Stability, Millie Carter, is ready for a change. I'd say it's about time after, what, thirty-five years? Same old job, same old life, day after day, night after night. Don't get me wrong. I'm not saying being a librarian is boring. It's been a great job for me, and I've loved it, but now I'm ready for a change."

"But what will you do?" Lydia asks like a fretful mother.

"I don't know, but something different."

"You're not doing something different just to escape the computers, are you, Millie? Because computers are everywhere these days," I say.

"No, that's not it. I just want to think about what I really want to do and go for it. If I don't go after my dream now, it will never happen. I don't want to end up on my deathbed with regrets for the missed opportunities."

I nod. "That's easy enough to understand," I say, thinking about Steve and wondering where our friendship will lead.

"I don't want regrets either," Lydia admits. "While I was in the woods, I asked God to take care of my boys, and then I thought of all the things I wished I'd done but instead let my fears keep me from experiencing them."

"Such as?" I probe.

"Traveling, for one thing. Deep down inside, I love to travel, but my fears have held me steadfast at home. Don't get me wrong, I love to be home, but now that everyone is gone? Well, it's just not the same. I'm not ready to roll over and die."

"That's right. My goodness, we talk as if we have only a few years left in us. Who knows what we've got? Why, there's a lady who comes into the library who is eighty-seven years old, and do you know what she did?" Millie asks.

We shake our heads.

"Just before I left for this trip, she came into the library to show me her new braces."

"On her teeth?" I ask with disbelief.

"That's right."

"Unbelievable," Lydia says.

"It's the truth. She said she'd always wanted to have straight teeth, and she decided if she didn't do it now, she'd die with crooked teeth." Millie laughs.

"Good grief, I'd be happy just to have my own teeth at eighty-seven." Chewing on my popcorn, I'm thankful to have teeth.

We giggle together.

Just then my cell phone rings. "It's Rob," I say, looking at Millie and Lydia. I click on the phone. "Hello?"

"DeDe, please talk to me," I hear Rob plead.

"Rob, the only thing I have to say to you is that I want you to leave me alone. I've prayed about everything and finally got my life straightened out. I would advise you to do the same. Now please don't ever call me again."

"But we were so good together. Are you sure that's the way you want it?" he asks.

"It's exactly the way I want it."

"Okay, I get the picture. I'll miss you, precious. Bye."

I click off and look at the worried expressions on Millie's and Lydia's faces. "Don't worry. It's okay. I've never felt better about anything in my life," I say with a wide grin.

Only then do Millie and Lydia dare to breathe and talk excitedly about what the future may bring for us all.

"Funny how this trip has changed some things for us," I say after we settle down.

"Isn't it, though? It will be interesting to see where we all end up," Millie says.

"Only God knows," I say. "Only God knows."

Morning sunlight sprays across the forest leaves as we gather around the fire pit one last time to say good-bye. Millie clicks away on her camera, catching our candid shots, our smiles, our tears, our hugs. She steps aside when Eric approaches Lydia.

"It's been great to see you again, Lydia." Genuine sincerity covers his face. It's easy to see Eric had hoped for more than friendship from Lydia, but it's just not there for her. Still, he seems happy to be friends.

"You too, Eric. And believe it or not, I actually enjoyed those jaunts on your bike," she says with a laugh.

"You're more of a traveler than you think. You ought to consider the RVer's life. You just might enjoy yourself." Eric winks and gives her a hug. "Take care of yourself, okay?"

"Okay."

"And let's stay in touch. One can never have too many friends."

"You're right, Eric. Thanks for everything."

Beverly walks over to us. "So what are you going to do now that the camp is closing?" Millie asks.

"I'm not really sure. I'd like to travel, but, well, I'm not really keen on doing it alone," Beverly says.

"Sounds like someone else I know," I say. We all look at Lydia and laugh.

She smiles, then her face grows serious. Suddenly her eyes grow as wide as walnuts. "Beverly, what would you think about traveling with me?"

"What?"

We all look at Lydia as though she's lost her marbles.

"What's to stop us from traveling together? We can try it out, see how it goes. If it doesn't work out or we prefer to go back to our homes, no big deal. Nothing ventured, nothing gained."

"Call the police. An alien life-form took over Lydia's body while she was in the woods," I say.

Lydia smiles. "Well, why not? You guys are always telling me I shouldn't let my fears run my life. My family is gone; there is no better time to see a little bit of the country."

"Now you're talking," Millie says.

"That's a great idea," I agree.

We all turn to Beverly. "I would love it! I don't have to work for the money. I have enough to get by, but I want to keep busy." She claps her hands.

Before I hear any more of their plans, Steve approaches me and leads me a few paces away.

"Will you come with me for a minute?" he asks.

"Sure."

The excited chatter of our friends fades to mere murmurs as Steve leads me away from the crowd to a secluded spot beneath a canopy of pines.

He faces me, taking my hands in his. "I know we've just gotten reacquainted, and we're merely friends, but I'm looking forward to whatever the Lord has in store for both of us, DeDe."

Heat climbs my face, and I wonder if I'm going to have another hot flash.

"It's no accident that we met up again. Who knows where it might take us?" He holds up his hand. "But no pressure, I promise."

"I'm glad we had this time to get together too," I say, meaning it.

His eyes hold mine. "I'll miss you."

His words, the look on his face, his eyes, stir an emotion inside me that I had thought forever gone. "I'll miss you too."

He steps closer. His eyes search mine with such intensity, my knees start to buckle. Before I have a chance to fall, his arms reach around me and gently pull me to him. With his gaze fixed on mine, he lowers his head toward me until his lips touch mine with a sweetness that I've never known before.

By the time we pull apart, I feel as dazed as a seventeen-year-old after prom. Steve holds me in an embrace, and I surrender to the warmth of his strong arms around me. I think of Lydia's and Greg's initials carved on the camp entrance logs. This camp changed their lives, their future. Maybe it's doing the same for me.

It's obvious we don't want to say good-bye. Our little group lingers, no one wanting to be the first to leave. We still have a few hours before we take Waldo in for repair, so we continue to visit, hug, and laugh with the others.

Steve walks over to Millie, who is standing beside me. "You know, Millie, the guys and I were talking. This may be a little premature, but if we pull off buying this place, we're going to need someone to help us run it. They'll have to employ counselors, workers; there will be all kinds of things to do."

"That's true. We have a little time before we have to worry about that. We can put an ad in the paper or something." Millie's professional voice takes over.

Steve seems to consider this. "Still, it would be great if we could put someone in charge we have complete confidence in."

"Yes, it would," she agreed.

I'm wondering where he's going with this until I see the amusement in his eyes.

"You have anyone in mind?" Millie is completely clueless.

"Well, the boys and I talked it over, and what with Beverly deciding to travel, we thought you would be the perfect fit."

Millie's jaw drops like the mouth of a nutcracker.

Steve holds up his hand. "Now, I know you've been at your

job for years, and you probably don't want to give it up. I'm just asking that you think about it. I'll call you, and we can talk further if the sale goes through."

"Will you have computers?"

I purse my lips to hold back a giggle.

Steve fingers his jawline. "Probably."

Millie grimaces.

"But since you'd have a small office, they wouldn't be all that hard to learn," he says. Millie looks away a minute, and Steve winks at me. "Well, I'll be in touch." He pats her arm and walks away.

We lock eyes.

"What do you make of that?" Millie asks.

I smile. "This could be the very thing for you, Millie."

She scans the area, seeming to take in every inch of the place. A look of excitement replaces the concern on her face. "You know, you're right." A grin lights up her face. "It could very well be just the thing."

Lydia walks up to join us. "So are you and Beverly going to become world travelers?" I ask.

"We are! Can you believe it? I'm going home, get things ready for travel, and she's going to fly to my place after we get the corporation set up and she ties up the loose ends." Lydia flicks a pine needle from her shoulder. "We're going to try it for a month or two and see how it goes."

"Any idea where you're headed?" I ask.

"We're going to think about it and discuss it once we get together."

"When the weather turns cold, you could always come to Florida for a visit," I say, flashing a grin.

Lydia brightens. "We just might take you up on that."

We continue making the rounds, hugging others, saying our good-byes, until one by one we reluctantly head toward our vehicles to leave.

Steve comes over to me once more. "Hey, keep me posted on your business, okay?"

"Sure," I say. "Thanks for your help on that."

He grabs my hand, giving it a lingering squeeze. "I'll be in touch."

I squeeze back. "I'll look forward to it." One glance at Lydia and Millie, and embarrassment warms my cheeks.

"You girls stay out of trouble," he says to Lydia and Millie.

"You're barking up the wrong tree," Millie says, pointing to me.

His eyebrows rise. "Oh, that's right. Stay out of jail, DeDe." He winks and grins.

"No promises."

"No promises?" he asks as if there's a double meaning. His eyes hold mine, and my pulse stumbles.

"Hey, we're over here. I believe you were saying good-bye to us," Millie says with an ornery glint in her eyes.

Lydia tries to hide her grin behind her hand. Now Steve turns red, and we all laugh.

A shy grin lights Steve's face. "Talk to you soon, Dee." He turns and walks away.

Lydia, Millie, and I make our way back to Waldo.

"Hmm, that little exchange was interesting. Do I detect a bit of romance in the air?" Millie asks.

"Maybe." A smile touches my lips, and my feet feel so light, I think I'm floating.

"This from the girl who insisted she would never love again?" Millie pushes.

"I'm surprised too. Like I said, this trip has changed me in more ways than one." I look at Lydia and Millie. "In fact, I think it's changed all of us."

Lydia nods. "So true. My little jaunt into the woods got my attention in a real way. The entire trip, I've been rethinking some things, but my time in the woods just made me all the more determined to make some changes."

I pick up a stray cup from the picnic table at our campsite and throw it in the trash. "How about you, Millie?"

"Well, I've rethought some things. Made a lot of mistakes with Bruce. I'm not in the market for another husband, but I realize if I'm going to enjoy anything in this life, I need to do my part to make it happen."

"Like maybe considering the new job that might open here at the camp?" Lydia asks.

"Right. I'm going to go back to the library and throw myself into the new computer system, but if we all buy the camp and a position materializes, I'm very open to it. In other words, I'm not running from the library job and the computer stuff. I'm just allowing myself the freedom to change if my dreams take me there."

"Okay, who are you and what have you done with Millie?" I tease.

A chuckle escapes her. "You know, I was just thinking the same thing."

My thoughts turn serious. "I'll be praying for you, Millie." I squeeze her hand.

A look of appreciation shines on her face. "Thanks."

"Well, it's just about time to take Waldo in for repair. Beverly will pick us up from the shop in a few minutes so we don't have to stay there," Lydia says, opening Waldo's door. We step inside.

"So where we going next year?" Millie asks. The shock on Lydia's face matches my fear. "I think we should go on a trip together every year, don't you?"

A smile tugs at the corners of Lydia's lips and spreads into a full-scale grin. "And why not?"

"In Waldo?" I can't believe I'm actually calling him that. *Please say no.*

Millie brightens. "I was thinking something a little different next time."

"Why is it I have this sinking feeling that I don't want to hear this?"

Millie waves her hand. "Oh, DeDe, you'll get used to the idea."

Uh-huh, that's what they said this time.

Millie leans in, eyes sparkling. "I was thinking a houseboat."

I gasp.

She steps back and looks at us as though she's just announced the answer to world peace. Trust me on this one. The three of us on a houseboat does not spell world peace.

"You, Lydia, me—us in a houseboat, away from civilization, traveling down some forgotten waterway, in the heart of a thick jungle. Haven't you ever seen *Anaconda*?"

Millie gives me a hard stare. "I was thinking more along the lines of a nice, peaceful river."

"Leave it with Huckleberry Finn," I say.

"I think it's a great idea," Lydia says. "And if Beverly is still traveling with me, she could join us."

"Right," Millie says with a snap of her head. The two of them walk down the hall, and I watch after them, wondering what in the world my future will hold.

If I've learned anything on this trip, it's that every day is a journey. And one thing I know for sure, the journey is easier when traveling with friends—well, most of the time.

Still, if I have my way about it, I'll be spending my next vacation at a spa. And call me spoiled, but I have every intention of getting there in less than one day in the comfort of an airplane.

Special thanks to:

- Mr. and Mrs. Bill Darrough for allowing my husband and me to tour their beautiful facilities at Camp Timberline in Estes Park, Colorado.

- Jim and Daphna Bickerstaff for answering my endless RV questions.

- The great folks at DeBrand Fine Chocolates for the world's greatest truffles that constantly feed my inspiration!

- My readers for traveling these pages with me. Because of you, I have a job. Thank you!

- My husband, Jim, who will, one day, be thrown into jail for forcing my books upon people. Thanks for believing in me, honey. I love you!

- My daughter, Amber Zimmerman, and her husband, Kyle, for making sure my books are face out in the bookstores. My son, Aaron Hunt, and his wife, Megan, for selling my book to the lady at the bookstore. I love you all!

- My granddaughters, Macy, Micah, and Zoe Zimmerman and Abby Hunt: I pray I will leave you a legacy of laughter.

- My writing friends, Colleen Coble, Kristin Billerbeck, and Denise Hunter. The journey wouldn't be nearly as fun without you.

- My awesome agent, Karen Solem, for her infinite wisdom in the publishing world.

- My in-house WestBow editor, Ami McConnell, for her amazing insight and creativity. Thank you for making midlife (well, it is if I live to be one hundred) my best years yet!

- Editor Natalie Gillespie, who cleans my words until they sparkle.

- The creative team at WestBow Press: Allen Arnold, Jennifer Deshler in marketing, Caroline Craddock in publicity, Natalie Hanemann, the book cover creators, the copyeditors, the sales reps—all of you are totally amazing!

- The friends I have made over the years. I am blessed to know you, and I thank God for your influence on my life.

Study Questions for RV There Yet?

1. DeDe had a real struggle with temptation during much of the story. Knowing she had that temptation kept her filled with guilt. She finally learned that temptation in itself is not wrong, but rather it's the "giving into it" that many times brings about sin. Have you experienced temptation in your life? How did you handle it? Do you wish you would have handled it differently? Why or why not?

2. Lydia found herself starting over without her husband or her children. Have you ever felt lonely? How did you deal with it? Did it help?

3. Millie experienced great disappointment in her life when her husband left her. Maybe you've been through a divorce and understand that pain, or maybe you've had another type of disappointment. What got you through the struggle? Do you know others who might be experiencing disappointment? What are some ways you might reach out and help them?

4. DeDe had been involved in a relationship that was wrong for her. She knew it was wrong; still, the thought of starting over almost brought about panic. Do you struggle with letting go of someone or something that has a hold on your life? What are some steps you might take to make a fresh start?

5. DeDe turned to chocolate, Millie turned to whipped cream, and Lydia cooked for comfort. What kinds of things calm you during your crisis moments? Do they truly comfort you, or are they just temporary fixes? Can you think of what might offer more than a temporary fix?

6. DeDe and Millie faced new job challenges. DeDe needed different strategies, and Millie had to enter the computer world. Does your job require you to rethink some things? Are you closed to new ideas,

or do you insist on doing things the way you have always done them? Can you think of ways you might stretch yourself beyond your comfort zone?

7. Lydia struggled with fear on many levels and finally surrendered her fears to the Lord. Do fears plague you? Have you taken them to the Lord? How has He helped you?

8. Though Millie has not accepted Christ into her life by the end of the story, her girlfriends have planted the seeds. Did a friend tell you about the Lord? How did you react? If you have accepted Him into your life, have you told other friends about your experience? Have you led them to the Lord? If you have not accepted Him into your life, what are you waiting for?

9. DeDe, Lydia, and Millie had their occasional tiffs, but all in all they had a great journey together. Can you think of friends who have made your journey through life easier? Have you ever told them how much you appreciate them? In what ways did you let them know? If not, what can you do to show them?

10. Friends are among God's greatest blessings to us. It's a blessing not only to have friends but to be a friend. Are you a friend to others? What are some ways you can be a better friend than you have been in the past?

11. DeDe, Lydia, and Millie had been friends for years. At one point their contact had dwindled down to annual Christmas cards. Do you have friends in your life who have meant a great deal to you, but with whom you have lost contact? Can you think of steps you might take to renew those relationships? What are they?

12. DeDe didn't always have the best attitude. Do you ever have days like that? What do you do? Lock yourself in a padded cell? Eat chocolate? Go shopping? What might you do the next time?

13. Life is a journey filled with roadblocks, detours, breakdowns, and wrong turns. Still, DeDe, Lydia, and Millie found that the journey was sweeter with friends. Who are the people in your life who help you through the difficulties of life? Who are the people you help through life's struggles?

14. Sometimes the vehicle in which we travel isn't all we had hoped it would be. Think Waldo the aging RV. What are some ways we can come to terms with our changing bodies?

15. Are you satisfied with the road you've taken up to now? Do you wish you had traveled another way? Just as DeDe, Lydia, and Millie discovered, it's never too late to start over. The choice is yours. You can go it alone or make the journey with the Friend who sticks closer than a brother. What will you do?